chickpea del and the fabled tree of destiny

A Merlin's Tale

Maya Kaathryn Bohnhoff

BOOK VIEW CAFE

chickpea del and the fabled tree of destiny

Maya Kaathryn Bohnhoff

https://www.bookviewcafe.com/
Book View Café 2nd edition
February 25, 2025
978-1-63632-315-2

dedication

*To my diminutive protagonist, who introduced himself by
name, then regaled me with the epic tale of "the last little
war" between the kingdoms of Embarcadero and Potrero
Taraval ... as I was driving home from work on a winding
mountain road.*

*No, I'm not kidding. And I have it on the authority of the
late, much beloved Ursula LeGuin that these things happen
to writers all the time.*

*Here's to you, Chickpea Del, Merlin to the King of
Embarcadero.*

epigraph

It is an odd thing, but every one who disappears is said to be seen in San Francisco. It must be a delightful city, and possess all the attractions of the next world.

— Oscar Wilde (1854–1900),
Lord Henry in *The Picture of Dorian Gray*

contents

first: something's up

LORD E LORDY wanted the Wiz. That's where the Last Little War got started.

You see, Lord E Lordy—he's Alcalde of the next-door kingdom of Potrero-Taraval—was of a mind to conquer. This was not unusual. Lord E was always of that mind. Potrero has been spreading all the time, bit by bit, south and east toward Excelsior and Merced.

It started doing this when Lord E's daddy was Alcalde of Potrero. He was an expansive SOB. He pushed Potrero-Taraval down against tiny Bernal in the southeast and up against Embarcadero all the way to the Farm. He even gobbled up the Buena Vista, whereupon the Embarcaderans beat him back, but not before some folks died.

Folks like mi madre y padre.

Lord E'd like to be an expansive SOB, too, but he's fortunately not as good at it as his daddy. Once in a while he sends his knighties against the Border between Embar and Potrero, but they always turn back—usually about the time they see our knighties with their body-armor and AKs, and decide knives and crowbars won't cut it.

But this time, Lord E determined that he would leave his knighties at home and send only sméagols over the Border. 'Cause Lord E had a new merlin and Lord E's new merlin had a plan.

It is my eternal shame that I didn't know this. It was Deadend, sméagol extraordinaire, who brought the smell to Hismajesty's attention.

"Somethin's up," he says.

We are hanging in the Throneroom of the Regency Palace when he comes in and makes this pronouncement.

"What's up?" asks Squire, 'cause that's his job. Hismajesty don't talk to sméagols.

"It's an ill wind from Potrero-Taraval," says Deadend, "Lubejob's been skulking around the Farm."

"Says who?" asks Squire, scathing-like. "Or are you fabricatin'?"

"Kaymart and Bags put me onto the rumble. I saw the sméagol myself. It was Lubejob. I put a tail on him. Followed him all the way back to the Slot."

"Ask the sméagol, 'then what?'" orders Hismajesty.

"Then what?" asks Squire.

"Then he huddles with his gang. Mark me, Squire, there's evil afoot—we're being scoped."

Hismajesty looks to me. "Had you an inkling of this perfidy, merlin?" he asks me.

"The branches of the Tree of Destiny did quiver," I say and cross my fingers, 'cause the TOD was sitting on the balcony in a stiff breeze at the time. "I perceived no cause."

Hismajesty's brows go all gnarly. "Summon Scrawl," he tells Squire and Squire turns to the gofer next to him and says, "Gofer Scrawl."

Hismajesty's brows are still looking like smooshed black caterpillars. "Prepare to read the runes," he says to me.

I do, and damn quick. Hismajesty's an ace dude if you're square with him, but if he thinks you let him down—wham!— you could be deadjim in no appreciable time. I don't wish to be deadjim, so I get my rune can and hustle back to the Throneroom.

Scrawl is there when I get back, and Firescape and Cinderblock, too, 'cause this looks like it could be a job for the military.

She's a piece of work. Firescape, I mean. Number one jade— all rigged out in black leather and red spandies and redder hair, with her Magic Weapon slung at her hip. My pants get uncomfortable. I shake my rune can to announce myself and get my hormones' attention off Firescape.

Hismajesty waves a hand at me. He's not scowly now— mostly, I think, 'cause of Hermajesty, who is sitting in his lap. Hermajesty's name is really Ampam as she was born in the produce bin of a mini-mart on Columbus, but His M doesn't care, though he is of higher origin, having come into this world in the back seat of a Mercedes-Benz.

There is a circular pit in Hismajesty's Throneroom. We call it the Pit. Here, we gather to read runes and jam on Saturday nights. This is where Scrawl and I go now.

While the Majesties and the others sit in the soft cushions around the shallow edge, Scrawl and I move down onto the stone floor and begin to circle each other. She shakes her rune bag at me; I shake my can at her. It is a bright red can and says "Hills Bros" on it. There is a picture of a merlin drinking a cup of coffee on the front, and it is this I direct at her so she will remember that I am a merlin and she is only Scrawl.

She yields, of course, 'cause that's protocol, and I am the first to spill my runes on the center of the great Mandala in the floor of the Pit. We both hunker down to ponder them.

Scrawl makes humming noises and nods as if she sees auspicious stuff. I see nothing but broken chips of glass and bottle caps. There is even a matchstick or two and a button from the fly of my jeans. There is also a rotten old peach pit; someone's used my rune can for a garbage receptacle. I snag the pit and chuck it over my shoulder.

Scrawl "ahems" at me, then waves her hand over the stuff like she is stirring a pot. I look at her face but her big, watery eyes are mum. I wonder if she is wondering what I see.

I squint at the runes, then my eyes go wonky like they do. I see a shape. Looks like a giraffe, but that doesn't make sense. I look at it some more and it gets to be a crane—the kind there is near some of the big skyscraper carcasses downtown.

"A crane," I say and nod, then see something else. "And a scales."

Scrawl comes to peer over my shoulder. "Yeah," she says. "Could be."

I move to another angle. My wonky eyes see a mountain . . . or a pyramid . . . or maybe it's the Regency Palace.

I say, "Mountain," and Scrawl mumbles, "My turn, Chickpea-face." She moves, too, giving me the hairy eyeball. Then she screeches, "Danger! Danger! They's after something!"

"Sooth!" says Firescape. "Of course, they's after something. Lord E's always after something."

I begin to suspect that Scrawl sees less in the runes than I do, but while I am trying to make sense out of "crane," "scales" and "mountain," she stands up straight as a lamp post, clutches her head and says in her best Voice-O-Doom, "They's after Hermajesty!"

The Majesties don't like this pronouncement. They look at each other and get all scowly again.

I check my higher consciousness, trying to sense out what this has to do with cranes and scales and mountains. When I think of mountains, I think of trees. Mountains have lots of trees—more than the Farm, even. And they are much bigger than the Fabled Tree of Destiny—Giants. This makes me think I am supposed to be thinking of the Fabled TOD.

I say as much. "I think of the Tree of Destiny. Runes are not enough. The Tree must be consulted."

Scrawl sees that Hismajesty likes this pronouncement better

than hers, so she gives me the hairy eyeball again. I am the only one who can talk to the Tree. Still, she pretends to be agreeable.

"Chickpea's right," she says, "meanwhile, I shall consult the wall runes."

We are dismissed and I make my way up the Great Crystal Elevator to my chambers on the top floor of the Palace. The Palace is much narrower at the top than it is at the bottom. On my floor there are only eight big rooms, joined two and two. Four are the Majesty's; four are mine, although I've considered asking Firescape to share them with me. Two of the four have beds so I have my choice of sleeping places. Naturally, I have in mind that she should share the beds, too.

I go to the room I use as a workshop. There, out on the balcony, is the Fabled Tree. He is enjoying the sun, and the tips of his branches reach upward, waving. I am sorry to disturb him, but I must, taking my seat beside him at the balcony.

He's a Douglas Fir. I know this 'cause of the Wiz. I also know that Trees have sexes just like people and animals. It just so happens that Doug is a boy, which is good, 'cause the name fits better.

"O Tree of Destiny," I say. Normally, I call him Doug, but this is ritual stuff. "O Tree of Destiny, we have a problem. Lord E Lordy has spies upon us. His head sméagol's been seen in Embar. All the little sméagols've been seen too. So says Kaymart, Bags and Deadend. O Tree of Destiny, we fear the kingdom of Embarcadero is jeopardized by these skulkings. Scrawl says Lord E wants Hermajesty. I need to know is this so and how he means to get her."

I bend my face to the little Tree. The boughs brush my cheek. I close my eyes and breathe in the firry smell. It reminds me of the Farm that now is all that divides southwestern Embarcadero from Potrero-Taraval, and where I spent many child-days.

Nothing happens, except I can almost see the Farm with its giant Trees and flowers and strange buildings. Which lack of something makes me wonder—like I always wonder—how I got to be a merlin. I know it's 'cause I got the Tree. I say a thanks prayer that Doug chose me and not somebody else (like Scrawl, for instance).

When I open my eyes again, I see something odd. I see a knightie looking up at me from the plaza outside. This is not unusual except that she is half-hiding behind an old trolleycar and she is not wearing Firescape's colors. She is wearing the yellow and black of the Virgin Guard, the knighties who patrol the Richmond near the Farm.

She sees me just as I see her and disappears behind the trolleycar. A chill goes down my spine. I pick up Doug—pot and all—and head back to the Throneroom. The Majesties are surprised to see me lugging the TOD out of the Great Crystal Elevator.

"What the hell?" says His M and salutes the Tree. Hermajesty throws him a kiss.

I ask Firescape if she knows any reason one of Sweetie's Virgin Guard would be wharfside instead of on her normal beat around the Richmond Virgin. She can't think of any, and when I tell her the Tree inspired me to know there was a yellow knightie in the courtyard, skulking, she and her sidekick, Cinderblock, unsafety their magic AKs and head for the street.

"Well, merlin?" Hismajesty is looking kingly at me. "Well? What has the Tree of Destiny revealed?"

"The Tree says," I say, though I am clueless, "there are sméagols all about us."

I set Doug's pot down and dust off my hands, catching a whiff of his nice firry smell and trying to think of something more to say. I do.

"The Farm must be watched night and day. This knightie the Tree saw is ersatz. Which means that, most likely, one of Sweetie's gang is deadjim. Maybe more than one. First, sméagols around the Farm, now sméagols in disguise, at the heart of it all. Think of it, sire. If you wanted something close to Lord E, what better way than to disguise yourself as someone who could get real close?"

His M is nodding. "Yeah. Like a knightie. But why a Yellow

Knightie from the Virgin Guard? Lord E's gotta know the Palace is guarded by Red Knighties."

I shrug. "She had to get past all kinds of eyes, Majesty. I suspect she cacked the first knightie she came across."

His M is still nodding. "But is she after my queen?"

I don't know the answer to this, but I'm not about to say that. Scrawl saves me from having to open my mouth. She comes in wailing like a house on fire. "Oi!" she's saying. "Oi! They've left signs! Th'arrogance of 'em!"

They left signs, alright. LORD E RULES! was the sign. Plastered all over the side of the old trolleycar. I didn't have to guess who did it. Only question is, why so bold?

Hismajesty doesn't ask me again if Lord E is after Hermajesty. He has Firescape set a guard on her and puts all the knighties in Embarcadero on alert.

Rumbles start flying. All kinds of scuttlebutt. I hear all of it, of course, 'cause I'm listening. A good merlin has "ears" all over the place. A better merlin is pro-active. I go down to the Gee Gah to hang around the steamy stalls and shops that smell of fish and herbs and incense. That's where I hear that Lord E's shopping queens. According to the rumble along the Du Pon Gai, he's lost another lady-lord to the dolores. Childbirth, says the rumble.

The old ladies and gents in their shops and stalls chatter like pigeons, blaming it on the water, the food, the air in Potrero. On the outside, I think they're right. It could be any of those things. Potrero got its problems, that's a surely, foremost of which is a King who don't give a fig about what he can't stick in his treasure house. And there's a lot of sicklies, too. But I know there's always something inside the outside—something that makes the outside work bad. In the case of Potrero-Taraval, that thing is the dolores.

A long time ago, see, way before the Getting Out—hell, before there was even a city here—this whole place belonged to a people called Ohlone. They named it Awaa-te and lived close to the water. One day, they woke up to find aliens—my own ancestors—staring at them from inside these silly tin hats.

My ancestors put them all into a dios house called Dolores, which means "sad." In this dios house, the Ohlone caught the alien's diseases and died. There are thousands of them buried around the Dolores dios house. I learned this from the Wiz.

By the time the folks who called themselves Americans sent a government agent to check up on the Ohlone, there was only one left—an old man named Pedro Alcantara. Pedro told the agent that he had lost his son and asked if the agent couldn't help to find him. And then he said, "I am all that is left of my people—I am alone."

The Dolores dios house lies smack inside the boundaries of the northern-most Potreran barrio. You can see the top of it from Embar. That, I thought, was why Potrero was so sickly and so sad —those spirits were still there—the Ohlone dolores.

I am pondering this when I bump into my good buddy, Creepy Lou.

"Thay!" he says to me. "Thay Chickpea!" (Which is 'cause he's missing a few teeth. He'd call me Cicerone, but Chickpea is easier on both of us.) "Thay, Chickpea! You be scopin' the rumble? Lord E lost hithelf another lordette."

"I be hearing that," I say. "Third one."

He nods, looking sad. "Third one. Young, too. . . . Thecond trimethter."

This pokes my Alice bone. "Where'd you hear that?"

Creepy Lou scratches around in his scraggy hair, making dust and leaves rain onto his shoulders. "Shmeagols."

Interesting. "Deadend?"

"Naw, *little* shmeagol," he says, and jerks his head three times to the right. "One of his hangabouts. Shmeagol says, uh, Lord E thinks we got some kinda magic. 'Cause Hermatchsty has three babies, already, no hitches, no glitches."

The last word comes out in a shower of saliva. I blink and shake my head.

"No, really. Th' Alcalde thinks our women are magic." His face lights up; big holey grin, a little wicked. He pumps his left knee up and down and jerks his head three times to the right. "I think tho too."

Makes sense, I s'pose. Odd sense. Lord E didn't have such good family luck. He hadn't produced an heir yet. His M has three—two girls and a boy. So, Lord E might think if he has the right queen—a *magic* queen—he can have heirs too. And slit Hismajesty's throat to the bargain.

I shake my head, this time meaning it. "Our women aren't magic," I say, "just healthy."

Lou nods, stamps his right foot, and grabs at something I can't see. "It's the water. Damn bad water in Potrero."

"Damn bad attitude," I answer, knowing it's the Dolores.

second: his diminutive self

 **CICERONE.** That's what mi madre called me. Means "chickpea". Other kids picked up on that and, well, you can probably guess how that went down. You got any idea how small a chickpea is? Pretty damned small. Got called "Peanut" a lot, too. And some other stuff not as complimentary. I wished heartily that mi madre had craved kung pao or seen a seagull or heard sea breezes after I popped out, but no—she had to eat chickpeas.

Mi madre said there was a chance I'd get bigger as I got older, but it never happened. Didn't really expect it to. It's got a lot to do with diet and that mi madre didn't eat too well when I was a babe. There was food and all, but they were new here and didn't know the what-how. You get the best veggies in the Sang Yee Gah, but we lived at the other end of the kingdom. I think I saw my first broccoli when I was five. Thought somebody'd shrunk up a shrubbery.

You don't notice stuff when you're little 'cause you think life just goes on and on, and that whatever life's like, it'll always be just like that. My kid life was pretty bueno, you know? Mi padre got a job at a beanery in the neighborhood and mi madre learned how to grow green stuff in a garden on the roof. They got integrated, I guess you'd call it. Which was more than they'd done all the other places they'd been.

It might've been a foggy old dead city to the folks from Outside, but to mi madre y padre it was the Gam Saan—the Golden Mountain—which I guess to them, was sort of like Eldorado.

It was the Economy that killed the cities, Kaymart says. What with one thing and another (like the fact that some Economic Centers were an earthquake, volcano, or hurricane away from Complete Ruin) people just started Getting Out. They went to Rural Places—Planned Communities, Kaymart calls them, where there were no dumpsters or indigents, no rats the size of hub caps, no syringes in the gutters, and where nobody planted their backside on your front porch and called it homesteading.

According to History, folks just sort of drained out of The Cities like corn meal through a slit bag—first trickle-trickle, and then a steady pour and then let's-get-the-hell-out-o-here. It took a while, but finally everybody who could Got Out. What Kaymart calls the Economic Base went with them.

That left people like mi madre y padre, who did a lot of wandering before they found a place that wanted them. And people like Creepy Lou, who isn't much wanted either, 'cause no one likes to be around a dude that makes them twitch. And people like Firescape's madre who just got born in the wrong barrio. And people like Lord E who saw the Getting Out as a Golden Opportunity. (Oh, I'm not saying Lord E is that old, 'cause he isn't. But there's always been guys just like him, even before the Getting Out, according to Kaymart.)

Anyway, mi madre y padre fit in here, so I just sort of fit in with them and I thought fitting in was something you just did and that just was.

I remember Cinco de Mayo festivals that'd go on early into the next spring morning; the streets all clogged up with folks and torches; the air so stuffed with music and laughter I didn't see how anybody could move. After I was s'posed to be in bed, I'd lean out over the fire escape and listen and watch and think that maybe I could just float right out the window, and that all that noise and heat and life would let me down to the alley as light as a feather.

I was ten when mi madre y padre were killed.

We lived real close to the Border between Potrero and Embarcadero—just north of the Mission Dolores, I found out later on. Lord E's daddy was especially expansive that summer so the strip right along the Border wasn't the safest place to be. I don't think mi madre y padre knew this, or that it wasn't the best place to go treasure hunting. But there they were, poking through the empty buildings when the Alcalde's knighties put in an appearance.

Mi madre had wanted some little bit of furniture to festive up the room we ate in and stayed warm in when the temp dropped— that's why they were there. A stick of furniture seems like such an oddball thing to die for.

I still don't know how it happened really. Just that I was playing in the alley with Fredo and Pigeon when all of a sudden Mrs. Lopez-Alvero, whose husband called her Acorn, was standing in front of me with all her big self trembling and her eyes wetting her rust-colored cheeks. She put her arms around me, too, I remember. And I remember thinking, that here I was, two years short of my Coming of Age Rite, and now there would be no one to do it with me.

There was more than that inside me, but I couldn't let it out just then—only later on Mrs. Lopez-Alvero's big, soft shoulder.

I think that was the first time I heard the Whispers—while I was grieving all over Mrs. Lopez-Alvero. I thought it was Mrs. Lopez-Alvero at first, saying Ave Marias in my ear. But it wasn't her; her mouth had closed up shop and gone all grim and sad.

The Whispers didn't mean anything to me 'cause I didn't understand what they were saying, but I heard them as if they were air being sucked through the Lopez-Alvero's actually working window fan. But the window fan wasn't on that day 'cause of the fog and fog doesn't whisper. I thought it might be rain and that the sky was crying for mi madre y padre—but there wasn't any rain, either. Just fog—a wu pesado so thick and still no sound could move in it.

So, I lay in Mrs. Lopez-Alvero's overly padded lap and listened to Whispers I didn't understand or even really hear all that well. I decided to believe it was mi madre y padre whispering to me from the Abhá Kingdom, and that somehow made me feel a little put back together. When I pray, I still see mi madre y padre with a ten-year-old's eyes. They were day and night; mi madre with sun-colored hair and pale skin and mi padre with midnight locks and skin like burnished copper. I take after mi padre, mostly, but he always said I had her eyes and her smile. I suppose I am what you'd call a legacy—a pretty sad one, if you ask me.

Well, there was someone to do my Coming of Age rite with me, after all; there was Mrs. Lopez-Alvero, who sat with me at the table when I had turned twelve, and gave me my first coffee in a hand-thrown cup, and spoke to me about the Grown Up Things —choosing mates and raising families and finding Something To Do in the world.

I had my coffee with cream and no sugar. And then I packed my stuff and moved north, away from the neighborhood and away from anyplace where I could look up and perhaps see the sad old building where mi madre y padre had died for a stick of furniture.

I stayed for the Day of the Dead that year—my twelfth year—and I painted my face like a skull and I carried a torch and I prayed for the Departed Ones. I sat up late and listened to Whisperers say nothing to me. Then I moved on up into the Hollow.

Now, let me tell you that I was a sorry citizen at that time. I had officially Come of Age, which meant two Big Things. One: I was now responsible for furthering my education because Two: In three years I'd be looked at to choose my Calling and I didn't have the veriest glimmer of one.

Maybe this doesn't seem like such a problem. I s'pose wherever you're from it might not be. But here, where there are so many jobs that need to get done just to keep Decay from taking over the kingdom, its the Most Important Thing you do before you're grown up. It's what you're growing up for. I knew this as well as anybody. But here I was, heading toward the big ONE-FIVE with no Calling in sight. At least none that I figured I could pull off. I was no kind of cook, so following in mi padre's footsteps was out of the question, and I couldn't grow a thing to save my sorry life. So there it was.

At twelve, in the Hollow, I was a lonely solo with nobody but the street kids to rub up against.

Oh, and I had this cat . . . well, I can't exactly say I had the cat, but we shared my cozy. He was a cat of many colors and bad attitudes and smells. We were not what I would call friends, but we got along okay. I called him Bunuelo 'cause he looked like one of those fat little buns that come out of bakery ovens around Christmastime. He sure as hell ate better than I did, mostly 'cause I always brought dinner. He hardly ever returned the favor.

I could talk to Bunuelo about the Whisperers. I still couldn't hear them clear enough to make out one word of what they were saying, but they were there on and off, kinda like a bowu mist. Sometimes I thought I saw them, too, the way you think you see Something out of the tail of your eye, and the Something jerks your head around, but there's nothing there.

One thing about cats I can surely appreciate. This is that they are good listeners. You can learn much about the art of listening from a cat.

Bunuelo never laughed at me when I spoke of the Whisperers. He never gave me pitiful looks like Mrs. Lopez-Alvero, or swatted my behind like Mr. Lopez-Alvero, or called me "that jingbing ghost boy" like my so-called friends and acquaintances. My teachers at the Wiz consulted the Fiche and took my questions about Whisperers into the Holy of Holies, but I never got more from them than the same sort of pitiful looks I got from Mrs. Lopez-Alvero.

Bunuelo even purred when I spoke to him about the Whisperers. Sometimes he also gave himself a bath, but I knew he was still listening. I suspect we were friends after all, and just too macho to admit it.

Eh, stupid idea, now that I think of it. Bunuelo may have had the genes for macho, but I sure didn't.

Bunuelo disappeared the year Hismajesty became King. I s'pose I should've seen a sign in this, but I didn't. I just saw that I was really alone this time. When I got tired of being alone, I had two options: I could go into the street, where other kids would call me names to remind me of how little I was, or I could go to the Wiz where I could hear all sorts of Important Stuff that might further my education and put me in mind of a Calling.

Nine out of ten, I went to the Wiz. Problem was, I had to go into the street to get there, which meant I'd arrive late for my classes with a sorry attitude and a few new cuts and bruises to show for it.

One night, after coming home from the Wiz with even more bruises than usual, I decided I was sick of it. I addressed God and the Whisperers, saying, "O Lord . . . and you Whispering guys, whoever you are. Know that I, Cicerone Del, am mighty tired of suffering abuse day in and day out from people who think it is somehow their right and responsibility to cream me every time I budge outside my cozy. If there is anything you can do about this state of affairs, together or independent, I should surely be much obliged. Thank you, amen, and insh'allah."

The next morning I met Hoot.

He's sitting up on top of a bunch of packing crates that are choking the open end of the alley below my cozy. Red hair—duck-back slick—levis, black boots with those nasty little chains around the ankles that mean, I'm bad. And he's wearing this jacket—this black, leather jacket—but it's like 80 degrees in this stinking alley which is steaming like a crab pot, and this dude's not even breaking a sweat.

I gotta admire that, even while I'm thinking, This jake's gonna kick my sorry little chickpea butt from here to the Wharf.

"Well," he says, and pulls these shiny shades down from out of his hair as if to see me better. "Well, if it ain't His Diminutive Self. What's shakin' Chickpea?"

Okay, could've been worse. I mean, there's a lot worse stuff he could've called me, and he could've called me nothing at all but just commenced to kicking my butt down the alley. I figure, this is not so inauspicious, and I say, "I'm shakin'."

"No kidding?" he says. "Why's that? D'I scare you?"

"Voices from the sky kind of, you know, weird me out."

He tilts his head sidewise like one of those window-sill-sitting pigeons and says, "That's not what I hear. I hear voices from the sky's pretty vanilla to yourself."

Damned if I know what to say to that, 'cause I surely expected to be getting kicked by now, so I just squint up at him for a few and then I start up the alley like I'm bored with the whole business.

"Hey!" he shouts and starts to climb down off his crate.

I know I'm in for a kicking now, and I try to hurry, but this jake's fast, and he comes down in front of me before I can make the street. He's twice my size, easy . . . well, okay, so I exaggerate a little. But he's big and he's got his hands on his hips and he's staring at me outta these shiny, scratched up shades and I'm really shaking now, 'cause I can't read his eyes and I just suddenly realize how important that has been to my survival up to now.

"So what do they say?" he asks me.

Since I expected to be flat on my back, perusing sky by now, this question comes as a great relief. I ask back at him, "Who?"

His head waggles and I swear I see his eyes roll behind the shades. "The voices from the sky, Chickpea-brain. What've we been chewin' on here?"

I been chewin' on the inside of my left cheek, but I wax all sassy anyway and say, "Who says they come from the sky? I never said they come from the sky. I don't know where they come from."

"Well, what do they say, anyway?"

"Stuff," I say, and before he can ask the inevitable, I add, "Real secret stuff. If I tell anybody what it is, there'll be hell to pay." (Well, I'm not about to tell him I don't know what they say.)

"Okay. But what kind of stuff do they say? I mean, do they do mah jongg tournaments so you win a lot of swag, they tell the weather—what?"

I make something up on the fly. "Well, they told me I'd be meeting you this morning."

He seems real interested now. "Yeah? What else they tell you about me?"

To hell with secrets, I figure. "They said you'd be a real neon dude. Number one jade. Too cool for words."

I am lying like I got no conscience. Which is not true—I got plenty of conscience. But I also got an appreciable survival instinct. Anyway, this works. This jake is smiling at me—grinning at me. He likes this stuff.

"Where you going—the Wiz?" he asks, to which I nod. "Okay." And he turns around and starts to walk with me.

"So," he asks as we stroll, "these voices from wherever they're from—they guy voices or girl voices?"

I fabricate that they are girl voices as I suspect this will hit big with Hoot. (He is called Hoot, he informs me, because the singular thing his madre laid ears on after she'd popped was his padre crowing like hoot-owl.) The girl voices are a very big hit, and Hoot walks me all the way to the Wiz. The net effect of which is that I arrive with no more bruises and abrasions than I started out with that morning.

Hoot is outside my cozy every morning for over a week and then on and off after that. Got so it didn't matter whether he was there or not. My bruises and abrasions healed right up and were not added unto. Needless to say, I was sincerely grateful for this and thanked both God and Whisperers accordingly.

third: something goes down

I AM asleep in my favorite room when I hear the ruckus. Out in the hallway, voices are ricocheting off the walls. As I reach the door I hear Hismajesty roaring, "Get 'em, for cry-aye! Get 'em!" and the thunder of feet. I pop out my head and I see knighties galore, heading for the secret elevator. That's the first thing I see. The second thing I see is His M standing out in the hallway in his boxers with Her M sucked up to him like a limpet.

He spies me out of the corner of his eye and says, "How come you didn't see this, merlin? Where were you while all this was going down?"

I was asleep, Majesty, doesn't sound too good, so I don't say this. I say something equally dumb: "See what, Majesty?"

He splutters and waves his arms. "This attempt on my queen! Dastardly!"

He sees I'm not tracking him and lets go of Hermajesty to come and drag me into their rooms. He drags me all the way to the balcony where he points down the long, sloping wall with its little rectangle pocket gardens and windows. A doubled cable dangles through a piton sunk in the flank of the palace. I know it's a piton 'cause of the Wiz, where I learned about mountain-climbers and Sherpas.

"Wall-crawlers!" snarls Hismajesty, his finger shaking. "Wall-crawlers after my queen! What do you have to say for yourself, merlin?"

His brows crushed together like fighting kittens, he glares at me. The breeze is chill and I realize I am shivering and he is not, though he is wearing mostly skin. I am about to say that the Alcalde's merlin must have some serious magic at his disposal, but the thought of Scrawl inheriting Doug sends me on another tack altogether.

I draw myself up smartly. "I knew of this, Majesty," I say and raise my finger skyward. "I saw a crane in the runes, and a scale." I don't mention the mountain, which it seems was the Regency Palace after all.

The kittens wriggle mightily. "So?"

"Normally, a crane would be needed to reach this height," I explain. "And the scale . . ." I point to the rope, threaded through the clip on the piton. "A counter balance."

"Why didn't you warn me?"

"Because I also saw that the attempt would fail. If I told you, you might've done something to change that. At the very least you'd have worried yourself sleepless. I saw no need to disturb you or frighten Hermajesty."

Hermajesty is sweetly pleased. She smiles at me.

"Thanks, Chickpea."

Hismajesty's face struggles. Finally, he says, "Well done, merlin," and dismisses me.

By the skin of my teeth, I think, and slink back to my rooms.

By dawn, we know that the wall-crawlers were Noe Valley Ninjas—the Alcalde's crack troops—the only ones, I figure, who could've gotten past our best defenses without being seen. By mid-morning we know exactly how they did it. They came by sea.

"Up from China Basin most likely," says Firescape. "Under the wharf at the Point. Stowed their boats under the docks and came up the back way from Fish Alley. Left one of their dinghies behind as a calling card."

Firescape is angry and offended and her skin is all flushed rose-gold. This makes her eyes extra dark, which makes her extra beautiful. Firescape is the only red-headed Chinese girl I know. Her mother's name was Flannigan, she told me once, and she'll name her firstborn that.

I hope to be the father of her firstborn. Flannigan is fine with me.

Hismajesty is also angry. He looks to Squire and Firescape and me. "Advise me," he says.

"Bring in more knighties from downtown," Squire says. "Put Wharfside on heavy alert."

Firescape shakes her head, making all that red hair gleam in the light from the morning streets. "Leaves our southwest flank exposed. I say we move Hermajesty to a more defensible position. The Summer Palace or the Grace."

Squire spocks an eyebrow. "I say we do both."

I am nodding when His M gets to me.

"You agree, merlin?"

I keep nodding. "A deft move."

"Which one? The Summer Palace or the Grace?"

I consider this, watching Firescape's face, which is no hardship. The Summer Palace is in a walled compound near the Marina—a wildy sort of place called the Presidio, ringed by the farms that produce about two-thirds of our food. Problem is, it's close to the water. Water, we now know, is hard to defend. The Grace is a dios house, but it's built like a fortress—reinforced concrete. Problem is, it's as close to the Border as the Regency Palace. I decide this is a decision I must take to the Wiz and say as much.

Hismajesty respects my words, but warns me: "Make it quick, merlin. Lord E Lordy is scoping the mother of my children. If anything happens to her . . ."

I don't need to hear the end of that. I cut for the Wiz direct. Firescape goes along—as my military adviser, she says.

The Wiz is quiet as a dios house this morning—full of chatter and the sound of pages turning. There's no singing or chanting here, though. Firescape and I move on through the main chamber and into the private places in the back. Here, there are maps of the city's five kingdoms. Here, I can strategize.

"What first?" asks Firescape when we reach the sanctum of the map room. It's very quiet here and her voice is hushed.

"The Fiche," I say and approach that Relic with reverence, genuflecting before her. "Fiche," I say, "maps and aerials. North of the Slot."

"Specify," Fiche responds in her tinny voice, "Define 'slot.'"

I forget sometimes how literal The Fiche is. The title is short for Micro-Fiche and I figure this literalism is the micro part.

"Embarcadero. North of the Bayshore. Include the Richmond, north of the Farm."

"Specify 'farm.'"

Fiche, being an antiquity, tends to think like one except where the Knowledge Maintenance Team has changed her programming. She uses the pre-Getting Out names for just about everything. A good merlin has to be steeped in local history.

"Golden Gate Park," I say.

Fiche's flat faceplate displays a map. On it, I locate the Regency Palace, the Summer Palace and the Grace. Firescape stands so close, she is almost touching my shoulder, though Fiche's screen is broad and could be seen from further back. I take this as a sign that my love incantations are working.

"Outline these locations," I say, trying not to tremble. I poke my finger at the screen, touching the two palaces and the dios house. After a moment of thought, I add the Virgin, another huge place of worship buried in the Richmond, and the Tin Hau, a dios house behind the Gee Gah. The spots are circled in five bright colors.

I study the avenues of access, feeling Firescape's breath soft on my cheek. This makes it hard to concentrate, but I see what I need to see. I clear my throat.

"It seems to me that the Regency Palace is already the safest place for Hermajesty. I see no reason to move her."

"But it's so close to the Border."

"And the Border is fortified and guarded."

Firescape is unsure. "The Tin Hau would be hardest to get to. No wilds, no down-looks, no tunnels . . . But, the Virgin is built like a keep. I vote for the Virgin."

I glance at her, chill. "May I remind you that it was a Potrero knightie in Virgin's clothing that the Tree revealed to me this morning?"

She is abashed and I feel guilty for pulling rank.

"Summer Palace, then," she suggests.

I look at the whole picture again. Part of me wants to agree with Firescape. Forge a bond. Be on the same uplink. But deep down in my soul I feel it is wrong to move Hermajesty at all, though I'm not sure why.

"I must cast the runes," I say, and back we go to the Palace, pausing just outside the doors of the Wiz to genuflect.

It isn't far from the Wiz to the Palace—a bunch of blocks on Columbus is all. We are back again in notime to find the Majesties waiting for us.

Scrawl waits too, Face-O-Doom. I wonder if the Wiz has a spell to get rid of Scrawl. Then I pinch myself for this unworthy thought.

"Well, merlin," says Hismajesty, "where do we relocate?"

"I must cast the runes," I say.

Scrawl snorts.

"You must cast the runes," repeats Squire. "You always gotta do something. You consult the Wiz, you gotta to cast the runes; you cast the runes, you gotta talk to the Tree."

His M is nodding in agreement. "This is my queen's fate we're chewin' on, merlin. Don't you have any revelations?"

"I do," I say, wondering what they are. I realize something

new has happened. Something that's got Scrawl all smug and Squire and Hismajesty all twigged.

"Tell me," His M demands. "Tell me your revelations."

"It is revealed to me by the Wiz that the Regency Palace is the most defensible place for Hermajesty to be kept. I feel it would be unwise to relocate."

Hermajesty, juggling her youngest princess on her knee, is pleased. "Good. I don't wanna move. I like it here. The beds are soft."

Firescape gives me a strange glance, then steps forward. "Majesty, I must disagree with the noble merlin. I believe we should move the Royal Family to the Summer Palace."

Hermajesty's face screws up prettily. "But it's not summer! There's fog every morning and the Summer Palace is so friggin' cold. And the beds are hard and the rooms are too big and echoey."

I forget sometimes that for all Ampam has been Hermajesty for three years (with a prince and two princesses to show for it), she is no more than a child, herself—even at sixteen. This outburst reminds me. I think of her in the hands of the Alcalde of Potrero-Taraval—a man with a bad rep when it comes to his ladies' lifespans—and my blood runs deepfreeze. She'd be joining his other lordettes singing with the Ohlone dolores in no appreciable time.

My face must show fear, for Scrawl looks smugger'n ever.

"So," she says, cackle-voiced. "So, you think this is a safe place for Her M, huh? Let me show you the runes I been reading, Chickpea."

She and Squire take me and Firescape out of the Palace and along the pavement to its southeast flank, where there is a shaded overhang. There, she strikes a grand pose—wrath of God stuff, like a beard-free Moses. I expect lightning to drip from her finger.

There's no lightning, but might as well be. Our knightie night visitors have left a message beneath the overhang on the haunch of our Majesties' home. It is a semi-cubist mural showing, in vivid detail, what Lord E Lordy plans for our queen. Up to and including a one way trip into China Basin if she doesn't plop forth an heir. The artist has a bold sense of color and a flair for the dramatic.

I can almost hear Firescape's hair standing up on her head. "Has Hermajesty seen this?"

"Are you kidding?" snorts Squire. "We'd have to peel her off the sidewalk. His M wanted you to see it before we paint it out. Thought it might help to clarify the situation."

I hackle. Squire is a spiky so-and-so at the best of times. Now, he's just plain offensive.

"The situation is clear, thank you. But I feel moving the Royal Family is . . . well, not a good move," I finish, lame. "I am the King's merlin, after all. Gut calls are what I do. They're the tools of my trade."

Scrawl snorts again and pokes a crooky thumb at the mural. "When those damn sméagols got the time to paint a whole friggin' peep show on the backside of Hismajesty's roost, your gut calls ain't worth squiddle. Firescape's got the idea. Move the royal family to the Presidio. And quick, before our artists strike again. Maybe paint a love note on Her M's door while they's dragging her to doom city."

Squire is nodding and Firescape is looking at me, sad-eyes. I'm going to lose this one. Firescape's mind is made up and His M listens to Firescape more than just about anybody.

That night I cast the runes in my workshop. I've just emptied the can when Firescape shows up at my door. For once, the Magic Weapon is nowhere in sight.

She doesn't say anything, at first, just looks at me, and I get nervous.

"I'm casting runes," I say, as if that isn't clear as bluesky, and when she hesitates, I crook my finger at her.

She comes in, and my merlin robe is suddenly too warm. I strip down to my shirt and jeans and feel no cooler. I clear my throat.

"I'm sorry, Del," she says, before I can say something dumb and nervous.

I'm surprised. "For what?"

"For siding with Scrawl and Squire."

"You didn't side with them. It was your idea to move Her M. They sided with you."

My intention is to make her feel better. I have the opposite effect; her pretty mouth droops further at its perfect corners.

"I'm very sorry, Del. I . . . I really thought it was a better place . . . tactically, I mean. It's a ways from the Border . . ." Her voice gives up.

"I was just tagging a hunch," I say. "I got nothing to back it up, really."

She glances over my shoulder. "What do the runes say?"

"Not a whole lot . . ." I begin, looking at them—buttons and bottle caps and chips of glass. There's even a sea shell or two and a seagull beak. Looks like a little orange pincers. The peach pit is back again. And now there are some little tacks or nails in there too. This makes me a little testy—I would surely like to know who keeps tossing trash into my rune can. A merlin's rune can is sacred—no place to be depositing junk. I pick out the tacks, chuck the pit, and give my full attention to the runes.

My eyes go suddenly wonky.

Pincers. What the hell does that mean?

They're clamped around a splinter of driftwood. The Whisperers are screaming at me to *get it*. I shake my head. I don't get it. Some merlin I am.

"I gotta talk to the Tree," I say, and start to turn, but Firescape's hand is on my arm—on my bare arm—and lava is bubbling somewhere down below. I can feel it.

"Do you really think it's not good to move Her M? You feel that, deep?" Her eyes are like chocolates sprinkled with gold dust.

I feel something deep. I nod.

"Then I'll back you with Hismajesty. We can defend the Regency . . . I trust you," she adds.

"How old are you, Firescape?" I ask.

She frowns. "Old enough," she says, and pulls herself up as tall as she can and gives me this LOOK. "I'm sixteen—according to Wiz time."

Sixteen. Sixteen and not married and no children. A career woman.

"So," I say, "you figure to quit the Service someday and settle down to have Flannigans?"

Her tilted eyes slip sidewise to the windows and she toes the carpet and shrugs. "Why settle down? Sure, I'd have to take leave while I was . . . you know." She puts her hands out around an invisible belly. "But I could do both . . . with the right dude . . ." She shrugs again and her eyes slide back over and kind of bump into mine.

I have no idea, at this point, what my face is doing, so I compose my features and nod sagely.

"Don't you think?" she adds.

"Sounds good to me," I improvise. "I'd want you to be careful, though. If it was me. If the dude was me, I mean."

Lame, Chickpea. Really lame.

She takes a step closer, the frown coming back. I can smell her shampoo—jasmine.

"Yeah? How careful?"

I lick my lips, which are suddenly muy dry. "Well, no hazardous duty. You gotta think of all the little Flannigans, right?"

She's right in my face now—her head tilted back so her chin almost meets mine. The frown sort of melts, but she looks sort of . . . puzzled. "All the little Flannigans," she repeats, and I think those are the sexiest words I've ever heard in my life.

Our lips are nearly touching and I'm counting Flannigans,

when someone pounds on the door. We part company. Someone turns out to be Cinderblock, looking for her General, Firescape's magic AK in hand. Duty calls, and all I end up with is a sad chocolate-gold glance as Firescape slips out of my room.

I return to the runes. Bird beaks and driftwood. What the hell does that mean?

I talk to the Tree. I try being all formal, at first, but soon, Doug gets to me, and I'm caressing his boughs and pouring out my feelings for Firescape.

Doug understands. He gives me the idea that I need to make a love potion for Firescape. Like most of my ideas, this one comes to me in his perfume. By morning, with his blessing, I have made an attar of fir for Firescape, which I hope will do more than just smell good on her.

fourth: firescape

THE SUN WAS SHINING the day I first saw Firescape.

It was chun jie. I think this is significant if for no other reason than, at that time of year, Embarcadero gets less sun than the North Pole. I never been to the North Pole, but I got the Wiz's word on it. Where I been, lo, these many years, is here, and I can count on one hand the Spring Festivals in which I haven't just about chattered the teeth right out of my head.

The big event of chun jie is the parade. It's a long parade that winds all along the Wharf and the Sang Yee Gah for hours, then ends up in the Gee Gah around sunset, where it sort of crumbles into a big block party. Then there are fireworks and bonfires and dancing and mountains of food.

Pandemonium. Chaos. That's the chun jie. Doug likes it—the noise, the people milling, the smells. When he was just a shrub, we'd watch from this second floor flat over the Gee Gah where I sometimes overnighted when I didn't feel up to dragging my tail back to the Farm after a day downtown. I'd sit in the window casing and Doug'd perch out on the fire escape in his little clay pot while the sun went down and the fireworks went up and the whole universe paraded by underneath.

Later on, he liked to be right down in it, which is hao with me —just fine, you know—'cause Doug'd gotten bigger and that new brass pot Kaymart got him was nothing I'd be yearning to haul up a flight of busted stairs and out a window.

So this particular year, we're mingling with the universe and tailing the parade through the Sang Yee Gah when I feel this sort of tugging at my immortal soul.

I look to Doug, naturally, 'cause usually this means he has a message of import for me. But he's just soaking up chun jie with his boughs waving and his needles all quivering in the thrill of it all. (Which, since I asked, he's intimated to me he enjoys because it reminds him of the frisky winds that blow up the slopes of Mount Diablo. How he knows this, I don't savvy, since I am not Tree.)

Anyway, I get, right off, that this tugging at my immortal soul is not of Doug and I glance around to see where it might originate. And that is when I see Firescape for the first time. She is standing next to a baozi wagon along the parade route waiting for a taste of the wares. I suspect her stare—which, as I glance at her, goes someplace else—was the source of the tugging at my immortal soul.

And why should she stare at me? I'm no great shakes to look at, let me tell you, unless you happen to like small, dark and stringy. But I am in company with a venerable Radio Flyer and Doug, and I am aware that any guy dragging a red wagon with a Tree in it attracts attention, even here.

She-who-is-no-longer-staring-at-me is a vision in black and red. Black silk quilted jacket with red collar and cuffs, black silk quilted leggings with red leather hi-tops. An assault weapon hangs jauntily from one shoulder.

The vendor hands her a paper-wrapped bao into which she bites delicately, then wipes her chin on the back of one dainty hand. This gives her the opportunity to glance at us again without seeming to.

She is a China-doll, her flower-face golden, her eyes like teardrop chips of dark amber. But unlike any of the hundreds of Chinese girls I've seen along the Sang Yee Gah, her hair is the color of October trees—a shade of red you see only once a year.

I am smitten. So smitten, Kipling pops into my head, courtesy of Archaic Literature 101, Professor Lombard Street instructing: San Francisco, Kipling said, is a mad city—inhabited for the most part by perfectly insane people whose women are of a remarkable beauty.

My heart sighs. Mr. Kipling said a mouthful.

A breeze stirs and Doug brushes my hand with a scented bough. I am urged to cross the street and meet this vision. I look for an opportunity and see one—there, between the dragon boat and the Dog of Heaven.

I manage to get me, my wagon and my Tree through the parade and across the street. I get yelled at, and some firecrackers go off right under the wagon, but we make it.

Too late. The red-haired Chinese girl is gone, red hi-tops, assault rifle and all.

I feel like a deflated balloon. Then I have the hopeful thought that the vendor might know the girl.

"What girl?" he says.

"Ninja-girl in black and red. Red hair. You just now sold her a bao."

The vendor shrugs. "I sell lots of baos."

"Not to red-haired Chinese girls carrying AKs, I'll bet not."

"Why you wanna know, chico?" the vendor asks, suspicious-like.

Honesty, I decide, is the best policy. "I'm smitten," I say.

"What the hell's that—smitten?"

I blush. "I think she's neon. Number one jade."

He laughs. "You jingbing, chico. She's King's Guard. Colonel, by the pips on her uni."

My heart beats a little faster. I have tumbled at first gander for a Colonel of the King's elite knighties. What a ditz. I might as well have fallen for a goddess. It's hopeless.

I ask the vendor if he saw which way the knightie Colonel went.

He jerks his head up the street toward where the parade will end in a wild melee. "After the King's float, where else?"

I follow the parade, tugging Doug after me in the Flyer, trying to catch the head of the beast. The Sun is setting, torches are flaring, and the shadows in the street are taking on a life of their own. It is hard to see things that are black and red. I pray to find the King's float before it reaches the end of its route, but my prayers don't make it to the Big Ear and I find myself swept into the courtyard where the parade melts into chaos.

This is where the Sang Yee Gah and several narrow cross-alleys meet in a long, cobbled yard. Right now it is a sea of floats and dancing dragons and stilt walkers and music. People flow past me, around me. An old Chinese guy smiles at me as he shuffles by, a couple of young women look at me slyly, some kids jostle my wagon and pat at Doug's boughs.

Then I can no longer make out individuals. I am awash in the crowd and lose all hope of finding the red-haired ninja knightie, when Doug brushes the hand that holds the wagon tongue. Simultaneously, I feel the tugs—his, which I recognize, hers, which is new. Then hers is gone.

I glance at Doug. He is waving me to the right along the wall of a brick building. I go, but even here, the crush of bodies is intense. Fireworks are beginning to go off, painting the crowd and the buildings and the far-off sky with rainbows, and I head toward the balcony where the King's float will stop.

By tradition, Hismajesty climbs off the float onto the balcony, where he will watch from a throne as his subjects entertain him through the night and into the next morning—a lot like Cinco de Mayo in my old barrio, but a lot chillier. Beijing's just gotta be warmer in February than Embarcadero or this festival would've never gotten off the ground.

I can see the balcony and the throne when the crowd gets so dense I can't move forward. I give up and step up into a doorway and there she is.

We just stare at each other for a moment and then Doug gives me this fir-scented nudge.

"Hello," I say intelligently, "I've never shared a doorway with a Colonel before. I never even met a Colonel before."

She looks at me with these big, smoky topaz eyes and I can see fireworks and torch light reflected in them.

"Firescape," she says. "Colonel Firescape. King's knightie. Who're you?"

"Cicerone," I say, and then decide to go for the whole enchilada. "Cicerone Del. And this is Doug."

Her eyes widen, then go to my Tree. "You named a tree?"

"He's not just a tree," I explain. "He's a close personal friend."

She nods, shifting her AK in her arms, which reminds me to be circumspect. Then she bends down and shakes one of Doug's boughs.

"You got some interesting friends, Doug," she tells him. "They say only loco people give up their real and secret names to total strangers. Is your friend loco?"

If Doug answers her, I don't hear it, so I say, "I don't think I'm loco. But I do hear voices sometimes. Whispers, really."

She looks impressed. "Yeah? What do they say?"

I shrug. "Wish I knew. I get words sometimes now . . . at least, I think they're words. Well, of course they're words, I'm just not sure what language they're in."

Her mouth makes a little 'o.'

"So you're guarding Hismajesty?"

Now, her mouth twists a little. "Not right now. Right now, I'm talking to a possibly jingbing dude who names trees and hauls them around in little red wagons."

She is gazing up over my shoulder, and I turn my head so I can see what she sees. It's Hismajesty, King of Embarcadero, and he and his float are approaching the Royal balcony.

This is when I feel another tug at my immortal soul—third one tonight. Only this one isn't so much a tug as it is a yank—a cold, shivering yank. This is not Doug, of that I am certain. And it's not Colonel Firescape 'cause she's standing right in front of me and this is coming from somewhere else.

Doug's branches are waving like crazy all of a sudden, and I know something bad is shakin'. Then, I hear the whisper, "Wiwe," it says, which is something I don't know, then, "bu hao," which I do know.

"Bu hao," I repeat.

"What?" says Colonel Firescape. "What's no good?"

Across the courtyard in a window is a shadow. It's Someone. I don't know who, but then I look at the window and Doug's boughs are brushing my hand and I see fire leaping up the wall and taking hold of the balcony where, in two minutes, Hismajesty will be roosting.

"Don't let him get on the balcony," I tell the Colonel. "Don't let him get anywhere near the balcony. Get him off the float!" I say this very low and earnest, so she won't think I'm loco.

"Esta loco?" she says, and her hands tighten on her AK.

"Fire," I say, "I see fire. If he gets to the balcony—"

"How d'you know? You a merlin or something?"

"Yeah. Or something." I'll say anything, I'm so sure about this.

She gives me this look, then jumps down off the doorstep, using her AK like a battering ram.

"Make a hole!" she yells, and I can hear her voice clear as a seagull's cry over the crowd noise.

But the place is jam-packed and Hismajesty's float is moving faster than she is. I get down there with her, hoping Doug and I can help. We're maybe two yards from the float, from which His M is waving and grinning at his subjects, when Firescape gets wild and fires her AK into the air. This makes us a hole. We reach the float just as it draws up to the balcony. It's all adrenaline, I s'pose, but I don't think I've ever leapt as far in a single bound as I did to get up on that float. She made it look easy, like she could fly—submachine gun and all. We land amid the flowers (from Kaymart's glass gardens, I suspect) and grab Hismajesty and drag him off the float.

When we hit the cobbles, we have to drag him a few feet on this backside so he is not a happy monarch. He fights himself upright, sees that his float has docked without him and roars, "What the hell was that?" and "Who's this scum?" (Meaning me.)

We all blink at each other, then Firescape says, "He said—he said there'd be a fire."

"You think so? Maybe he meant someone'd get fired!" snarls the surly sovereign.

And then his float explodes.

Well, it doesn't so much explode as the front of it, which is docked under the balcony, just goes whoosh in this pillar of fire. The fire takes the balcony, the fire escape that leads to it and the throne that sits on it.

About 10,000 things happen all at once. Fireworks continue to go off and everybody stops whatever they're doing and finds themselves doing something else they hadn't even thought of doing two seconds ago: screaming, maybe—mostly the ones with singed eyebrows—oooh-ing and ahhhh-ing, running for cover.

Hismajesty is struck speechless, which is a condition, I come to know, so unusual as to cause great consternation among those who know him.

Faster than I can breathe again, we are surrounded by knighties in red and black and whisked away into a dark corner of the square. Whisking is almost impossible with a 30 pound tree in a wagon, but they do it. While they are whisking, I get that yanked at feeling in my soul again and look away across the courtyard. What I see, as though he was the only one out there, is this old Chinese guy—the one who smiled at me. He is like something out of a history video—which is to say, he looks like a lot of old

Chinese guys I know. But he's staring at me across all that dark and fire and all those bobbing heads and, for a second, we are connected and I am sure this is the coldest chun jie I have ever known.

I am not given any time to contemplate this, however. The knighties continue to whisk most efficiently, and my view of the OCG is cut off. And a good thing—I was on the verge of mental frost bite. Next thing I know, we are in a dark, close place and the shouting of the crowd is smothered.

"Palace," says Hismajesty and before I can steady my heart, Doug and I are standing in the very Throneroom of the very Lord of Embarcadero, gazing up at the ensconced monarch and his very pregnant Lady Queen—Hermajesty to all and sundry—with knocking knees.

Well, that is, my knees are knocking. Doug, being Tree, doesn't have knees to knock.

"I owe you a debt of gratitude," says His M in a voice-o-majesty. "For this eve—according to Firescape—you have saved my life and years of senseless grief and anarchy among your fellow Embarcaderans. What have you to say for yourself, merlin?"

Merlin. My mind has completely slipped over the fact that I made such a claim. I wonder if I can retract it. I bow. Doug bows a little too, although without aid of a breeze this is hard for him.

"I'm glad to have been of service," I say and leave the merlin thing unaddressed. Then I'm tongue-tied.

There is an awkward silence—or a weighty one, depending on your POV—then Hismajesty asks, "By what strange and wonderful magic did you accomplish this?"

"It was Doug," I say and nod toward the Tree.

All eyes turn to Doug, who waves congenially.

"The tree? My life has been saved by a magic shrubbery?" asks Hismajesty, and eyeballs me real good. "Who are you?"

I open my mouth to say I'm just Chickpea from the Farm and the weirdest stuff comes out. "I am Cicerone Del—merlin—and this is the Fabled Tree of Destiny, the rustling of whose boughs did save your royal posterior."

Now there is an even weightier silence and Hismajesty is looking at me muy strangely and says, "So you talk to the Tree and it . . ."

"Talks to me. Not in so many words, ni dong, but the Tree of Destiny makes itself understood to me alone, and what it had me to understand this eve was that your majesty's float was significantly doomed."

"You foresaw the fireball?"

"Poof," I say with a flourish, and the next thing I know I am entering the realm of merlinhood and Firescape has been promoted to General for not assuming me to be loco.

Hismajesty confides in me that he's been having merlin trouble. His previous merlin has gone AWOL and hasn't been heard from for weeks. As it turns out, he is at the bottom of the Bay. Had I known this, merlinry would've lost much of its appeal.

"You aren't really a merlin," says General Firescape later.

I am struck almost speechless. "I'm not?" I plan to bluster a little with indignation, but she doesn't give me a chance.

"I know what you said, but you didn't mean it. You just wanted me not to think you were loco. In the Throneroom tonight, you meant it."

I am amazed by this, let me tell you. It's like she reads me.

"Actually," I say, before my brain can stop me, "I didn't know I was a merlin."

"I kind of thought so. But you're a merlin now." She gives me this LOOK and I melt. And she asks, "So what happened? I mean, was it just fireworks?"

Yeah, it was fireworks, all right.

Oh, the poof, she means. "I don't know," I say, then, hopping on a memory, "No. It wasn't just fireworks. There was gasoline in the grate under the balcony. I smelled it."

She nods. "Lord E."

"Huh?" I say.

"Who planned the poof. It was Lord E . . . wasn't it?"

"I don't know. I s'pose it could've been."

For some reason I resist telling her about the creepy old Chinese guy. He might've had nothing to do with this. Then again, I got this feeling he had everything to do with this. I wonder if he connects to Lord E somehow.

"Does Lord E do stuff like this often?" I ask.

"No. He'd sure like to get rid of Hismajesty, though. That's solid." She looks a little suspicious at me. "Can't you tell? If it was Lord E, I mean."

"Merlinry," I tell her, as serioso as I can, "is not an exact science."

I do not tell her that, despite her conviction, I am not exactly a merlin, but just a dude lucky enough to dig up a very talented Tree.

When I tell Bags and Kaymart what has happened to me and Doug, they are awfully proud. I tell them it was Doug, not me, but Bags winks and says it's both Doug and me.

"It takes two," he says. "A merlin and his channel. You got it made, Del. You been called."

They help me move my stuff into the Regency Palace where I would now live. Then they take me to a fanguan to celebrate with some hot and fishy noodles.

Called. I think about it that night while I lay in my new bed, holding Doug's bough for comfort against the strangeness of sleeping twenty stories high in a building that shivers when the wind hits it.

"Doug," I ask him, "why'd you make me say all that stuff about being a merlin?"

He doesn't answer me, but I think I hear him laugh.

fifth: there is more going down than i think

 FIRESCAPE'S RECONSIDERING of the move doesn't impress Hismajesty. He is determined to follow Scrawl's advice and bug out. I can tell she's been chewin on his ear. Giving her best ooga-booga doom talk.

I bring up the bird beak and driftwood and Scrawl is quick to announce that it's a portent. The Alcalde will attempt to seize our queen by way of the Sea. Since the Regency Palace is practically on top of the Sea, that goes down like the Titanic. I note that Her M has nothing in common with driftwood, but no one hears me. The royal family is packed up and spirited away (belongings and household to follow) until such time as Firescape and the other Generals can put a stop to the threat.

Firescape, herself, is assigned to Hermajesty's personal guard. Net result, I will be separated from her until I can pack up my workshop and all my magic crap and make the move.

"I have a bad feeling about this," I quote as we say polite goodbyes in the plaza before the Palace.

"Me too," she admits. "I should stay and guard you and the Tree. Cinderblock could handle the Royal Family."

"No, I understand. Hismajesty wants the best. That's you, General Firescape." I smile and give her a tiny bottle of attar.

Her eyes get big. "What is it, a potion?"

I blush. "Attar of Fir. Smell it."

She does. "It smells just like the Tree!"

I can tell she's pleased.

"He helped me make it. It's from his needles."

She smiles and puts some on her neck, then tilts her head to one side. "Does it smell good on me, d'you think?"

I read this as an invitation to get close, so I do. Close enough to feel warmth coming off her skin.

"Smells great, General."

"Jade," she murmurs, tilting her head so she's looking right into my eyes. "Jade Berengaria."

"What?" I say, not daring to hope the potion is really working, and so soon.

"My real and secret names. Jade from my father; Berengaria from my mother. It means Spear Maiden. She picked it out at the Wiz. She wanted me to have a career in the Service—like her. She's with the Border Guard, southeast." She smiles, then gives me a kiss on the cheek. "See ya, Cicerone Del."

I hold my cheek and marvel. She has given me her real and secret names. *Jade Berengaria.* I roll the syllables in my head, let them fall from my tongue in a whisper. A precious jewel and a warrior maid. Perfect. Number one jade. I am boggled solemn with the significance of this: in two words, Firescape (Jade Berengaria Firescape) has given me the key to her very soul.

Late that night, an explosion rocks the neighborhood. It's an old boat shed down on the Wharf that burns. A BIG boat shed. Lights up the waterfront for miles. When I reach the Wharf, a crowd has already gathered. I spy Creepy Lou standing there in the bright haze, scratching his head.

"You see it?" I ask.

"Just about. Looky-dooky." He points at the pavement at his feet. In the wriggling light, the colors seem to move.

I squat. Effigy. And still wet. Hismajesty, by the painted crown, I think. And next to that, a cubist-looking Ampam struts off with—

"Lordy-lordy," says Creepy Lou. "Voo-doo."

"Naw. Scare tactics."

Same style as the mural. I stand and look about the street. Kids are trying to get close enough to toast hoarded marshmallows or sausages from the knacker's up on Mason. Other folks have brought buckets and stuff to carry away the leftover coals.

"Anybody see who did this?" I ask.

"Not much traffic along here."

Creepy Lou unrolls his favorite blue hat and crams it over his head. Tufts of bleached yellow stick out around his ears like straw. He reminds me of the Scarecrow in the Oz books.

He grins at me. "If I only had a brain."

I hate it when he does that. "You see anybody?"

"Sure. Thaw a bunch of kids and a clown I know from the Gee Gah. But he lives here."

There is a big, hot whoosh as the roof of the shed falls in. The marshmallow roasters and coal collectors cheer and jostle.

"Huh," says Lou. "Used to live here."

I am appalled. "He wasn't in there, was he?"

Creepy Lou shakes his head and I imagine I see a spider rappelling down his gaunt cheek.

"Naw. Look."

I follow his scarecrow point to where a dejected looking clown wilts in the heat. I sidle over and Lou follows.

"S'cuse me," I say. "This your place?"

The clown eyes me, realizes who and what I am and clutches

my sleeve. "Oh, please, great merlin! Please make the fire un-eat my digs!"

The fireknighties have arrived now in a blast of sirens and air horns. The front wall collapses as they reel out, making the marsh-mallow crowd scatter.

I tell the clown that I regret his loss. Can't do nothing for his old digs, but I for sure can get him new. I ask how he'd like to live in the Regency Palace for a while. Then, while he is kissing the hem of my sleeve, I ask if he saw how the fire started.

He shakes his purple frowze, tears trickling away his white-face. "Just got home. Just opening the door when something hits me—bonk—on the pate. It's a fish head. Geez, I think, who'd throw fish heads at a clown? I'm pissed, see, so I head back across the pier to see who did the throwing. I get out there"—he points to the half-burnt planks that lead from the pavement to the big, smoking cinder—"and I hear this popple-popple-popple! Then roar-*whoosh*! No more house."

"Anybody about?"

He shrugs, his lips tremble. "Nobody that shouldn'a been."

"You see the fish head tosser?"

"Just his butt for a flash." He shrugs again. "Big butt, red happy-coat. Dime a billion around here."

The clown is right. Among the residents of Embarcadero a red happy-coat is like brown eyes and black hair; everybody and his aunt Whoopee got 'em. Hell, I got two.

"Poor dumb schlub," says Creepy Lou when I have sent the clown over to the Palace with a note for the steward. Then he grins. "Gonna make old Scrawl see reddy-red-red."

"How so?"

"Hates clowns. Thays they give her creepy-crawlers. I thay she oughta check out the mirror." He shivers enthusiastically. "Ooga-booga! Hates this clown most special 'cause he dumped her ath!" He wheezes laughter. "Now he's gonna be livin' with her!"

Lou goes off cackling while I wait for the Firebrigade to wrap things. I see Cinderblock about, playing detective. I go over to ask if she's got anything. She does, but not much.

"Cheap fireworks from Wang's Novelty on Du Pon Gai," she says, holding up a wrinkled scrap of paper. Her nose is wrinkled, too. "Cheap fireworks and ethanol. Nasty combo."

"Arson."

"Count on it. Question is, why and who?" She squints at the major pile of charcoal. "I got my suspicions. Good thing we moved Hermajesty, huh?"

"Yeah. Looks that way."

I am holding a hunk of crispy-fried wood, about to chuck it into my belt pouch, when suddenly, I feel like one of Creepy Lou's spiders is crawling down my back.

"S'cuse me. I gotta talk to a clown."

The Palace is empty without the majesties and their close, personal servants. It feels strange, creepy. The left-behind knighties are just straggling back in from the fire, their red and black jackets and spandies sooty. The smell of smoke follows them in.

I talk to the clown, whose name is Winky, but he can't tell me anything more. Red happy-coat, he says and mumbles that somebody's trying to kill him.

"Woulda been in there, 'cept for that fish head. Saved my life. S'miracle."

I'm not so sure.

Upstairs, I can't shake the feeling that something is wrong—that I am missing something. From my balcony I can see the glow of the ex-boat shed. The marshmallow people have moved in real close, stuff bobbing at the ends of their sticks. The coal collectors work around them.

I take Doug to the railing to show him the damage. He quivers and I apologize. I forget how nervous fire makes him.

He's restless tonight and his boughs wave fitfully in the barest breeze. He leans west toward the Presidio. Of course, this is 'cause the wind blows that way. My thoughts lean that way, too, 'cause I worry about Firescape. This is stupid, of course, 'cause Firescape is good at taking care of herself. Better than I am, I'm pretty sure.

I put my face to Doug's needles to smell what is now Firescape's scent, but the fragrance is carried away from me.

I close my eyes and beg to understand the runes I cast the night before. Nothing comes to me . . . except I can still see that dumb bird beak. After that, all I get is a rehash of stuff—the mural under the overhang, the one on the sidewalk. Same artist, I think—some Noe Valley sméagol with artistic flair. I see the sad, homeless clown that Scrawl hates and a firestarter in a red happy-coat.

Cheap fireworks from the Gee Gah and ethanol. And nobody sees nothing. Gotta have connections to get ethanol, or you gotta rob a stash. Or you gotta have a secret stash of your own.

There haven't been any stash robberies since God knows. The ethanol might've come from Potrero-Taraval, which also doesn't make sense 'cause our sméagols been telling us there's no running machinery in Potrero—no cars, no buses, no lawn mowers, nada. And if you don't have machinery what the hell do you need with ethanol?

Of course, maybe they just use it to blow things up. Which still leaves me with where the flammables came from. I just can't picture somebody sneaking all the way from the Borderlands with a big old can of ethanol. Of course, the wall-crawlers and mural painters came in by boat. Two boats, Firescape said, one of which they left behind. Maybe they left behind more than a boat.

A thought comes to me which I throw away, not liking the smell. What if this too-close-to-home stuff isn't Potreran do? What if somebody here is helping out? Somebody who could cadge fireworks from the Gee Gah and ethanol from a stash without getting the hairy eyeball.

I think for a split second about the old Chinese guy that I was convinced for five seconds once upon a time had tried to assassinate my liege lord. The whole idea seems pretty silly to me now. I mean, why would some old Chinese guy want to do in

Hismajesty? Unless, of course, he was in the employ of Lord E Lordy.

Okay, that's a maybe.

Another thought comes—a question. Why now? Hermajesty is at the Summer Palace by now, shivering in front of a giant fireplace, moping 'cause the beds are so hard. First I think maybe the firestarter doesn't know this. Then I think maybe the fire doesn't have anything to do with Hermajesty.

Then I think maybe somebody just doesn't like clowns.

In the morning nothing is clearer. I'd stop thinking about it except that Doug is so upset. His little boughs quiver like a cat's whiskers. I move him to where the wreckage of the clown's digs are not visible, but he is still twigged.

The air smells like soggy ashes. I ask if this is the problem. I inhale his perfume and close my eyes, but all I know is that I don't see the Royal Party or Firescape. All I see is the burning boat shed.

Satisfied that Doug is merely feeling the effects of a wood-burner so close at hand, I go about my day's business, packing a little here and there. Like Her M, I don't really want to leave the Palace. But it's damn lonely here, with the place so empty. The fire's brought more knighties down to patrol the Wharf. Some of them are from the Knob and the Richmond and other areas, wearing a rainbow of colors. But most are Red Knighties and this makes me miss Firescape.

I'd even speak to Scrawl this morning, but she's mad at me 'cause of the clown and shakes her bony finger at me and gives me the Look-O-Doom.

"Bad times for you, Chickpea Face," she says, "Bad times."

I tell myself I'm not worried, but I cast runes anyway. First, I make certain the rotten old peach pit and tacks are where I left them on the shelf next to my can. They are. I study the rune-fall, looking for patterns. The damn bird beak is still there, so's the piece of driftwood. Being lighter than the other stuff, they fall one way, the glass and metal and pebbles bounce away into a raggedy line along the edge of the table, like a sort of phalanx. I notice I missed a few tacks. They're strewn amongst the pebbles and stuff; I don't feel like picking them out, so I leave them there.

A little piece of paper lies between the beak and the wood. I pick it up and see that it's the torn corner of the page from a book. There are page numbers on both sides: five and six. That makes eleven . . . or fifty-six, depending. Eleven or fifty-six what? Or is that even important?

Books. The torn corner is from a book. I decide this means I must consult the Wiz. But not now. It's dark, late, and my head hurts. I sleep.

Sometime in the night, there is a big brouhaha. Pounding in the halls, noise in the streets. Eyes open, I see light dancing and weaving across the ceiling and walls of my room. I check all my windows and realize there is another fire somewhere on the Wharf. I dress and go out. In the street, knighties galore are headed for the piers and I hear the Firebrigade's air horns.

The fire's a monster—down near the Old Ferry Building, maybe it *is* the Old Ferry Building. That would be terrible; there are a lot of fisher families in that old place.

When I reach the Wharf road, I see it's not the Ferry Building burning, but the two derelict hulks beached next door. Fireknighties are already pumping water onto them out of the Bay. While I watch, another troop comes along and starts spraying the Ferry Building. All I can do is stand there and mutter incantations to Tam Kung, who specializes in extinguishing fires, praying for a cold, thick fog—a helado at the very least—with no breeze.

Despite that my prayers are answered with a fog so thick it is almost wu pesado, the hulks burn for hours. Once the flames leap to the roof of the Ferry Building, making the crowds shriek and the Fireknighties scramble to pour on more water. They get it under control when the keel of the biggest boat collapses and the whole thing slides into the Bay. The water burns now, too—oily sheets of flame, little bonfires of floating junk. But the Ferry Building is safe.

When there's nothing left onshore but embers, the coal collectors swarm in. Poor pickins—most of the coals are in the Bay. I stay till the end; till all the coal-gatherers have gone, till Cinderblock and her troops have gone over the area.

"Arson?" I ask.

She shakes her head. "Hard to tell. Not much left. But . . ."— she looks out at the smoldering water—". . . sure was a hell of a lot of fuel on those old barges. Oil, gasoline. Big loss for those fishers."

About which the fisher families are understandably pissed. I remind them that whoever did this could more easily have set fire to their old warehouses and then none of them would be here to bitch about it. I leave them grumbling and drag myself home, thanking God for the wu helado without which things might have been much different.

Back at the Palace that awful feeling comes over me again, so strong this time, I almost shake. Something is wrong. I try to reason with myself. It's just the quiet. I'm not used to the Palace being so quiet, not any time of the day or night. There's always somebody playing music or gaming or fighting or snooping the kitchens. There's always something going on.

Now there's nothing. No guardian knighties on patrol, no Squire and Squire's many ladies. Nada. *Something is wrong*, says this little voice in my head. I don't realize how wrong until I'm in my room again with the lights on. I feel kicked in the head. The walls bleed glossy red with graffiti—one word over and over: GOTCHA. Just that: GOTCHA. Sure as hell did.

Doug is gone, pot and all.

sixth: pot and all (i begin to take this personally)

 NOW I UNDERSTAND ALL the quivering. Now, when it's too late. *Some merlin I am*, I think. *Some stupid, Chickpea-faced merlin I am.*

I send out knighties, but they're about wilted after the fire and I know it won't do any good. I been away hours, fire-watching—like my prayers could do something about the physics of firecrackers and oily goo. Worst of it is, I understand that bird beak now. And the wood chip.

Huh. Some light bulb I got. Now it comes on. They were never after Hermajesty. They were after Doug. They emptied the Palace, got us to split our knighties between the Wharf and the Presidio, snuck up on our big bare ass and got away clean . . . with Doug.

I send one of Firescape's girls to the Presidio with the news, then, just to keep from going shining, I cast runes. This time, the crap just looks like crap. My eyes don't go wonky no matter what I do. And there are no Whispers. Zip. And to add insult to injury, the damned garbage is back in the can. I start to pick out the pit and the tacks and chuck them again, then think, why bother?

Instead, I just put the stuff back in the can. That's when I find another slip of paper, which is neatly folded and sticking to the underside of the peach pit. It's kind of a lavender rice paper, fine quality.

I open it. There is a strange symbol I don't know in one corner of the little page and a series of Chinese characters, which I do know, in the middle of it. *He sends the vultures,* they say. He sure does.

For one miserable moment, I take this as Lord E's way of saying "Up yours," then realize he's already done that with the GOTCHAs. Suddenly, the message don't figure. I mean, Lord E barely speaks Chinglish, let alone Chinese proper. And a neatly folded note has never been in his repertoire. But if it's not from Lord E, then who? And why? Was somebody trying to warn me about the tree-napping?

With my cosmic sense of timing, that'd make about perfect sense. I get the warning after the crime.

Disgusted, I pocket the little hunk of driftwood and the note and head for the Wiz. Can't wait no more. Shoulda gone when I first saw that torn book page. Too late now, but at least I can go to The Fiche and study maps.

"Show me the quickest way from here to Lord E Lordy's palace in Potrero-Taraval."

"Specify," says Fiche, "which Palace. There are three." And Fiche pops up a map with three bright spots on it.

One of Lord E's places is in a Conservatory, another one is in the old Trans-Bay Terminal—spitting distance; no way he'll be there. The last one is buried in the Sunset south of the Farm. Far and away from the Border; that's where I put my money.

"SF State," I say.

All the spots wink out but one, and Fiche draws me a ziggy-zaggy red line all the way from the Wiz to the old University. The line is etched into my pea-brain. I genuflect respectfully, then I am on my way to the Farm—my last stopping-off point before I venture into Potrero-Taraval.

The Farm is beautiful this time of year. The leafy trees are all different colors—yellows, oranges, the purply-red of the little maples. Only the giant conifers are green still. Usually when I walk through them, smelling their sweet pine musk, they remind me of Doug, and I'm happy. Now they remind me of Doug and I want to cry.

I'm not a brave person. It's all I can do not to cry when I finally see Bags and Kaymart gathering cones under the Giants. They're surprised to see me. I realize it's been weeks since I came out to see them.

Guilt is one of the quickest emotions I know—quicker than anger, even.

"Great harvest, Merlin Cicerone!" Bags thanks me. "Number one jade. Biggest squashes we've ever had. Thanks a lot."

Most times I'd be glad to take the praise for my merlinish ministrations. Now . . . who cares?

"Most welcome," I say, anyway. "You seen any skulking action down here? Last night, maybe?"

Kaymart frowns, cuddling a monster pine cone. "It's funny you should ask. I thought the dogs were up to something last night. They sure were raising Cain. Woke me up, oh, about moon-set, I guess."

Bags scratches in his grizzly beard. "I didn't hear nothin'."

"You," says Kaymart, "sleep like the proverbial log." She turns back to me. "What's wrong, Del? Somehow I seriously doubt you've just come home for dinner."

Kaymart talks like the Videoschool Teachers in the Wiz's AV Shrine. This is because she is (or was, I guess) a Professor of Anthropology before the Getting Out. She didn't leave, she told me, 'cause she saw the Getting Out as surrender and wasn't inclined to do so. Then she met Bags, who was living under the back porch of her walk-up in Cow Hollow, and that was that.

Sometimes it's hard to understand Kaymart. She got all these quaint aphorisms. Right now, I'm having trouble understanding what my problems have to do with her dogs growing sugar. And they grow beets here, anyway, not cane.

Right about now I realize how wore out I am.

"It's Doug," I say. "The Potreros snatched him last night. I think they may be headed for the Palace at SFU."

Bags and Kaymart are blown about sidewise by this news. They helped me raise Doug practically from a fir cone—they're like his grandparents—and they take it hard. I feel terrible. Doug is gone and it's my fault. Bags wants to go with me into Potrero-Taraval. Kaymart wants me to stay with them and rest until nightfall.

"You're dead tired, Del. You probably haven't eaten since God-knows-when. It'll be dark in about three hours. Stay and rest."

I start to protest, but she gives me a Mom Look. "You're not going to do Doug any good in the condition you're in. Just look at that; your hands are shaking."

She's right, and I submit. It's hard to argue with Kaymart when she's in Mom mode.

For dinner, we eat squashes stuffed with spinach, acorns, and goat cheese and talk about my plans to rescue Doug. I talk Bags out of going with me; he's pretty old and so much like my own padre, I sure wouldn't want anything to happen to him.

One thing leads to another and next thing I know we're reminiscing about Doug's seed-hood and way back past that to when I first found my way to the Farm.

It was Hoot that brought me there, really—Hoot with all his questions about the Whisperers. He is, like, fascinated by the idea that there're these voices in my head that I can't tune in.

"Maybe you got a bad filling," he says. He's read comics where guys with bad fillings hear voices in their heads. Me, I got no fillings. Hoot is disappointed, but the questions don't stop.

"So, d'you think it might be a directional thing, anyway, like a radio transmitter? I know all about radio transmitters. That's what I do—fix radios and things like that when they go fizz. Now with radio signals, you gotta get the antennae oriented so they can pick up the signal clear. Ever thought of that? Are your Whispers clearer some places than others?"

I had not thought of that and did not want to think of that. I was spending most of my time cogitating on a Calling—which, I figure, has nothing to do with radio signals or Whispers or antennae.

"I don't have antennae," I say, but Hoot will not leave it alone, even though he has now determined I am not something he can take a screw-driver to.

"Look, Hoot," I say, finally, "I don't think this is that type of reception problem. I think it's more of a spiritual nature, comprendé?"

He looks at me like I'm speaking in tongues. "You think angels are trying to talk to you?"

"Not angels maybe. I don't know. I just don't think it's a mechanical thing."

"Okay. You prayed about it then?"

"On occasion."

"Yeah, but did you ever just say, 'Hey, God, could you tune in these Whisperers a little better so I can understand what the hell they're chewin' on?' Did you say that?"

"I don't talk to God that way," I answer.

Before I know it, we are on a quest. We are taking a walking tour of Embarcadero and local environs to see if there are places where the Whispers are clearer than others. I make a point of stopping at every dios house we pass to go in and offer prayers for the clarity of Whispers.

I am thinking the day is destined to be uneventful by the time we have walked all the way around Embar and have wound up tracing the Slot up toward Potrero-Taraval. I am tired and tending toward grumpiness and am getting ready to grumble about all and sundry when I hear a Whisper that is a real word: *Dolores*.

I stop in my tracks and turn all around.

"What?" asks Hoot.

"Dolores."

In answer to my non-answer, he turns and points across the Border between Potrero and Embar. There's a trench that runs the whole length of the parklands on southside, just below the Farm—used to be a street. Maps show it was dug up to put in electronics for the masstransit, but it never got done, 'cause right about then everybody was outward bound. On the Embarcadero side there's a brick wall with gates, where there are Checkpoints with knighties on constant patrol. On the Potrero side is terra incognito, which means the 'big unknown.'

"There?" asks Hoot, still pointing. "There's a Mission over there named Dolores."

Since this is inside enemy territory, I do not think that can be what the Whisperers are talking about.

"No," I say, "that can't be it."

The Whisper in my ear is suddenly more of a little shout: *Dolores!* Damned insistent all of a sudden, these Whisperers.

"We can't get there from here," I say, half to Hoot and half to the Whisperers.

Dolores, insist the Whisperers, and Hoot grins at me, like he can tell what's going on in my head.

"I can get us across, no problem."

He does, at a place where the abandoned masstransit dig lets us disappear on one side of the border and pop up again on the other. Trick is, we have to wait for dark to get across, so in the meantime, Hoot suggests we visit the Farm.

My only real association with the Farm up till now has been dietary. Like anybody else in Embarcadero, I eat stuff that's been grown there. Most greens eaten here—except for the ones from rooftop gardens—come from the Farm, or from the plot of land set aside at the Presidio. The Farm is almost a mythical place to me, but I never actually been there.

Hoot acts like he owns the place. He acts like that everywhere, and here, he just marches me up to this little log house and onto its big front porch and I meet Bags and Kaymart who will very soon change my sorry life, though I don't know it yet.

Bags is a crusty old dude with one dead front tooth and a lot of gray and white hair. Grizzled. That's the word I read in books to describe a guy like Bags. He laughs a lot—sometimes at nothing I can hear or see—and he always looks like he's got a secret and is thinking of letting you in on it. I can't tell what color his eyes are. I don't think they are any color at all, but they twinkle with his secret. I can't help but wonder what it is.

Kaymart, now she's a different sort of person altogether. I feel like she's studying me—not in a bad way, but like I'm something really interesting. She thinks a lot, Kaymart does, and even from the beginning, she thought things about me.

I'm not used to that. People thinking about me, I mean. She asked me all sorts of questions about the Whisperers once Hoot told them what we were doing. I felt pretty dumb, let me tell you.

"Voices?" Kaymart says. "What do they say?"

"I don't know," I answer, and Hoot pipes up and says, "Dolores. They said dolores just now."

"Dolores? As in sad?" asks Kaymart, and Bags says, "I hear voices sometimes. Not as often as I used to, but I hear 'em."

"As in the Mission Dolores," says Hoot and jerks his head in that general direction. "Which is why we're planning a forage into the land of darkness."

"I think you mean foray," Kaymart says and looks at me studyingly. "Is that what you think it means?"

"I don't know," I say. "But it was a damned insistent voice and seemed righteously pushy when I tried to offer another explanation as to its intent."

"Well, that's not good," says Bags. "Damned dangerous territory just over there. Mission's haunted, you know."

"Haunted? By what?"

"Whisperers, I should say," says Kaymart, and gives her old man this look. "Don't scare the boys now, Mr. Bags. They seem to be on a quest of sorts—a fine thing to be on, in my opinion. Better than a lot of other things boys their age could be on."

Bags nods. "Be careful, anyway—just in case what the Mission's haunted with is Potreros."

Hoot just grins. He likes quests.

I am not in the mood for a quest of any sort by the time we leave the Farm. I would rather, I decide, hang here among the giant trees and the strange, whimsical buildings and follow Kaymart around asking dumb questions about vegetables.

I like the way the Farm smells—like spicy perfume. I do not like the smell of Potrero at all, which unless you've ever been up along the Border between Potrero and Embar you can't fully appreciate. Potrero stinks 'cause Lord E doesn't give a toot about garbage pickup.

Still, when darkness falls, we are at the trench from which Hoot will lead me, most likely, to my death. We do not go anywhere near the Checkpoints and I find myself wishing some knightie would spy us, stop us, and send us packing.

None does.

On the Potrero side of the Trench there's another wall made of old junked cars and trucks and trolleys laced together with razorbarb wire. Runs for miles.

Sméagols say there are no running trolleys in Potrero-Taraval. No running anything—water, electricity, you name it. All sorts of stories come out of Potrero-Taraval on the tongues of sméagols. Stories about gangs and burnings and rapes and horrible diseases; people stealing to eat, starving if they can't steal. Sounds like something out of Mad Max to me. Like I said, we hear this stuff from Deadend and that bunch. Don't know whether to believe them or not. I've never known truth to stand between a sméagol and a good story.

All this haunts me; I realize I'm about to find out for myself if any of it is true. We go down into the trench where, if I stand on tiptoe, I can see over the lip. I move along behind Hoot, popping my head up here and there, while he looks for a place to slip through the machine wall.

It's a clear, calm night with only a shadowless sliver of moon —almost the kind I'd've prayed for if I'd thought of it. But I didn't, so I thank God for thinking of me without being asked.

About a quarter mile from where we drop into the trench, Hoot spies a chink between an old trolley and a mangled dumpster. About sméagol-sized. We go up over the edge, scat over to the wall of dead machines and squeeze through REAL careful.

Peeking out from the little chink, we see the streets are empty. No. Scratch that. More-than-empty. I see nobody. No knighties, no by-standers, no bikers, no mimes, no street-vendors, nothing. Not, I s'pose, that I should expect to see ordinary people so close to the fringes, but I'm looking up a long hill and there's nobody there, either. Besides which it is un-friggin'-believably dark in Potrero-Taraval. No street lamps, no fire-cans, no light bulbs, not even a candle.

Maybe, I think, the knighties are hiding in the buildings. I take a look. But I can see from here that these buildings are also more-than-empty. Fact is, when I look up at the ones crowding the street, I can see right through some of them—and I'm not talking windows here, either.

I shiver. It's like looking through somebody's flesh and seeing clear bluesky through their skeletals. *Oogabooga*, as Creepy Lou would say.

Hoot nudges me. "Two blocks," he whispers. "Easy streets— you'll see."

I get the sudden feeling Hoot has done this before. "Just for the record," I say, "I'm not hearing any Whispers at the moment."

But just then, as if to make a liar of me, they whisper, *Dolores* again, and then something I don't know—*tsiaiaruka ka ruk*. I shake my head, wishing they'd go away.

"You were saying?" asks Hoot, somehow knowing.

"Let's go," I say.

I am known to exaggerate, but I do not exaggerate when I tell you that it was so dark on the Potrero side of the wall, I started to think the darkness was like fog. Not just any fog, but wu planchar, which is the kind that when you push it, it pushes back.

This was that kind of darkness—pressing in all over. I could feel it kneading my face, weighing down on my shoulders, flattening my hair. I was sure if I ever got back to Embarcadero (Kingdom of welcome light!), I'd find the stuff on the bottom of my shoes.

I can just see Hoot ahead of me in the dark, moving—so, I am moving too. I tug at his jacket.

"Yeah?" he says, and the unexpected sound of his voice just about turns me into an abject coward, as opposed, say, to a merely trepidatious one.

I start to hush him, but he says, "S'okay, Chickpea, just past new moon. The knighties are all up around Lord E's headquarters, tucked in for the nighty." He chuckles over his own dumb pun. "They tighten the perimeters when the moon's new. That's when the Haunts're out."

Now, I'd never heard of these Haunts until Bags mentioned them back at the Farm, and I say as much, which launches Hoot into a description of these ghosts that about curdles my blood.

I am pretending not to believe any of this, but as I am a dude who hears Whispers, and who is on his way to try to locate source of same. I feel I have very little grounds for bluster. But I say it anyway: "I don't believe in ghosts."

In my head, the Whisperers say, *cat-ta-us*, which makes no sense, but which somehow makes me feel . . . okay. I mean, okay as in I am not scared spitless all of a sudden, though I realize my lack of belief in ghosts is possibly uninformed.

"Which way?" I ask.

"Down that way," Hoot comes back, but as he is wearing his black leather jacket (can't say I've ever seen him not wear his black leather jacket), I don't see which way "that way" is.

"Straight down two blocks," he adds a moment later. "And you don't have to whisper. I'm not jazzin' about the Haunts. They're really here." There is a flash of almost white from where I think his mouth might be. "Well, at least the Potreros think so. They don't come around the Mission at night."

"How they figure to guard their border if they're afraid to come down here?"

Hoot giggles, which is a source of amazement to me. Big, cool dudes don't, as a rule, giggle much. It tends to spoil the effect of being big and cool.

"They think the Haunts are guarding the Mission border for 'em."

My feeling of okay-ness slips a little and I pray that the Potreros are dead wrong about this. We plow through the heavy darkness for the longest two blocks I have ever skulked. I can barely see the broken buildings that hover over us, but I can feel them. Without eyes, they are watching.

"Are you sure there's nobody here?" I ask Hoot and then almost walk up his back when he just stops.

"Here," he says and I struggle to see where "here" is.

I find an iron fence in front of me—the kind that's like a row of spears stuck shaft first in the ground. I peer through the bars and am amazed that I can actually see something by the thin curve of moonlight.

It is big and ghost-gray against the smothering darkness. Tatters of wu seda fly like silky banners from the bell tower. I begin to see where this whole Haunt idea came from. The Mission Dolores is not a home of ghosts, it *is* a ghost, a ghost in a monk's habit of black wool and silver silk and gauze.

Though the dark seems less heavy here, I still feel something pushing, pressing, pulling at me—reaching all the way to my immortal soul.

Cattaus. My son, say the Whisperers, loud and clear.

Whoa. Now, that part I understand. I just don't understand what it means. I been hearing these Whispers for almost a year and this is the first time they come up with a word in any language I get. The possibilities mad-dash through my head—foremostly that I'm the sole survivor of a family of ghosts. So, now what—they're calling me to the Glorious Place?

"You hearing 'em?" asks Hoot, and I'm all but knocked sideways because I've forgotten he's there.

"They called me 'son.'"

"*Zhende?*" he says. "No kidding? Huh. Well, c'mon then."

"Where?"

"Inside. C'mon."

He moves off and I barely have time to peel my fingers off the cold iron bars and follow him.

"We don't gotta go inside," I protest.

"Yeah, we do. This is important. We got us a quest."

"How do you know that? How do you know it's important?"

Hoot makes a rude noise. "What—you think this stuff happens to everybody?"

I can't answer that. Or maybe I just don't want to.

Deeper into Potrero-Taraval we go, about half a block. Then we turn east. I can see a little better now, though I can't say how. There is still no light to speak of, and now a sly fog has begun to creep about us. It's a shabu dong—that's Chinglish for Moving Form of Gauze—and it makes my skin crawl when I pass through it—like walking through a ghost, according to Supernatural lore.

Hoot takes me to a large and stiffly-leafed bush that has climbed all over the Mission's outer wall. I think I'm s'posed to climb and start feeling for a branch to grab when Hoot clamps a hand on my ankle.

I make this noise I had no idea could come out of a human throat and hit the dirt.

"Geez, Chickpea! You wanna bring the whole of Potrero-Terribal down on us? C'mon!" And he drags me down and stuffs me under the bush.

The next thing I know, I am standing in a strange forest of frozen stone. The shabu dong is here, too, and wraps itself around the strange shapes and around me and around what I think might be trees, but am not sure. Hoot comes up next to me.

"Where the hell are we?" I ask.

"Graveyard," says Hoot. "How're the Whispers?"

"Whispering," I say, and they are—like crazy.

One big voice, a lot of little ones, all saying God-knows-what. It isn't English or Chinese or Spanish or even Chinglish—which is what most Embarcaderans speak day-to-day—but it sounds vaguely like a cross between the last two. In between all the unintelligibles.

I hear it again, *Cattaus—my son*.

"Let's stroll," says Hoot, and we do.

I've gone about a dozen steps before I realize something. "Graveyard? We're scopin' ghosts?"

"You don't believe in ghosts," Hoot reminds me, and leads on through a garden gone loco. (At least I hope all the light-sucking black stuff among the not-so-black stuff is greenery.) Through the graves we creep, and it occurs to me as we scuttle, to ask Hoot how he comes to know this side of the Border so well.

For a moment, the only answer is the creak of leather as he moves. "I'm just a curious guy, I guess . . . and kinda stupid." There is a flash of white as he smiles back at me. "Thrills, y'know? The Potreros, the Haunts. Besides, I like this place, I guess. It's got something."

It does. And that something suddenly reaches out and hauls me to a dead stop (you should pardon the term). Something ahead of us looms like a small mountain. By the sliver of moon and the silver of fog I see it as a jumble of pale stone. The shabu dong curls around and over it like giant see-through cat—gray fluff everywhere. And the Whisperers aren't whispering now, they're talking out loud.

My son! they insist, but this is not mi madre y padre, that much I know for sure.

"Who are you?" I ask, not really expecting an answer, but I get one, and it makes my insides quiver.

Amah.

The word is alien. I don't know it . . . but I *feel* it. It feels old. Older than the walls of this Mission, old as the rocks in this little mountain, old as . . .

"What is this place?" I ask Hoot.

"Don't know. Part of the graveyard, I guess. There's some sort of plaque or something on the other side, but it's real worn. I can't read it. You might be able to make it out. Maybe we could make some light."

"Rather not," I say, and turn my attention back on the Whisperers. "I wish I understood you guys," I tell them.

There is no answer, but for no particular reason my hair stands up all over my head. The shabu dong around the pile of rocks is doing something most unshabu dong-like. It's all moving toward the same spot, which is about ten feet from the tip of my nose. It's a little chilly in the graveyard, but where I'm standing it's sub-zero. I am aware that my mouth is hanging open, sucking in mist.

Beside me, Hoot says, "Cool. What is it?" Like I should know.

"It" was starting to look less and less like fog and more and more like something else—something sort of person-shaped.

"Huh," says Hoot. Then he tugs at my sleeve. "We should zhou now."

I shake my head. I'm scared spitless, but I don't want to miss this—whatever it is.

"No. I mean it," Hoot tells me. "Let's go. Now."

About the time he says "now," I hear something most un-ghost-like. Like shouting, for example, and the pounding of many non-ghost feet. And about this same time, Hoot just grabs me and shoves me into some overgrown bushes.

"Zhou!" he says—which is to say, "scram most diligently."

I do, momentarily forgetting the not-shabu-dong thing forming by the rock pile.

Hoot and I scramble for yards on our hands and knees—him leading, me praying I don't lose him in the shrubbery and wondering if he knows where the hell we are going. Suddenly, I realize there are no more bushes and Hoot is hauling me to my feet.

"Zhou!" he says again, as if I need any more encouragement.

We are in the open street now between the Mission and the Border. Behind us is the Mission wall; before us is another wall—a wall of fog. It's a woolly zhentou—thick and silent and impossible to see through. We dive in and lose ourselves to Potrero-Taraval. I pray we don't lose ourselves, period.

We don't. Oddly, the zhentou stops right at the Border, and it is clear where we drop into the long, deep ditch. Behind us, I can still hear shouting, and the fog lights up with the flicker of torches.

"I thought you said the Potreros never went there," I say as we come out into the lesser dark of Embarcadero.

Hoot blinks up at me from the trolley car wreck.

"Things change, Chickpea," he tells me.

They do. They change muy mucho and all at once. The next night Hoot goes back into Potrero-Taraval, pulled by his own Whisperers, I suspect. He does not come back.

As a result of this, I spend the next month or so—every day— at the Wiz, trying to do two things: One is to make sense of the loneliness; two is to figure out my Calling. I read. I listen. I watch. I VR. I talk to the Keepers of Wisdom and History. No ideas come to me.

The Whisperers are of no particular help, either. I'm getting more words I can understand, but not make sense of, 'cause I got no context. Sometimes now, I think I hear Hoot, too—in the alley outside my cozy—but I know that's only the loneliness talking. I think a lot about finding another cat. I also read a lot about the California mission system. This does not inspire me to happy thoughts, but the subject sucks my interest like a vacuum.

I mean the Haunts, ni dong. The Haunts that Hoot took me to meet that night at the Mission Dolores. I didn't know what they were then, but now I was beginning to get the picture.

Long ago, the Ohlone people lived here. There were many tribes, all of which referred to themselves as The People. This is called 'ethnocentricity.' Everybody does it. The thing that made my blood run deep-freeze was learning that that Mission—Dolores—had about 5,000 Ohlone buried somewhere around it as a more or less direct result of my daddy's Spanish ancestors' attempting to save their souls.

Hoot and I'd been standing on a burial ground, and that pile of rock where the shabu dong did its little dance was a memorial—a tribute to the dead Ohlone. I'm not thrilled with this idea. Besides, it's confusing. I mean, why would 5,000 dead Indians be talking to *me*? The only answer I can come up with isn't comforting, considering that some of my ancestors were responsible for their demise.

Anyway, I am sitting in the Wiz staring at a History book without seeing the words when someone sits down cross-table. It's the old man Bags, and he's looking at me like I'm an unreadable subway sign.

"History," he says. "Good subject. Never figure out where you're goin' if you don't know where you been."

I nod, feeling as if he's saying more than he's saying.

He taps his finger on the page I have not been reading. "Mount Diablo," he says. "Big magic there. Very sacred ground to the Ohlone people. They say that's where they met the first Spaniards."

I nod again. "I read about it. The Spaniards met an Ohlone holy man and thought he was their Devil."

"Yeah, well, I bet that old Indian shaman thought the same thing about the Spaniards."

His eyes are twinkling at me and, for some reason, I smile.

"Yeah, well, I guess he'd've been right."

"They were powerful, those shamans. And wise. Shamanry is a great calling."

He nods at his own pronouncement, very solemn, then turns the other books I have collected so he can read the spines. What he sees is another book about the Ohlone and the first of the Books of Kingdom.

"Ah, you study the Classics."

"Sure," I say, and don't add, "Doesn't everybody?"

Fact is, I've probably read all the primary Books of Kingdom more than most folks I know except maybe the reigning monarch. I can almost recite them by heart.

"Who d'you read for?"

"Huh?" seems the only likely thing to say.

"Who d'you read the books for? Arthur? Aragorn? Galadriel?"

"Oh. Merlin, I guess. And Gandalf."

He reads me up and down and I fidget. "You're about how old—twelve?"

"Thirteen," I say quickly.

"Two years from choosing your Calling . . . thinking of going into merlinry, are you?"

His question strikes me both kinds of dumb. Only in the deepest recesses of my little chickpea heart had I ever dreamed of being a merlin, and I had hidden it so well that I didn't even know it until the old guy spit it out.

"No way," I answer. "I just like the books."

"That so? Then what you planning to do?"

I shrug. "Dunno."

He squints like the sun is in his eye, which it is not, 'cause the Wiz is usually kept kind of dark except for the little reading lamps at the tables. This is more economical and does not waste resources. Regardless of this general dimness, Bags squints up one eye, then the other, then says, "Your friend Hoot said you got some magic."

The mention of Hoot pushes me out of mopey into depression. There is now a big fat lump in my throat, and my stomach is wriggling, and my heart feels like someone is scrunching it into a little, tight ball.

"Sorry you lost him. He was a good kid . . . So you think he's right about the magic?"

"Beats me."

"You still hear them voices?"

"Yeah. I get every third or fourth word. But I don't get 'em, y'know?"

"Yup. I know. It was like that with my plants at first. Only caught little itty bits of what they were sayin' to me."

Now that tickles my Alice bone. "You hear whispers?"

"Surely." He leans toward me across the table. "Green things, Cicerone," he tells me. "Green things speak to the heart of any man—or woman—who'll listen. You've seen Kaymart's greenhouse. Green things talk to her, too. Of course, you'll never hear her admit it."

I recall the overgrown garden of the Mission Dolores. "D'you think it's green things talking to me?"

"Could be."

"What would they be saying? Why would they call me their son?"

"Well, I don't know that, Cicerone. Probably don't mean it literal. Whispers are pretty individual; they say different things to different folks."

"What do yours say?"

"Oh, they tell me when to plant and when to harvest, and they tell me how much food there'll be for market and how much to put up for me and Kaymart. They tell me when it's gonna rain and whether the rain'll be a gentle shower or a hell-bent-for-wet thunderstorm. They talk to me about cold snaps and hot spells. The maples tell me when the syrup is up and if there'll be an early fall. The pines tell me how the water table's doin. They tell me other stuff too. Secret stuff."

I am impressed. I had no idea plants could be so vocal. I say as much.

Bags cocks his head sidewise in a way that reminds me of Hoot.

"You want to find out more about your Whisperers? You want to find a Calling?" he asks.

"In a big way," I answer.

"Why don't you come on out to the Farm? Maybe the answers are out there. I know mine were. Come on, boy," he adds, when I don't speak up right away. "Explore the possibilities. What've you got to lose?"

Truth is—nothing. I got no Calling in heart or mind other than merlinry—a striving for which I have no suit. I could, I think, be a farmer like Bags. It would be a most useful Calling, after all.

"Maybe I'll do that," I say. "I do thank you for the kind invitation."

"Most welcome." He gets up and winks at me. "'Sides, Kaymart's all set she's gonna feed you up. Put some meat on your bones. Anyway, son, you're welcome there any time you care to show up."

I show up the next morning, early. Suddenly, my cozy doesn't seem so cozy. Seems damn hard to sleep in. 'Specially as I have not heard anybody call me 'son' lo these many years except for the Whisperers. On the lips of Mr. Bags, it is awesomely sweet.

Another reason I hit the Farm early is to try to do some green listening. I hear wind in the boughs of the pines and firs and sequoias. I hear insects and birds waking to talk amongst themselves. And that's nothing compared to what I smell. I smell the green. I swear.

Then, when I've almost given up listening for smelling, I hear, in my inner ear, "*Tsiaiaruk ka ruk.*"

"Huh?" I say.

"I said 'welcome home,' son," says Bags from suddenly in front of me. He has a very large fork in his hand and grass in his hair. "Let me introduce you around."

Green things did not talk to me that day. In fact, they never talked to me—at least not in the way they talk to Bags. Which is not to say they didn't communicate stuff. I learned to tell in other ways about harvests and frosts and heat waves.

I'm talking about ordinary, general green things now. There's green things and there's Doug, which is entirely different. I have what Kaymart calls an Affinity for Conifers—which means that trees that make cones and have needles like me. I notice it right away. Conifers are just different from other trees. They have this smell that just about makes me float away. My bed in my room (my very own room) in the Farm House is a pile of fragrant boughs. I could sit and stroke the shiny needles for hours, and would, if Bags and Kaymart didn't keep me moving. It was my special job to collect dropped cones, for which I thank the trees most humbly as Bags taught me.

One day I'm trekking through the Farm dogging Bags' tracks and picking up cones, incidentally sucking up attar of evergreen and Bags' lore, when I see Doug for the first time. He's just a little guy, growing cupped between two roots of this great big sequoia gramma (or maybe grampa—you can never be real sure with trees).

"Bags," I say, "isn't it hard for a little guy like that to grow all hunkered on top of those big old roots?"

Bags snorts so loud, a flock of quail takes off twenty yards downhill.

"Hard? S'damn near impossible. Can't put down his taproot. Won't last the winter, most likely."

"Then, why'd God put him here?"

"It's a legit mystery, son."

I look down at the little tree and feel my guts start to quiver. It was the first time I'd ever felt that. I hear the Whisperers say that familiar word, *Cattaus*, and the next thing I know my eyes go all wonky and I see that little, tiny seedling in a clay pot, and the clay pot is in my arms.

"What'd happen, Bags," I ask, "if I dug that little tree up and put it in a nice pot and took care of it all year round?"

Bags' funny no-color eyes glint at me. "Well, I s'pose it'd stand a whole lot better chance of survival."

"Can we? Dig it up, I mean?"

Bags makes every last one of his nine hundred ninety-nine thoughtful faces. He knows how bad I want him to say, "yes." And he knows what having to stand there and watch all those nine hundred ninety-nine faces is doing to my twisty guts. No good, that's what. Finally, he nods.

"Let's get us a shovel and a pot," he says.

We do, and dig Doug up and put him in a pot. (I don't know he's Doug yet, of course.) I insist I can carry him home on my own.

Bags watches me hug that big old pot in my arms. "Well, now," he says, "you still wondering why God let that little tree grow there?"

I've always been impressed with how well Bags understands God. Kaymart's always been impressed, too.

"That's one of the reasons I married him," she tells me once. "You could go to the Wiz every day and never come home with even a smidgen of the wisdom in that old bean. I'd trade his savvy for my magna cum laude any day."

I didn't know what a magma-come-loud was and asked if it had anything to do with volcanoes, which I was studying in Videoschool at the Wiz. Kaymart just laughed. Much later I find out it has to do with going to a university, which we don't have any of around here anymore. Unless, of course, you count the Wiz.

It's as I'm carrying Doug back to the Farm House in his old clay pot that I come to a peculiar understanding: I have sort of just made a Green Thing my son. If Bags is right, may be Green Things are also calling me 'son.'

I have gone from orphaned to lousy-with-family in short order. I find I like this.

Forgive me, I have meandered bigtime down memory lane. Wandering back, I am sitting at table with Bags and Kaymart, preparing to make only my second-ever foray into the darkness that is Potrero-Taraval, and my eyes are watering something fierce, for Doug and Hoot both.

"You rescued him afore, f'sure," Bags reassures me. "You'll do it again. You'll see. No doubt about it."

I shake my head. "Back then he was only being guarded by a giant redwood, and that old redwood wasn't likely to pull her roots up out of the ground and come chasing after me for tree-napping."

"Yeah," Bags concedes, "but back then, you weren't no merlin either."

"I'm not sure I'm one now," I admit. "Sometimes I think I'm just making it all up."

Kaymart's having none of this. "Nonsense, Del," she tells me, her eyes looking fierce under her frizz of gray hair. "You're most certainly a merlin. I've seen you work. You've got some kind of special ability, that much I know. Your only problem is a lack of confidence. You just need to bolster your self-esteem."

I almost understand what she's saying before Bags butts in with a loud bray and exclaims, "She means you need to grow some cojones, boy!"

I have cojones, of course. Five seconds in close quarters with Firescape is enough to prove that. But I know what Bags and Kaymart mean. I don't have a lot of confidence, but sometime between then and nightfall, I gotta get some.

seventh: potrero-taraval

 **BY DUSK'S EARLY DARK,** my cojones are no bigger than usual. I decide I'll have to do without. There is a certain cowardly lion I remind me of. If I were the King of the Forest, I'd likely go hide in it someplace. But I got to do this, 'cause it's Doug who needs me.

Kaymart and Bags give me some drabs to wear; if I go over into Potrero in my merlin gear, I'll have knighties all over me in no appreciable time. (There's only one knightie I want all over me, thanks.) I have brought along a tiny flask of the attar of Doug to help bolster my aforementioned cojones, to keep me focused and to ward off the bad smells I recall from my first trek into Potrero-Taraval.

Kaymart helps me braid my yard or so of wild black hair and tuck it under a burnoose and I take off for the Border, all green and brown, looking like a cross between Robinhood and Lawrence of Arabia.

This time before I dive into Potrero, I report to the Green border knighties that I'm on a mission from God. They respectfully let me pass. It's a semi-foggy, moonless night—darker, even, than the first night I was here, if that's possible.

About a quarter mile from where I drop into the trench I spy Hoot's chink between the trolley and the dumpster. I imagine it's seen a lot of action lately. In notime, I'm in Potrero again, and Potrero is no less empty and godforsaken than it was the first time I was here.

A wind frisks up and papers and other light crap blow around on the asphalt and dance in little tornadoes. The wind makes a crying sound and I think of the Ohlone dolores lying in the grave-yard my ancestors made for them. As I think of them, I also hear them, whispering encouragement at me—at least, I think that's what they're whispering. They are most assuredly urging me on.

Being a merlin (if not much of one) I know a few incantations for protection. I choose one called Chouyan, which means "Smoke". It's a very ancient incantation, so I have some confi-dence in it. In fact, it's about the only incantation I can do well— which means it actually gets results. I mumble it now and squeeze out onto the street. It really is empty—so empty the buildings whistle to keep from being lonely.

I recall The Fiche's map. A few blocks west of here there is a long, wooded avenue. It runs just about straight to Lord E's Palace. I suspect it will be well-guarded, so I go west only one block and begin to work my way south through the haunted streets.

As I get further from the Border, I don't see a whole lot of difference in the scenery. I smell a difference, though. Bu hao! There is a stink like a red tide. It could be the garbage, which seems to be everywhere, or it could be something else I don't want to know about. Either way, I don't go look, but just keep heading south, sniffing attar of Doug and dipping in and out of shadows, my feet making soft scratches in the grit. The attar does better than ward off the smells—it makes me feel more and more like I can do this thing.

I count blocks as I go, and when I think I've gone far enough,

I cut west again. Then, there are people. I don't see them. But I hear them. First, I think it's the wind, blowing through the empty alleys and crumbling eaves. Then I realize it's voices I hear as I pass by the tired buildings. Whispers and moans in front of this one; I hurry. Laughter here; I relax a little. Rage rolls out of an upstairs window; I hurry again. I hear a child crying, a mother trying to shush it, a man swearing and demanding quiet. As I pass by, the woman begins to sing. I almost stop to listen, but I remember Doug and move on.

My math's a little off, 'cause I end up a block off from where I think I should be and see that I'm still short of Lord E's compound. Not only that, but now I see fires deep in the alleys and winking from windows and between the cracks of bad-fitting doorjambs. Out on the wooded avenue, people hang on corners and stuff, warming their hands around barrels full of fire.

I look toward the Palace and see a bunch of folks at the gates just kind of milling around. I think of joining in when I realize they're not getting inside. They're just milling and yelling and dodging stuff coming at them over the fence. Inside the fence are torches and I think I see who's doing the throwing—the first knighties I've seen since I came here.

I don't understand this. I duck back into the side street and jog, beneath whispers and shouts, to the next southbound road. The smell is worse here, where the people are, and I think Deadend must be right about no running water. It makes me homesick for the perfumes of the Gee Gah. Hell, even the fish-mart smells better than this.

Three more blocks and I cut west again, sneaking up on the back of Lord E's place. There're trees and bushes inside the tall chain fence and I think this might be easier than I thought.

I find a place in the fence where the razorbarb across the top has fallen away and start climbing. I climb the fence okay. Up, over, and right into the branches of a giant oak. The tree has a big spread and I see I can make the roof on the other side of it. I'm a tree-climber from way back and I move like the wind through the branches.

I'm feeling pretty good about myself, merlin-wise, as I come down onto the roof of the nearest building. Looking down, I can see guards patrolling the grounds. My incantations hold; they don't see me.

There is a stairwell leading down from this roof, but I ignore it. This isn't the main building of the Palace compound—that's about four buildings farther south, according to sméagols, and I can see the top floor from here, lit up like a party-boat with flickering lights. I head in that direction, skulking low to the roof.

The first two buildings are easy—real close together. I make the jump with no trouble. But the last one is different—a good two-and-a-half yards if it's an inch. And the leap won't take me to the roof, just to a ledge . . . a very narrow ledge. A ledge with windows.

I think about going to ground, but I'm afraid someone might see me. So, I back way off and take a running jump. I make the jump okay, except one of the windows opens up right in my face.

I fall. The fall is long, but doesn't feel like it. Feels real short. Fortunately, there is some tall dead grass between the two buildings, so I don't get hurt. Talk about wonky, though—my whole body is wonky. It takes me a moment to get up, a bit longer for my eyes to straighten out. When they do, I do not see what I expect to see—the walls of two buildings and a badly lit sidewalk twenty feet away. I see the walls of two buildings and four badly lit people about eight feet away and closing. They are just big, dark outlines of people—no faces.

This is creepy, so I turn to run. There are three more big, badly lit people behind me. They have faces, which, I discover is just as creepy.

I do what anybody would do, I surrender.

eighth: treed!

LORD E LORDY'S hangout is a strangely shaped building with a big dome on top—kind of like an upside down bowl. This is a planetarium. There's another one just like it in one of the buildings on the Farm. Scientists used these to show people stuff about the stars and planets they couldn't see 'cause the city lights were so bright back then.

Scientists are a kind of merlin.

This planetarium isn't as well preserved as the one at the Farm. It's practically a ruin. I'm taken up a flight of grody stairs and down a hallway into the heart of this building. The place is truly gross. Smells like wet camp gear and the carpets are stained and holey like old socks. I think about these things 'cause it helps me not shake so much. Behind thinking about moldy junk, I'm having crazy thoughts about being chopped into little pieces and fed to the fishes. I've heard Lord E has big dogs and I wonder if I'm going to meet them.

And I wonder about Doug.

They take me to the Throneroom. I guess that's what it is, anyway. It's a round room, dark, with chairs all the way around like in a theater. In the middle of the room is this big, round platform with a—well, I'd have to call it a robot—standing up on it. The thing's all black and scary looking—kind of like a giant robot spider—and its shadow is all over the curved wall behind it.

All I can do is stare. I hear this clanking sound and the robot-thing starts to turn around and flickery lights go on inside it. I realize there's stuff happening on the ceiling, but I'm too scared to look.

Can this robot-thing be Lord E Lordy? No wonder he's had such bad luck with his lordettes, I think. But no, there's a man under the robot-thing. A man sitting in a big chair. Light from the thing falls, quavery yellow, over his face, making him look like a jaundiced mime.

I gulp. I've never seen the Alcalde of Potrero-Taraval. I could've lived without.

There is something riding on the platform with him. Something in the dark at his feet. In the funny, pin-prickly light from the robot-thing, I see that it's Doug. I reach for him without thinking. A hand clamps on my shoulder.

"Wait jussa minute, littleguy. Bow before th' Alcalde." And he pushes me to my knees, whoever the hell he is.

I topple.

"Don't look much like a merlin," says the man on the platform. "Looks like a street monkey."

The man behind me wheezes. "Oh, this is the merlin, alrighty." And he pulls the burnoose off my head. "Cicerone Del, at our service."

The man in the chair leans forward and in the quivering light his hair glistens like an oil-slick.

"Don't look like much of anything. You really a merlin?" he asks me.

I raise my head. "I am." I have some pride.

He points at Doug. "This yours?"

"That," I say, calm-sounding, I hope, "is the fabled Tree of Destiny."

"Yeah. That's what we thought." He pokes his finger into Doug's needles. "So, how does it work?"

I don't tell them, of course. And, of course, I end up in the dungeon—a foul and nasty place of dripping water and cold, hard tile floors. Used to be a toilet, I'm pretty sure. If they use their toilets for dungeons, I gotta wonder where they pee. I also don't tell them I'm not sure myself how the TOD works. It just does.

I have visitors in the dungeon—besides the Whisperers, of course, who seem to go everywhere with me, these days. They are Lubejob, who I recognize as the other guy in the Throneroom, and some Big Ugly Dudes with safety pins and earrings stuck in places I don't think they belong. Not a good sign.

They are here, Lubejob tells me, to provide some incentive. What they really do is beat the crap out of me. Another thing I could live without. They don't really hurt me, though—not in the lasting-effects sense, anyway. I resist telling them anything about Doug. When the tile floors have collected enough of my blood, they just stop.

Lubejob gives me this really weird look and says, "You a guy? Really?"

I'm not about to show him. "Yeah." I mumble 'cause my lips hurt. "'Course I'm a guy."

Lubejob makes a rude noise. "No kidding. That ain't what I meant. I meant, are you people?"

"I didn't bleed enough for you?"

Sometimes I can't seem to keep myself from being a smartass.

He comes a little closer to where I'm lying in a wasted little heap under a sink. His nose wrinkles and makes snuffy noises.

"You don't smell like people," he tells me and takes his two pin-cushion friends out of my face.

When they're gone, I just lie there and smart for awhile. When I close my eyes I can almost see the forests around the Farm. Hell, almost! I can see them. And smell them. The smell of conifers is getting stronger by the second, which reminds me, suddenly, of Firescape, which makes me want to cry.

I begin to think I'm having an olfactory hallucination. Then I decide it's a new kind of vision—a nose vision—and I'm sure Firescape will come for me. I know she will. No doubt about it.

Feeling a little better about having been beaten to smithereens, I get up and discover that the water in these sinks sort of still runs. It dribbles, and that's better than squiddle.

It's when I lean against the sink that I feel something prick my thigh and realize something's broken in my pocket and I've just cut myself on it. It turns out to be the little flask of attar. I'm not sure whether to be amazed or depressed. I decide I like amazed better. Just think, I tell myself, even attar of Doug can give you visions. That's something. But the fact is, I'm separated from Doug like I haven't been from the day I pulled him out from under that redwood tree.

I start thinking about the first real vision I ever had, sitting in the Wiz reading about the first Merlin, namesake of all who followed. Doug was there in his little pot, beside me on the reading table. First, I saw his little boughs tremble, then I got a whiff of his firry perfume, then my eyes went all wonky. I daydreamed I was merlin and in my daydream I warned Bags that one of the Giants was going to fall in the next big wind.

Funny thing was, when I cleared my head, I still knew that tree was going to fall. I remember looking out and seeing leaves blowing in the street and knowing the wind was coming up. I hopped my bike, dumped Doug in the basket and rode as fast as I could to the Farm. I told Bags about that Giant falling and I even pointed out which one and which way.

"Why that," he says, "that'd take out our new greenhouse."

I apologized, but couldn't think of anything else to say.

There wasn't much in the greenhouse 'cause he was just now putting stuff into it, but he gave me this look out of his no-color eyes, then told me to help him move the stuff he'd already put in back out.

Another funny thing—I was right. The wind came up a screamer and that old Giant fell—*whammo*—right down on the new greenhouse and I knew right then that there was this thing between me and Doug and I had my first wild hope that I might someday be a merlin.

And now look at me.

I'm starting to get depressed, when I realize the little flask of Doug's attar probably just saved my life. In fact, I'm sure it did. Someone's still looking out for old Chickpea.

I spend about three days in the dungeon with only the Whisperers to talk to before they try again to get me to tell them about Doug. When I'm dragged into the Throneroom this time, there's lamplight—some kind of oil by the smell. And one of those battery camp things, stolen from Embarcadero, no doubt.

There's another dude there, too—an old dude with one squinty eye and wearing a long, scraggy beard and a ton of chains and beads. Looks like a court jester, but gotta be the Alcalde's new merlin, I figure, of which I have heard only rumor.

I'm right. The old dude comes up to me and gives me an eyeball no less hairy than Scrawl's finest. Then he sniffs at me: sniff! snuff! snuffle! All the hair stands up on my body, 'cause one of the rumors making the rounds in Embar is that in Potrero-Taraval, Soylent Green is people, if you index my reference.

Holy Maya, Mother of Buddha! I think, and start praying.

But this weird old merlin dude doesn't pull out his knife and chopsticks. Instead, he opens this squinty eye of his and says, "Are you a tree?"

I ponder this, realizing that THIS IS IMPORTANT. I am reminded of something from the Videoschool at the Wiz—which is, when someone asks "Are you a god?" say Yes.

I say, "Yes."

"Damn," says the old dude and turns to the Alcalde under his weird robot (which I realize with a bit of embarrassment is just a piece of planetarium machinery). "Damn and snap, he's a tree."

Lord E sits back in his throne and eyes me up. "So, then, this is your bro, hey?" He points to where Doug sits in his brass pot.

I look, and the breath sticks halfway up my throat. The pot

looks worse than my face—dinged up, I mean. Like they've been playing soccer with it. Worse, some of Doug's branches are bent and broken and the little blanket of moss I laid over his earth is gone. The earth is so dry, I can see cracks in it.

Suddenly, I can't swallow; my mouth is bone dry and my whole body's shaking like I'm standing on a fault line, which I am.

Diablo, say the Whisperers.

"Diablo!" I repeat. "What've you done to my Tree?"

Lord E giggles—which reminds me weirdly of Hoot. "Your Tree? *Your* Tree? *My* Tree, I think. It's sittin' in my Throneroom. All we did was play a little Q and A. It won't tell us how you work either. So . . ." He looks all bright and sunny at me. "Which one of you bites it first?"

Looking at Doug, I'm afraid he's gonna bite it immediate. I scowl menacingly. "Clearly, you have no idea what you're dealing with here. This—" I point at Doug, handquake—"is the Fabled Tree of Destiny, the Great Oracle through whose branches blow the winds of Fate and the secrets of Eternity. In this immortal conifer are the answers to all the major wheres and whyfores asked since time immemorial. This is the repository of wisdoms galore. Through this Tree, the future is seen and secrets are known . . . and all that."

"And I s'pose," says the squinty old dude, "you're the only one who knows how to get answers out of it, huh?"

I nod, squinting back.

"So . . . one of you's no good without the other, right?"

"You got it."

This makes the squinty dude do a dance and hi-five the thin air, which makes me muy nervous. I glance at Lord E, and Lube-job, who are also looking pretty pleased.

"We got it," says the Alcalde. "Lubejob, get on the grapevine and see that our dear bud, Mercedes, gets the rumble. We got both his merlin and his damn—uh, what'd you call that thing . . . Ora—"

"Oracle," I mumble, my heart doing a hindenberg.

It's clear to me that I have, once again, gone clueless. I thought I was leading them; all the time, they were leading me. Worse, I still don't know what they really want. I mean, first I think it's Hermajesty, then I think it's Doug and, for a moment, I even think it's me. I'm feeling truly sorry for myself when something hits me: Lord E called Hismajesty "Mercedes".

"How'd you know-?"

"The real and secret name of your lamebrain King?" the Alcalde finishes for me. He grins, showing yellow teeth and I wonder what they do for dental hygiene here. "We got our ways."

Yeah. I'll bet. Up to and including inside sméagols.

"What do you want, Alcalde?" I ask, trying to look fierce and merlinly.

He leans down from his throne, still grinning. "For now, I got what I want. I got you and I got your Tree. Two of the things that make Embarcadero tick."

I glance at Doug again, seeing how pathetic he looks. "You won't have us for long if you don't feed us. The Tree is dying."

Lord E twists to give Doug a sharp look. "How the hell do you feed a tree?"

"You give it water. If you don't give it water it dies. Then you can forget about having one up on Hismajesty."

Lord E scratches in his greasy beard. "That's it—water?"

"I feed him other things, too—coffee grounds, oak mulch, fish emulsion—"

He waves me down. "Sounds like merlin stuff to me. Discuss it with Squint." He thumbs at the squinty old dude, then tells him, "Keep them alive . . . for now." Lord E's leer is one of those things you could go through your whole life without seeing.

Squint gets a couple of Big Ugly Dudes to escort me and Doug to his workshop. I'm impressed. With his workshop, I mean. It's a little gross in some ways—a little on the primitive side —but number one jade in others. It's a big room with high, dark rafters and this one cool window that's like a wall only slanted in like a roof.

There's all sorts of fire pots hanging all over the place, giving off this scented smoke like the incense in a dios house. It smells kind of nice, which is more than I can say for the rest of Potrero-Taraval.

Squint's escort puts Doug down by the window and my heart drops into my shoes when I see how pale his needles are. I want to cry, but this would be unmerlinly, so I bite the inside of my cheek instead. Squint gets water from a rain barrel and brings it to me.

"Where's his mouth?"

I am bewoggled by the sheer ignorance of him. "Under the earth. He drinks and eats through his root system."

"Yeah?" Squint watches me pour the water into the pot. "You too?"

This old dude really thinks I'm a tree. "No. I drink like a person. Part of my schtick. You know—merlin stuff."

"How'd you get like this? People-like, I mean?"

"Evolution."

He shakes his head. "I don't know that spell."

Didn't think so.

"Look," I say, "you got anything he can eat? Fish emulsion, coffee grounds—?"

He's shaking his head. "Never heard of the stuff."

"You guys eat fish?"

"Yeah, sure."

"So, get me a fish."

"So, don't give me orders, tree man."

"Please," I say.

I show him how to make fish emulsion and explain that it's also good for people and makes a great, if stinky, salve for burns. I figure maybe I can make friends with this guy—schmooze a little, merlin to merlin, etal. I'm schmoozing away, listening to him rattle on about fertility spells that don't work, when I see something outside the window. It's a grey day, kind of foggy, but I think I see a flash of red and black between some scrubby-looking bushes.

My heart flips over a couple of times. I'm sure Squint can hear it, but he just keeps talking.

When Squint's all through with me, he puts me in a better room. I tell him a few things about the way the TOD works—like that he needs a certain amount of sunlight. I'm hoping for a downstairs room with windows; I get an upstairs room with a skylight.

Good enough, I hope, 'cause I'm pretty sure I know that red and black flash. I think Doug knows too, 'cause his needles start quivering the moment I see the flash and don't stop even when we are in our new room.

It's a sign of some sort, I figure, and I stare at him until my eyes go wonky and it seems like he's waving at the skylight. Suddenly, I get it. He wants me to rig a signal. But what would Firescape see and recognize that the Potreran Knighties wouldn't? In the moment I ponder this, it seems to me that Doug waves even harder, filling the air with scent and making one of his bent boughs dance.

All at once I understand; Doug is offering the injured bough as a beacon. Overcome by this selfless gesture, I remove the branch as gently as I can, praying I don't hurt him much. Still, I feel a horrible twinge in my gut when the bough comes free. Doug brushes my hand to reassure me.

I take the branch—it's about as long as my forearm—and climb up on a table to reach the only window in this place. It's half boarded up and half covered with stiff mesh. Inside the mesh is broken glass. I stuff the branch through a fist-sized hole in the glass and out through the mesh. Then, I let go of it, praying it will stay. It does.

Doug sends me a waft of perfume that prompts me to gently remove the other broken tips from his boughs. I use them to rub more scent on myself, too, and put the crushed remains in my pocket.

We settle down to wait.

ninth: attar of doug

AROMATHERAPY. That's what Bags calls the medicine side of it—the funny things smells do to you, I mean. Smells, he told me, early in my farmerly training, are powerful stuff. I was exceedingly doubtful at the time.

I remember he grabbed a handful of the dirt from the hole he was digging at the feet of this big cedar and stuck it under my nose and said, "Sniff it."

I obey of course. I always obey Bags. All the little apprentice farmers obey Bags. Obeying Bags and Kaymart has a kind of soothing effect. In my case, I'm making up for all the years I had nobody to obey but a cat.

I sniff. I smell rich loam, moss, wet grass, cedary perfume. "Yeah?"

"Do you think this soil's fertile?"

I nod.

"Because why?"

"Because it's got good mulch in it, so it's rich, but it's light, so it should drain well."

I'm very proud of this pronouncement. Bags has taught me a

lot and I like the chance to show off, even times like now, when none of the other little apprentices are around.

"Yeah? How can you tell all that?"

"Because it . . ." I get the point. "The smell. Okay, so smell can tell me stuff about stuff."

He squints at me in that way he has when he is delivering wisdom. "It can do more than that." He reaches off to one side and picks up something from the ground and rubs it between his fingers. "Close your eyes and sniff."

I obey. I smell attar of fir.

"What's that remind you of?"

"Doug," I say and can almost see him sitting on the front porch of the Farmhouse, enjoying the sunshine. I smile.

"How's that make you feel?"

"Real good. Happy." It's true. My heart seems to swell up with Doug feelings.

"Powerful feeling, ain't it?"

I nod.

"And all from a little attar of Doug."

He's right, I realize. The smell of fir or pine or cedar or cypress all make me feel fine—I mean, *really* fine. Almost like I'm floating in a warm, glowing place. I realize now that there are other smells I been taking for granted all my life that do powerful things to me —the smell of Mrs. Lopez-Alvero's tortillas, of rain-wet concrete, of salt-fog, of tar-soaked wharves, of the Hau Bau bakery on Market. I remember the clean, cold scent of Bunuelo's fur when he'd just come in from outdoors. I spent a lot of time with my nose buried in that old cat's fur, which is funny, considering how I pretended not to like him. Funny, too, as much as he pretended to be above me, he never seemed to mind.

Now that Bags has scored some points about the power of smells, he goes on to teach me more about them. We dig up the mulch we're after and head back to the house with it. Smoke curls from the chimney and mingles with a light wu gau that floats above, aloof as Bunuelo. Bags stops to look at it.

"Smell that?" he asks.

"Yeah." I love the smell of wood smoke.

"What's that smoke say to you, Del?"

"Home."

It's true. Wood smoke was home long ago, too, when home meant mi madre y padre. When I'd been out in the cold and wet longer than I should, that smell always said there were people waiting for me who would make me warm and glad to have even a drafty four walls to come home to.

"We all got smells that make us feel alright," Bags says. "And we got smells that make us feel rotten. But there's more to it than that. That wood smoke smell, that reminds you of your mom and dad, don't it?"

I nod.

"Bet you can almost see 'em, huh?"

I nod again, feeling sad now, and kind of wishing Bags'd get onto something else.

"Smells evoke memories," he tells me, sounding more like Kaymart than Bags. "They make you call up things you might've forgot." He smiles funny. "Could be a good interrogation tool."

I snort. "Yeah? And what'm I gonna interrogate—asparagus?"

"Smells can do other stuff, too," he says, ignoring me. "They can soothe the up-tight breast, calm the jangled nerve, heal the wounded soul."

"Now you're jinkin' me."

He stops at the porch steps and looks at me most somber. "No, Del," he says in all seriosity. "I wouldn't do that. Smell is a greatly powerful thing." He hands me the sprig of evergreen he has crushed in his fingers. "A greatly powerful thing. Now, you get cleaned up and help Kaymart with dinner."

He shoulders his shovel and heads off for the tool shed, leaving me with the bags of rich-smelling dirt. It takes me a moment to realize that Kaymart has come out of the Farmhouse and is standing on the top step watching him. When I look up, I see in her eyes that she really loves that old guy like crazy. I pray someday somebody looks at me like that. The prayer is answered only by the strong smell of crushed fir needles.

I shake my head. "He's a weird old dude. I sure wish I knew what the power of smells has to do with farming."

"Farming?" Kaymart echoes.

"Yeah. And he's always doing that. I mean, yesterday he was showing me how to plant corn, when he gets this weird bug in his noodle and starts telling me how a seed has to sacrifice itself to the tree, and how the tree gives everything it's got to its cones or fruit or whatever it uses to give birth to its seeds."

Kaymart nods. "And then it starts all over again."

"That's what he said," I note.

"What's so odd about that, Del?"

"Well, it just doesn't sound like farming."

She laughs at me—just outright laughs. "Is that what you think he's teaching you?" she asks.

"Yeah, sure. What else? Isn't that what he's teaching all the kids?"

She's stopped laughing, except in her eyes, which are having rare old time. "Well, he may be teaching *them* farming, but he's teaching you magic."

"Magic? What'd he know about that?"

She shrugs. "Ask him. He hasn't always been a Farmer, you know." When I twitch to go after the old guy, she adds, "After you've helped me fix dinner. I need you to husk some pine nuts."

I sit on what Kaymart says for over a week. I mean, it seems too weird, you know—Bags, a merlin? I mean, if he'd been a merlin, what the hell was he doing vegetating down on the Farm? I'm afraid if I ask such a jingbing question ("So, Mr. Bags, is it true you were a merlin, once upon a time?") he'll laugh at me. And I hate to be the source of guffaw for the old man. When Bags laughs at you, you feel like you've done something not just humanly stupid, but cosmically stupid.

Which is not to say that Bags *does* anything to make you feel cosmically stupid, it just happens. It's like with colors. Red is red, but it looks really, truly, redly red when you put it next to green, say, or blue. I gotta admit, too, that in my recollection, Bags doesn't wax esoteric around the other apprentices. At least, not that I've ever heard.

So anyway, I sit on all this for about a week, trying to think of a way to ask THE QUESTION without asking THE QUESTION, and one day I come up with something I think is not too cosmically stupid.

We are sitting on the front porch of the Farmhouse, me shelling acorns, him petting this old rag-eared cat named Zorro— when I say slyly (I think), "That stuff you put on the tomatoes sure got up a good crop."

"Yeah," says Bags. "Best ever."

"Magic, huh?"

He spocks an eyebrow at me. "Science. Been working on that formula for a couple o' years. Finally got it right. Gonna have to get some to Felicidad for his plots over at the Presidio."

Huh. That went nowhere. I sit and contemplate my options and lean toward forgetting the whole thing when Bags says, "You interested in magic, are you?"

"I like reading about the first Merlin and Gandalf and those guys." Now, I try to get sly again. "I studied the latter day merlins too, like Joseph Braghorn, merlin to King Levi Menorah, and the amazing Stanley Nemecec, merlin to the illustrious and artful Troubadour." I watch him out of the tail of my eye.

He's smiling and I see several toothless holes. "Joseph Braghorn," he repeats. "Stanley Nemecec. Those are names I han't heard for a month of Feast days."

"You know 'em?"

"Well, I remember seeing Joseph when I was a boy. He was an old man even then. Great merlin. The best."

I wax bold. "You know anything about merlinry?"

His eyes sting my face. "You care, do you?"

"Yeah."

He nods and strokes the cat's tatty old carcass. "I know a few things . . . You wanna be a merlin, do you?"

I laugh out loud—too loud. "Me? I got no merlin stuff. I'd have to be a certifiable ditz to think I got that Calling."

"Then I s'pose that means I'm a certifiable ditz, too, 'cause I think you've got merlin stuff. Fact is, I wouldn't have you here if you didn't have magic in you."

"But, I'm—I'm too small," I babble. "I got no aplomb, no erudition, no sense of import. Hell, I couldn't even get a damn cat to look up to me. A merlin's got to have aplomb and erudition and-and—"

"A merlin," he tells me, pointing a crooked finger at my nose, "don't need none of that. A merlin only needs a channel."

"A channel?"

"A sort of cell-phone to the Almighty. A cellphone that picks up all those little whispers in the Universe."

"What sort of channel?" I ask.

"Well, that depends on the merlin. Me, I had a cat named Pearl. A gray cat. And my Pearl'd whisper all the little secrets she knew—which was lots. But a channel, now, could be anything—anything at all."

"Anything?" I try to feature God whispering to me through one of the acorns in the palm of my hand.

Bags cocks his head, also looking at the acorns. "Well, any living thing."

There is this supreme MOMENT of silence in the Universe, after which I say, "Like . . . like a tree, for instance?"

"A tree would make a righteous good channel. God's partial to trees."

There is more silence, mostly from my end of the Universe, as I ponder this. No, "ponder" is the wrong word. There's no brain action happening here—this is all metaphysical stuff. At the center of it is a little Doug fir in a clay pot.

Right about the time the silence has waxed lengthy, something tickles my Alice bone most outrageously. I remember that there are questions lying around unanswered. I pick one up and give it a shake.

"So, after Pearl the Cat whispered all this stuff into your ear, whose ear'd you whisper it into?"

He strokes the cat a few times and says, "Troubadour's for one, and then there was Hismajesty's daddy for a while."

"But, Troubadour's merlin was Stanley Nemecec."

"Yep. That'd be me."

"But then . . . what're you doing here?"

"What's wrong with here?" he wants to know.

"Well, nothing, it's just not merlining. S'posing you were—are—the great Stanley Nemecec—why'd you quit?"

"Well, there's no simple answer to that one. First, there was the death of Hismajesty the First, who was more to me than just a sovereign lord; he was a friend. And then there was Kaymart and the Farm, and the green things tuggin' at my old heart-strings. And there were kids—Kaymart's apprentices—who needed a full-time father-figure, so she said. I told the young Majesty he oughta find hisself a younger merlin and recommended an apprentice of mine for the job. That'd be Mad Jin Gao. I suspect he's doin' a fair job of it. Haven't heard any complaints from His M, and His M the Second being the son of His M the First, I reckon I would, if there was a problem. There, that satisfy your Alice bone?"

I'm torn. I don't know whether to scoff or be very impressed. I decide to be impressed. Bags may seem like a crazy old man, but I'd been with him long enough by now to believe that crazy is just something he does so folks will size him up all wrong.

Needless to say, I am taking notes.

tenth: rescued?

IT'S NEARLY dusk when Squint shows up again, bringing food and a bottle of cola. The food isn't much—some scraggy veggies and undercooked potatoes—but I am truly amazed by the cola. I didn't think the Potreros had any of the niceties of civilized life left. They've always seemed sort of down on technology. I used to think Lord E was just hogging it for himself, but it sure hasn't seemed that way up till now.

Squint waves the bottle at me. "You rate bigtime, merlin," he tells me. "This is from the Alcalde's private, personal and very secret stock. I don't even get this stuff unless I done something mega."

"Take a swig," I offer, seeing another way to suck up.

He swigs quite adequately before passing me the bottle. Then he watches me while I eat and drink.

"So," he says after a while of making my skin crawl, "so, you eat regular food . . . How come you don't eat fish emulsion and bone meal like your bro?"

"Appearances," I fabricate. "I wanna maintain a people shape,

I gotta eat people food. Otherwise, weird shit happens. It's part of the magic."

Squint is interested. "Weird shit, huh? Like what?"

"Like, you know, my hair goes green and spiky, my skin gets barky, my toes start wriggling around, looking for dirt."

"Whoa," says Squint.

"Pretty scary," I agree.

"So, where'd you learn your stuff? Turning into people, etal."

"Oh, uh . . . the Wiz."

For the first time, he looks like he maybe doesn't believe me. "How does a tree get into the Wiz? Somebody plant you in there?"

"Sort of. You see, the last merlin of Embarcadero was a normal guy. He had a Tree . . . me. When he came to the end of his long and illustrious career, he had no apprentices that suited him. So, he created himself an apprentice via transmogrification."

It's scary how easy this stuff comes out of me sometimes.

I can tell by Squint's expression that I've lost him, but he doesn't let on, really, just nods like, uh-huh, sure, I got it. "So," he says, turning his nod to Doug, "he's like your apprentice, then, huh? You gonna do the same thing with him, when you start creakin'?"

"Yeah," I say, and take another swig of cola.

My eyes wander up over Squint's head to the darkening skylight. A face is peering in at me through the grimy glass— Firescape's face. I gulp, nearly choke myself, and hand Squint the bottle.

"Here, have some more," I say, but it's hard to hear myself over the racket my blood is making pounding around in my head.

While he's swigging, eyes closed, I glance up again at Firescape. She makes a little sign. *Get rid of him.*

Yeah. Like I haven't already considered this myself.

Squint hands me back the bottle—one swallow left. I kill it and give him the empty, though I don't s'pose they recycle over here.

"Tell Lord E thanks for the special treatment."

Squint actually grins at me. "You're a special dude." He doesn't leave though. Just keeps grinning and squinting. "So, you get all your schtick from the Wiz, too, huh?"

Jeez. "Everybody gets their schtick from the Wiz . . . or one of the little Wizlets. Where else?"

"Everybody? Including Hismajesty?"

"Sure," I say, and try not to sound testy. I can see Firescape hovering up there, waiting. "All the kids go there. They start off in the AV Shrine with Videoschool. Then they do books. When they're old enough, they find their calling and go with it."

"Calling?"

I twitch nervously. "You know—where they fit in. What they want to do and what needs doing. The Service, Firebrigade, teacher, butcher, baker, candle-maker, artist, merlin . . . court jester. Whatever."

Squint frowns. "Those're callings? You got people who just do that stuff? I mean, like a kid says, 'I wanna paint pictures' or 'I wanna bake stuff' and then they just do it?"

"Yeah, well, they get the inside on it from the Wiz and when they're ready, they do it."

"Why?"

Why? Duh. "'Cause they like to do it and it needs to get done. Somebody's got to do it, right?"

Squint scratches his head. "Hismajesty says, huh?"

"It needs to get done," I repeat, not getting why this guy is so dense, "or Embarcadero don't work." I don't feel quite so unworthy to call myself a merlin, all of a sudden. "Look, Merlin Squint, I'd love to jaw all night, but I'm really dragged and the TOD wishes to consult with me about some stuff."

Squint's left eye pops almost open. "He told you that?"

I nod.

"Just now?"

I nod.

"I didn't hear nothin'."

"He only speaks to one man," I say, and point to my chest.

"I get it. You understand him 'cause you're a tree, too."

I nod.

"Jeez. Can I watch?"

"No way. Communications between a merlin and his Tree are privileged."

"Huh?"

"He's shy."

"Oh. Oh, yeah. Well, any guy who eats through his feet." He shrugs. "S'cuse me."

At last! I look up as Squint vacates and see Firescape giving me the thumbs up.

"Uh . . . one more thing, Merlin Cicerone," Squint says from the doorway.

I gulp, jerk my head back down. "Uh, yeah?"

"Where'd you get your Tree?"

"The Farm."

"The Farm. That's that park across the Border, right? Where the old dude and dudette hang?"

I nod.

"Weird couple of ducks. Always digging around in the dirt—feeding the trees, I guess." His eyes get real big and he points at Doug, all reverent. "Wow, like that one, huh?"

"Yeah, like that one."

"Course, you can't get the big ones out of the ground, I bet. I mean, they can't, like, get up and move or nothin'."

"No," I agree, about to cry. "Not usually."

He scratches his beard, nods. Stands there for another minute. I want to scream and Doug is quivering like, well, like a tree, I guess.

Squint squints one last time, then leaves.

By now little sparklies are swarming around inside my eyes. But I hear Firescape above me, tapping on the skylight, and I look up. Through the swarm of sparklies she signs me to move back out of the way. I do, and the next thing I hear is the crunch of breaking glass.

In no appreciable time, Firescape is standing in front of me and I'm wondering if I should hug her. She doesn't wait for me to decide. She takes things into her own hands—or arms, as the case may be.

"Chickpea Del, you lamebrain!" she murmurs lovingly (I hope). "You gotta screw loose, or what? I couldn't believe—! When Geranium told me . . . You yutz!"

She gives me this big, outrageous kiss, right on the lips. Hard. Then she socks my jaw. Also hard.

"I love you," I say, which hurts, but who cares?

Her nose wrinkles. "And you tell me I gotta be careful. C'mon. Grab the TOD and let's scramble."

I look up along the rope that brought Firescape down to me. "How're we supposed to get Doug up there?"

She points up the rope. "I'll go up first. You make a cradle around the pot. I'll hoist him, then I'll send the rope back down for you. By the way," she adds, before ascending, "I love you too."

Good plan. We do it. And, as I am floating on a cloud of love, everything goes pretty smooth. Not a drop of soil lost. Blood neither.

Out on the roof, though, we got a problem. We gotta slide the pot to the back edge without (1) making a hell of a racket and (2) accidentally rolling Doug off the sloping roof (also, coincidentally, making a hell of a racket). We finally link arms and pick up the pot so we are face to face on either side, looking at each other through the boughs. They tickle my nose. For a guy who's just been starved for three days, Doug sure feels heavy.

"You just watered him, didn't you?" Firescape whispers.

I nod and stifle a sneeze.

We have to crab-walk to the back edge of the roof. Our footsteps sound like thundering hordes and I slip twice and skid some inches toward the edge of the roof. Then I get the hang of it.

I also get a little cocky, and the very moment I think about already being through the Fence, I slip, I fall, I take a long, lonely skid on my furry tummy, right for the edge of the roof.

Suddenly, there is air under my feet and space opening its big yawp below me and a big, hairy scream building up in my throat. Then, a hand clamps on the back of my jacket and I just stop, legs swinging in the air, a rain-gutter crimping my ribs.

Firescape, clinging to a rope, puts her face next to mine and hisses, "Hold me."

I'd like nothing better. I wrap my arms around her waist and dig my fingers under her belt. Together, we crawl back up the slope to where Doug waits, Firescape's climbing hook sunk into the tiles behind his pot.

"Thank you," I whisper, but Firescape merely detaches herself from me and says, "Thank me when we're outta here."

We start moving again; sidle-sidle, slip-slip, ouch-ouch. It seems to take forever, but at last we are at the back edge of the building and do the cradle thing again, this time going down.

Okay, I think, this is it. We've done it. But I've forgotten about the Fence. Now, I remember it. Which, I think, says something to me about the nature of reality. The Fence will not go away just 'cause I need it to. Neither will the curls of truly wicked razorbarb across the top.

While I pause to reflect on this, Firescape hunkers down and disappears behind a bush. Before I can ask what she's doing, the bush rolls clear over, showing a little hacked-off trunk and Firescape standing behind. She's pulling on the wire which parts like, well, like cut wire.

She holds the edges apart and grins at me. "After you, Merlin Cicerone," she says.

"After the Tree of Destiny," I correct, and drag Doug over to the hole.

It takes both of us to hoist him through the hole, then I follow while Firescape covers us with her Magic Weapon. I'm just straightening on the other side of the Fence when I hear her say,

"Damn," in that tone of voice that can only mean one of two things: Damn, I have stepped in something unpleasant, or Damn, we have been discovered. In this case, it is the latter.

"How," I ask Firescape as we are herded along by five Big Ugly Dudes, "did they get the drop on you?"

She scowls ferociously. "I got caught in the damn Fence, coming through after you. Couldn't even get the damn muzzle up." She snorts, glancing to where her AK rests in the hands of one of the aforementioned Dudes. "Some Magic Weapon."

Now, I am scared. I didn't think old Squint had it in him to thwart the magic of an Embarcaderan Weapon. I have learned an important lesson: Never underestimate a fellow merlin, no matter how much like a court jester he is.

That merlin and his lord are grinning ear to ear when the Big Ugly Dudes bring us in. I notice the grins get even bigger when they gander Firescape. My insides get freezer burn.

"Bonus prize!" squeals Squint and Lord E says, "Merlin Cicerone, you've brought some really good stuff my way these days, but this takes the garbanzo. How'd you know I was down a lordette?" And the two of them wink and yuk it up.

I realize suddenly that I have been had six ways from Sunday. I grip one of Doug's little boughs tight enough to draw sap. A wave of perfume hits my schnozzle and makes its way to my weeny brain.

"Scrawl," I say aloud. "You got Scrawl to say all that garbage about deadjim lordettes."

"Not garbage, exactly," says Lord E. "It's true, y'know. I really do go through lady-lords pretty fast. But, yeah, it didn't hurt to have Scrawl mouthing off."

"Yeah," Squint guffaws. "That old hag is so hot to crumble your tortilla, she'd buy the Baybridge from a blue whale if it'd do the job. Passin' along Lord E's sad, sad story was nothin'."

"And the wall-scrawl? She did that herself, huh?"

"She's got imagination," says Lord E.

"Yeah, and a source of ethanol and fireworks," I guess.

It comes clear, at last. The only thing I'm not sure of is what these two are really after. Huh—I mean, what I've helped them get besides, possibly, me and Doug and Firescape. I grab her hand and think real hard about what I've said.

Somewhere in the middle of all this thinking, it comes to me —where all Squint's questions were headed—straight to the Wiz.

eleventh: straight to
the wiz

IN THE END, we meet at the Border across the trench—Alcalde to King, sméagol to sméagol, Squire to Squint.

Today, the dead Potreran buildings are full of eyes. I feel them prickle my skin. A bridge has been laid over the Trench for this momentous occasion, and on the Embar side old Scrawl looks smugger'n hell. She figures my goose is paté. She's probably right.

Firescape and Doug and I are brought front and center while one really Big, really Ugly Dude holds Firescape's AK on us. He does not know how to use it. Strangely, this is not comforting.

"As you can see, Mercedes," says Lord E, and Hismajesty winces at the sound of his real and secret name on Potreran lips, "we got yer merlin, yer Tree, and one very pretty knightie—a General, she tells me. I bet you'd like to have them back, hey?"

His M snarls. "Scunge," he calls. "Slime. Of course, I want them back, scum. Your terms, scuzz, your terms."

The Alcalde is unaffected by this heroic speech. He merely chuckles.

"My terms—simple: Let me at the Wiz."

Hismajesty's eyes all but pop out of his royal head. Squire's too and, to my irrelevant satisfaction, Scrawl's.

"The Wiz?" repeats Hismajesty. "But I thought—"

"Ha-ha!" crows the Alcalde, and Squint cuts a caper. "As you were meant to think, Mercedes, old bud. 'Cause what I really want is all the other stuff you got—guns, ammo, running water, electric light, warm clothes that don't come second hand from dead folks. I want to keep the cold out and the warm in. I want a merlin who can do more than just rattle his beads and chains and dance the oingo-boingo."

Squint goes all surly when he hears this, but Lord E forges on: "I want to keep my lordettes from cacking before they plop forth an heir. I want more of my favorite cola. Shortly, Merc, I want the magic you been hoggin' in that place. And don't tell me it's not there. I know what I seen and I seen all the good shit you guys got. Plus I got it on grapevine and a hot say-so that this Wiz is the bonanza of all good shit."

His M blinks at Squire, who shrugs.

"He says," I translate, "that he's got it on good authority that the Wiz is the fountainhead of all our knowledge." I don't mention I'm the authority of which we speak.

"I see," says His M, looking majestically pained. "And if I accept your terms . . ."

"You get your property back."

"You don't have my property," says Hismajesty, taking a literal tack, "you have my General, my merlin, and the Fabled Tree of Destiny—all of which better be none the worse for wear."

"Whatever."

"And if I decline?"

"Huh?"

"He asks what'll happen if he says, 'no,'" I translate.

Squint and Lord E and that scum, Lubejob, all light up like Winky's ex-boathouse.

"Well," says Lord E, "in that case, we'll just keep your merlin, your General and your Tree and thank you kindly. See, I need a mother for my heirs, and my merlin, here, could sure as hell use some help merlining, and as for the Tree, well, there's no telling what I could do with that kind of magic. So you see, what I got here is a win-win."

More grinning.

At this point, Firescape leans over to me and whispers in one of my red hot little ears, "Del, do something. I don't wanna be the mother of little Alcaldes. I wanna be the mother of little Chickpea Flannigans. I mean it, Del, I'd rather be deadjim."

She means it, and in this moment of great desperation, as I see my Majesty deliberating on what is the lesser of two evils, I don't care what happens to me. But for Firescape—for Jade—I gotta do something. As usual, I look to Doug for help.

Okay—stupid, I s'pose. I mean, maybe he is just a pet tree. And maybe I do sort of exaggerate a few things about me and him and us. And maybe I feel wonky sometimes (like right now) 'cause I'm just naturally wonky.

But then, maybe not.

I look at Doug sitting there in the watery sunshine in his poor, dented pot and see his boughs and needles all a-quiver and a-shimmer with weird light and time stops. It comes to me, then, like Doug whispered in my ear: *Everything's gonna be okay, Chickpea-boy. Let them into the Wiz—the Wiz will take care of itself, you'll see. 'Cause it really is magic.*

I'm convinced. Yeah, convinced I'm muy loco. But hell, what's a merlin to do?

"May I speak to my lord?" I ask Lord E. "I think I can, uh, speed things up . . . maybe."

The Alcalde gives me the eye. "You ain't gonna split on me, are you?"

I am so incensed, the hair jumps up on my head. "And leave my Tree and my true love in your slimy hands? I'd sooner leave you my liver. I'll be back."

The Alcalde gives me the go-ahead.

As I walk across the bridge, I feel something behind me. Hairs stand up on my neck and say, "howdy!" and I know it's the sméagol, Lubejob. I sweat. What I got to say to Hismajesty is not for the ears of sméagols. But here I am, face to scowling face with my Majesty and I gotta say something. I can almost feel Doug quivering the air behind me. Wonky whispers come to my inner ear.

I bow to my King. "Majesty," I say, "have no trepidation. The TOD informs your worthless, despicable merlin that we are to evince no concern. I am assured that all will proceed felicitously to a satisfactory conclusion. Go ahead and let Lord E Lordy at the Wiz," I add for Lubejob's benefit. "No deleterious effects will accrue. You have the Tree's word on it." And I wink slowly for emphasis.

Hismajesty's left brow spocks upward and I detect an itty-bitty grin at the corner of the royal mouth. "I see," he says, "a bit of subterfuge is afoot."

"Indubitably," I affirm, though I feel clueless.

"So be it," says my liege. He raises his head, peers across the trench and waves. "You got it—the Wiz is your oyster. Elvis, come on down!"

Elvis?

A glance at Lord E proves he is none too pleased to have his own real and secret name flapping around on enemy lips. Huh. He can dish it out, but he can't take it. Big surprise.

"What goes around, comes around," HisMajesty growls. "Now you know what the 'E' stands for."

We proceed to the Wiz in a strange and wondrous procession. His M calls out the royal vehicles; a fleet of flip-top Mercedes (natch), flanked by a rainbow of knighties on steel chargers—Vespas, actually.

Lord Elvis is impressed as hell and practically licking his lips, 'cause he just knows the Wiz is gonna give him all this good stuff too. There goes our strategic advantage . . . and my head with it, I don't doubt. About now, I'm racking my chickpea-brain trying to figure out how the Wiz is not gonna give all this good stuff away.

The loud procession winds through the streets of Embar-cadero, watched on by the good and confused citizens of same, who surely deserve a merlin better than me. Elvis and Squint and the arch-sméagol ride in one of the Mercedes, keeping Doug and Firescape between them just in case. I ride with His M, all the time feeling Scrawl's beady blues digging holes in the back of my head. She's mad as hell, 'cause she had to be hoping His M was gonna strand my butt in Potrero-Taraval.

Scrawl and I go way back . . . unfortunately. Back to when I was still in my probationary period as a merlin. I had a wonky vision of a freak storm, which, since everything else I had wonky visions about happened, I took to His M. Scrawl laughed right in my face, but Hismajesty took some cautions in spite of the fact that no one else had said squiddle about a storm. As it happened, I was right. The storm came and it was a doozy. Which made Doug and I look like the Good Witch of the West and Chief Engineer Montgomery Scott rolled into one, and made Scrawl look like a quack. Scrawl has not cared much for either of us since.

But back to the present crisis. Lord E-for-Elvis is just about glowing as he and his right and left hand dudes and the Big and Ugly squad stand and gaze up at the sign that hangs above those hallowed doors—the sign that devoted acolytes have kept bright and new and spiffy clean for decade upon decade.

CITY LIGHTS BOOKSTORE, it says in letters two feet tall.

The Alcalde looks at me. "This the place?"

I sigh, praying I am not just naturally wonky, that I have really heard and smelled Doug's firry whispers. "Yeah, this is it."

He scowls. "Don't be yankin' me, Chickpea-face."

"He's not," says Lubejob. "I been here. I seen it. This is where they do their magic. Pictures that move . . . cars, boats, bikes, even people. The cars are in these little boxes and they drive them right out of the pictures, I bet. I ain't no merlin, but I seen the moving pictures."

What the hell? I think, but old Elvis the Alcalde is already on the move.

"Good enough," he says, and leads his sméagol and his merlin and his Big Ugly Dudes into the Wiz.

I am appalled. They don't even genuflect. I breathe a prayer that if the sky falls, Chicken Little, the good people of Embarcadero will be able to dodge the pieces. We genuflect, I can tell you, which bewoggles the Potreros.

Once inside, Lord E just stands there and gapes like a beached fish, turning and turning, not even aware that he has interrupted scads of folks in the worshipful act of reading. I know how he feels, though. Whenever I lay my unworthy eyes on these knowledge-crammed walls, I am overwhelmed and awed.

Finally, Lord E stops turning and gaping and says to me, "So, where's all this great stuff, all this magic and what-not you guys promised?"

I am perplexed. "It's here. All around you."

"Show me. Show me how you guys get all your stuff."

I choose the book upon which our government rests. It is called ARTHUR 'cause it's about that great father of all monarchs and his magic kingdom. I hand the book to Lord Elvis who gives its colorful cover a long look before opening it. He stares at the first page, then begins flipping quickly through the book, stopping here and there to look at the pictures, which are beautiful. Finally, he slams the book closed.

"These pictures don't move," he says to me, then looks at Lubejob. "They don't move. They just sit there." He waves the book at me. "Are they all like this?"

"Yes and no," I say. "That one is about government. Its companion volume—uh, the next book in the series—is about the very first Merlin. The others are about . . . well, everything."

"About? How can it be about anything? It's full of pictures of-of big dudes in tin cans on fat horses. And what do these scrawls mean?" He pops the book open making me fear for the binding. "Are these the magic runes?"

Finally, I understand. "Those are words," I say. "Those tell the story, not the pictures."

"What's he mean?" he asks Squint, but Squint just shrugs and squints and jumps like a scared cat when the Alcalde tosses the book into his hands. "Read the runes, merlin," he demands.

But Squint can't read them either. "I can't," he says and looks about ready to cry, and I actually feel sorry for the geezer.

The Alcalde grabs the book and points it at me again. "You're trying to tell me these runes tell you how to make electric light and feed all these fat people?"

"Not those runes, particularly, but others."

"Bullshit," says Lord E. "All bullshit. What good are runes my merlin can't read? You're yankin' me, Chickpea-face. These ain't magic. Hell, we use this crap for fire-starters." And he dumps ARTHUR back into my hands with no ceremony whatsoever. "Where're the moving pictures, merlin? Where's the real magic?"

Of course, what he means is the videos. I tilt my head toward the AV Shrine, and kind of let my eyes wander that way like I really don't want them to.

He grins at me and waves a hand at the Big Ugly Dudes. "What we want's back there. I don't know what it is, but Lubejob will know when we find it, won't you, Lubejob?"

Lubejob agrees that he will know it immediate, and with that, they take off into the back rooms and begin searching for this magical stuff they think we're hiding. Which, of course, we're not hiding at all.

Hismajesty sidles up to me as we tag along. "What's up, Cicerone?" he asks. "Can't these Philistines read?"

I shake my head. "It would appear not."

His M grins. "Then the Wiz can't do them any good."

I cross my fingers. "We'll see. There's still the videos," I say, which goes down like the Titanic.

His M's grin goes flat.

By now I hear noises of great turmoil from the AV Shrine. His M gives me a little shove and I hurry to investigate, Hismajesty, Squire, and Firescape on my heels. The Big Ugly Dudes have cleared one whole shelf of video discs and have piled them on a table in the center of the room. Squint stands by, a disc in each hand, clearly clueless as to what to do with them.

"What is this stuff?" he wheezes at me, while behind him, Lubejob mutters, "This is the place. Yeah, this is the place. This is where I saw the magic pictures. There was a box. And the pictures were in the box."

I point at a Learning Booth, then gingerly open the smoky plastic door. A Video Disc Player and screen are set up inside.

"Yeah!" says Lubejob. "Yeah!"

"You can watch a video in one of these booths," I explain, "or go to one of the Videoschool rooms."

"Now we're getting somewhere," says Lord Elvis. "Show me how this works."

Squint shoves a disc into my hands and stands back, arms folded, looking like a squinty, grubby Pharaoh (*Yo, Moses, make with the serpents, already!*). I go into the learning booth and slip the disc he's chosen into the player. It is Stephen Hawking's A BRIEF HISTORY OF TIME—PBS version. This should be interesting.

The video screen comes to life and a voice says, "This program is brought to you through a grant from Cornell University and —" The voice rattles off a list of sponsors (which are like patron saints) and the Big Ugly Dudes hunker down and glance about shifty-eyed.

Then the program starts: pictures of black holes, nebulae, comets whirl about while cosmic music plays. Then, for a word of introduction, appears the man we reverence as The Sagan. He is smiling (he is always smiling, 'cause knowledge brings happiness) and he tells us how we go about our lives knowing almost nothing of our world. How we don't even think about where sunlight comes from or how come life even is or why we can stand and walk and run on a big ball spinning in space without ending up in space ourselves. And chaos—he mentions chaos. And then there are pictures of the solar system and a close-up of Earth with an arrow that points to the blob that contains Embarcadero and Potrero-Taraval and a whole lot else and says, YOU ARE HERE.

"What's this? What's this?" Elvis snarls.

"Physics," I say calmly and send silent praise to the Wiz and the all-knowing Dios Who gave it into our unworthy hands.

"Fizz-what?" says Elvis, and Lubejob all but spits at me. "What's with the marbles? Where're the cars and the bikes and all the great-looking food?"

Squint shoves another video at me. "What's this one? It's got cars on the box; does it do cars?"

"That's THE ART AND BUSINESS OF AUTO MAINTE-NANCE. It shows how to fix cars when they break down."

Lord E howls. "I don't want to fix cars, dammit! I just want to *have* cars!" He gets in my face, then. "What the hell is this stuff? Where's all the magic stuff you promised me?"

"Right here, Lord E. In the books, the videos—"

I can tell he doesn't believe me, 'cause he throws a video at me. Shortly, he and his BUDs (the aforementioned Big Ugly Dudes) have torn the place apart, looking for the magic that makes Embarcadero work. They topple shelves, upset reading tables (not to mention readers), and put a dent in The Fiche's console. When they are finished, the Wiz is one humongous mess. I can only pray they don't torch the place.

They don't. They snarl and snap at Hismajesty and demand cars at AK point. By now, His M has gotten into the spirit of the thing. He enjoys seeing old Elvis all sweated up. He jerks a thumb at the front doors.

"You want cars? Go get 'em."

They do. It takes them all of two minutes to discover that cars do not magically drive themselves. And these guys drive about as well as they read. Surprise, surprise. They get so busy seething and frothing that Doug and Firescape and I slip from under gunpoint and get the drop on them. In the end, they hoof it back to Potrero with no Tree, no Wiz, no magic, just one, lonely little AK with less than half a magazine of ammo. They are not Real Clever Boys, so I don't expect they'll learn how to make more.

His M yuks it up real big when they've all gone, and pounds me on the back. "Well done, merlin! Well done! Those guys make bozos look like Rhodes Scholars. But tell me, why did you allow all the chicanery to impact our idyllic lifestyle?"

"Well, sire," I say, vamping, "I was trying to smoke out a mole; Lord E has a most secret double-sméagol in our court."

Already Scrawl is sidling away. She is forced to sidle all the way to the Borderland where she is politely ushered to the Potrero side and the bridge rolled up behind her.

I, meanwhile, am a hero. I eat this up for a while, then the niggling starts. Don't get me wrong—being a hero is a muy cool thing. I could definitely get used to it. But in the back of my mind is this little voice that says, "You are an impostor, Chickpea Del. A faux pas. What'd you do, anyway? A whole lot of nada is what. You get Doug tree-napped, you get yourself merlin-napped, put Firescape, the Wiz, and the whole of Embarcadero in dire jeopardy. You generally screwed up bigtime."

All true, I admit. It is through the grace of a very patient God and the illiteracy of Elvis and company that I have pulled my chestnuts (and a few other things) out of the fire. So, even though I am enjoying the hell out of being a hero, in the back of my chickpea brain is the idea that I will not feel better until I have done something truly heroic.

twelfth: we spring a leak

BACK IN MY STREET-MONKEY DAYS, I had occasion to meet all sorts of interesting, unexpected and potentially dangerous people. Hoot stands out as a prime example of this. I mean, first glance told me he was probably in my alley to beat the living crap out of me, but he wasn't and he didn't and the rest, as they say, is history.

Meeting these unexpected people almost always did strange things to my head in terms of worldview, if you know what I mean. Let me give you a for instance.

For instance, once upon a time, there was this rat pack that called themselves the Jade Dragon. They liked to pretend they were the heirs to the old Tongs and pretty much high-nosed the new Tongs under whose auspices they ate and slept and got doctored after close encounters of the bloody kind.

I gotta figure that since the real Tongs had gotten out of the lording-it business, and just took general care of things, that must've created a sort of lord-it vacuum, into which the Jade Dragon figured it would one day step when it grew up.

Now, you gotta understand that the average age in the Jade

Dragon was about thirteen, which I guess makes it a Tong-ette, and that these were just kids who, like yours truly, didn't have family or probably even a cat. I guess I escaped getting sucked into something like the Jade Dragon by virtue of not fitting in. All things considered and in retrospect, I'm muy grateful for that mercy, as wretched as it seemed at the time.

It is the way of a gang like the Jade Dragon that it eats its own tail. What I mean is, it don't allow for ideas or much of anything else to come in from the outside, so it sort of lives on itself—recycling old ideas and attitudes and trying to make everything outside the gang fit inside that old stuff instead of the other way around.

What that meant, mostly, was that members of the Jade Dragon stole when they didn't have to and fought for turf that wasn't particularly in dispute or even worth having. That way, they could recycle the attitude that they survived against all odds in a cruel and terrible world that didn't give them squiddle, and that they had to fight for everything they needed, and that life, dammit, just plain sucks.

Comes a day I am trekking through the streets with a book on window box gardens under one arm, chewing on a lunch of dried fruit prepared by the loving hands of Kaymart. I am heading back to the Farm where Bags has hopes of using the book (checked out of the Wiz on his authority) to get some new techniques for farming rooftop veggies and fruits. As I traverse the Slot, I am set upon by the aforementioned Jade Dragon, who knock me sideways, down, back, and over and then pounce to see what they've taken.

Not much, they decide. (Did I mention that the Jade Dragon isn't too sharp about picking targets?) But they are very keen on my little pouch of dried fruit, which they have never seen anything like, and quickly devour so as to be unlikely to see anything like in future. When they have eaten my lunch for me, they gather around and demand more.

"Sorry," I say, quaking and clutching my book. "I don't have any more on me."

"Then show us where you got it," says the oldest of them—a tall, stringy kid with waist-length black hair.

I admire his hair, which, unlike mine, is board straight, and ask, "You really want to know?"

They do, and I really want to get back to the safety of the Farm, so I grovel a little and whine and finally tell them to follow me. They are bewoggled as they walk amongst the giants, and just about all drop their teeth when Kaymart's big old glass house comes in to view. Bags, bless him, is out in front, working away at a mulch pile.

It is to him that I point and say, "This is where I got it. From that old dude, there."

Then I run . . . straight to the old dude.

I trip all over myself trying to tell him what happened—the Jade Dragon knocked me down and stole my lunch, and look, there's even a scratch in the cover of the book he sent me for and woe is me, etc.

Well, Bags, he looks up and over to where the Jade Dragon is sort of eddying around under a tree trying to figure if they can take the two of us, and he waves them in. "Come on, boys!" he calls and then says to me, "Cicerone, run into the house and get some bags of fruit jerky outta the pantry."

"But why?" I ask, agog.

"'Cause these boys are hungry, that's why."

I go, confused as hell, and when I get back, I see that the Jade Dragon has joined Bags in the orchard where he is giving them a taste of his wares. I drag the fruit over there and hand it over, to which he responds by handing it over in turn to the Jade Dragon.

"Now, boys," he tells them. "If ever you want some more of this stuff, you just come on up to the house over there and ask me or Kaymart—she's my wife—or Cicerone, here. That ain't gonna keep you fed all the time, but it'll help."

The littlest Dragons start to go for the bag, immediate, but their Head Dragon—the tall one with the cool hair—stops them.

"You givin' us this stuff, old man?" he asks. "'Cause we don't take charity."

The littler Dragons pinched little faces say that they'd most certainly make an exception to the charity clause in their Tong membership contracts just this once, but the Dragon Head is adamant.

"Not charity," says Bags. "It's a reward for not breaking my kid in two." And he pats me on the shoulder.

The Dragons look from one to the other like they're wondering what planet they're on, then dive into the biggest bag of fruit and start stuffing their mouths most prodigiously.

That's when Bags spies the book on box farms, which I still got under my arm. He snags it.

"Wanna see something?" he asks, and waits for no reply. He plops the book open and shows the Tong-ette a double-page spread on window box veggies that just about pops their eyes out of their heads.

"What is that?" asks the Dragon Head.

"L'ks like veg't'bles," says another kid, his mouth still full of dried figs.

He draws a glare from the Dragon Head, who, I think, is supposed to do the speaking and thinking for the whole Dragon.

"They are vegetables," confirms Bags.

"Growing in a window sill?" asks Dragon Head.

"Window sill, fire escape, rooftop—whatever you got."

"How'd you do that? Magic?"

Bags smiles and listens to them all chew for a moment, then says, "Yep. Magic. And . . ." He glances around and leans in toward Dragon Head as if he's got some grand secret. "I can show you guys how to do it. That'll give you the magic to grow your own food. It's powerful magic," he adds.

"We don't take charity," repeats the Dragon Head. "We make our own way in the world. We're the Jade Dragon."

The other kids nod and puff out their scrawny little chests and gnaw chunks off their fruit. They look like pint-size pirates, chawing jerky.

Bags looks surprised. "I told you, I ain't offering any charity. What you take me for, a Tong? I'm offering a deal. You leave my kid alone and I'll show you some magic to keep your bellies full."

The Jade Dragon chews and studies the picture and smells the orchard and tastes the sweet fruit.

Me, I hold my breath. What the hell is Bags up to?

"Yeah," says the Dragon Head, at last. "Yeah. You teach us the magic and we'll maybe leave your kid alone."

Bags smiles. "Good. Now, first, why don't you all go over to that tree there and get yourself a nice juicy peach? I'll be right along."

He turns back and finds me gawping at him.

"Now, Cicerone," he says, "I want you to go get Juk and Fircone and have them scare up some big sacks to put earth in and then . . ." He squints at me. "What is it?"

"Why'd you do that?" I demand. "They were gonna steal from you. They did steal from me. And you're just gonna give away magic to 'em?"

"Tell me something, Del. Why'd they eat your lunch?"

"'Cause they're tin-plated gangsters with delusions of dragonhood!"

"'Cause they're hungry." He bends a bit so he can look me in the face and pokes a grubby, stubby finger into my solar plexus. "Give a man fruit jerky and one man will get one meal. Teach him to *make* fruit jerky and he'll feed hisself and maybe others till there's no more dirt and water. And he won't need to steal anybody's lunch. You get me? These little dragons are a parasite, Del. We got to teach 'em symbiosis. Now, get on after Juk and Fircone, pronto."

Well, I do, but I have some serious misgivings about what my old man has done. I even foster dire predictions of what will happen because of his jingbing idea. Such as that now, the creepy little jakes will start up a black market fruit and vegetable business and gouge their fellow street-monkeys for food.

I share these predictions with Kaymart and Juk and Fircone, which only increases my acute embarrassment when reality refuses to match said predictions for direness.

First, the Dragon Head and two of his cohorts go on to study agriculture at the Wiz and the Jade Dragon becomes the Jade Dragon Co-op which does reasonably fair barter for produce and farming supplies among its fellow Tong-ettes. It also becomes a halfway house for street-monkeys with too much time on their hands and a fondness for loot and pillage.

The punishment for pillaging the Co-ops gardens is apprenticeship to Bags or Farmer Felicidad of the Presidio; the net result of this that both end up with more apprentices than you can shake a stick at. They train the kids up and send them back into the 'hoods to start rooftop farms. So, I guess you could say that because Chickpea lost his lunch, the Tenderloin is now a prime agricultural district. Go figure.

All of the above is why when Doug proposes to me a preposterous idea for something heroic we can do for the Potreros, I neither scoff nor sneeze him off.

Anyhoo, it is about a week and a half after Elvis's Great Embarrassment. To illustrate how quickly things can change, I am now a Married Merlin. A *very* happily Married Merlin and learning a whole 'nother kind of magic—magic of a very intimate nature. I am in the Wiz with Doug and my beautiful bride, Jade Berengaria Firescape, helping to clean up the mess and sort the books and videos when he sends me a whiff of firry perfume from where he sits in the sun on a reading table.

"Cicerone Del," he says to me, though not in so many words, ni dong. "Cicerone Del, Potrero needs educating." And a little later, he hits me with this outrageous idea: "Del," he says, "find a way to share the magic."

Well, let me tell you, this knocks me six ways from Sunday. Not just the thought of selling Hismajesty on a Potreran literacy campaign (which makes my guts jiggle), but the idea of selling the Potreros on it. I already know what Bags will think of the idea, so I consult with my lovely wife, who thinks it's a great thing to help the Potreros.

"You know if the children could be taught to read," she tells me, "they could teach the grown-ups. Then we could do vocational rehab."

Yeah, if. Big IF. I know it's not as easy as all that. Even if His M would go for it, Lord E wouldn't. I mean, first of all, knowledge isn't food.

Okay well, yes, knowledge is food, but it doesn't make your belly stop growling right away. You gotta apply it first. So, while it'd be easy to get the Potreros to take our food, it ain't gonna be similarly easy to get them to take our wisdom. 'Cause there's a Wall between Embarcadero and Potrero-Taraval—and I don't mean the one along the Border made of old junk.

Okay, well, this one's made of old junk, too, I guess, but it's a different kind of junk. It's inside junk. Like I said before—it's the inside stuff that makes the outside stuff bad.

One big thing I learned from seeing Lord E and his guys in the Wiz: We don't think the same. And the difference is . . . well, I guess it's this: Lord E thinks magic is about *having* things; in Embar, we know it's about *knowing* things.

I admit I also realize that there could be certain benefits to bringing Enlightenment to Potrero-Taraval. Not only will it improve the lot of those miserable Potreros, cause Elvis to consider Hismajesty an ally instead of an enemy, and bring down the Wall between their kingdoms, but will allow a certain merlin to visit the Mission Dolores without fear for his life.

Now, lest anyone think my motives are ulterior, I must say that I do truly and urgently care about the miserable Potreros, and feel real sorry for them, but I got a memory of the Mission and the fog that wasn't fog, and voices that are yammering at me like crazy in any unguarded moment. I think they are trying to tell me something different now—something about fire.

It is Firescape who gives me a clue about how to handle our King. She tells me that the best way to get to Hismajesty is through *Her*majesty. I know this, of course, 'cause that's what landed us in this mess in the first place: His M being scared for Her M.

"No," says Firescape. "That's not what I mean at all. I mean if you tell Her M about your—I mean, about Doug's idea—and wait a week or so, His M will be boggled to pieces when you come tell him the Fabled Tree's just recommended the very thing he's been pondering for ever-so-long."

I have long suspected Firescape is a natural merlin. Now, I'm sure of it. And I am not only a hero, but a humanitarian. But there is still this PROBLEM, which is how to convince His M to share our magic with the Potreros. Then there's this other PROBLEM, which is how to convince Lord E that he should accept our largesse.

I don't even bother with the rune can. Doug is on a roll—the visions, the premonitions, the words coming out of my mouth before I can even think them, etal. I take the PROBLEM straight to him.

Doug says we should spring a leak. A magical leak, so that knowledge can just trickle south little by little. So, I start looking for a place to make a hole—just a tiny, little hole—in that wall of old junk that separates Embarcadero from Potrero-Taraval. As it happens, I find the perfect place—right along the Border where it parallels the Farm. Bags and Kaymart aid and abet, of course. We leak food and knowledge about certain things, and we start teaching some little Potreros interesting things like how to read.

Meanwhile, I decide I must work on the Royal Conscience. I speak to the Majesties almost daily about the sad plight of our neighbors—especially the children. His M doesn't react much, and Squire is most offensively and eloquently derisive of my concern, but Her Sweet Majesty wrinkles her lovely brow and pouts.

While I am working hard to raise sympathy in the Royal

Quarter, our leak backflows—the Borders of Embarcadero become the scene of illicit immigration. At first, I take this as a Bad Thing. Hismajesty is perturbed, Hermajesty is scared, and Squire is a grumpy sonofabitch. All eyes turn to me again, and I am expected to determine our response to this fine state of affairs. I thank the Patient God that no one knows how appropriate that is (seeing as how this is All My Fault).

Our first response is to double the knighties along the entire length of the Slot, which means recruitment goes up and piffle crime right along with it. With the knighties concentrated out on the edge of Embarcadero, folks in the heart of it who are so inclined find it easier to indulge their klepto tendencies. On a walk through the Gee Gah, you hear cries of, "Stop thief!" almost as often as you hear haggling. This makes Hismajesty more perturbed, Hermajesty more scared, and Squire more grumpy.

Meanwhile, along the Borders, I decide to follow the advice of a great philosopher, whose name I cannot remember, but who said: *If God gives you a lemon, make lemonade.* It is with lemonade in mind that I instruct our knighties to turn back all wannabe Embarcaderans . . . except for women with small children, which is to say, except most of them. I make sure they get right into remedial reading programs at the Wiz and Wizlets. This puts a strain on our kingdom's Social Services, of course, and makes Lord E cranky enough to send unveiled threats along to Hismajesty via a particularly bold and nasty Lubejob.

No lemonade yet.

My prayers become quite beseeching, Doug trembles as if in anticipation, the Whisperers whisper, and Squire continues to grump. In this climate, a king of Hismajesty's ilk naturally consults his merlin (me), and his merlin tells him that the problem is one of ignorance.

"Lord E's pathetic population," says Hismajesty's merlin, "is scopin' ours truly because it's quantum leaps better than the usual. We got stuff they don't, which can only breed a horrible, deep sort of longing, which, if left unchecked, will eventually transmogrify into envy, and envy into jealousy. And when the pathetic populace of Potrero-Taraval is as jealous of your royal immensitude as is their terrible Lord, Elvis, well then, Majesty, we got problems."

"Problems?" he repeats, eyebrows meeting head to furry head above his royal nose.

"Immense problems."

"How immense?"

"War," I say.

He pales. "But Potreros have become lazy and feckless. They aren't up to the vicissitudes of war."

"Lazy and feckless," I agree. "But jealousy will make them reckless." True—and it scans, yet.

Hismajesty grips the arms of his throne and stares off into the immensity of his throneroom. He is imagining the world at war. Not a pretty thought. I feel a niggle of guilt because I don't really think Lord E could organize a picnic lunch, let alone a whole war.

"Options," demands my liege.

I begin to pace around the Fabled TOD, whose shiny new pot I have rolled into the middle of Hismajesty's throne room where sunlight will hit it and render it blinding. It is partly cloudy today, so the Sun is on and off, but the effect is still great. He is glowing right now like a house afire.

"It is jealousy of what we have that makes the Potreros connive to slip across our Borders," I say. "If they had what we have, they wouldn't need to do either conniving or slipping, and their warlike tendencies could be nipped in the bud."

"You want to give away the farm?" he asks, scandalized.

I pause. "Majesty, I would never suggest we give away the Farm. As you know, it represents a significant food source. I think we could get Bags and Kaymart to grow extra stuff for them, though."

Hismajesty is waving his hands at me. "No, no. I meant—you wanna give them what we've got, literally speaking? What the hell does that mean?"

I hold up a finger and cock my head as if listening. "What?" I say, and Doug, playing along, waves his boughs.

"What's he saying?" asks His M.

"The Tree says: If you read a man a book, he will hear a story, but if you teach him to read, he can learn until the cows come back to Cow Hollow." I nod as if I am considering this and glance at Hismajesty. I don't think he is getting it. "All of our stuff comes by way of the Wiz. By the light of literacy and knowledge we know the secrets of the ages."

His M nods. "Yes. Yes, of course." Then he gives me the sharpest look I have ever seen in those eyes. "The Potreros' problems all stem from their incredible lack of smarts, illiterate sods that they are. If we educate the sods, they will know how to make stuff happen, instead of stealing it after *we* make it happen. They'll understand how to feed themselves, how to clothe themselves, how to repair their infrastructure. Perhaps Lord E might even learn how to govern wisely."

That's pushing the envelope, I suspect, but what the hell— His M is clearly primed and ready to go off. "Majesty, your insights amaze me. It's no mystery why you are king."

"Don't jink me around, merlin. My young and spunky (if not overly bright) bride has already pitched the idea in her ingenuous manner. I suspected it must have come from you and yours." He slants a glance at the Tree. "I been musing upon it."

"Huh," I say. "This did, indeed, come from the Tree. I am merely the messenger boy."

Hismajesty leans down toward me, eyes still weirdly keen. "I see that there are advantages to this idea, merlin, but tell me how we are to keep our advantage over the Potreros if we pursue it. Explain to me how this knowledge you propose to give them will not make them more dangerous to us."

Okay. Straight shootin' time. "It's this way, Majesty—as anyone who has ever traveled through Dog Patch can aver, a wild dog is most dangerous when it's hungry, and right now, there are a lot of hungry dogs in Potrero-Taraval. Now the difference between dogs and Potreros is: Potreros are gonna look ahead to the next meal. They're not likely to do things to put that meal in jeopardy. Think of it, Majesty, if you'd been dumb and hungry all your life, and suddenly you got to be smart and well-fed, how eager would you be to slink back to dumb and hungry?"

Now, His M is a man who appreciates a well-mixed metaphor. "Got it," he says and sits back, waving his arm expansively. "Mobilize your forces of enlightenment, O most excellent merlin. I give you Executive Carte Blanche."

"Your largesse shall become legend," I intone, bowing. I bow my way out of the room—which is tough to do, hauling Doug's increasingly heavy wagon.

"You know, Squire isn't gonna like this," I tell Doug as we take our Executive Carte Blanche and prepare to run with it.

thirteenth: the neutral zone

 I SEND Deadend in to Potrero-Taraval. Not because I'm afraid to go myself, ni dong, but because this is protocol. Sméagols always go in first. As I have already been where sméagols fear to tread, Deadend doesn't dare beg off.

I am on pine cones and needles until he returns with his report.

"Lord E is inclined to disbelief," he tells me. "Actually, he said monkeys would fly from the nether regions of his royal anatomy ere he believed your intent was benign."

"I expected as much," I have to admit, and cannot contain a sigh.

"I ain't finished yet," Deadend informs me. "Lord E thinks this is all crap, but it seems he's got hisself yet another new merlin, and this new merlin advises him he ought to hear me out. So he does, see. Then the new merlin tells him he's got nothing to lose by accepting our most benign offer. And damned if old Elvis don't turn right back around to me and say, 'Well, I got nothin' to lose by accepting your most benign offer.' I tell you, Chickpea, it was like somethin' out of Star Wars—creepy."

I am immediately suspicious. "So, who's this new merlin?"

Deadend shrugs. "Clueless, your merlinhood. Some smilin' jack he found under a dumpster someplace, I guess. Like I said—righteously creepy."

"Creepy?" I try to get details.

"Creepy. Never stopped smiling. Not once. Ooooga-booga." He does a reasonable Creepy Lou impression.

"So, we're on?"

Deadend nods. "You got a high level conference to be held at the location of your choice—as long as it's in Potrero."

I have no problem with that. There's only one place I'd want to hold this conference, Potrero or no.

The Mission Dolores seems almost a part of the real world in the unusually bright and wintry day. There is no shabu dong nor any other fog-like substance in evidence. The stones of the courtyard are smudged and pale and, in the sunlight, the graveyard isn't scary, just sad. I try to remember how long it has been since I was here. Six years; seems like a hundred.

Elvis keeps me waiting. I expect as much. It is his way of exerting Authority. Fine by me; he can exert all he wants in ways that don't mean a sneeze. For my part, I go for the whole enchilada: I braid up the sidelocks of my hair and wear my best jeans, my brightest and best merlinly robes and a rat skin amulet bag that contains a vial of Attar of Doug. I hang this on a thong around my neck, since according to the Books of Kingdom, this is the way merlins have worn them since time immemorial . . . and since I have determined that a glass vial in the pocket is a Bad Idea.

The negotiations take less time than they would if Potrero's Lord and Master half-cared about details. But he doesn't. He doesn't even bring his new merlin, who is, he tells me, minding the 'ranch' while he's away. In the end, I get classes set up for young Potreros both on home ground and in Embar. Lord E will get private tutoring from our finest teachers, and the Mission Dolores, and all approaches thereunto, are declared The Neutral Zone.

I only have to put up with about a dozen suggestions, whines, wheedles, pleas, growls and long-winded soliloquies all of which indicate that, 1) we ought to consider just giving them cars and stuff and teaching them how to drive them and, 2) I ought to think about the advantages of being merlin to Elvis instead of Mercedes. This I pointedly ignore, mostly because I am listening for Whispers. I hear a word now and again, usually punctuating something Elvis has said—sort of like "harrumphs" or other expressions of skepticism.

When the whole thing is over and done, and I have Lord E's squiggly and thumbprint on a contract he can't read (but swears his new "ear man" can), I hear one great Whisper from out of everywhere.

Good, it says. Just, good, like a giant's sigh, or like wind soughing through the sequoia, which I guess is the same thing. I am pleased they approve, whoever the heck they are.

After the Agreement, I go up to the Mission at least once a week, usually alone, except sometimes for Doug. The Mission seems a peaceful place to me now. Peaceful, but filled with a kind of bottomless sorrow. The Whisperers speak to me most clearly when I am here. I am understanding about every other word, but the words sometimes make no sense whatsoever. Like *amnah* they say, and then *people*. And then *cattaus*, they say, and *son*.

I severely regret having something so chickpea-like for a brain. All I can do is sit before the rock pile, rolling strange syllables around on my tongue, while my language lessons provide entertainment for a bunch of slack-jawed Potreros.

One day, I have given up on the rock pile and am wandering about in the ruined sanctuary of the old church. It's silent but for the sound of pigeons in the rafters, and it is still but for the fluttering of their wings and the slow sifting of the dust they send raining onto the gritty floor. Light pokes into the place through every hole, every broken window, every rotted-out eave, every door half off its hinges.

I move through the shattered light to the altar because I am drawn there. And when I am there, I get down on my knees in the grit to pray. I am in the middle of a conversation with the Almighty when something creeps up my spine and makes my hair stand on end. It is a portentous Moment, and I am surprised I recognize it, being that all I have of Doug on me is the attar in my amulet bag. I wait for the Moment to unfold, but what unfolds instead is a wheezy, hacky, snuffly sound behind me. I freeze.

"Hell, Chickpea, I didn't know you was Catholic."

The pigeons freak. I jump up and turn around to see Scrawl standing in the aisle in a mad rain of feathers and dust and other crap.

She folds up on herself just a little when my eyes hit her. Then she kind of sidles down the aisle toward me, making these little mewing noises. Simpering, I think they call it. When her face comes into the puddle of light where I am standing, she blinks and looks aside so she doesn't have to meet my eyes.

"I'm not," I say.

She just nods, then glances around like a kid who's just been told to apologize to somebody by a mother who is watching from close enough by to land a solid blow.

"I got somethin' to say t'you, Chickpea," she says. "It's important. 'Cause I hate bad enough goin' down in history for somethin' I did. I can't stand goin' down for somethin' I didn't."

"Meaning what?" I ask.

"Meaning, you got me righteous on two counts for burning out that old bum and scopin' for Lord E. But I had nothin' to do, no way, with that fire on the pier. That wasn't me. I did the old clown's digs 'cause I was s'posed to create a distraction and I figured, why not get sweet revenge while I'm at it? They was s'posed to grab the Tree right then and there, but when you sent old Winky into the Palace and then got back pronto yourself, they couldn't do it. The night of the big fire, all I did was let Lord E's sméagols know you was out of the Palace. That fire wasn't me— I'd've never burnt out no innocent fisherfolk. That was someone else."

She holds up her left hand. "On a stack of Holy Books," she adds, with great conviction.

Something in my heart of souls tells me this is muy important to the old girl. "You're serious—a stack of Holy Books?"

The hand doesn't waver. "Bhagavad Gita, Iqán, everything in between."

"Someone else, you said. Like who—Lubejob?"

"Naw. Don't think so. Lubejob an' that bunch was caught nappin'. When I went to tell 'em you was out of the house, they had to scramble to snatch the Tree. I don't know who done it. I can only tell you what I seed." She stops right there. Good old Scrawl, still knows how to milk a mystery.

"Which was?"

She takes a step toward me, so her face is in weird shadows, and lowers her voice, like the pigeons might hear something they shouldn't.

"Ninjas," she says and nods once, emphatic.

"Ninjas?"

"Little hurry-scurry guys all in black. Like shadows. Like big old cats. Like the shadows of big old cats."

"At the Wharf?"

"Down by the Old Ferry Building, just after the fire started. They was watching the hulks burn. I seen 'em afore that, too."

"Where?" I prompt.

"Around. Just around. Around the Palace and the Gee Gah, mostly. Always at night."

"Yeah? Got any theories?" I invite her to feel as if I am consulting with her. Equal to equal.

"I think they're evil spirits. Demons." She steps closer and lowers her voice even more—those pigeons are gonna catch none of this. "Nasgul," she intones, then makes a high-pitched whiny sound and signs at the altar. "Oi! Bad ju-ju."

I thank her kindly for this revelation and assure her three times that I believe her before she will leave me alone to think. And what I think is that I don't know what to think. I sit in the dust and debris on the floor, stare at the carvings behind the altar, and finger my amulet bag.

Five nameless, painted saints stand frozen in niches, looking for all the world as if they are about to leap from the windows of a very fancy building. There was once a crucifix in the middle niche of the first row. I can tell because of the light spot in the back of the niche.

A crucifix is a wooden cross, by the way, that has a carved, wooden Jesus hanging on it. But He's gone, and there's a funny shaped light spot in His place.

"So let's say I believe old Scrawl," I say to the saints. I expect no response, ni dong, but I get one, from the pigeons, who flap crap all over the place. "What's the story—bad ju-ju ninjas from Godknowswhere start a fat old fire on a couple of barges and Lord E opportunes into a Tree-napping? Why?"

The saints do not answer. No surprise there. I wish I had Doug or my rune can or both with me right about now. I doodle in the dust beyond my knees and try to order my assumptions. Then, on a whim, I take out the vial of attar and twist out the cork.

"Okay, first things first: do I believe Scrawl?"

I inhale.

Dui, says Somebody, which is about as 'yes' as you can get in Chinglish.

For a moment, I imagine it's the saints, then feel foolish for thinking some painted wooden guys are talking at me. It's the Whisperers, of course, suddenly speaking perfect Chinglish—and most emphatically, too, I must say.

I draw another deep breath and ask, "Who besides Lord E would send ninjas to set fire to the pier?"

Wiwe, say the Whisperers and I sigh. We're back to verba incognita again.

"Look," I say, "ni shi shei? Who the hell are you?"

Yelamu, Ssaisen, Huimen, Saclan. The names roll out of the mist, then the whisper dies to a murmur, like a stream as you walk away.

I know these names. These are the names of tribes to which the Spanish gave the name Ohlone for their common language, and Costano, because of where they lived. To my padre's ancestors the many were one. They couldn't tell the Yelamu from the Ssaisen, or the Tuibun from the Huimen. They were all just Indians—Ohlone. I read these names in a book once, five—maybe six—years ago.

Then I tried to forget them.

My suspicions, which I have buried for lo, these many years (having other things to occupy my mind), have been verified. I have been talking to the Ohlone Dolores (or rather, they have been talking to me) in a state of self-imposed cluelessness. As I said, it is my ancestors who put these poor guys in the ground. You can't blame me for not wanting to think about what they might want from me.

I have read the history of the Mission in the Micro-Fiche archives of the old Diocese, but it lacks a certain perspective and detail, I guess you could say. Like, for example, it doesn't tell the tales of cruelty, of overwork, of desperate escapes, and the diseases that swept the Ohlone into the grave. The Diocese records count each Ohlone soul won for the Church; the Ohlone counted each soul and family and tribe lost—Tuibun, Tatcan, Rumsen, Chupcan, Chiguan—like lights going out in a neighborhood as households go to sleep. When night came, their world shrank from the forever horizons to the four walls of their mission rooms.

Five years ago, having read those names and seen those lights go out in my head, I hadn't wanted to know more. Now I did.

I went home. I shared what I had found with Firescape and Doug. They went with me to the Wiz to learn more. What I learned was that while the Ohlone had disappeared into the missions (and into the earth) they had risen again, tattered, on the rancherias—lands deeded to them by the new American government, or bequeathed to them by the Californios, the New World Spanish families—they had served.

I might have breathed easier but for one thing: that last Ohlone, Pedro Alcantara, didn't know any of this. He had died believing he was the End. For some reason, this bothered me most outrageously. I mean, try to imagine being among aliens and thinking everyone you love is dead and that after you, there'll be no more them or you or anything. No more family, no more tribe, no more Ohlone.

Gone. History.

Pedro Alcantara was an old man when he died—an old, lonely man. A man whose son had run away from the Mission and had never come back. Pedro never knew whether he'd escaped to the east, or had been killed by the soldiers sent to stop the runaways.

I know what losing folks is like. Losing my parents was the worst. But I gotta believe it's worse to watch your children die before you. 'Cause it's not natural, y'know? It's just not natural. I couldn't even bring myself to think about having a little Flannigan with Firescape only to lose him or her.

I don't get anything more out of the Whisperers that day, though I try. All I get is the same litany of tribal names. After a while, even that stops.

Later, Firescape and Doug and I wonder aloud about where Pedro's son might've run away to and what he might've found there. We pray aloud that he made it to wherever he was going. Some of them must have made it or Pedro really would have been The End.

I glance over at Doug, who is playing with the dust motes in a ruddy sunbeam and checking out a video on the Great Sequoias of the North Coast. Firescape sits just beyond him, squinting into a book of history.

"Am I being a ditz?" I ask them. "'Cause this is what I'm

thinking. I'm thinking that maybe if I tell the Dolores they weren't the last, they'll get it. Then they'll tell Pedro. Who knows, maybe that's all they need to be free. To be able to stop hanging around the Dolores."

Doug stops playing with the motes and Firescape turns to look at me.

Firescape says, "Don't you s'pose they might already know? I mean, after all, they've—y'know—gone on." Her eyes graze the ceiling. "I thought that meant they knew more than us."

Well, there's an interesting theological quandary.

"Huh," I say. "I guess I've always thought that way about ghosts—when I've thought about ghosts at all, I mean, which isn't much. But why would they know any more than we do? Or maybe they do know more about some things but not so much about other things. I gotta think there's some reason the Dolores are still haunting that Mission. Some reason they're still here."

She frowns, wrinkling her delicate nose. "Maybe this Pedro is waiting for his son. Isn't that what the Whispers call you—son? Maybe Pedro thinks you're his son."

I gotta admit, this is something I've given a little thought to myself. It's a creepy-crawly kind of thought—I mean, having a bunch of haunts think you're kin. Of course, mi madre y padre being dead, I guess you could say I was already the son of ghosts. But then, mi madre y padre have not, to my knowledge been haunting anything.

Whoa. Now, that is a scary thought and it raises this horrible specter (you should pardon the pun) of a building somewhere in the Buena Vista where mi madre y padre are permanent residents.

I shake myself real hard. No. I can't believe that. I celebrated them at the Day of the Dead. I laid them to rest myself, with my prayers. Which is something Pedro Alcantara never got to do for his son and which I gotta think there was never anyone to do for poor old Pedro himself.

"Del?" says Firescape. "What're you thinking?"

"That it's better to be safe than sorry. I want to make sure that Pedro knows he wasn't the last. And that I'm not his son."

Doug's boughs quiver and I know I'm right.

"Maybe if I tell the other Dolores they can, like, get a message to Pedro. And . . . I think maybe we gotta do something to celebrate them. I mean, maybe that's part of why they're still here—nobody prayed for them, nobody cared. What do you think?"

Firescape nods and smiles at me in that way that says she really likes what she sees. "When are you going to do it?"

"Tomorrow, I guess."

Doug's boughs more than quiver, they wave.

Firescape gives him a sideways look. "I think maybe you'd better go now."

I leap up, full of resolve or beans or something. "You wanna come?"

She rises and her hair bursts into flame as sunlight strikes it.

"You'd really let me come? This is part of your vision thing."

"Jade, you're my wife," I say. "What I have is yours. No weird secrets."

She grins. "Neon. I'll get my AK."

We set out for Potrero-Taraval with the Sun burning down behind the tall buildings pulling the color out of the sky. I drag Doug in his Radio Flyer, which also carries candles and some incense so we can say prayers properly. I bring my rune can and a battery torch, too, thinking if the Mission is as strong a place as I suspect, I might cast things there I'd never cast somewhere else. Firescape watches everything, casual-like, her AK at her side. She looks relaxed. She's not.

On the way, I think about fires and ghosts and ninjas all in black. The Dolores seemed to know that Scrawl was truth-telling. I wonder if they know who the ninjas belong to.

The Sun sets while we are traversing The Neutral Zone. A gauzy shabu rises up the walls of the unnatural canyons, and every step of our feet, every squeak of Doug's wagon comes back at us like the chitters and shrieks of demons. I do not like the thoughts I have here. I really got to get more positive.

We go to call on the Dolores in their rock pile, which I tell Firescape is a memorial to the thousands of Ohlone buried around and about. While she looks on, I sit cross-legged in the chilly, weed-eaten courtyard in the yellow glare of the torch, hoping my cheeks don't freeze to the stones. I set out and light the candles and the incense and say some prayers for the departed. Then I wait, wondering if I have just sent the Dolores on to the Abhá Kingdom.

I have not. Out of nowhere comes something like a humongous sigh, and then I hear "*Cattaus.*"

"But I'm not!" I exclaim. "I'm not your son. I'm Chick—I mean, Cicerone Del, merlin to Hismajesty, King of Embarcadero and Keeper of the Fabled Tree of Destiny." I grab one of Doug's boughs and squeeze, praying for his assistance. "This Tree, here."

Diablo, say the Whisperers, apropos to nothing. They go clammy again.

I decide I might as well say what I come to say. "Pedro? Pedro Alcantara? If you're in there, or out here, or wherever—I need to tell you something."

The shabu over the rock pile shifts ever so slowly, and there is a great silence, like the whole place is holding its breath. I feel light-headed and little sparks fly before my eyes. I begin to think this is significant, then I realize I have been holding my breath. I suck up some air and let my head settle down. Through wonky eyes I see that the rock pile is the same as ever. I determine to deliver my message.

"Pedro, you gotta know that I'm not your son. I'm muy honored and all if you thought that, but I'm not him. I said some prayers for him just now, though, and for you too, but I don't know where he is . . . or was. I also want you to know, Pedro, if you can hear me, that you weren't the last one—the last of the Ohlone, I mean. There are still Ohlone . . . somewhere. I don't know any personally, I don't think, but I s'pose I might. Well, anyway, that's all I wanted to say."

I wait, but there is no word from the Dolores. *Great*, I think, *all these years they yammer at me, then when I finally got something important to say, they clam up.*

I'm a little upset, I gotta admit, and I start to get up to leave when I knock over my rune can. I don't really feel like casting runes right now, but somehow when the can is in my hand, I turn it upside-down in front of me on the flagstones. Then I lean close, squinting in the lamplight.

Firescape leaves her guard post and comes to look over my shoulder. The shadows are bizarre and my eyes go wonky before I can even focus on the rune junk. Even so, I can tell this is one of the weirdest castings I've ever thrown. The rotting peach pit is circled by general junk; a fly-button from my jeans, a thimble, an acorn, some blue and green glass chips, some pebbles and some raisins that are just as hard. The usual bottle caps and coins are there, and so is the sea gull beak, which is about to clamp down on the fly button. Surrounding all of this is a ring of nails and tacks.

With a sigh, I chuck the peach pit and sweep the nails aside.

Firescape's hand lights on my shoulder. "Are you supposed to do that?" she asks. "I thought the rules of runing said you gotta take what you get, no matter what."

Irritation doesn't tickle; it burns like stomach acid in those funny old commercials. "Who said that?" I ask, trying to sound arch.

"Bags did," she tells me. "He said a merlin gotta work with available materiel. And that God maybe puts that stuff there for a reason."

"God didn't put that stuff there. Somebody else did." I think of Scrawl.

"Does it matter who put it there?" she asks.

I don't answer, but just shrug and go back to the runes. Truth is, I feel a little guilty about tossing the pit and the nails, 'cause

Firescape has cited Bags pretty accurately, but it doesn't change the essential message of the runes, which is that there's some sort of squeeze play happening here. And if, as I suddenly suspect, that bird beak is still Lord E and that little silver fly button is me—I'm caught between a beak and a hard place.

The Whisperers choose this time to break their silence again. *Wiwe*, they tell me, and a chill dribbles down my spine. They have said this word to me before. Now, I decide it's time to find out what it means.

fourteenth: shaman

 I DON'T FIND Wiwe in any dictionary at the disposal of the Wiz. Even The Fiche draws blanks and she has access to multi-lingual databases. Doug seems to be as clueless as I am, which does not inspire confidence. Whatever or whoever this Wiwe is, it's not a good thing, that much I think I get. I file this in the back of my brain and move on to more politically charged matters, such as how I break it to Hismajesty that the runes suggest old Bird Beak (AKA Elvis), whom we have befriended at my personal say-so, may be planning an attack on us, his noble benefactors.

I s'pose there's no way to do it than just do it. To that end, I compose my words ("Majesty, it has come to my attention that the very Potreros we have taken under our wing are about to be sold out by their treacherous Lord.") and I puff myself up.

Then I procrastinate. I will sleep on it, I decide. What's one more day more or less?

By morning I am glad to be a practicing procrastinator, for I dream. I am in the courtyard of the Mission, then I am in the sanctuary, then I am in a small place full of dense smoke or one hellacious helado. Then I am in a place that is all three and none of the above, all at once. I am sitting cross-legged on a sandy floor, and a voice says, *Shaman*. I don't say anything, and the voice says again, *Shaman*, and I realize it's talking to me.

"I'm not a shaman," I say, feeling acute shame.

A hand points out of the smoke, which I can now smell, and directs my attention to the gritty floor beyond my knees.

Cast them, says the Voice, and I realize my rune can is in my hands.

I spill the rune junk out onto the sand.

Deja view: I've been here before. The stuff lays out just the way it did in the Mission courtyard. Exactly—peach pit and nails and all.

Okay. I get it.

The nails form a circle and their points are turned in toward the other junk. The peach pit is in the middle of it all, and I realize this has been so since the first time it turned up. Suddenly, my eyes go wonky bigtime and the runes become features on a map. Instead of pebbles and chips of glass, I see land and water and Embar and Potrero. Instead of nails, I see a Threat coming from across the Bay and I see a mysterious, black pit at the middle of it all.

Shame makes me blush, or would, if I was real. The peach pit wasn't just a piece of garbage, it was the center of the rune. When I think how many times it turned up in my can and how many times I chucked it overboard, I want to sink through the dream floor and dribble away into the Bay. I am no longer so sure about Lord E Lordy. Is he attacking me or flanking me? Is he friend or foe? And what the hell is in that pit?

Wiwe, the Voice says, on cue.

This is important; I want to be very sure I understand. I reach my hand out and point to the pit. "Qué es?" I ask.

Wiwe, says the Voice, again. *Carrier away of souls*.

Well, I gotta say, that's good for a soul-deep chill. Freezing, I break into a sweat. I can feel it creeping, icy on my dream-skin. My voice comes out of my dream-throat like it's squeezed from a concertina. "Whose . . . whose souls?"

Make the world safe from Wiwe.

Make the world safe? "Wiwe carries away souls. Is that what you mean? Did he . . . carry away the souls of the Ohlone Dolores?"

We are here, the Voice informs me.

"Is Wiwe holding you guys captive? Do you need to be rescued?"

Make the world safe from Wiwe.

Are they asking me to rescue them? I take a deep breath.

"What do I do?"

Before the dream me can exhale, the place changes again. The walls and ceiling suck in until it's close and round and I can see it's made of mud and wood. Someone sits across from me in the sand and a fire burns between us. I can't see him; he is just a shadow, a form, less than either.

"When I was a young man," he says, and his voice is like a sigh, "I dreamed of the Mountain. It told me, 'You will live to an old age, for nothing can hurt you.' After this, the Mountain would come to me in times of trouble and tell me I would be alright. I would talk to the power of the Mountain in my dreams and it would answer me.

"One day, as I traveled, I grew very sick—so sick I was afraid I would die and my spirit would go South. I was afraid the Mountain had forgotten me, for I had forgotten it. As I lay beneath a fir tree dying, a shaman came to me. He said my Mountain had sent him. He put a stick into my hands and said, 'This is a soul stick. Seize this and look to your power and your soul will cease its journey South.'

"I grasped the stick and remembered my Mountain and turned my eyes to it. And it was as the shaman said. I became well. Then the shaman told me something else, 'You are called,' he said. 'Your Mountain calls you to become a shaman, like me.' I looked to the Mountain and felt it was so. But I saw that if I were to become a shaman, the Mountain's power might fail me before my old age and I would die. So I refused. Still, the Mountain kept its promise to keep me safe in times of trouble, and I did not forget it again.

"Later, after my son was born, the Mountain asked again, 'Will you become a shaman, a healer?' Again, I refused. I knew the work was dangerous. I dreamed and knew I would die if I became a shaman. I refused the power because I wanted to become an old man. This I did, for the Mountain's promise was true. But my wife went South before me; my son went before me; my people went before me. And that left only me—an old man.

"And what is a man?" he asks me. "A man is nothing. He is less than nothing—less than a beetle, or the dung in which the beetle crawls. A man must be with his family. The family is everything. No man should forget this and think his life is important apart from that. I refused the Mountain, though its claim on my soul was great. I refused to save the souls from Wiwe. And so I lived to be old . . . and alone."

In the silence of the dream, I hear the snap of flame, the sigh of wind; I smell smoke, fir, dried spices, sweat; I see nothing but the smoke and the fire; I feel the heat of flame on my face; I feel this man sitting across from me, watching me, and I feel as if I'm being given some kind of choice.

I open my mouth to speak, to ask what this means, and he says again, "Save the world from Wiwe."

The place and the man are gone and I lie in the dark trembling. Firescape wakes up, rolls over, and touches my face.

"What?" she asks.

"I don't know," I say.

And I truly don't. I determine to take some time to consider the possibilities. But just then, all I want is for Firescape to melt the ice off my skin and out of my veins. She does it so well, I'm in no hurry to consider anything for quite a while.

In the morning it becomes clear that time is not something I have. The first thing I notice by dawn's early light is that Firescape has already gone to work; her AK is gone from its rack by the bed. The second thing I notice is that Doug, who is perched in the big old window by the balcony, is trembling like crazy. He's leaning toward the glass, too; if he had a nose, it'd be making tracks on the pane.

I get out of bed, pad over there and put my arm around him.

"What is it, Doug?" I ask.

I put my face to his branches and breathe in his perfume, but all I get is a stomach full of anxious flutters. I can't tell if that's him or me, but I'm the only one here who's got a stomach. I look out the window, even press my nose against the glass, trying to see what he sees. All I get is that something's crawling around out there and I gotta get it before it gets me. This will require a quest.

I determine to refuel before I begin questing, and take Doug and myself off to the Sang Yee Gah for breakfast. We go to Doug's favorite juk shop, the Dragon Boat. It's kind of a grand name for a place whose main food item is rice porridge. Still, it's a great place for thoughtful silences if you can ignore the noise: dishes clatter, people chatter, somewhere cooking oil snaps and pops like a pot of mad. The smells here are twice as loud as the sounds. They are black and red and gold smells, smoked and spiced and soaked in sesame oil. Sometimes the din sets my poor brain off on a runaway trolley and I end up miles from where I mean to be, someplace I've never been and don't know how I got there.

Today is like that—my mind is all over the place. Thanks to a little tug at my immortal soul and an accompanying whiff of fir, I finally get it under control and the loud noises and smells become a background for eating and thinking. I eat rice porridge and drink hot green tea and think about impending doom. I determine that I will cast runes in the Dolores courtyard again, and this time I will pay attention and remember that the line between omens and junk is . . . well, there is no line between omens and junk. You could be looking at either, so, in most cases, it's safest to err on the side of omens.

I'm getting up from my chair when I realize that Doug has

sprouted a small square of rice paper, which is caught in his topmost branches. The paper has a familiar lavender tint and has been neatly folded. Deja view. I unfold it. In one corner of the paper there is a strange symbol, which I recognize but still don't know. In the middle of the paper are Chinese characters I do recognize. They form two words: *Tin Hau.*

This is the Chinese name of the Queen of Heaven. She's one of the Immortals. She's also the Goddess of Waters, which is appropriate. According to legend, she was born as a mortal on the island of Mei-Chou in Fukien province. Her padre was a sort of mayor or something like that.

She had these dreams, see, about saving fishing boats near her village. The weird thing was, every time she had one of these dreams, some boatload of fishermen would come limping back into port talking about how they'd been saved from certain doom by some freak happenstance. By the time Tin Hau was twenty-eight, she was perfect, so she died and became an Immortal. (I gotta admit, I'm very glad my Jade isn't quite perfect. It's her temper, ni dong, which I won't say I encourage, but I sure don't regret.)

Anyway, Tin Hau got recalled to the Abhá kingdom, and her story was inscribed on some temple walls in Hangchow somewhere around 1228. About fifty years later, the powerful Mongol leader Kublai Khan read the wall scrawl, had her declared a goddess and started calling her Queen of Heaven. He was a Buddhist, you know.

Anyway, she got to be known as the Imperial Consort, which made her second in rank only to the Jade Emperor. She started out being a protector of boats and fishermen and ended up being general goddess of the general waters of the earth. We celebrate her on the twenty-third day of the third month.

Since it isn't anywhere near Tin Hau's Feast day, I gotta believe this note is in reference to her temple over on Waverly.

"What do you think, O Tree?" I ask Doug formally, hoping he

can hear me in the chaos sounds from the Dragon Boat's kitchen. "Do we go to the Tin Hau?"

A waiter speeds by, nearly tripping over me and almost making me miss Doug's thoughtful nod. Accordingly, I take myself off in the direction of Waverly street. It's not a bad idea, I tell Doug, to get a little divine intercession while I'm at it.

The Tin Hau is on the fourth floor of the building, which leaves me with a choice to make—lug Doug up the stairs, leave him behind in the lobby, or trust the ancient and enigmatic elevator. Since I got not idea one of what sort of situation awaits me, and Doug is getting to be almost as tall as I am (empotted), I do the latter.

When I cross the upper foyer and step into the sanctuary, I am almost immediately overwhelmed with more of the Sang Yee Gah's smoky smells. Braziers ooze fragrant incense and, at several altars, little offerings send nice smells toward heaven. The main altar at the head of the room is dedicated to Tin Hau, herself, but the room is a clutter of smaller, less impressive shrines. I stop to take stock and to absorb the serenity in the smoky scent of meat and flower and incense.

I have not even bothered to ask myself why I have been summoned here or by whom, and this brings me to a sudden profound realization about myself and my life. I am, pure and simple, a reactor. I let myself be dragged through life by my nose. Who, you might ask, is doing the dragging? Everyone from the Wiz to Doug to a fat ginger cat, that's who. Everyone, including Bags and Kaymart and Firescape and Hoot and Lord E and even the Whisperers . . . maybe even most especially the Whisperers.

A ugly little thought wriggles into the back of my mind and tells me this makes me a fool, but I honestly can't work up much indignation. Fact is, I got nothing better to do with my time and, with the possible exception of old Elvis, none of these nose draggers mean any harm. Hell, Firescape can drag me any-damn-where she wants. Besides which, I was the one who settled myself on a career in merlinry, no one else. Bags just gave me a push.

I shake my head and bring myself back to my study of the sanctuary. There are several worshippers in the room, kneeling in various places. Two of them are paying their respects to Tin Hau. None of them so much as twitches as I enter the room hauling the Radio Flyer and Tree. As I approach the main altar, though, one of the monks rises and makes his way back through the room in a route that will take him right past me.

He sees Doug and pauses to smile and bow deferentially. "Nin hao, Wondrous Tree. And greetings to you also, distinguished merlin. You have come to seek the blessings of the Queen?"

I return the bow, not quite as deferentially, so as to be culturally correct. He is a young monk—possibly even younger than I am—and has a face that reminds me of Firescape's. Except for the eyes, which are really strange in some way I can't quite wrap my mind around.

"After a fashion," I answer. "I have received a message to come here. Does anyone here seem to be in a state of waiting?"

The monk's smile deepens. "Everyone, merlin, is in a state of waiting. But this you already know." He bows again and disappears behind a thoroughly carved screen at the rear of the room.

I make my way to the main altar, twitching a little like I always do after a dialogue with a monk. I feel like part of me has been communicating while another part of me has been whistling dixie. In this case, I am doubly bothered by this guy's eyes.

I kneel to the left of the remaining monk, placing Doug in between and slightly behind. The monk is a wizened little fellow, and I wonder how long he has been kneeling here with his nose wedged between his folded hands. He is making a raspy little sound that's almost as wizened as he is, and I realize that he's snoring.

As I am pondering how to wake him—for after all, he could be the one who sent me the message—Doug takes matters into his own hands—or branches as the case may be. He tickles the old fellow's cheek.

The monk's a happy napper and comes to with a big smile on

his face. His watermelon seed eyes take in first Doug and then me and he bows low at the waist.

"Nin hao, effulgent Tree. And felicitations to you, as well, most enlightened merlin. May the Queen of Heaven bless you."

Then he goes back to his devotions.

Okay, no help here, I guess. I glance about the sanctuary, seeing altars, hanging braziers and lots of smoke. Behind me, the other monks are frozen lumps of dark and light linen. Only their prayers stir the heavy air.

I sigh and turn my gaze up to Tin Hau. She is beautiful. Very similar of face to my beloved Jade Berengaria Firescape. Her two companions, however, are not terribly beautiful. They are terribly terrible. Wherever she goes, you see, Tin Hau is accompanied by Thousand League Eyes and Favoring Wind Ears. You just gotta imagine what they look like; my words could never do them justice.

It is while I am pondering Thousand League Eyes that I feel this immensely powerful yank at my immortal soul. It is not a pleasant feeling, nothing like Doug's tugs or Firescape's but, *Damn*, I think, *I been here before*. This is a familiar yank from a very cold place.

My instincts get very weird on me at this point. Part of me wants to scram most diligently; part of me wants to crawl under the altar; part of me wants to rise up and face the Watcher, saying, "Hey you! Get your butt out here!"

I am a man of too many parts at this moment. I fight the impulse to turn around and get an eyeball on Mr. Thousand League Eyes. Instead, I keep my head down and glance sideways into a polished brass gong. The monks behind me are still praying away, eyes straight ahead, prayer beads whispering through their fingers. Beyond them lies a clutter of shrines and the big old dragon screen where the friendly young monk disappeared. The second my eyes light on the thing, I know that's where he is—the Watcher.

I sweat. What I need now is the powers of a real shaman. What I got is the Tree and Tin Hau and the Whisperers.

"Is this the Peach Pit?" I ask the Dolores under my breath and am scared spitless when the name *Wiwe* sputters out of a brazier practically under my nose. I grasp one of Doug's boughs and break one tiny needle. The scent gets to me even through the smoke. I look up at Tin Hau.

I need stuff, O Queen, I think at her. *Real stuff.* What I need is to be invisible, or at least hard to see.

I fasten my eyeballs on the smoke around Tin Hau's head and begin the Chouyan incantation. I think of smoke. With a little more effort, I begin to think like smoke. I become smoke. My eyes are wonky as hell, and my brain feels like it's full of sandal-wood and jasmine. I sink very low next to Doug and the old monk, and ooze back to the next shrine, and the next, and the next.

When I stop oozing I'm behind the small shrine of Men Shen, Protector Against Demons, who is guarding the screened door-way, his tiny bow and arrow aimed at the dragon panel. On the opposite side of the doorway is a shrine to Chang Tao Ling, God of the Afterlife.

This is not a comforting juxtaposition.

Now I am two steps from the screen and there are no more shrines to ooze behind. I rise up from behind Men Shen, thinking smoky thoughts. I see a ripple of plum silk through the coiled, carved serpents of the screen.

"Chickpea! Thay, watcha doin'? We been lookin' all over for you!"

Creepy Lou's voice freezes me where I stand. So much for being smoke. The plum silk flashes behind the knotted serpents and disappears in the snick of a door latch.

"Damn!" I cry, and leap forward to squeeze behind the screen.

I am face to face with a closed door. I fumble with the latch, while behind me Creepy Lou is jostling up and down, back and forth going, "Thay Chickpea, what's rumblin'?" and I hear the voice of my own gemlike Jade saying, "What the hell are you doing? I gotta talk to you!"

The door is not locked, and it swings open onto a broad, east-west hallway with a muy low ceiling and about a godzillian doors, all closed. I experience claustrophobia because of the ceiling and brain freeze because of all the doors, but before I can shake off these conditions and move my ass, I realize that a monk has appeared at my elbow with smokelike stealth. It is the friendly young monk I saw disappear behind this very screen.

Where the hell'd he come from, my inquiring mind wants to know. I immediately suspect magic.

The monk no longer looks particularly friendly. He is still smiling, but it is a strange veil of a smile, which is not helped by those eyes. "You are disturbing our devotions, merlin," he tells me. "I must ask that you leave."

Creepy Lou has gone round the screen and pops up behind the monk, jouncing and jostling, up-down-side-side. He waves at me. Behind him Firescape appears, also waving.

"Who uses these rooms?" I ask the monk.

"We use them," he says and repeats: "I must ask you to leave, merlin. And take your too energetic friends with you." His eyes don't seem to move, but I can feel their gaze shift.

"Someone in plum silk was eye-balling me from behind this screen," I say.

His eyebrows rise, and his smile gets bigger. "We monks," he says, "do not wear silk."

Duh. "I know. Who does? Who might use these rooms?" I add.

He tips his head. "Our . . . master dresses himself in silk." His face gets this funny, pinched look. "I could not reveal his name, even were I to know it."

"You gotta call him something."

"We call him Master Chen. But that is not his name. That is his station. You have been asked to leave. My brothers and I wish to continue our devotions." He gestures at the door to the foyer.

"I need to talk to Master Chen."

"Master Chen has left the temple."

"I just saw him—"

"He is no longer here." Again he gestures at the exit.

Creepy Lou and Firescape are gesturing at the exit too.

I give the Cheshire monk a look I hope is particularly fierce. I try to bore right on into his eyes, and that is when I realize what it is about them that gives me the oooga-boogas. They are not a monk's eyes. A monk's eyes are sunny little bowls of peace, contentment, and kindness. There is none of that in these eyes; these eyes are full of something wild and dark and dizzy-making as a bottomless pit. And they are entirely black.

Inside my chest, my heart shrivels to a prune, and it occurs to me to wonder, somewhere in the back of my suddenly frost bitten little brain, if he's even real. Real people, I mean, 'cause I got the distinct impression that the lights are on, but there's nobody home—at least, not the rightful owner.

I'm outta here. I head back to the main altar to retrieve Doug, who has been waiting patiently beside the old monk. I bow hastily to Tin Hau and, as my knee touches the floor, I feel a tug at my shirt.

I glance at the old monk. He doesn't raise his head, but only turns his face toward me. His eyes grab me and wrap me in a straight jacket. Unlike the young monk's eyes, these eyes are bright and clear and burrow right into my soul. Without seeming to move, he slips something into my free hand. Then he retreats into his devotions again.

I am about to ask him something, anything, when I catch movement out of the corner of my eye. The young monk is approaching from the rear of the room. I slip whatever it is the old monk has given me into a pocket and leave the temple with Creepy Lou and Firescape practically on top of me.

Out on the street, the two of them start talking at once. I don't get one word of it, just white noise.

"Stop!" I cry, and they do.

I turn to General Firescape. "What?"

"Creepy Lou has a report of great urgency," she says and nudges him with the muzzle of her AK.

He's nodding like a bobbing doll and tugging at his left ear. "Yeah. Report. Yow! You're not gonna believe it, Chickpea. There're cars and trucks and people!"

"What? Where?"

I glance at Firescape for some sense of what he means, but she's still looking at Lou, and I don't like the expression on her most expressive face.

"Theen 'em comin' down the Slot," Lou goes on. "Next thing I know they're all over the Mission."

My heart takes a dive down a dark hole. "The Mission," I repeat stupidly.

"The Dolores," says Firescape.

"Yeah, the Doloreth." Lou nods wildly and snatches at air. "Ghost Town. Whithper-ville."

"Who are they?" I ask. "What're they doing?"

"Don't know. Uh-uh. Nada clue. But they're mean SOBs."

"They've got all kinds of machinery," Firescape volunteers. "Trucks and hoes and cats and jeeps and some stuff I've never seen before. And these big cranes on tank treads. And they got weapons that'd make your eyes bug out. They gotta have way more fire power than these things." She bounces her AK on her hip. "According to the rumble, the Potreros took these goons on somewhere along 16th and they shot up the place with lightning bolts. Oh, and they got winnebagos. Dozens, of 'em. In working condition."

"Maybe they're refugees from somewhere. Gypsies."

"With heavy machinery, serious firepower, and a fleet of winnebagos?" my wife asks doubtfully. "They don't act like refugees. They act like an invasion force or at least like guys on a mission. They knew exactly where they were going, as in bee-line. And this is the chiller-diller: sméagols say they came in over the Bay Bridge."

That is a chiller-diller, 'cause the Bay Bridge has been less of a bridge and more of a barrier for a muy long time. This is because in the third year of the reign of Levi Menorah, son of King Jerry Steinmetz, there was a quake that did some damage to all and sundry, but mostly to the Bay Bridge which had fallen into general disrepair. The then king of Treasure Island, who liked to call himself Blackbeard for literary reasons, helped things along a little with a hefty charge of dynamite. I'm not sure whether he wanted to keep T-Islanders from coming into the Gam Saan or if he wanted to keep the Gam Saan from coming out, but two collapsed sections of deck did the job pretty well either way.

The significance of all this is that these alien guys had to have fixed the Bridge before they could come across it, which says stuff about their techno-power I don't much like. It also means there could be a whole mob of truly angry T-Islanders in their backtrail. We have not had much in the way of contact with the Island for more years than I've been around, so I got no idea what to expect from that quarter.

Great. Another Big Unknown.

Firescape watches all of this flicker across my face like a message from our sponsor, then says, "Deadend's got sméagols posted on the Bridge. Just in case something else decides to come across. There's a squad of Wharfside knighties up there with."

"These aliens," I say, not without some quivering, "what are they like?"

Lou shrugs. "Just guys. Folkth. A few women, I think. Hard t'tell from a far away. But they look like people, pretty much. They're drethed funny, though—like for thkulking." He stamps his right foot and yanks at his hair. Dust flies.

Firescape nods.

"You've seen them, too?" I ask her.

She nods again. "Me and Deadend saw them coming down the Potrero side of the Slot. I got knighties out skulking STAT and told Deadend to mobilize all sméagols. Then I came looking for you."

"So Deadend hasn't talked to His M?"

"He scrammed. Like I said, I told him to get out sméagols and he don't generally procrastinate on a direct order from a superior officer."

Here I am, chasing some invisible dude in plum silk, while funny-dressing guys with winnebagos are taking over the Dolores. And me the last to know. I got it backwards again as usual: I'm scopin' the Peach Pit, when I should've been keeping an eye out for the Nails.

Damn. And why, I gotta wonder, didn't the Dolores say anything? Here their stomping grounds are being overrun and they go all clammy on me. Then my dream washes back over me and I get this horrible feeling that the Dolores did say something. They told me I had to save the world from Wiwe and now it looks like Wiwe has driven his winnebago right down the Bayshore into the heart of the Gam Saan.

Suddenly I realize I'm confused and scared—a truly dynamite combination. I look at Doug. His boughs are droopy and quivering all at once. He must be as scared as I am. Not a good sign.

"Firescape," I say, "we gotta head back to the Palace to reassure the Majesties and begin a plan of action. I'll need you to call in at least half a dozen of your best knighties and a couple of Deadend's slinkiest sméagols. We got some serious scopin' to do."

fifteenth: aliens, ghosts, and unquiet spirits

 **THE NEWS IS GRIM.** According to the best reports of Deadend's sméagols and other eyewitnesses, the Mission Dolores is now home to bonafide aliens who are not above taking serious pot-shots at the natives with guns that shoot lightning bolts.

"Not so much phasers as photon torpedoes," says a sméagol who calls himself Berk. "'Course, not exactly torpedoes either, seeing as how they ain't aqua-nautical, but they're enough to make a person seriously deadjim, or so's the rumble. Potreros are fleeing like someone stood up and yelled 'bath!' I'm telling you, your merlinship, this is serious shit. It's a pogrom."

"A what?" asks Cinderblock, whose studies in history were, I suspect, slim-to-none.

"The end of the world as we know it," says Berk the Sméagol, and I want to rap him upside the head for saying this stuff in front of our watchful and impressionable Majesties.

Berk thinks everything is a pogrom.

"It's not a pogrom," I say. "We don't know what it is yet. So at the moment, it's just a visitation by-by—"

"Aliens," says Creepy Lou, soberly, "in winnebagos."

"Armored winnebagos," adds my wife. "And some righteous weaponry. Recon says eaves were falling along 16th. If we have to fight these jakes, our best bet is a joint military action."

"Joint," repeats His M. "How joint?"

"I recommend we dispatch envoys, Majesty," I say, picking up the cue, "to all monarchs, elected or otherwise, in the Gam Saan. Whether our response must be military or diplomatic"—here I pause to glance at General Firescape—"remains to be seen. But even diplomatic measures will be best taken in multilateral harmony."

"Sounds like a friggin' choir!" snorts Squire. "You don't stand a chance in a billion of getting cooperation out of those bozos. I say we deploy all our knighties and blast 'em."

"Oh, right, fish-head," says Cinderblock most scathingly. "Our measly AKs and handguns against their Trek-tech. In case you hadn't noticed, the last of our winnebagos is home to a family of five over on Geary."

"Yeah! They run a hot-dog stand out the back window," adds Creepy Lou with enthusiasm. "Great dogth!"

"They got two dozen winnebagos, Berkowitz," Cinderblock continues, ignoring Lou. "Plus the jeeps, also armored, and the trucks and the earth-moving equipment. What're we supposed to do, shoot out their tires?"

"There will be no shooting," I say, "unless and until we're sure they're hostile aliens. They might just be . . . tourists. Tourists were once wont to travel by winnebago."

"Were they also wont to carry ray guns?" asks Squire. "I'm with Berk, Majesty. I say we take them out before they take us out."

"You're not listening, Squire," says my wife. "I'm not sure we *can* take them out. Especially not if there are more where they came from."

"What's the news from Treasure Island?" asks His M, to

which Deadend replies, "No news, Majesty. Nada peep. No one's set foot on that Bridge since the aliens crossed over."

Hismajesty has a peculiar look on his face, which I recognize and don't much like. He is thinking. He says, "So far these alien guys have just moved in on the old Mission, right?"

"Yes, Majesty," I reply.

"And they haven't set one little alien foot inside the Embarcadero, right?"

"Yes, Majesty. I mean, no, Majesty, no feet."

"Then, they're all part of the SEP field, my merlin. It's Simply Elvis's Problem. Let him deal with it."

Squire and his cronies break out in suck-up laughter, and Hismajesty looks pleased with his dispensing of wisdom and waves his hands to zhou us out.

"You're all dismissed. I expect our sméagol corps to keep an eye on things, but don't offer provocations. We'll see if old Elvis can sort this out."

"And if he can't?" This comes from my wife, who is surely thinking that our liege has something like egg foo yung between his royal ears.

"Then Elvis is stew meat. Or maybe Elvis comes running to Ours Truly for help. Either way, Elvis is out of the Alcalde business. Who's to say our new neighbors won't be better than the old ones? Now, you're dismissed. Except for my royal merlin," he adds and my heart skips three beats or so—not enough to kill me.

"First of all," Hismajesty says when all and sundry have left, and it's just him and me and Tree, "why didn't you foresee this alien inroad?"

Truth is, of course, I did, but didn't know I did. Truth, in this case, is bu hao.

"Well, Majesty," I fabricate, "as you yourself so ably noted, the aliens invaded Potrero, not Embarcadero. I do not usually tune myself to Potreran frequencies, nor does the Fabled Tree. I did, as it happens, foresee an influx of some sort, but as it seemed to indicate no injury to our beloved homeland, I said nothing, not wishing to upset my Majesties after such distress in our recent past. The moment I see a clear threat to us and ours, I'll let you know."

"Good enough. Now, here's the second thing." He leans way forward out of his throne and points a regal finger at me. "Get your butt over to the alien encampment and suck up bigtime. Establish diplomatic relations. Initiate trade. They're here, maybe nothing we can do about that, but we sure as hell can see what's in it for us. Like I said, we may like these new neighbors better than the old ones. Oh, and while you're at it, get the skinny on their intent and their force. Any questions?"

"None, your royal sagacity," I say, and scram.

We approach the Mission Dolores carefully. Doug is carrying a white flag, which I hope means the same thing to the aliens that it does to us. We appear to be alone, but we are not alone. There are knighties flanking us above, below, and on the ground. The walk to the Mission seems longer than usual. Fear has this weird effect on things—especially time.

Fidgeting, I dig my hands deep into my pockets and run into the Tin Hau note and the thing the old monk gave me. I bring the thing out into the uncertain Potreran daylight and look at it for the first time. It's made of stone and shaped like one of the little arched niches in the sanctuary of the Mission Dolores. It has a symbol engraved on it, the same symbol that's on the note in my pocket. On this hunk of smooth stone it doesn't look at all Chinese, it looks Egyptian. I wish I'd paid more attention in Kaymart's cultural anthropology class.

Why would an old Chinese monk give me an Egyptian artifact? That's a mystery I don't have time to solve at the moment. I put the thing into my amulet bag and grimace at the sheer audacity of the Tin Hau's so-called master.

Master Chen, the young monk said, was not a name, but a station. If that's so, the master's ego has gone seriously napoleon. Chen, for those who don't know, means Great and Vast.

It's weird, too, for the head of a religious order to trick himself out in plum silk. Like the monk said, monks do not wear silk. Huh. Maybe Master Chen wasn't a monk. But if that's so, how'd he come to be the master of a monkish order?

We do not get blasted when we come up to the Mission's front gate. This is a relief. The alien guards look at us funny and chuckle, but they let us in when I ask to see their leader. They look just like Embarcaderans, but their skin tones are a little more extreme—white and black mostly, with only some in shades of gold and brown. It's kind of a kick to see alien Latinos. I wonder if I seem alien to them.

Their clothes look like uniforms, but they're the drabbest uniforms I've ever seen. The guards call another man, a very dark brown man wearing mirrored shades against the swift changes of light, to be our escort. He chuckles at us too, then leads us into the compound.

The Whisperers are still silent, like they been almost since this started. This is scary, 'cause I been hearing them inside my head for close to ten years now. I hope Doug is having more luck tuning them in than I am. He's here as sort of an instrument package, like those things tornado chasers dump out in the middle of cornfields. (Not the cornfields here, ni dong. We don't have tornadoes in Embarcadero, just the occasional earthquake, some wicked winter storms, and the thirty-four known varieties of fog.) Right now, Doug's every needle is tuned to the metaphysical; he is a Dolores radar.

We are led across the courtyard to one of the winnebagos. Along the way, I notice much about the alien goings-on. The winnebagos are parked all about the central courtyard; none are very near the fences or walls even though the aliens have put up a thick, tall chain-link fence where the walls and fence-o-spears are busted.

In the very center of the courtyard is a trailer platform with something on it. I can't see what the something is, but it's pretty big. Big as a car, maybe, not as big as the winnebagos, which, I notice, are armored, like Firescape said, and have satellite dishes on top of them. These are for the purpose of catching rumbles out of the air, according to Hoot and the Wiz. We got some dishes here, but none of them work. The satellites won't talk to them anymore. I gotta assume these do work and wonder what kind of rumbles they catch and from where.

Aliens hustle all around, going here and there, carrying stuff, and there are piles of building materials lying about. I almost trip over myself when I see that a scaffold is starting to go up around the church and aliens are moving in and out of the broken doors. I see one guy with what looks like a video camera. He's videoing the guys who're working.

What the hell are they doing?

At the winnebago, our escort pokes his head through the open door and says, "Hey, John. There's a little guy with a tree here to see you."

I'm surprised all over again that they speak a dialect I grok, though the accent's a little oddball.

John proves to be a big guy with a red beard and electric blue eyes. He has unnaturally short hair, like most of the guys I seen since I got here, but his has this well-mannered little queue that dangles down his back like a Chinese patriarch's. I take this as a badge of leadership, at first, then realize that several other guys also wear the little queues. Huh. Maybe it's just a fashion statement.

I notice all this as he is standing in the door of his winnebago gawping at me and laughing with his buddy. Then the electric eyes are on me full blast and I realize he is addressing me directly.

"Who—ha—w-who the he-hell are you, little guy?" He

glances down at his friend, who is leaning against the side of the winnebago, grinning. "Doesn't he talk?"

"He was talking just fine a mo' ago."

"Apologies," I say. "I'm Cicerone Del, merlin to Hismajesty, King of the next-door realm of Embarcadero. This is the Fabled Tree of Destiny," I introduce Doug.

"The-the wh-what?" John is having trouble controlling his mirth. "What are you, some sort of an environmentalist?"

"I'm a merlin. This is the Tree of Destiny. My channel."

"Your channel. Aw, and I thought he was a housewarming present."

I'm on guard immediately, but calm myself when I see that the winnebago has no chimney. "No, he's the Tree of Destiny, a sort of cell-phone to the Almighty. God is partial to trees."

The two aliens exchange glances and my escort says, "Local color, I guess."

"I'm John Makepeace," says the red-beard. "What do you want?"

Makepeace. I like it. An auspicious name. I relax a little. "Hismajesty, King of Embarcadero, wishes to extend to you the hand of friendship, and inquires about your intentions toward the Mission in particular and this territory in general. (Okay, so I fib —I'm the only one who gives a rat's tuckus about his intentions toward the Mission.) He also wishes to know if there are needful things we might provide to you during your sojourn in our land."

"Needful things?" repeats John. "Such as?"

"Fresh produce and fish. Fresh water—there's not much of that in Potrero-Taraval. Info. Guides . . . ?"

"We brought our own food and water; yours would probably kill us. We've got all the information we need and we already have guides." He squats in the doorway so we are nearly eye to eye. "Now, as to our intentions: we're here to save San Francisco. Or at least to salvage what's left of it." His eyes, which have been boring into mine, take a hike around the courtyard.

"Save it?" I repeat, my mind going to the Peach Pit and from there to the Tin Hau and to the Egyptian thing in my amulet bag. "From what?"

"From disintegration and decay. From rot and ruin. From you." He pokes a big finger at my chest. "We're going to put San Francisco back on the map, Cicerone. We're going to bring it back to life one cultural treasure at a time."

I'm confused as hell. "But it's not dead. Well, sure, here seems a little falling down, 'cause it is. But this is Potrero. It's not like this all over the Gam Saan. It's not like this right over there." I wave north toward Embar. "Lord E Lordy's Alcalde here. He's a bit of a barbarian. Hismajesty's working at improving that, though, through a strict regime of education and better hygiene." I ignore the fact that they're laughing at me again, and plow onward. "You picked a bad place to roost, John. You oughta see the Regency Palace, the Farm, the Wiz."

"Oh, I'll see all of San Francisco in due time. I intend to assess it very thoroughly. But right now, this is where we set up camp." He puts this big hand on my shoulder and talks to me like I'm a little kid. "You see, I'm in the renovation business, Cicerone. Do you know what renovation means?"

I nod, but he defines it anyway. "It means to make new. That's what I'm going to do to San Francisco. I'm going to take old run-down places like this and make them new. Then I'm going to make access to them easy and safe, and open them up so that people can come and see them every day."

"People already see them every day," I argue.

He chuckles. "Well, Cicerone, that's just a handful of folks who don't know what kind of treasure they're sitting on. The people I want to bring here are people who will pay money to see these places, money that will keep them new for all time. These treasures will never get abandoned or forgotten or buried again. Gam Saan, you called it. Do you know what that means?"

"Of course, I know what it means," I say, getting a little testy under his condescending scrutiny. "It means Golden Mountain."

"That's right." He has the effrontery to look surprised that I know this. "And I'm going to put the gold back into the Golden Mountain. Now, you go tell your king to keep his knights and serfs out of the way of my work crews and everything will be just fine. There were some . . . problems when we arrived yesterday. I'd like to avoid that. Renovation, young man, is not a spectator sport." He rises and panic goes up right alongside.

"But this is a sacred place!" I cry. "There are spirits here—"

The look he gives me scares the words right back down into my throat. He moves his eyes to the other man and I breathe again and realize that the unease I taste now is not purely mine.

John Makepeace smiles at me, but it is not a real smile, and he is not looking at me, but at the dark brown man. "There are no spirits here or any place else in this city. It's a heap of decaying buildings populated by indigents." He laughs, but it's not a real laugh. "Jesus Lord, what rampant superstition!"

I am comforted that he seems to be on friendly terms with Jesus, but this seems at odds with his disbelief in spirits. I protest: "But they're here. The Dolores are here. They speak to me."

"I don't hear them, do you, Ty?"

The very dark brown man shakes his head and reaches up to adjust his shades. "Nope. Nary a whisper."

"But that's just it!" I plead, desperate. "Since you been here, they're silent. I gotta know why. Please, let me go into the grave-yard and try to-to reach them."

The look passes between them again and Ty glances over his shoulder as if to make sure no one's dropping.

"Who are these . . . Dolores?" he asks.

"They're nothing," says John Makepeace, as if he knew diddly about the Dolores.

"They're the spirits of the five thousand Ohlone Indians buried around here. That rock pile over there is their memorial." I point across the courtyard toward the gardens.

The sun chooses this auspicious moment to breach the clouds. A shaft of light falls onto the garden splashing color everywhere.

"Don't you know the history of the Mission?" I ask.

This time Ty tries to pass a look to John, but John declines to take it.

"You could come to the Wiz and learn the history," I suggest.

"I know the history," says John, then, "Get him out of here, Ty. We have work to do. Can't spend all day making friendly with the locals."

The door of the winnebago shuts in my face.

On the way back to the front gate, Ty watches me. At the gate, he says, "What you said about the Indians, is that true?"

I nod forlornly. All I can think about is this big silence in my head. I want to cry.

"Five thousand?"

"The diseases the Spaniards brought and the heavy work and bad food wiped them out. Having the spirit squeezed out of them didn't help, either. There were survivors, though. Some of them ran away."

"Yeah, but the ones who didn't . . ." He glances back at the Mission church.

His unease tickles my nose. "Are buried all over the place here," I finish for him.

"And they talk to you," he says. A smile is trying to crawl out onto his face.

This man is scared. I can see it, feel it, smell it. I store the knowledge for the future: some aliens are afraid of spirits. Maybe the reverse is also true; maybe some spirits are afraid of aliens.

"Not any more," I say, turning to go. "Not since you got here."

Across the street from the Mission, I park Doug and try to think orderly thoughts. I see that Ty is still watching me. He does this for a moment then says something to the guards and hustles off toward John's winnebago. The sun breaches again just then and turns the walls of the old church white-gold and the broken tile roof almost red.

I think about salvation. John Makepeace and I both want to

save the Mission from each other. A paradox. My ancestors wanted to redeem what they thought was a wasted land populated by wasted souls. Another paradox.

I don't think either needed redemption—the people, or the land—not like that, anyway. Which I think is why my ancestors failed. They didn't have the say-so over either the souls or the land, but their arrogance made them believe they did and the payoff was disaster, death and generally bad karma.

The hugeness of this suddenly plops square on my shoulders and I sink down next to Doug in his wagon. I am staggered by the idea that history is repeating on itself and that I am at what they call the crux of the situation. I am also staggered by what I don't know. I don't know how much of our Golden Mountain John Makepeace wants, and I don't know what he'll do to get it. I don't know what'll happen if he wants something that's important to more than this little Chickpea, and I don't know if we got the wherewithal to do diddly about it.

But the biggest I-don't-know is this: I don't know how many people there are where John Makepeace came from. I gotta believe there're lots—thousands, millions, maybe. I know that the population of the City before The Getting Out was in the hundreds of thousands. I try to imagine thousands of people coming back to Embarcadero, even just to gander, with all their stuff—cars, trucks, winnebagos—and my little mind tilts bigtime.

What will we do among those hundreds of thousands? Where will we go? What will become of the world we built?

I decide I have to ask John Makepeace these questions. I also decide I am spitting mad. John Makepeace's people had this Golden Mountain—this Gam Saan Francisco—and left it to rot. We stopped the rot and put the broken bits back together. Okay, so maybe our glue is lo-tech, but it works. Everybody in Embarcadero got a place to call home and food to eat and folks to check up on them. What happens to all that if the aliens take over the world?

I think I already know the answer 'cause I've read it in the

Books of History. I got this horrible feeling we're doing a sort of historical instant replay. They say a year is a day in the sight of God. If that's so, then He's just seen this. I know He can't want to see it again. Somehow, we gotta make things different this time.

I feel a soft, firry something touch my ear.

"What d'you think, Doug?" I ask. A quick breeze stirs and Doug's limbs flutter wildly in a sort of conifer war dance.

I get up and pull the Radio Flyer out of sight of the Mission. The guards watch us go, laughing.

This is gonna be one strange war.

Firescape meets me at the corner of Church and 18th. Cinderblock is with.

"What were you doing, sitting there like that?" Firescape asks. "Incanting?"

"Meditating on salvation and symmetry," I say. "We're off to Lord E's."

We are, and pronto. Lubejob meets us and escorts us in, asking all sorts of questions about my visit to the alien camp. I don't tell much.

Lord E is in rare form. In fact, I haven't seen him in such manic spirits since the Great Embarrassment. This is not the humbler, more sober Elvis I have come to know and tolerate, this is a smug Elvis, an I-know-something-you-don't Elvis, a possibly on-heavy-pharmaceuticals Elvis (though where he could've gotten heavy pharmaceuticals, I sure couldn't say.)

He side-steps all talk of unified efforts and executive summit meetings. When I remind him that so far the aliens have only invaded his turf and how much he stands to gain from a strong alliance, he giggles like a three-year-old and casts sideways looks at his new merlin, a shadowy personage who affects a cloak and cowl, an old monk's get-up.

All during the audience, the merlin-monk speaks only when spoken to, and then in monotone monosyllables. It occurs to me to wonder if this jake has gone napoleon—or Rasputin, as the case may be—and if he's responsible for Lord E's new smugness. Not liking any of this much, we take our leave. Elvis makes us pick our own way out of his palace—a diplomatic slap in the face. We are making our way silently down a long hallway that seems to be heading streetward when I sense my two-knightie escort tighten up.

A nanosecond later someone calls out, "Merlin!"

I stop and turn. Firescape and Cinderblock already have their weapons aimed at the heart of the Alcalde's new merlin. He stands atop a flight of stairs to an upper hallway, sunlight cascading all over his cowled shoulders. This has a stunning effect in that it makes him hard to look at, so I don't try very hard, just sort of look in his general direction.

"You want?" I ask.

He makes a funny little gesture with his hand as if pushing something aside.

"Don't matter," he says. "Watch yer back."

"'Cause why?"

"'Cause th' Alcalde's got his own agenda, besides being a ditz. It's not the same as yours. You know Lord E, he don't change."

"He was changing," I say accusingly. "He was finding out how much he didn't know. The first step to learning. The first step to wisdom."

The merlin shakes his cowled head. "Damn, but you're naive. You can throw all the learning you want at old Elvis. The only stuff that sticks to him is what he can use in the next five seconds." He sticks his hands into his sleeves, monk-like. "Watch yer back," he says again, and turns to go.

"Hey!" calls Firescape before I can twitch. "Why're you giving us advice? You're th' Alcalde's man."

"I'm nobody's man, General. I'm *my* man."

"Then you got an agenda, too," my wife persists. "Care to share it with us?"

He's moving away from us down the upper hall, but pauses. "You been east of the Mission on 16th?"

"No," Firescape answers.

"Go home that way," he says and disappears.

Accordingly, once we find our way out of Lord E's palace, we angle east on our way back into Embar. Firescape and Cinderblock are joined by a handful of other knighties. At least all I see is a handful. They're from all different neighborhoods and wearing diverse uniforms. The two in yellow are from the Richmond, one is in the green of the Presidio Guard, another in Tenderloin teal, a couple more in the black and burgundy of Russian Hill's crack troops.

They are wary as we bypass the Mission a block away and make our way up to Guerrero where we turn north again and head up toward 16th. They suspect a trap of some sort, given that a Potreran merlin has sent us here.

There's no trap. What there is, is a war zone. On Guerrero, before we even reach 16th, buildings are blasted, eaves fallen, walls caved in or out. Charred spots pock what's left standing.

"Bu hao," breathes Cinderblock, "This must be where the aliens came through."

Once we turn onto 16th, it gets worse—smashed houses and storefronts, scorched masonry, debris everywhere. I am wondering how far up John Makepeace's backtrail this sort of thing goes, when I hear Firescape cry out.

I stop, realizing that every knightie around me has frozen. When they unfreeze they dash toward where Firescape stands near a blasted out pile of rubble that was once someone's front steps. I dash too, though Doug slows me a bit, because now I can see that there is more than rubble here. There is a body.

I draw close against my will, and find there are two bodies, both horribly broken. One is a woman—or was—in her twenties or thirties maybe. The other is a little boy—about four, I guess. They lie close together, almost embracing, the woman's body partly covering the boy's. Mother and son, I think. Even broken and torn there's a strong resemblance.

One of Doug's boughs brushes my neck and I see it in a flash: the street, a battle zone, Potreros pelting the invading vehicles from sidewalk and rooftop with bricks and bottles. An occasional shot is fired from a handgun. The little boy and his mother are in the street. They have frozen there, terrified by the other-worldly vehicles moving toward them. A rock strikes one of the winnebagos' satellite dishes and the invaders begin to shoot back.

The mother and son flee, the mother trying to shield her little boy from the stuff flying around. They head for this building, where they live, where they will be safe, but they've waited too long to move. An alien weapon strikes the staircase as they step onto it and shatters it and them beyond repair.

The vision passes, and I stand in the broken street weeping.

Firescape's hand falls gently on my shoulder. "They left together," she says, and I see that she is crying too, thinking of Flannigans as yet unborn.

There is a silence in which I can hear the distant sounds of renovation from the Mission to the west. Then Cinderblock says, "We should bury them."

"All of them?"

This comes from one of the Tenderloin knighties. Her eyes are turned ahead, up the block.

There are over a dozen more—fourteen, to be exact—mostly men and boys, but not all. In the end, we use the rubble to make neat cairns over them and mark them with strips torn from the bright scarves and headbands of our knightie escort, which has inexplicably grown.

As we work, I think again about history. I guess we're not repeating it exactly, after all; at first, the monks smiled and held out gifts. The dying didn't come until later. I give a moment's thought to Treasure Island. There was a whole kingdom there, once. I wonder what's left after the aliens came through. Maybe there hasn't been anybody scoping the Bridge at that end 'cause there's no one left to do the scoping—or at least, no one who cares to try.

We head home, gray as the day. After a while, my mouth just sort of runs off without me, and I talk to Firescape about salvation and the symmetry of history. She listens and doesn't say a lot, just looks sort of grim and sad. Cinderblock looks angry and doesn't say anything at all.

"Tell me something, Del," my wife says, when I have run down a little. "When you were up at the Tin Hau, chasing your mysterious message man . . . how'd Creepy Lou know about the Whisperers?"

Whatever I might've expected her to ask, it wasn't that. I'm caught off guard both by the question and the answer.

"I dunno. I never told him. . . . You're sure he—"

"He called the Mission 'Whisperville.' I just wondered how he knew."

Now, so do I. I silently thank Jade Berengaria Firescape for giving me something besides death to think about.

sixteenth: chen

 **WHAT WITH ONE** thing and another, I don't get to ask Creepy Lou about Whisperers or anything else for awhile. First, I have to give my disturbing report to Hismajesty. It is both scary and gratifying to see him look truly grim when I'm done. Sometimes he gets cocky—a dangerous condition for a king.

After this, I make sure our perimeters are well-guarded. As much as I hate to do it, I recommend that we break out our heaviest weaponry. Firescape concurs and calls a war council with her officers. Our sméagols go out in force.

Knowing Embar is in good hands, I take off to the Farm on a twofold mission. One is to warn Bags and Kaymart about the activity to the southeast. The other is to call upon Kaymart's expertise. Her eyes get big when I take the thing the old monk gave me out of my pocket and lay it on the kitchen table. She picks it up and turns it over and over in her hands, touching it the way she touches her flowers.

Behind me, Bags looks over one shoulder; Doug looks over the other.

"Egyptian, right?" I ask.

Kaymart looks up at me, eyes bright. "Very good, Del. You remember your archaeology. Yes, it's Egyptian. Do you remember what this symbol is?"

She taps the carving with her finger. It's a funny not-quite-circle with a cross attached to it.

I shake my head. "Sorry. Chickpea brain."

"There's nothing wrong with your brain, Del," Kaymart assures me. "This is an ankh. It's a symbol of eternal life. Amulets like this were often placed at the feet of the dead to assure their eternal progress in the next world. They were thought to keep the soul out of the hands of Suti, the Lord of the Underworld. They're called shen."

My brain does this little woggle and I feel Doug's branches quivering against my back and Kaymart's eyes on my face.

"What's the matter, dear?" she asks and puts a hand over mine. "Why is this amulet so significant?"

"I'm not real sure," I say, and I tell her about the runes and the dreams, the Peach Pit and the Nails. I tell her about the first time felt the cold, dark yank on my immortal soul the night I saved Hismajesty from the fireball everybody figured had been set by Lord E Lordy's goons. I tell her about my trek up to the Tin Hau and the Watcher who calls himself Master Chen and feeling the same cold, dark yank there. I tell her about the young monk with black holes for eyes and the old monk who gave me this, and how he came to give it to me. I tell her, too, about the weird runes I been casting.

"Then this is a message about Master Chen, don't you suppose? The words are certainly similar. Chen," Kaymart says thoughtfully. "Great and Vast and Shen, an Egyptian death ward."

"Which is also Chinese for divine," I murmur.

"Not a coincidence, I'll bet. Is this a word game?"

If it is, I don't feel like playing. "Question is, what was the old monk trying to tell me? And why? Is this a warning or a clue? Or is it just a good luck charm? And what the hell is this Chen up to?"

"If he's your cold, dark yanker, it sounds like he doesn't like Hismajesty much," says Bags, who has a flair for understatement. "Maybe he's in cahoots with Lord E."

"I thought of that. It'd explain why the runes are warning me about him. But the Dolores are always chewin' on him, too. It's like they're . . . scared of him or something. They call him Wiwe."

"Wiwe?" repeats Kaymart. "Carrier Away of Souls?"

I've read about a person's jaw dropping, but this is the first time it's ever actually happened to me, personally. Though my chin is floor-bound, I manage to squawk out, "You know Wiwe?"

"Yes. It's a word in one of the Costanoan language groups. He's the Ohlone equivalent of—well, of Suti—the one these little amulets were supposed to guard against." She taps the shen with a fingertip. "Remember, this ankh is a symbol of eternal life—that means an escape from Suti. A seemingly universal quest. It's shaped the course of many religions, turning them from the here and now to the there and then. Taoist alchemy was essentially born out of a search for the elixir of immortality. I don't know how Master Chen fits into all this, but it seems the Dolores aren't the only ones trying to send you a message about him."

I get up and pace over to the lit hearth, which is about the cheeriest thing I've seen all day. "But what message? That he's a rotten spot in the universe? Okay, I can buy that. I mean, I think he's the one who tried to toast our sovereign lord. And he sure *feels* rotten. He wants to be immortal, maybe. Okay, but what's that got to do with me? Or the Dolores? And why are the Dolores telling me I gotta save the world from whatever-it-is? It's like you said, Kaymart, a game. Only I don't know what the game is and I don't know who the players are and I don't know what the rules are and I just don't know, period." All of which makes me muy cranky let me tell you.

"Trust your feelings, Del," Kaymart tells me. "Trust your intuition."

"She's right, son," says Bags. "Go with your gut. And your channels. Let them lead you." He gives Doug a little pat.

Doug waves his boughs and says nothing, but I know with a flash of certainty that he's more worried about Chen that he is about the aliens. In some strange way, so am I. I mean, you gotta have some kind of powerful juju to get a bunch of 400 year old spirits riled, right?

I look at the three of them sitting there, huddled around the lamp lit table, watching me—an old man, an old woman and a Tree—and I realize that here are three good reasons I got to figure out what Chen's game is.

That night I dream. I am before the fire in the smoky, upside-down bowl of a room, and I am alone. Really alone. I sense no presence but my own. I wait, but no Voice addresses me.

"Hello?" I say, then, "Where are you?"

The fire snaps and crackles without meaning, but nothing else speaks. Half wakeful, I toss and turn some, trying to escape the empty dream, trying to return to it. The perfume of fir washes over me and I am put firmly back on the sandy floor of the dream place. On the floor in front of me, where I cast runes before, there is a pile of stuff. Even through the dream smoke, I can tell it's native stuff—Ohlone stuff. There is a piece of folded cloth, a shirt maybe, with beads woven into it. On top of this is a head-dress, a pipe of clay, and a painted wooden stick stuck into a gourd that's wearing a horse-hair wig. Another, shorter stick is driven cross-wise through the gourd and the handle to hold them together. It kind of reminds me of the ankh, only 3D.

I smell fir again, and a voice—the Voice—says, *Shaman*.

"Yes!" I cry. "Yes?"

Save the world from Wiwe, it says, and there is no further message.

I wake with tears on my face and turn to see if I've waked up Jade, more than half-hoping I have. Something prickles my cheek, distracting me from my need for comfort. It is a Doug sprig, no more than three inches long.

I turn my head the other way, toward the window. "Thank you," I whisper. And wonder, Is Doug channeling the Dolores?

"Del?" My Jade is propped up on one elbow, looking at me. "You alright?"

"Glad you asked," I say, and let her wipe away my tears. Then I let her do other things that pull me, body and soul, away from everything but her.

"How'd you hear about the Dolores?" I ask Creepy Lou as we wend our way through the Sang Yee Gah, picking up alien gossip and trying to cool some of it down before we put it back in circulation.

"Huh?" he says and scratches his head. "You told me, remember? You studied hithtory and—"

"Not the Mission, the Ghosts, the Whisperers."

"Well, I didn't 'xactly hear about 'em. But it's hard not t'hear 'em."

I stop me and him both. "You hear the Whisperers?"

Lou's looking at me like I just asked him if the sky was gray. "Yeah. Am I not s'posed to?"

I grab his arm less gently than I mean to, making him jump. "Do you hear them now?"

He looks hangdog at me and shakes his head. "Nope. Not lately. Not since the alienth. At least, that's what I think." He screws up his face and stomps his left foot a couple of times. "You hear 'em, Chickpea?"

"Same as you—not since the aliens. D'you understand what they say?"

"Nope. Not a word. They just chant, ni dong. Kinda like the monkth. Never did understand all that. Guess God does though, huh? Must be neon t'understand every language there is."

My heart does a slow slide south. "So, what they say doesn't mean anything to you?"

He tugs at his ear and grins. "Nope. But sure is entertaining."

Okay, no hope here. I can't hear them, Lou can't understand them, and when I ask Doug what he picked up at the Mission, he lets me feel it: it's like the Gam Saan is holding its breath. I don't know what to make of that, but I know I gotta take action. With that in mind, I plan another trip to the Tin Hau.

Firescape is not in favor of my plan.

"Jeez, Del!" she says. "We got aliens camped next door and you gotta go off in search of more trouble? This is a hell of a time for a spirit quest."

"It's a gut call, Jade. It's what I do. Bags and Kaymart both told me I gotta go with my gut. I told you about the shen and the Peach Pit and Wiwe."

"Yeah, yeah. You told me." She scowls. "It's a ghost-chase, Del. Get your mind on the real problem: Makepeace and his damned aliens."

"I do got my mind on 'em," I say. "I've consulted every resource at my disposal. I spent the day scopin' the aliens and doing research at the Wiz. I've incanted until I'm blue in the face. I've done everything a merlin can do. This isn't a ghost-chase, Jade. It's important. I know it. I feel it. Doug feels it too."

She is unconvinced and angry and goes off mad as hell. I got no words to tell you how un-Jade-like this is. Still, there is nothing I can do about John Makepeace, so I gotta see if I can do something about Chen.

I wait until very late—or early, depending on how you look at these things—then get my butt out into the fog. It's a thick, chill, shaggy sabana, almost a jin rain, and hangs in pale banners that lap at the streets. The occasional neon light makes it pulse with color that runs, gold, red, blue, green across the wet pavement and into the gutters. In between the neon flash, the moon oozes down through it, silvery white.

The Gee Gah never really sleeps, but it bustles a little less in the early AM. Even so, I am dressed in black with my head all wrapped up in a black turban, trying to look as unlike myself as possible. Leaving Doug behind goes a long way toward this end, since he tends to make me kind of conspicuous. I carry a Doug talisman, though; the sprig that interrupted my dream last night is on the thong around my neck. The shen is there too, inside the amulet bag, on the chance that it is a talisman meant to protect me.

Still, this general Douglessness causes me no end of self-esteem problems. The closer I get to my destination, the shakier I am. By the time I have skulked my way through the darkness of Spofford Alley and around to the side of the Tin Hau, my nerves are on full alert. So, I'm not surprised when I start to see things, merely scared spitless.

I'm looking for the best way into the dark temple when the sabana seems to come to life. Out of the corner of my eye I see a dash, a slither, a scurry; out of the corner of my ear I hear a scrape, a swish, a bump, a murmur. I think of Scrawl's black ninjas and my insides woggle. I stop long enough to take myself severely to task. I get tough, and have just about talked myself out of the woggles when Something that is not fog—living or otherwise—rises up out of the darkness not four feet from my nose.

"What took you?" it asks, and I practically dissolve into the pavement.

I cover the four feet in a lick and get right in his face. "Lou! What d'you mean 'what took me?' What're you doing here?"

He scratches his head. "I dunno. I thought maybe you'd need company—being Treeleth and all."

"How did you know I was coming? Did you follow me?" I ask, wondering who else might've done the same thing.

He cocks his head sideways in a way that reminds me of a little kid or a dog and says, "Wiz, Chickpea—how could I follow you when I got here first?"

"Then—" Nah, it's not worth it, I decide. "I need a way in. Any ideas?"

"Front door? It's not locked, y'know."

We go in through the front door. I don't even try to talk Creepy Lou out of coming with me. I tell myself it's because he wouldn't listen anyway, and I ought to have him where I can keep an eye on him. This is all true, but I gotta admit, I'm glad of the company.

In the downstairs hall, Lou heads for the staircase before I can stop him. What the hell, I figure, and follow him. The elevator makes a lot of noise anyway. The stairs creak a little when I step on them, and I realize that they don't creak at all when Creepy Lou steps on them. He's juking from side to side, putting his feet right along the outside of each tread. I follow suit. Creepy Lou seems to know a lot about the silent climbing of stairs.

I lead the way into the sanctuary. It's dark except for the tiny red glow from the braziers at the scattered altars. The air is still almost chewy with incense, but it's the heavy scent of cooling embers. There are no worshippers, no monks, no one. I glance toward the Tin Hau altar and catch a chill from Thousand League Eyes. I shake myself and wish Doug was here to let me know if we're being watched by real people or just my active imagination.

The door behind the dragon screen is still unlocked and I get a little light-headed when it opens silently at my touch. The hallway beyond is dark. No, not just dark, black. My chickpea brain supplies a memory of how low the ceilings are here (for which I thank it kindly), and I duck a little without meaning to. I pause, trying to recall how the hallway is laid out. All I remember is a lot of doors and a couple of windows and, of course, that ceiling pressing down on my head.

The windows, I realize, are where the little glimmer of light is coming from—a very small, dull gray glimmer, useless to see by, unless you happen to be a cat. Not being a cat, I send a prayer heavenward that the sabana will politely step aside and let the moon through. I am sincerely surprised (and pleased) when it does and clear, silver light floods into the hall by which I see each heavy wooden door like a hole in the white washed walls. They're all the same. I suppose I could just start at one end and move to the other.

I glance left. There is a lone door at the end of the hall. Might as well start there, I guess. I start to move that way, but Creepy Lou clamps a hand on my shoulder and points to the other end of the hall. This end doesn't have a door. It has a tapestry—a big, silk one, covering practically the whole wall.

Okay, I'll bite. We go that way, moving like ninjas (or at least, the way I imagine ninjas move).

The tapestry hides a door. I quiver. Okay. Good place to start. My hand shakes as I turn the latch. I thank the monks for taking such good care of the place. This door is just as silent as the last one.

There is light here, too. The same silvery light as in the hallway, but much brighter. It cascades like ghost-water down the long, narrow staircase I am now staring up. At the top of the stairs is a window, and framed in that window is the moon, fat and round.

I am moonstruck for a moment, watching as the sabana trails across its face.

Creepy Lou whispers, "Pretty," snatches at the moonlight, and moves ahead of me up the stairs, feet going right, left, right against the walls. I close the door and follow. The latch makes only the tiniest snick!

At the head of the stairs, we stand in the moonlight and are amazed. The upstairs hallway is a tiny palace. Ivory and gold and flame-colored silk gleam against dark wood, lit by the moon and the light of flames hidden in clever little brass lamps. Across the stairwell from where we stand gawking is a set of double-wide doors, carved with all kinds of strange symbols—some I know, some I don't.

We tread on thick, soft carpets on our way to the doors. With every step, I'm more scared to open them. I got no idea what might be on the other side. I whiff conifer effluvium and realize

I'm squeezing my talisman. I am suddenly inspired to get down on hands and knees and put my nose to the bottom of the door.

Incense. The same heavy, cold smell as downstairs. This is a private shrine. I rise and try the door. It's locked. This does not boggle me. I have always had an affinity for locks. A good merlin must be able to waltz in and out of locked rooms like the wind. I pull a carefully twisted piece of stout wire out of a pocket and poke it delicately into the lock mechanism. I find the tumblers and tick them over one by one. *Tick. Tick. Tick. Click!*

I glance at Creepy Lou who grins at me and pushes the door. It glides open on silent hinges. It's like no shrine I've ever seen. More like an art gallery. Tables and stands of carved wood hold all sorts of oddments, and more stuff hangs on the walls.

"Wow!" says Lou softly, then mouths, "Sorry."

In the center of the room, I look down at my feet. Even the wooden floor is art. I'm standing in the middle of a five-pointed star all of inlaid brass. At each point of the star is a tall wooden stand with a twisting column. On one stand is a menorah, on another a Buddha sitting in a golden lotus, on a third is a golden, jeweled bowl of water, on the fourth, a bowl of fire. The fifth one is empty.

Closer to the walls are tables, massive and as intricately carved as the dragon screen downstairs. There's more stuff there: a Tibetan prayer wheel; a little doll with buggy eyes and a big ego; a glass ball with an ivory monkey in it; a piece of bone with funny burnt squiggles on it—an oracle bone, I suspect; an ankh; a strange, bee-hive shaped stone; some funny, twine-wrapped sticks with faces; a dragon; a drum with two heads; a ram's horn, decorated and wrapped in silk cord; some more shen and other medallions or amulets; all sorts of figurines and cups and bowls and knives.

I pause in my circuit of the room and look at Creepy Lou. He's standing in the middle of the star turning round and round staring at the walls and mouthing, "Wow!" at every turn. I step back and follow his eyes. More wonders: a sun disc with tiny hands at the end of each sunbeam; a carved wooden mask with angry eyes and major-league lips; a painting done all in sand; a mandala with a blue Krishna in the middle. There's clothing too, all kinds of ceremonial robes hang from the walls. And there's a crucifix.

This causes me to do a double-take. I get close. The size is right, the shape is right. It could be, I realize, the missing crucifix from the Mission Dolores. There are smaller, golden crucifixes around it.

"Looky," whispers Creepy Lou.

He is standing at the head of the room, opposite the doors, where there is an altar of sorts. On the altar is a din, which is a sort of three-legged stone offering pot that has great significance if you happen to be of the Chinese dynastic sort. Only emperors had them, because Emperors were the scions of God. Godlets, sort of. My mind asks the obvious question: Is the din just part of the collection, or is it another sign of Chen's elevated self-image?

Next to the din's altar is a cabinet of big dark wood, with lots of carving, just like all the rest of the furniture in the room. In the cabinet are herbs in bundles, bottles, boxes, tins—you name it. Next to the cabinet is a bookcase full of all sorts of books. I recognize a Bhagavad Gita, a Dhammapada, Pentateuch, Bible, Qur'an, Iqán, I Ching. There are scrolls, too. Next to the bookcase is a totem pole. Tlingit, I think.

So, Master Chen collects religious artifacts. That's nice. But it can't be why the runes, the Dolores, my Tree and an old monk have warned me about him. Further questing is clearly in order.

I give the room another eye sweep, hoping to see a door. I only see the ones we came in through. Okay, so it's hidden. I lean close to Lou's ear and whisper, "Gotta be a door hidden somewhere."

He nods and I wave him to the bookcase. I start behind the herb cabinet. Nothing. On the other side of the bookcase, Creepy Lou looks at me and shakes his head. He moves right, I move left, feeling the walls with our hands—we'll meet at the front doors.

I'm about halfway down my side of the room on my hands and knees when I hear Lou say, "Uh-oh."

I rise and turn and see Creepy Lou staring at me from the other side of the room. Well, actually, it's not me he's staring at, but the all in black, turbaned ninja who's just appeared between us in the middle of the room.

I freeze. It's like I'm looking into a mirror sideways, until the ninja turns his head to look at me. His eyes are like the young monk's eyes—big, black chaos orbs and nobody home with a vengeance. The ninja turns his head to look at Lou, then turns back to me and bows.

Okay, I figure, when in Little China . . . I bow back.

He inclines his head toward Lou. "Ta shi shei? Who's he?"

It takes me about two seconds to realize I'm the luckiest little *jing-bing* merlin in the Gam Saan. He thinks I'm one of him—a ninja, I mean. I look at Creepy Lou.

"Ta shi yishujia," I say quickly. "He's an artist. Master Chen, zai nar?" Good tactic, I figure—pretend to be seeking our unintentional host.

The ninja's eyes blink slowly. "Sleeping," he says. "Why are you here at this hour?"

"Looking for the broken table," Lou ad-libs, and I just about fall over before I pick up my cue.

"Dui. There's a crack in one of the tables—the carvings, ni dong. I just found this guy tonight. Had to track him down and pry him out of the Li Po." I make a drinking gesture and the ninja grimaces.

"An artist should be more disciplined," he says.

I shrug. "We couldn't find it anyway. I'll bring this guy back tomorrow—sober—so the Master can show us which table needs fixing. Must be one tiny crack."

"The Master . . . expects perfection," the ninja informs me, and his mouth twitches strangely.

I bow again and beckon Creepy Lou toward the door. The ninja's spooky eyes press against my back as I follow.

"Deng!"

Oh, shit, I think, and turn slightly, ready to bolt.

The ninja is holding out a Doug sprig to me. "You drop this?"

My hand wants to say "yes," but I demure. "Not me. You?" I look to Creepy Lou.

"Uh-uh." He shakes his head.

It strikes me suddenly that he hasn't ticked or grabbed or stomped since we came in here. Interesting. I shrug and open the door and we're outta there.

In the outer hall, I slow my steps waiting to see if the ninja will follow. He doesn't. And when he doesn't, I scurry back to the door and put my ear to it. Nada. I take a deep breath. I turn the latch, I open the door a crack—an excuse for coming back making itself up in my glib little brain.

I don't need it. The ninja is gone.

Damn. I was hoping to catch him making an exit, but the room is as empty as the thong around my neck. For a moment, I think of going back in, but I'm fresh out of good stories.

"Let's zhou," I whisper, and we do.

"Wo bu dong," I tell Firescape when she is awake and scowling at me sometime later, "I don't get it. I can't figure out who this guy Chen is, or who he thinks he is. I mean, okay, the runes say he's a rotten spot in the fabric of our fair kingdom, the Dolores say he's the Carrier Away of Souls, and I gotta admit, I've seen some guys around his place that sure look like their souls've been carried away somewhere. But he's, like, saving all this religious art. What's rotten about that? I don't get it."

I see that my wife's scowl has deepened. "Dammit, Del, can't you keep outta trouble? You're always in trouble. Every second of your life, you're in trouble. You're all worried about me being out in the street and here you are pokin' around some damned Carrier Away of Souls. It sucks. At least I got an AK. You got a-a twitchy guy and a Tree! What kind of protection is that?"

I don't get this either. I am not used to seeing my Jade in such an angst-ridden state. She is sitting up in our bed with her hands folded in her lap, her scowl flicking between me and Lou, who is kind of swaying back and forth in the middle of the bedroom. Behind him, I see Doug waving at me from the window, trying to get my attention.

In a sudden flash of insight and flashback, I do get it.

"You're pregnant!" I tell her.

She bursts into tears. Needless to say, I send Creepy Lou home and we discuss Master Chen no more this night.

Later, I dream. I dream about Creepy Lou and me searching Chen's gallery. But somewhere in the middle of the dream, it is the Mission Dolores we search, scrabbling through the dirt and debris. As we search, I know we are being sought, but whether by aliens or ninjas, or both, I can't say. At the very end of my dream, a weird thing happens. Yeah, sure, dreams are weird all over, but this is like . . . an intrusion. Like somebody's walking around in my dream with me, uninvited.

And then, I hear this Voice that asks, "Are you an ear? An eye? Or merely debris?"

Not only is this a pretty weird thing to say—kind of like a riddle, I guess—but this is not one of my familiar voices. It is one I haven't heard before—a slippery, laughing Voice that oozes through my head like a snake. I experience a wild, weird, woolly moment of vertigo as if I'm being lifted into the air. I wake up with a jolt, let me tell you. Then, I get to lie there in the dark and think about whether I (or something else) is an ear, an eye, or merely debris.

I am like that until morning, when I am informed that, once again, I have run out of time. In the morning, I learn that the aliens have taken the Farm.

seventeenth: i discover even aliens have fairy tales

 I CAN'T REMEMBER EVER SEEING Kaymart cry. She is crying now. Bags isn't, but I can tell he wants to and is just being strong for Kaymart. I think they call that role reversal 'cause usually it's the other way around. Bags, he'll cry over almost anything—an old tree coming down, a new tree coming up. But now, I guess seeing Kaymart weak means he's got to be strong, so he just is.

"It happened so fast," Kaymart tells me through her tears. "They were just there with these . . . these weapons pointed at us, telling us to get out."

"But why?" asks Firescape. "What'd they want?" She turns to me. "I thought you said they brought all their own food. What'd they want with our Farm?"

"They seemed most interested in the old museums. Especially once they saw how we were using them." Kaymart manages a weak smile. "I think your Mr. Makepeace was a bit upset with us 'ignorant squatters' and our hatchery. Somehow I think he imagined he'd find the old aquarium stocked with exotic species."

"That was when they tossed us," grumbled Bags. "Just like that. Damned marauders. Mannerless, uncivilized shits."

"Now, Bagsie. . . ." Kaymart's color is finally coming back. "That's just about what they said about us. I think they took exception to being attacked with pitchforks and spades. At least they let us all go back and take some of our personal belongings."

"Some, but not all," says one of their woebegone apprentice Farmers. He is the youngest, a usually scrappy little squirt named Hijack. He kind of reminds me of me when I was that age. "Who's going take care of the seedlings?"

This sends Bags off on what they call a tangent. "Hijack's right, you know," he tells Kaymart. "Who's gonna feed your damned fish and tend your precious vegetables and monitor your hydroponics experiments? Who's gonna do all that, old woman? Hm? You tell me. Any of those damned marauders look like botanists to you? Any of 'em look like they give a rat's hindmost about superior strains of broccoli?"

Now that Kaymart is recovering herself, Bags is edging toward losing his-self. All the little farmhands are looking from one to the other, wide-eyed and teary. I am preparing to say something helpful and merlin-like when Cinderblock makes a grim observation.

"This," she says, "is gonna severely jink up our food supply."

It doesn't take a merlin to do the math—the Farm yields about one-third of our food crops—veggies, fruits and nuts mostly. Except for Kaymart's experimental strains, all our grains are grown out at the Presidio. I look into Firescape's eyes and know she's thinking what I'm thinking.

She puts it into action. "Cinderblock, pack up the Royals and move 'em out to the Presidio. I'll draw the Wharfside Guard over to set up a perimeter. If we lose that land, we lose Embar."

The two of them move like red and black lightning and my heart goes deep-freeze in my chest.

"Be careful!" I shout after my beloved wife.

She pauses at the entrance to the Royal's private dining salon to grin at me. "Duh!" she says, and sails off, flying a banner of red.

"You know, Del," says Kaymart, "the Farm itself might not be in much danger. I don't think Makepeace has any intention of trying to hold the whole thing. He's only after the treasures, as he calls them, the things with historical significance. In fact, I'm not at all sure he could hold the whole thing, not if he intends to keep dividing his resources. Who knows—they might even lose interest in it once they realize the buildings aren't full of forgotten artifacts. We might be able to take back the parts that are important to us."

Bags is nodding. "Maybe we could even swing a deal with that rat's hiney. Get him to give back whatever we care about so long as we don't touch what he cares about."

Kaymart puts a hand up to stop him. She's looking at me. "What is it, dear?"

My face must be doing one of its freeform expressions, 'cause my eyes are wonky as hell.

"He's envisioning," whispers Bags.

I am. And what I am envisioning, among all this talk of treasures and galleries and dealing, is that Master Chen, with his gallery-o-magic is just the sort of individual John Makepeace would love to talk to. My blood thunders around in my head like it got elephant feet because I have the sudden intuition that Master Chen means to sell all that art he's collecting to the aliens. Now, I'm mad as hell at the thought that some guy with delusions of Immortal-hood has plans to sell off bits of everybody's history and faith. This makes me want to go down to the Tin Hau and give Master Chen a piece of my mind, but I realize I should save all the best pieces for John Makepeace.

When I tell Firescape and my liege lord this, however, they are of different minds altogether. Hismajesty has refused to pack himself off to the Summer Palace with his family and has called upon my sweet wife to take the Farm back by brute force. My Majesty, I realize, is fighting mad precisely and exactly because he is scared more spitless than I am. I am uncertain how to take this revelation; should I give myself congrats for superior cojones, or should I lose more spit over the fact that my very King—the supposedly omnipotent and invincible leader of the sovereign nation of Embarcadero—has gone into omnipotent and invincible flight-or-fight mode?

I do not want to fight. I'm no good at fighting. I'm better at talking. Except that, of course, where John Makepeace is concerned, I'm not even so good at that. I think it's possible that we speak different languages that only sound the same.

Firescape's battle plan is for a hand-picked force of knighties to go in under cover of pre-dawn dark and take important prisoners. She has studied her tactical manuals carefully; this is the only strategy she envisions working against interlopers with superior firepower and armored winnebagos.

Against my best advice and abject whining, the plan goes ahead. Hermajesty and the Junior Majesties are moved quickly to the Summer Palace at the Presidio, which is just as quickly put under the added protection of the crack patrols from the Virgin, Wharfside and Union Square. The regular Presidio Guard isn't that large; corn and rice don't need all that much policing, ni dong. The next thing I know, they're all cleaning their guns and getting out their black and gray skulking gear.

I can't talk to Jade when she's like this. She's not even really Jade, now; she's 120 percent General Firescape and this is the first time she's planned a raid this big against this strong an enemy. I don't dare let her see that I'm nervous about her and the little Flannigan within. So I say some protection incantations before the fact and insist on tagging along to lay down a cover of Chouyan when they go in.

It's two AM when they move into the Farm. Firescape and her troops melt into the bowu that rises from the grass like moist ghosts. They are like ghosts themselves—no one can see them, of that, I'm certain. I can't see them and I know they're there. In truth, they probably don't need my smoke screen, they're Firescape's best.

Anyway, they go in while I stand in the woods and make with Chouyan. I don't know how long I been there, incanting, when I hear this sound like demons singing. I don't know what singing demons sound like, really, but I imagine it's like this sound that pierces the brain and vibrates the bone. I see lights shoot up into the trees where the knighties have gone and then there's gunfire.

I run toward the lights. All I can think of is Jade, and I wish for a split second that this were the age when men were in charge and women were supposed to obey them. Well, okay, so it's just mythology, I realize, and Jade Berengaria Firescape Flannigan sure as hell wouldn't have obeyed me even if there'd ever been such an age, but it was one of those panicky if-onlies that happen when your adrenaline's gone rocket.

I don't get very far before I'm assailed by knighties flying out of the trees, looking wild-eyed and grim. I see Cinderblock and a couple of others I know. And finally, when I'm about adrenalined out, I run headmost into Firescape. She turns me about-face and pushes me into a run and we keep running till we're out of the woods and back in the streets.

"Que pasa?" I pant, when I can.

"I dunno. I'd swear we were silent. Nobody saw us, I'm sure. There were three winnebagos, some jeeps and tractors some big floodlights, no guards. I wasn't worried about the lights, what with the Chouyan and all. We get about five yards from their camp and all hell breaks loose. There's this sound like, like—"

"Singing demons?" I insert.

"Yeah, I guess. Like that. So loud, it just about split my head open. Damn, Del! I don't know what we did wrong. I'd swear no one could hear us or see us or smell us. I don't know what happened, but they were all over us. People popping out all over the place with those damn guns. I mean, once we lost surprise, well, we didn't have squat."

Our report to our liege is grim. We have wounded now, and

are lucky not to have lost anybody. We didn't lay a scratch on the aliens. The enemy has an early-warning system, which brings us to a renewed respect for the level of techno-magic John Makepeace is packing. We pack the entire royal household off to the Presidio, King and all, and I settle in for some earnest meditating.

Since I have not slept much or well lately, my earnest meditating kind of morphs into some earnest sleeping. Normally, I would say this was an unfortunate evidence of my complete ineptitude as a merlin, but I dream—and it's a doozy, as Bags would say.

I'm in a smoky place and I think it's my dream lodge, where I hear the Whisperers. But then, I get that this is the Tin Hau—his place, the Art Gallery. It's full of incense and stuff, and I know there are people here, I can feel them and they make me quiver.

A Voice asks, "What have you brought me?"

It is the snake's Voice—a Red Dragon's Voice, hot and slippery. Chen?

There is movement, and a walking bit of darkness comes out of the smoke. It's face is the face of a certain young monk's, and the eyes are his eyes. They are as big and black and empty as ever, and they gleam like cold, polished obsidian. Nobody home.

I vaguely see light now, and it seems to me the light is all around whatever the monk has in his hands.

Okay, Chickpea, says my dream brain, *this is important. Pay attention.*

The monk puts the lit-up thing on the empty stand in the gallery and I see that it is a folded strip of cloth with beads and bits of shell and feathers.

"This is all?" asks the Red Dragon Voice, sounding peevish.

"All, Master."

A hand comes out of the smoky darkness and picks up the beaded cloth and I feel as if the cloth is me. I can't breathe.

"More," says the Red Dragon Voice, "there must be more. Do not fail me. Shall I demonstrate what will happen if you fail me . . . Ho-win?"

This must be his real and secret name, 'cause the monk lets out this blood-curdling yelp and falls like his invisible puppet master cut his strings. He curls on the floor, his face lifted up into the smoky light. His lips move and he says, "Master, this is all that was found where you sent us."

"There is more," says the Red Dragon. "There must be more."

A swirl of purple robes and I am lifted up again. There is a blur above me and it reflects the smudges of light like a golden moon. I think it must be a face. I don't feel like looking at it right now though, so I let it be a blur.

The Red Dragon speaks: "Is there more?" it asks, and I fall.

This causes a drastic shift in my POV. I am in my dream lodge again, in the fire and smoke, and the sand is gritty under me. On the floor in front of me, I see the beaded shirt, the pipe and the funny stick and ball with its horse-hair wig.

Okay, the shaman stuff again. It takes me a moment to realize that something is missing; the beaded headdress is gone. And I've just been shown where it is. The meaning is clear as bluesky. Chen has somehow gotten hold of this thing and added it to his collection, and the Dolores are understandably upset. After all, it must be their stuff.

I have just come to this obvious conclusion when out of the smoke of the Lodge comes a single word: *Diablo*. This isn't spoken, exactly. I mean, it's really weird, but if I had to put a sense to it, I'd say I smelled the word.

Yeah, I dream-think, *if I could sum up Chen in a word, Diablo would be it*. And I sleep, smelling fir.

Sleep isn't awfully refreshing. I wake up knowing I got my work cut out for me. By the rustling of Doug's boughs, I gotta go see John Makepeace and try again to reason with the man.

When I head in that direction, Bags tags along.

"As far as the Wiz is all," he says. "I couldn't bear to see the homestead and not be able t'go home."

When we get to the Wiz, I let Doug and me get sucked inside

where I sit down to do some researching. I'm real curious to know what it is Chen's after besides the headdress. The beaded shirt's an easy savvy—that's shamanly vestments, like a priest's robes. The pipe, I get too, I guess. I mean peace pipes and all. But that horse-hair wigged stick, I don't get.

As it happens, I learn more than I reckon I will. I learn the pipe is sort of a general ceremonial pipe, not just for peace. It's like the Taoist-Buddhist monk's little braziers sort of, or like Chen's din; it's where the ceremonial herbs are burned to get the spirits' attention. And the horse-hair wigged thing, that's a spirit rattle. The shaman uses it to get the spirits he calls up to focus themselves on what needs done. It's more than that, too. The Books of Wisdom tell me it's like a staff of power. Every shamanly, wizardly type got one, from Gandalf to Cinderella's Fairy Godmom to . . . well, to me.

This all hits me like a 6.7 on the Richter 'cause I catch a whiff of the Tree as I'm contemplating. Doug is no mere channel, he's a talisman and he's a staff of power and every part of him is a stafflet of power, and it walks in and slaps me upside the head that that dream I just dreamed happened 'cause I dropped one of those self-same stafflets in the Tin Hau.

I find myself repeating Chen: "Are you an ear, an eye, or merely debris?"

I am struck with the wonder of it. Then, I am struck by the intriguing possibilities. With Doug flying our white-flag I head up to the Farm, but John Makepeace is not there. He has returned to his headquarters—the Mission Dolores—to oversee the work there. Fine by me.

It's late afternoon when I approach the Mission. I'm really surprised to get in this time, but I am welcomed by smiles that say, *We're laughing at you, not with you.*

I get it. They think I'm A Character—Local Color, like John Makepeace said before. Okay, I can live with that.

One of the guards takes me to his leader this time. He takes his sweet time about it, too, stopping to talk to folks so they can say funny and insulting stuff at me like I don't get it. While this is happening, I'm dropping little ears and eyes about everywhere, which is when I notice that the cover is off the big thing in the courtyard. Hard to miss, for sure—it's a giant version of the satellite dishes on top of the winnebagos. It's black—a matte, light-sucking black—and it's got shiny chrome stuff on it and it's tilted up to the sky. It reminds me a lot of the radio dishes the SETI people used to listen for aliens.

Ironic.

My escort finally leads me to the winnebago of John Make-peace, then makes me wait while he goes off to talk to someone else. While they look at me and chuckle, I note that my Tree is straining toward the vehicle with his little branch tips all aquiver. I step a little closer to the door and prick up my ears. I hear voices, and if I try real hard I can make out words.

". . . cathedral," someone is saying. "Those onion domes are amazing."

"Isn't that . . ." begins a new voice, then I lose it, then it says, "pretty damn deep. We don't want to split ourselves up too much."

"What are you afraid of, Gino?" says a third voice, louder and closer to me. I recognize John Makepeace. "Has this city shown you anything you should be afraid of besides a few stray shadows you can't account for? We're okay. We've got the satellite rig and the GPS. We're armed to the teeth. The only problem we've got right now is that we've got to pick and choose our targets as carefully as we can."

"Yeah, that and the little spooks," says Gino. "I'd sure like to know what that's all about."

"Overactive imagination," answers John Makepeace sharp-voiced.

"My guys say not. My guys are sure there's something there." There was kind of a funny pause, then Gino says, "I've seen them."

"We've been over this and over this, Gino. These spooks of

yours aren't real. They can't be. If they were real, they'd have tripped the security system . . . wouldn't they?"

"You haven't seen them," Gino accuses.

"Thank you for making my point for me. Now, can we get back to business?"

There's another pause, most people'd call it an awkward one. Then a softer voice says, "Where do we go next?" and I realize it's Ty.

"You guys ever hear of Jack Kerouac?" asks John Makepeace.

There are some noises that could mean 'no' or 'yes.' I've heard of Jack Kerouac. *On the Road*. Beat generation. Lost boy. Joined at the hip to the Wiz back in the days before Wiz-dom.

"He was a folk hero," says John Makepeace, "an iconoclast and an urban poet. Hung out at a place on Columbus called City Lights—a bookstore. I have it on good authority that the place has actually been kept up by the abos as a kind of shrine. It's a prime target."

"Prime target? It's a bookstore." This is a voice I haven't heard before.

"It's a potent historical icon. A monument to a bygone age. In fact, in 1997 it was accorded the status of an historical landmark by the state of California."

"It's a pet project, John," said Gino. "How many tourists are going to come here to see a bookstore? You said it just a mo' ago: We've gotta choose our targets carefully. If we don't, we lose our shirts."

"I think Gino might be right," says Ty. "I doubt there are so many history buffs at home that we can afford to waste resources on something like that. Besides, we'd have a real fight on our hands if we tried to take that bookstore. Like you said, the abos think it's some sort of shrine. I think we've got to go for easier targets that are more glitzy."

There is another silence. "You think so, do you? If the Spanish had felt that way, this place would have stayed a godforsaken swamp."

"I'm just trying to be practical, John. I think we need to look at what will convince our backers this venture is viable, don't you agree?"

I never get to hear if John Makepeace agrees because my escort comes back and knocks on the winnebago door.

I'm shaking like a 5.2 temblor. John Makepeace wants the Wiz. I don't make the mistake of thinking this is the same as Lord E Lordy wanting the Wiz. For one thing, I'm pretty sure John Makepeace can read. So, as I am thinking these deep and tremulous thoughts, I am once again struck silly and mute when the door of the winnebago opens.

"You again?" asks John Makepeace and he smiles at me in what they call an avuncular way, and then glances back into the room. "It's my little friend with the tree," he says. "What's up?" This is to me.

"It's about the Farm, John Makepeace. I need to talk with you about the Farm."

"What Farm?"

"The hunk-o-land you swallowed up the other evening— Golden Gate Park. It's a significant part of our food chain. You might have noticed some of the greens you trampled upon were a bit better organized than is normally the case in nature."

"Oh, yeah. I guess they were, at that. What about it?"

"We sort of need it back," I say, lame-o.

"Which is why you tried to attack us last night?"

"Well, not me in particular. My wife, General Firescape, actually, and her knighties. But, yeah, that was the general idea."

"Sorry . . . Cicerone, is it? But I can't let you have such a valuable piece of property. You wouldn't know what to do with it, for one thing."

"We grow food on it."

"My point, exactly. You have no idea of its real value."

I am getting a little hostile, at this point, and it comes through in my voice.

"Like hell," I say. "It may just be property to you, it's life and death to us. That's our food. We don't care about the buildings, except for the fish tanks and the greenhouses. All we really want is the land we got planted—the food crops and the tree farm. You can have the rest."

I look over John Makepeace's shoulder and realize other faces are looking at me. One of them is Ty's and he looks sort of pitying. Pity is not what I want, but I'm willing to settle. John Makepeace don't strike me as a guy who negotiates.

"Look, Cicerone, I would say 'yes,' but it would just be postponing the inevitable. You're going to have to move on anyway. The new San Francisco isn't going to have room in it for transients. I'm afraid you're going to have to accept that."

Even I know that transient is just an expensive word for homeless. I shake my head. "There haven't been transients in Embarcadero since anyone can recall," I say. "Everyone here has a home. Or did, until you came. If there are homeless people here, John Makepeace, you made 'em."

He gives me this long, thoughtful look, while Ty gives him the same, and hope springs eternal. But it gets dashed pretty damn quick.

"Sorry. But I can't let this city and all its marvels go to waste."

And that, as they say, is that. Deflated, I take my Tree and slink away across the compound. I find myself drawn to John Makepeace's big old talisman. I am staring it at, trying to fight down the despair I'm feeling and wishing I could get into the old church without being noticed when I hear someone calling me. It turns out to be Ty and he still has that kind of funny pitying look on his face. There's something else there, too—a little uneasiness, maybe, or shame.

"Hey, Cicerone," he says, then. "Should I call you 'Cicerone' or 'Del?'"

I take a calculated risk. He doesn't understand the power of names, I'm pretty sure. "Call me Del."

"Hey, Del, I'm awfully sorry about all that. About John, I

mean. He can be pretty abrasive when he's got his mind set on something."

"Not to mention greedy," I add, and feel guilty right off. "Sorry."

Ty tilts his head sideways and scrunches up his face. "Well, I don't know that a person ought to be sorry for speaking the truth. John is . . . ambitious."

"This is a big kingdom," I say. "The Gam Saan's even bigger. We could get used to sharing it, but he wants to grab everything and push us out. That's not good, Ty. This is our home. We stayed when everybody else left. We have lives here."

His brow wrinkles. "No, I don't suppose it is 'good,' at that."

"The Spirits don't like it," I say baldly.

He smiles, but it's a twitchy little thing, just a weak tugging of the corners of his mouth. "You really believe in your spirits, don't you?" His voice tries to sound pitying, and a little superior, but misses by about that much.

I give back a very direct look. "The Spirits are real, Ty. They speak to me."

Oh boy, I think, *now I sound like one of those old movie Indians.*

Ty glances at John Makepeace's winnebago, then sits against the platform under the satellite dish and opens his mouth.

"What's the dish for?" I ask, before he can say anything.

"Huh?" He jerks his eyes up to the thing. "The-the satellite dish? It, uh, talks to the other satellite dishes. What I mean is, I can talk to anybody else who's got one. It's, um, like, um—"

"It's a communication device," I supply. "Let's you phone home, huh?"

He looks surprised that the dumb transient "abo" would know something like that. "Yeah. Yeah, right."

While I give myself a mental kick for my cynicism, he says, "Can I ask you something?"

I nod. "Sure. Anything."

"We've heard all kinds of stories—legends, I guess you'd call them—about the lost cities."

"They aren't lost, Ty. They were abandoned."

Ty looks blank for a second. "Yeah, well. Anyway, there's a boatload of legends about these places—especially San Francisco. It's the quakes mostly. You learn about them in school and, well, I guess that's just a matter of geology, but they've got sort of a legendary quality to them. The World Series Quake especially."

I nod. "The Loma Prieta," I say. "A's and Giants."

He gives me that surprised look again, which is followed by a shifty glance around, like as if he doesn't want anybody to hear what he's going to say next. He leans towards me, his arms crossed over his chest.

"It's not just the quakes. There are other things too. Like Crips and Bloods."

"Like what?"

"You know, street gangs. Those women with guns . . . are those Crips and Bloods?"

"Those are knighties. They protect the realm. We got gangs here, but they mostly have tire irons and old baseball bats." I shrug. "Some knives. The Jade Dragon gang runs a food co-op over in Embar. I've never heard of Crips and Bloods, Ty. What do they do?"

"Well, the legends say they're like vampires or zombies or something—you know, undead, immortal, and invincible. They're involved in this eternal warfare, tearing the cities apart and sucking up innocent children. And Tongs," he adds, and I think there must be a whole truck full of legends in Ty's head. "There are stories about Chinese Tongs that own the city and run things behind the scenes. They sort of let the street gangs have their little wars because it suits them to keep the undead occupied."

I have to admire Ty's vivid imagination. "We got Tongs," I admit, "but they're not gangs. More like . . . community service organizations."

"No shit."

"No shit, Ty. They do all kinds of philanthropic stuff. Mostly keep the hospitals running, although they provide pre-schools, too, and organize the big market in the Sang Yee Gah."

Now Ty is ogling at me. "Hospitals? You got hospitals?"

"How else could we meet the medical needs of our community?" I ask.

He shakes his head. "Okay, how about the sewers?"

"Uh," I say. "They work, mostly."

"What about alligators? I've heard there are alligators in the sewers. Giant ones that feed on refuse. John says that's all bunkum, of course. I imagine he's right about that."

I think for a moment about saying that, of course, there are giant alligators in the sewers, in the church gardens and in the crypt under the church, but that kind of lie is pretty easy to debunkify.

"No alligators," I say.

"Nah. I didn't really think there would be. I suppose the dread diseases and plagues are all legends too, and the mutated animals and all."

Right about now, I'm staring at him like he's sprouted a horn between his eyeballs. Alligators, okay, that I can see. I mean, I read about how those kinds of stories got started in New York—urban legends, they're called—but mutated animals? Whoa.

"What kind of diseases?" I ask.

"Plague-type things, I guess. None of us were too sure about that, I think. We sort of expected we might find corpses in the streets. Even John. After the mass exodus out of here, well, we weren't sure what might have happened to the people that got left behind."

I reflect that the people who got left behind did just fine, thank you, and that the only corpses in the streets were the ones these guys put there. Ty seems like such a nice dude, I hate to remind myself that he was part of that. But I do.

"We have diseases," I say, nodding and looking muy thoughtful. "And plagues. Especially in the heat. Embarcadero is better about that than most of the kingdoms and Potrero is worse. They have awful sanitation problems here. I wouldn't drink the water."

"We noticed." His nose wrinkles. "We noticed how much cleaner it was over on your side of that trench." He pauses, looking at me real intent. "You have quite a culture over there, don't you?"

I nod, straight-faced, sober as can be. "Yes, Ty, we do."

He shakes his head and says nothing.

"Hey, Ty, fog's coming." This comes from one of the workmen bustling hither and yon.

Ty looks around. Indeed, the fog has come up since we started talking. It's a shabu, which I think is the Mission's pet variety of fog. I say as much.

"Shabu?" Ty repeats.

"Gauze. Usually, it's a shabu dong—Moving Gauze. But today it's just gauze."

Ty chuckles. "You got names for your fog?"

"Of course. When you got so much of something and it comes in so many different varieties, you gotta name it just so you can talk about it intelligently. There are thirty-four known varieties of fog in the Gam Saan. Some are quite localized. For example, you only see a real wu planchar dong on the Presidio. That's a truly heavy moving fog—oppressive."

"Uh-huh," he says, but seems distracted.

"What's the matter, Ty?" I entertain the idea that the fog is making him nervous, but that seems . . . well, silly. If these jakes are afraid of fog they couldn't have come to a worse place.

He confirms the silly. "Damn fog. Gives everybody jitters."

If I understand "jitters" right, he's just said fog makes 'em nervous. Well, you could knock me over with a pine cone. His eyes have the jitters too, glancing around between the winnebagos as if he expects giant alligators to pop out.

"Ty," I say patiently, "fog is a fact of life here. It's inescapable."

"It's not just the fog. It's this place . . . and the fog. And . . . and maybe something else."

Every hair on me stands up and says 'howdy.' "The Spirits," I say nodding and trying hard to look sage.

"Hell, no. Hallucinations is more like it."

I shrug and shake my head.

He scoots a little closer to me. "Sometimes, around dusk or at night or when the fog comes up like this, some of the guys . . . well, they've seen things. Little . . . somethings . . . slipping in and out of the fog and the dark, around the buildings. You wouldn't . . . you wouldn't know anything about that would you?"

"No, Ty, I wouldn't. Um, what sort of somethings . . . if you don't mind me asking?"

"Little, dark, darting figures."

"Like the shadows of big cats?" I ask.

He makes a funny noise. "I-I suppose so. Why?"

Ninjas! I'm thinking and try not to let my face do anything stupid. I wonder if Chen is scopin' out the aliens as a possible market for his—I mean our relics and magics. But back to the problem at hand: I contemplate going off about mutant animals, but say, "Doesn't sound like spirits. They're more foglike."

Ty laughs. It's shallow laughter that doesn't get all the way up to his eyes. "Yeah. Thanks, Del. Now, I think maybe you should get out of here. Things tend to clamp down a little more when the visibility's poor."

"I was wondering," I say, "if maybe you could let me go into the church. Just for a minute or two."

"To talk to your spirits?"

"Yeah. It's been a while, you know and, uh . . ."

He's shaking his head. "Sorry, Del. I'd like to, really, but John would have my head on a plate if I let you in there. You might disturb something."

I might disturb something? Yeah, right.

I leave, but not without looking back a whole bunch of times at the church and asking myself what Chen's ninjas want there. I don't much like the answer I'm imagining.

Out in the street, I take advantage of the shabu to disappear and double back. I feel this soul-deep need to talk to my Whisperers. The silence in my head is like hunger. I come back around to the place where, in another time, I entered the Dolores for the first time. There is a chain-link fence over the hole we used. Security system. Now I understand why Firescape's guerrilla attack failed. These guys got double-o-seven stuff. Which leads me to wonder how it is Chen's ninjas, who I am certain are causing the aliens' hallucinations, are getting in and out.

I twitch to investigate this, but I can't leave Doug alone out here. I hunker down beside him in the thickening shabu. His boughs wave and quiver. I don't wonder, considering what we just heard.

"I'm lost, O Tree," I say, rubbing his needles between my fingers. I inhale the perfume. "What I need is a miracle."

"What you need," says a voice from the shabu, "is a guide."

I jump about three feet in the air and come down facing a figure that is little more than a walking lump of fog. I recognize the voice, though. It's Lord E's strange, cocky new merlin. I glance at Doug, who has stopped waving and now seems merely watchful.

"And that'd be you?" I ask, trying not to choke on my heart.

"I know how you can get in," he says. "You interested?"

"Without setting off the alarms?"

"Yeah. Just like those little ninjas."

I prick up my ears. "You seen 'em?"

The fog bobs where his head must be. "Seen 'em go in and out, to and fro."

"I can't. I can't leave my Tree. And I sure as hell can't take him inside."

"I'll take care of him."

"Yeah, right." What's this guy think—I'm a born ditz?

He moves a step toward me, getting a little more solid. I hear the faint creak of leather. Not wearing his merlinly robes today, I guess.

"I mean it. I'll take care of him for you. Keep him safe and sound and get him back to you when you're done. Trust me."

"Why should I?"

"'Cause you need to go in there and you can't leave him alone. Because I'll swear, merlin to merlin. 'Cause I want what you want."

"Yeah? Which is?"

"To save the Gam Saan."

"You're Potreran."

"I'm from here," he says, pointing down at the ground under his feet. "Gam Saan."

"Why don't you go in there then?"

He laughs and the sound, muffled as it is, tickles my ears. "Because I don't got magic, Chickpea Del, and you do. I'll let you in on a little secret. I'm not really a merlin. Lord E only thinks I am."

"Why're you telling me this?" I ask, suspicious.

"So you'll know you can trust me. You got a secret on me, merlin. Here's another one to go with. Something I never told anybody." He hesitates. "Hector," he says.

"Hector?" I repeat.

"That's my name. My real and secret name. It's yours. You do what you want with it."

I suddenly realize that I'm smack in the middle of a MOMENT. Doug's boughs tickle my hand and I know without doubt that I can trust Lord E's not-merlin because for some reason unbeknownst to me, Doug trusts him. And because he has given me his name.

"Show me, Hector," I say, and he leads me to the place where the ninjas are getting into the Mission.

eighteenth: grave circumstances

 **THERE IS A VERY** tiny chink in the chain link fence, or rather in the ground beneath it, for the ninjas have dug a little hole to squeak through. It begins some yards away from the fence and goes under it and, I guess, comes up some yards from the fence on the inside.

"Trick is," says my guide, "you gotta not touch the fence. In fact, you gotta stay away from the fence altogether, so don't double back toward the perimeter, okay? Once you get inside, stay low—I mean flat on your belly low—until you've gone at least twenty feet toward the middle of the compound. You got that?"

"How do you know all this?" I ask.

"I'm just a curious guy, I guess."

Something I can't quite wrap my mind around pokes at me. "You'll be right here, when I come out?"

"Near here. I don't want the ninjas to see me. Halfway down the block toward 17th there's an alley. On the right. I'll be there. *We'll* be there."

I quiver inside as I prepare to go. "Remember," I tell him, "I know your name. And remember, Hector, that I am a powerful merlin."

He chuckles. "Tell me something I don't know."

I say good-bye to Doug, surprised all over again that he's being so calm about this, and prayerfully remove a six inch length of fir sprig. Then I tell myself I'm ready to go. I head for the broken earth, half-hidden by an ancient, twisted lilac.

As I prepare to descend into the hole, I am struck by a certain terrible thought. "If I don't come out," I say, "please take the Fabled Tree to Bags. He's the old man who—"

"I know," he tells me. "And you will come out. I got a feeling, ni dong?"

"Yeah? Your feelings any good?"

"Pretty good . . . for a non-merlin."

I accept that and dive under the bush. The hole is close and cold and damp. I hold the Doug sprig in my mouth so I can smell it. It's the only thing that keeps me from screaming as I scrape through the endless, black tube. Well, that and the smell of wet earth. It's one of my favorite smells and it calms me. I suspect I'm a closet claustrophobic. You can probably imagine my relief when I finally come out at the end of the line. The urge to yahoo is almost overwhelming. But I manage.

The Mission end of the tunnel comes up under a fallen statue that's over-hung by the limb of a big old cedar. I squeeze out from under and crawl with my belly flat to the ground for another twenty feet or so, then I go to my hands and knees through low shabu, until I just about collide with something. It turns out to be one of the alien winnebagos and its nose is pointing right where I want to go—the Mission graveyard.

Once my heart has ceased to hammer at my ribs, I roll underneath and begin moving forward till I am near the nose of the thing. That's when I realize there are voices coming from above me. One of them, I'm pretty sure, is John Makepeace's.

I'm not above a little eavesdropping. I am, in fact, beneath it, and therefore cannot help but fill my ears. Most of what I hear is about supplies and movements, although there is some talk about the ninjas and how nervous they make the fellow who is not John Makepeace. I think it must be Gino—his voice tends to get louder and louder when it seems John Makepeace is not taking him seriously, and right now John Makepeace is laughing.

That's when the conversation turns in a direction that makes my blood ice over.

"I think it's this damn boneyard we're sitting on. Just the thought of that mass grave makes me want to levitate. Jeez-us, John, we're walking on dead people. I don't know how you can be so sanguine about it."

"I'm not afraid of a few dead people," John Makepeace says, "but I can see that there are those who are. Now, now, Gino, I'm not ribbing you. I've been giving this some serious thought. And I've talked to a few of our backers about it. It's their considered opinion that tourists will not be excited by the knowledge that they are treading on the bones of someone's ancestors. In fact, indications are they'll find it quite disturbing."

"So, what are we supposed to do?"

"Lose the bones."

There is a moment of silence and I have the feeling that both Gino and I are scrambling to "get it."

Lose the bones? I think, and Gino says, "Lose the bones? What the hell does that mean—lose the bones?"

"Dig them up. Dump them in the Bay. The memorial plaques, too."

"And rewrite the history of the Mission?"

"Romance sells," says John Makepeace.

"You can't do that!"

For a moment, as I ride a sickening wave of absolute, heart-banging terror, I think I've spoken aloud, 'cause it's a safe bet Gino wouldn't have said that. But it isn't my voice, or Gino's. Someone else is in the winnebago—someone who's remained silent up until now.

"What do you mean—I can't do it? You see a problem?"

"A problem? John, that's sacred ground."

"Jesus Christ, Ty. What kind of superstitious gibberish is that? Of course, it's not sacred ground. What's gotten into you? Have you been fraternizing with that little wizard again?"

"John, they were people. You can't just dig them up and dump them like they were last week's garbage."

"They're four hundred-year-old bones, Ty. They haven't been people for centuries. Calm down. Think about this logically."

I can't think about this logically. And I gotta leave Ty to his own decision about whether he can. I'm outta there and on my way to the graveyard, packing a charge of adrenaline that just about turns me into a rocket. I gotta calm down, I know, 'cause when I'm like this, I'm deaf, dumb and blind, and I gotta find a grave.

It will be apart from the other Ohlone, I know, because it was made after the Americans took over this place.

In the shabu, I dare to bring out a tiny light—a foglite of deep yellow, which is the best color for seeing in a true wu. It looks almost like an ember in the deepening, darkening mist. I begin at the statue of the saint, which is the stand-out landmark in all the wildy green and broken stone.

Adrenaline aside, I wax philosophical as I look up toward the stony face. I can only see as far as his little stone-rope belt. The shabu has got hold of his head. Father Junipero Serra. I wonder how one guy's saint can be another guy's Satan. Somehow, the thought brings to mind John Makepeace.

I work my way from the so-called saint to the pile of rocks, and circumambulate, checking each gravestone. I hope he isn't in the crypt. If he's in the crypt, I could be in deep trouble, 'cause I never been there and I'm not even sure the aliens got it all dug out. And besides, the crypt is . . . well, it's underground. As I quiver in the dusky shabu with only my foglite and a sprig o' Doug for protection, I see (or almost see, or almost not see) a flash of more or less solid black at the gate of the graveyard—ninjas, scurrying to and fro, here and there. They are just like Ty said, little, dark, darting figures.

One of them pauses not so many feet away and I somehow know his (or her) eyes are turned on me—eye of the Eye, little watcher to the Big Watcher. I also know all he, she, or it can see is a faint amber pinprick of light quivering like mad in the shabu wu.

On a wild hare, I raise the light way up, then wave it around in swoopy, wiggly circles. The ninja vanishes. *Poof.*

Neon. I guess I make a good ghost. I go back to my task. It is completely and truly dark when I finally find what I'm looking for —a lone grave set apart under buckling flagstones. The grave of Pedro Alcantara.

First, I kneel on it, as if I were in a church, then I sit cross-legged as if I were in a temple. I clear my mind, but it seems there's as much fog in there as there is just lying around in general.

"I gotta talk to you," I whisper.

Nada happens.

"I need to warn you guys about John Makepeace. He wants to dump all you guys in the Bay 'cause the tourists won't like walking on you."

More nada. This is not good. Time to call in the heavy artillery. I get out my Doug talisman. I feel a tingle immediately. This is good. I clear my mind. I offer prayers. I incant. I plead. I intone (very quietly). But though the fog seems charged with electrical shivers, nothing real happens at all. It feels as if the place is about to sneeze. But it doesn't.

I don't know how long I hang there in the cold, tingly shabu when I decide nothing is going to happen. I don't understand this. For my whole adult life, the Dolores have talked to me, and now, when I really need them to talk to me, they're silent as a damn graveyard.

I give. I lay the little Doug sprig on Pedro's grave and try to orient myself in the fog. The moon has risen by now and is pouring its silvery self all over and into the shabu. Doug's sprig is a little dark slash on the white of Pedro Alcantara's grave.

Then, the shabu begins to misbehave. I rub my eyes. Really hard. 'Cause mist and moonlight don't usually do this. It's a little silver tornado at first, and then it's a million tiny little stars all swirling above Doug's little sprig, and then it's a man-shape made of a million tiny little stars, then it's a whole man, and he's looking at me like he's been watching me for a long time.

Finally, he speaks, and his voice is nothing like moonlight or mist. It's like the creaking of dry branches. It's the Voice I hear in my dreams, the Voice that belongs to the man of the smoky dream lodge.

"I know you," he tells me.

"I am Cicerone Del," I say and try not to let my voice wiggle, "merlin to Hismajesty, King of Embarcadero."

"I know you. You are the shaman. And you know me—we have spoken many times."

This is not really news to me by now. I get that Pedro is my main Whisperer. My spirit guide.

"You are much like my son," he informs me. "His name is Pedro, like me. Pedro Delmar Alcantara." His eyes stray to the hills which can't be seen because of the walls and the church and the city.

I can see his gravestone through him, and the rest of the grave-yard, a tumble of stones like broken teeth in the dark, overgrown earth, and the grotto of rocks that are his people's only memorial. He seems to notice this.

"He's not there, you know. He's not in their sacred ground. He ran away from here. They said they would find him, kill him, as they did others. But I never heard, so I think he got away from here. He would have gone to our sacred ground, to The Mountain."

"I hope he made it," I say sincerely.

He nods, still looking out at the invisible hills. "He did. Do you know the story? The story of how the Mountain got its name?"

My turn to nod. "The Spaniards met an Ohlone shaman when they climbed the mountain—"

He smiles. "They thought he was their Devil, that shaman. But they were wrong. They were our devil. I told him I was the last one. That I was alone."

I know he means the Indian agent the American government sent to see how many Ohlone the Spaniards and their bugs had left alive.

"I was wrong. We are still here. We are all still here, except the ones that fled to The Mountain." He looks right at me then, and I feel cold. "This demon," he says. "This demon would have us driven away. He would imprison the spirits of the Ohlone. He would turn our magics and spirits to his own purpose."

He is silent for a little bit and I wonder if he can see through me as easy as I can see through him.

"You must stop him, Cicerone Del, merlin. You must save the world from Wiwe."

Whoa. Suddenly I realize that Pedro and I aren't in the same book. He's talking real demons, and I'm just thinking your average, garden-variety human demons.

"You . . . you mean Chen?" I ask. "What about John Makepeace? He's gonna dig up your bones and dump them into the Bay. Doesn't this concern you just a little bit?"

"Makepeace is a man. The one who calls himself Chen wishes to be more than a man. He wishes to be Wiwe—beyond-man. He is a hungry soul. He devours magics hoping to spit them out again with power. He pulls at the spirits of things and seeks to own them."

I think of Chen's gallery of artifacts and the idea begins to dawn in my chickpea brain that I have seriously underestimated the competition. I've been thinking Chen is just a greedy materialist out to build up treasures here on earth. If Pedro's right, he's got a far more serious agenda.

"Makepeace is a threat to your homes and your families and your lives," Pedro tells me, as if he can see the thoughts ooze out of my head. "Wiwe is a threat to your souls. So, you must stop him. You must keep him from devouring all the magic and owning the spirits. It is through the spirits of things that he enslaves souls."

"W-what souls?" I ask this, but I think I already know the answer. I think I've seen them—priests and ninjas.

"Yes. You have seen them," Pedro tells me.

Ooga-booga.

Naturally, the next thing would be for me to ask how I might do anything about a Red Dragon who enslaves souls. But, also naturally, I'm a little loathe to ask this auspicious question. I think I already have half a clue, anyway.

"It's the shaman stuff, isn't it? That's what will help save the world from Wiwe."

Pedro says, "When the last great shaman of my people came to this place to stay, he converted to the ways of our captors and took up their religion. He laid aside his magics, powers, and vestments. A great show was made of this, Cicerone Del, merlin. The leaders among the tribes were brought to see how their priest, their holy man, bowed before the icons of the Spanish priests. The monks took from him his vestments, his symbols of power, and put them into a casket, and sealed them away beneath the altar in their sanctuary. This, so that all would see that our ways, our magics, were buried, and that the Christian magics had triumphed over them. It is these things that have kept us bound to this place. It is these things that Wiwe wishes to own."

"He has the headdress," I say. "But there's still a beaded shirt, a pipe and a-a—"

"Spirit rattle," Pedro says.

"Yeah, one of those. But if this stuff was all buried together, how come the ninjas only found the one thing?"

He shakes his starry head. "We do not know, our memories

say they are in the altar. Perhaps they are not. But they are still here, in your Gam Saan, or we would be gone."

"But you guys are spirits. Shouldn't you know this stuff?"

"It's been a long four hundred years."

Under any other circumstances, I'd think he was joking with me, but there's nothing very funny about any of this.

"We are our memories," he adds after a moment. "The world you live in is . . . mist and shadow to us."

The feeling is mutual. "What about Makepeace? He's planning to take over the place and chase us all out—including you."

"We can do nothing, Cicerone Del, merlin. The presence of Makepeace is disturbing to us, but it is Wiwe who stops our voices from speaking to you . . . to each other."

"I was wondering about that," I say. "How come you're speaking to me now?"

"Diablo," he says, and his hand drifts downward toward his feet, beneath which the Doug sprig lies upon the stone. "You have brought with you a token of the spirit of our sacred Mountain."

Doug? Well, this is a surprise. "But Doug was born on the Farm and grew up in a pot," I explain. "How can he be a token of the sacred Mountain?"

Pedro seems to shrug in a misty, foggy sort of way. "These things happen."

"Okay, so this ritual stuff—Chen needs the whole enchilada, right? And you want me to stop him, right?"

"You must find the shaman's tools before he does."

Sounds simple enough. I get a sudden clue. "Wait . . . you said the shaman stuff held you here, right? So, if I were to find it and take it to the sacred Mountain, you'd be able go there, right? And then . . . would it matter about the bones?"

He's silent for a moment and I know I've hit on something. But his next words aren't what I think I'm gonna hear at all.

"Burn them."

My mind does a neat somersault. "B-burn—?"

"The implements—you must burn them. Destroy them. Then, they will be forever safe from Wiwe."

"But-but, what'll that do to you guys?"

"I don't know."

This honesty is not comforting. "I can't do that. Not if you guys will . . ." I have a horrible image of 5,000 Ohlone spirits going *poof*! in a puff of holy smoke.

"My world is lost," he tells me. "If you would not lose your own, you must do as I say. John Makepeace is not your worst enemy, shaman. Nor is he ours."

I believe him. I do. But I can't help myself; the thought of saving our bacon while the Dolores are at the bottom of the Bay makes my stomach hurt.

"Find the magics and destroy them," he says again, as if he can read my thoughts. No surprise there. "If they remain in this City, all is at risk."

I got my mouth open to continue the argument, but suddenly there's no one to argue with. It's like he's been sucked up by a vacuum. I can't believe how close I come to shouting out loud. Fortunately, I realize I'm hearing the voices of live folks and don't do this. Instead, I hunker down low to the ground and zhou the hell out of there.

My first thought when I crawl out of the hole is Doug. I head right for the alley. The first thing I see when I turn the corner and squeeze past some crates is Doug sitting in his wagon in a spot of moonlight. This makes me realize the fog has lifted and thinned a lot. It's a wu gao huichen—high and billowy. It's as if the narrow alley has squeezed the frothy stuff up between its high walls. Ghostly puffs hang just over my head. The place is dead quiet except for the scuffle of small critters. I am immediately on my guard. In videos, this is where the music goes all creepy and you, the Watcher, are s'posed to be thinking, "It's a trap, you ditz! Don't go in there!" So, I am thinking this at myself, but since I am playing the role of the ditz, and as Doug does not seem alarmed, but only happy to see me, I do go in there.

Doug is downright chipper, considering, and I am wondering where the other merlin is, when I hear him somewhere above me along the wall.

"What's up with the Mission?" he asks and his voice echoes softly off everything.

I realize he is sitting up on a rusting fire escape almost behind me. Good thing it wasn't a trap, I guess. I turn and squint up at him, but all I can see is a pair of scuffed up boots at about eye level, and a dark, hunkered shape above that. This boy sure loves his sense-o-mystery.

"It's not good," I say, and am swallowed by sudden despair. "I heard John Makepeace saying he was going to dig up the Dolores and dump their bones into the Bay. The Dolores," I add, "are the Ohlone spirits that—"

"I know," he interrupts and shifts on the fire escape so it groans and clanks. The sounds bounce around dully under the blanket of gao huichen. "Why the hell'd this goony alien want to do shit like that?"

"Tourism. Survey says his folks won't want to walk on dead folks, and there's a regular carpet-o-corpses under that place."

"So, for that, he's gonna feed them to the whales?"

"Whales aren't carnivores," I point out, "or scavengers either, for that matter. I guess tourism is big on the outside."

Now the fire escape shrieks. "So, we got us a quest then, eh?"

This stops my brain in its tracks. We? So, now I got a sidekick? I sit myself down on the end of Doug's wagon and focus my eyes on the other merlin's boots.

"More to it than that. He don't want us to save the bones."

"He who?"

"Pedro. Pedro Alcantara. He's sort of the head Whisperer— a shaman . . . sort of. He says we got bigger problems than that."

Lord E's merlin makes a noise like a cat hocking up a fur ball. "And what might those be?"

"There's this old Chinese shaman guy—"

He moves further down the stairs, making them groan again. Now I can see his knees.

"Master Chen?"

Why, I wonder, does everybody else seem to know more than I do? I have this feeling that when I tell him about the weird shrine/art gallery and the religious artifacts, he'll just say, "So what?" Then it occurs to me to wonder why I'm telling him anything at all.

I glance at Doug, whose branches drape across my shoulder. He's comfy as a clam. I wriggle my butt down into the wagon and tell the other merlin everything I know about Chen.

He doesn't say, "So what?" when I stop talking. He says, "Shit," with much gusto. "And I thought he was just playin' at this shaman business."

My Alice bone twinges. "How d'you know about Chen, if I might ask?"

"He's been a visitor to the court of my lord," he says. The tone of his voice adds he doesn't think much of his lord. "Looking for objets d'arte, especially religious stuff. Lord E's had sméagols crawling through every church and temple in Potrero-Taraval along side those creepy ninjas. They came up with some stuff. I thought he was just a collector at first, then I got the drift that he was playing at being a wizard. My . . . sources say he's about trying to reinvent the Tong along the lines of the olden days. Wants to topple the current order—or lack thereof—and set himself up as Emperor." He pauses for a moment, then adds, "It was him put the bug in Lord E's brain about takin' the Wiz. I figure he was hoping our respective lords would take each other out or at least demolish each others' forces pretty good. Which didn't happen, thanks to you."

I am so staggered at this revelation, I can only woggle. I finally manage to fill my lungs with air. "Are you . . . are you sure?"

"Oh, yeah."

I am yet suspicious. "You said sources. What sources?"

He chuckles. "I got someone in the Tin Hau. A friend."

I accept this for the moment. "I thought he was looking to sell our sacred stuff off to Makepeace for his tourists until I talked to Pedro," I admit.

"So, what's the quest?" he asks.

"I gotta get the Ohlone sacred stuff and . . . Pedro wants me to burn it."

"Zhende? Really? And that's supposed to call off Chen? What about Makepeace? How does he get had?"

"He doesn't." Suddenly, I can't sit down; I leap to my feet. "Don't you get it? Makepeace isn't the Big Demon, Chen is. According to Pedro, this guy can get our souls, not just the place they live. Pedro says the magic stuff's gotta be burned."

"So . . . what, you wait till Chen gets 'em and burn down the Tin Hau?"

Now the very idea of burning down a House of Worship, even to save souls, tastes like bad kim chee, but with all that sacred stuff inside . . . "That . . . that'd be one way to do it."

"But it won't save the Gam Saan from Makepeace. And it won't save the Dolores, either, will it?"

I shake my head.

"This sucks, Del."

"This is not news," I say.

"Isn't there anything we can do about Makepeace?"

We again. Like we were Scully and Mulder, Sam and Dean Winchester, Dr. Who and the companion de jour. I am bewoggled by his willingness to fraternize with one-time enemies, but happy to have an ally. I wonder if something I been thinking might just be worth something. I start pacing around the wagon.

"I had an idea," I say. "But Pedro got real testy when I mentioned it."

"Give over," he says and the fire stair whines.

"Okay, it's like this: Diablo is their sacred Mountain—the Dolores', ni dong. It's where the shaman met the first Spaniards. It's where they're from, spiritually speaking, it's where the sacred things are from, too. If we can get the sacred stuff all together—or even some of it, I think—and get it to the Mountain, the Dolores' spirits will be able to go there too."

"You sure about this?"

"Pretty sure. Pedro said they were bound here because the shaman's things are here. So I figure, if they're on the Mountain, muy better, right, because then they got the power of the whole Mountain behind them, too. Then they'll be in control of their own magics, or maybe the Mountain will, and Chen won't be able to use them."

The fire stair honks like a goose. "Wo dong! I get it! All the sacred energy sort of . . . lines up—the Mountain, the shaman stuff, the Dolores . . ."

I am equally excited by this prospect. "Only they won't be Dolores any more. They'll be free."

"Still leaves us with Makepeace," he observes. "But two out of three ain't crap. What do we do?"

I am struck by two things, standing there in the dark, dirty, foggy alley. One is that there really is a We here, the other is that We haven't got a clue.

nineteenth: who are we and what are we doing?

 I **TRY** to calculate how long it will take me to hustle back to Embarcadero, round up reinforcements and get back to the Mission. Then, of course, I got to get everybody under the fence and into the church, et al, without raising the alarms.

"D'you s'pose the ninjas know where to look?" Hector the Ersatz Merlin asks.

I gotta figure they don't, of course, 'cause they have not been jawing with actual witnesses to the events of centuries ago and I have. This gives me hope We might have some time after all.

"I'm going for help," I decide.

I leave Doug with my new amigo, Hector, whose name I will certainly not forget and which I will most certainly abuse should anything happen to the Tree.

I am just to the Potrero side of the Trench when I sense I'm being scoped. I know I should just keep hustling (after all, we are engaged in détente, so I supposedly can come and go as I please without fear of Potreran ill will), but I stop and peer at the sneaky mist that's wandered into my back trail.

"Jeez-Louise, Chickpea! You are so not-street-savvy. How'd you manage to stay alive for so long?"

Lieutenant Cinderblock seems to rise up from the street. My wife rises up behind her.

"By looking as feckless as possible," I say, and Firescape asks, "Where the hell have you been? You got idea one what I been imagining?"

She is close to tears and I am immediately plunged into sticky, steamy guilt. I feel a sudden kinship with our crustacean population. A good quest should distract her from what she's been imagining, I imagine, so I drop one on her.

"I'm okay," I say, "but we got one big job to do. I talked to the Whisperers again, only this time face to very face . . . as it were."

Cinderblock and Firescape share a LOOK.

"I talked to Pedro. Pedro Alcantara. The shaman in my dreams."

Firescape's eyes say she is getting it. I explain further as we jog back to the alley where Hector waits (I sincerely hope) with Doug. By the time we reach the alley, I realize I would be more surprised to find no Hector and Doug than to find Hector and Doug.

My faith is not betrayed; Hector and Doug are just where I left them. I am most pleased with this, of course, but it occurs to me, when the General and the Lieutenant go all prickly on me, that I have neglected to fill them in on an important development. I do some quick filling in and they become less prickly, though my wife is suspicious when she hears that, once again, Hector is prepared to Tree-sit while the three of us return to the Mission.

"You really got no problem with this jake?" she asks me just before we dive under the lilac.

"So far, he's been an upstanding citizen," I reply. "And Doug is okay with him."

Again, the LOOK passes between Hismajesty's knighties. "You coulda told me that before I embarrassed myself," Firescape informs me. "I never, never, would have threatened to whack off his cojones and lob them into the nearest sewer if you'd given me a little advance notice."

"Ditto," says Cinderblock.

Talk ends here. We are quiet as any of the thirty-four known varieties of fog once we are inside the walls of the Mission. I see no ninjas; hear no ninjas; feel no ninjas. I am surprised, when we ooze into the church (with me Chouyan-ing like a house afire) that there are no ninjas here, either.

For a minute I'm afraid this means Something—like as in, we are too late and they've found what we're all looking for. But then Cinderblock, who's on point, signs me that they're scopin' the graveyard and the crypt.

I try to squash my apprehension and murmur a quick prayer that the rest of the treasure is still where Pedro's memory says it is. While the ninjas scurry around amongst the tombstones, we go straight for the altar.

It's darker than dark in here, and the air is close and cold and heavy. I get out the foglite. It helps a little. I have forgotten a few things about the altar. Like, for instance, that it is very big and made of very solid stone.

"How are we supposed to get inside?" Firescape signs and whispers.

This is a good question. It had not occurred to me that when the padres buried the shaman stuff under their altar, they meant it to stay there for all eternity, amen. I am about to become very depressed when I realize that the altar is not quite all very solid stone. There is a front piece on it made of three bronze panels held together by a bronze frame.

"That solid, too?" asks Cinderblock, then answers her own question by thumping the middle panel with the butt of her AK. It makes a satisfyingly unsolid clank.

Neon, I think, when my heart stops pounding in fear that ninjas will soon be all over us. I hunker down in front of the panels and start poking. When that does squiddle, I try prodding. Ditto. I try pulling, and get a wiggle and an itsy-bitsy groan of

protest from the bronze frame. Before I can ask, Firescape and
Cinderblock are down on their knees, knives out, prying at the
panels.

I don't have a knife 'cause a merlin's only weapon is his magic
—that's part of the code of merlinly ethics. So the only useful
thing I can do is pray. I decide a Remover of Difficulties will be
most effective.

It is, but not in any predictable way, which is often the case
with prayer—one of the Almighty's more playful aspects. Before
the prayer has quite slipped off my whispering lips, a presence
makes itself known.

"Howdy," it whispers. "Need help?"

"Jeez-Louise, merlin," fires back Cinderblock, twitching in
the dark. "You got a death-wish, or what?"

She ignores the fact that if Hector'd been an enemy, he'd've
had the drop on her.

I do not ignore the fact that if Hector is here, Doug must be
somewhere else.

"What have you done with the Tree, Hector?" I ask, my heart
pumping something cold into my veins. I hold his real and secret
name as if between two fingers, ready to give a good pinch.

"Relax, Del," murmurs Hector, with some mirth in his
murmur. "The inestimable Tree is with your good friend, Creepy
Lou. Caught him pokin' around the lilac bush. Figured you
wouldn't want the alarms going off, so I thought I'd give him
something useful to do. What's holding things up?"

I let go of his name and gesture with the foglite at the altar so
he can see what's holding things up. He leans into the light a bit,
his face shadowed by his cowl and a lot of hair that pitches over
his eyes. I can just see that he has one of those pointy beards like
the Three Musketeers wore. Jeez, talk about affectations. Makes
his face look saturnine, which I think means like the god Saturn.
Never seen him. Musketeers will have to do as a reference point.

The Musketeer pokes his fingernail under the edge of a panel.
"Huh. You tried prying this up?"

"Yeah. Just about broke my knife blade," says Firescape.

"Too hard for a knife blade." Hector pulls a screwdriver out of somewhere and wedges it in under a corner of the panel.

It takes a while of wiggling and prying and yanking, but at long last, one screwdriver, two knives and twenty fingers (counting thumbs) make the panel come loose with a sharp metallic *ka-chunk*!

Cinderblock, who has gone to guard our flank, hisses and jerks in the darkness. Above, pigeons flap crap onto us. I push the little foglite inside the hole we have left in the side of the altar and follow it up with my head. I don't know what I expect to see, but it is not what I do see which is absolutely nothing.

I pull my head out of the altar in a hurry, 'cause the air is pretty rarified in there.

"There's nothing in there," I whisper.

It seems no one believes me. One by one, they grab the light and poke their heads into the hole. Then we sit back in silence looking at it, until Lord E's Musketeer-merlin says, "Huh. 1907."

"1907, what?" asks Firescape.

"This altar was put here in 1907."

He is rubbing a finger over something on the front of the bronze panel we have removed. I hold the foglite to it. The number 1907 leaps out.

This is not the original altar. Duh.

"The year after the Great Earthquake," I note. "The first one, that is. "The first altar must have been damaged. And replaced." More to the point.

"So, where's the magical stuff?" asks Firescape.

"I don't know," I say.

"Does Master Chen?" asks Hector, effectively stopping my heart for a second.

"He couldn't. I mean, if he does, the ninjas wouldn't still be here, would they?" It hits me right away that the fact that there are now ninjas in the crypt only means that they haven't found all the stuff.

I suddenly got this intense itch to know if Chen has picked up any more of the shamanly stuff in the time I been knocking around Whisperville. I have a wild woolly what-if: There's a Doug sprig in Chen's gallery and a Doug sprig here; what if I can just fly into Chen's secret shrine on the wings of smell?

"I gotta do something you're probably gonna think is kind of creepy and weird," I say.

"Weirder than normal?" asks my wife.

I ignore this. "I got sort of a channel to Chen's gallery. I think I can use it to find out if he's got any more of the shaman stuff. But I think I gotta go into a trance or something like that, so you're gonna have to watch out for me."

Surprise: I do not hear a whispered chorus of "Are you loco?" And by foglite, I see only Very Serious Expressions.

"What do we do?" asks Hector.

I pull open my amulet bag and take out the Doug sprig. "Just keep an eye out for ninjas."

"He's going to have a nose vision," says Firescape solemnly. "We gotta not distract him."

I sit monk-like before the altar and close my eyes, holding the Doug sprig up in front of my nose. I dig a fingernail into a needle and inhale the perfume. I can still smell the musty stillness of the church and the chemical smell of the cleaning stuff the aliens have been using in here, but that fades. I break a second needle and try to make my mind as empty as this broken sanctuary. Well, as empty as it would be if you took out the pigeons and the people. I think about the Tin Hau—about Chen's gallery. I think about the little coniferous spy I left there. I think of smoke and I think like smoke and I feel the place around me change.

The cold of the sanctuary seeps away and I am wrapped in scented warmth. I can see the wobbly light of flames and hear them lick the air. I break a third needle, squeezing more fir scent out of my talisman. Everything focuses. I am looking across Chen's gallery from the big altar at the end of the room. I'm up in the air and my memory tells me I got the din's-eye view of the place. I imagine myself turning my eyes to sweep the little stands where the artifacts are kept. There is the menorah, the Buddha in His lotus, the golden bowl, the cup of fire.

The head-dress sits, alone, on its stand. I heave a huge sigh of relief and thank God aloud.

"Ah, there you are," says the Red Dragon Voice, and the light in the vision is overcome by shadow. "I see you peering at me from this tiny form. Clever. It would be a shame to waste such cleverness."

Just like that, I am airborne. My stomach does flip-flops and the room spins. When it stops spinning, I see all the riches of Chen's shrine laid out before me. I am agog.

The Red Dragon speaks again: "This room is filled with the magic of ages. Each object in it is a doorway to power. Combined, they form a gateway broad, terrible, and infinite. Would you not like to step through this gateway, little wizard? Aid me in putting an end to the reign of these petty tyrants who divide the Gam Saan and impose hardship upon its people—my people. Do this, and in return I will open the gate to you. Though you show some little promise, you are a puny wizard. An insect. I could teach you to be a shaman of the highest order. Among these monks I have found none who are worthy of my tutelage. Are you worthy, merlin?"

The room spins again. I swear I'm gonna heave. Then I'm back on the grate on top of the din.

"Should you wonder what will become of you if you do not accept my instruction, allow me to illustrate."

A ball of fire flies at me out of nowhere and *poof!* I'm a bar-b-cue. I shriek, naturally, and a petite iron hand clamps over my mouth.

"What the hell was that?" The voice is urgently dulcet. It is my own sweet Jade. "You want ninjas all over us?" she demands.

"No," I pant, sweating cold and hot and cold again. The flames are gone, along with the scented shrine and its nasty master.

"What happened?"

I decide I won't tell her about Chen or the bar-b-cue. Hell, I'm not even sure that was real, although I hate to think my imagination would come up with something like that all on its own.

"He's only got the head-dress," I say. "We're still in business."

"Okay," says Hector. "We got half a chance."

"Better than half," I say. "We got the Wiz."

We remove ourselves to the Wiz with all the energy of the living dead as filmed in black and white by George Romero. All except for Creepy Lou and Hector, that is. They've had a reasonably easy time of it, after all; haven't been on 24-hour duty like our noble knighties; haven't done a whole lot of crawling or scrambling or having visions or anything. They tend to get ahead of us a lot, then have to wait for us to catch up, Hector just looking too cool for words and Lou bobbing around like he's on a spring.

It occurs to me as I am dragging my little red wagon down Mission Street that Lord E's ersatz merlin sure knows his way around Embarcadero awfully well for a Potrero. Reason dictates this is probably because he rose from the ranks of Lubejob's sméagols. Although, I ponder, perhaps old Hector is a defector, who is now undefecting. I already know he thinks squat about his Lord and Master.

As we shamble up Columbus, I draw up within yakking distance of him. "Hey, merlin," I say. "You don't like Lord E much, do you?"

"Oh," he says, "I'm an amiable sort of dude. I like just about everybody."

I decide to come right out and ask the Big Q. "Are you defecting?"

I guess the Big Q strikes him funny and upside-the-head all at once, 'cause he uncorks this high-pitched whinny. Creepy Lou, walking to his other side, snorts and chortles for no particular reason, except that laughter is contagious.

"From what?" Hector asks.

"From Potrero-Taraval and its Alcalde."

"I told you, Chickpea, I'm from the Gam Saan. I don't see the need to boundrify it. I kinda thought we were of a mind about that."

"We are," I say. "But in case you hadn't noticed, we aren't kings or alcaldes."

"No, we're merlins, which is better right? The power beside the throne."

"I thought it was the power behind the throne."

"Hell, no," says Hector. "I ain't standin' behind anything."

He's in a rare mood. Makes me tired just watching him stride along beside me, his hiked-up monks robes flapping in the fog. I slow down again and let him get on up ahead.

When we arrive at the Wiz, the acolytes and Keepers are none too pleased to see us (after hours is when they get to do their own research, ni dong). But seeing as how I'm their merlin, and in close company with a General, her Lieutenant, and the Tree, there's not much they can do but let us in.

I lead us directly to the Fiche. All except for Lou, who pops off to the video room to watch Dr. Who. I think he likes to imagine himself as a time traveler's companion, or maybe even as the Time Traveler, himself. Considering what we been up to lately —400-year-old ghosts and all—he's gotta be thinking truth is stranger than fiction, if he even makes the connection.

I glance at the Fabled Tree as we enter the Shrine. Tree as TARDIS—an interesting idea. Trees live for centuries, after all, and it's just possible, I s'pose, that one of Doug's relatives was a native of Mount Diablo. In fact, Pedro more or less said that the Tree was a—how'd he put it?—a token of the sacred Mountain. I s'pose that makes him a time machine of sorts.

Anyway, I am not at all certain the Venerable Fiche has access to the kind of information I need, but you never know. I ask her about city records first. She has those, she informs me, and asks me to specify. If you hadn't guessed, "specify" is Fiche's favorite word.

"Mission Dolores' records," I specify.

"Specify year or range of years."

"1907 to 1914."

Fiche ponders this, then requests I specify a subject.

My turn to ponder.

"Earthquake damage to the church," suggests Hector.

More pondering. "The church sustained some damage from the 1906 earthquake, most specifically to the roof, bell tower, and altar."

"The altar!" I say quickly, lest Fiche ramble off on one of her long expositions. "Details about the altar."

"The altar of the Mission church was replaced after it received damage in the earthquake of 1906 as the result of falling eaves."

Not her usual, chatty self, Fiche seems to think this is sufficient.

"What about the Indian stuff?" asks Firescape.

"Specify Indian stuff."

"Ohlone artifacts," says Hector over my shoulder. "Ohlone artifacts related to shamanry or shamanism."

"Searching database for 'Mission Dolores' and 'Ohlone artifacts,' and 'shamanry' or 'shamanism,'" says Fiche, and proceeds to ponder briefly. "Two finds," she says. "First find, dated 1829. A Tuibun shaman named Paguin converted to Catholicism at the Mission Dolores in that year. His ritual implements were ceremonially removed at his baptism, whereon he received the Hispanic name Diego. These artifacts were interred in the altar of the church at that time as a symbolic surrender of the old ways to the new."

Fiche displays a picture of an Ohlone man. He is wearing a loin cloth and a shirt that is really more of a vest. On his head is a feathered, beaded head-dress; in one hand is a rattle. There's a bag of something hanging around his neck. Some sort of amulet bag, most likely, just like the one I keep stuff in.

"Cite references?" Fiche asks.

"No," I say. "Next find, please."

"Year: 1907. A casket containing Ohlone artifacts was found within the altar of the Mission Dolores when it was dismantled following earthquake damage. The artifacts were not replaced when the altar was renovated."

"Where did the artifacts go?" I ask, dry-mouth.

"They were removed from the altar," says Fiche, as if this were not perfectly obvious.

"Sheesh," says Hector. "Removed to friggin' where?"

"The artifacts in question were handed over to a local historical society called Friends of San Francisco."

The lady knights make rude noises and Hector sighs. "And then what?" he asks. "Did they end up in a museum or what?"

The Fiche is momentarily speechless. "I have no further records pertaining to the artifacts in question," she says at last. "I do not have access to the records of the Friends of San Francisco. I can cite references to relevant books and periodicals, if you care to examine the written record."

Which would take forever. "Thanks," I say and realize I am sitting down and do not recall having done so. It just seems to have happened.

I feel Firescape's hand on my shoulder. "Del," she says, "I gotta sleep. You gotta sleep. Hell, I bet even Doug gotta sleep. Come on home."

She looks ready to drop. So does Lieutenant Cinderblock.

"You go on," I say. "I'll come in a bit. I gotta think what's next."

"Maybe," she tells me, "maybe there is no what's next."

I shake my head, knowing I can't accept this and knowing that she can't either, really, she's just that worn down.

"Pedro wouldn't have brought me this far for nothing. Those

things are somewhere in the Gam Saan and not presently in the hands of Chen. I gotta find them."

Her brows all knit up and I think she's gonna unload on me bigtime, but she doesn't. She squeezes my shoulder and smiles into my eyes in that way that makes them tear up and says, "Let me get about four hours and I'll be ready to go again."

"Okay," I say, and she kisses me—one of those long, soft kisses that I find very . . . stirring. Then she hauls herself and Cinderblock out of there and back to the Palace.

"Neon," says Hector.

I nod, knowing he means my Jade is absolutely hao, but I am looking at the Fiche's display which still shows the shaman and his artifacts (sans pipe) as they may or may not have looked in real life. I am drawing one big blank. Should I cast the runes, I wonder? Should I go back and try to talk to Pedro again? I glance at Doug. His boughs are waving thoughtfully up and down, back and forth. Where would an historical society put historical stuff?

Beats me. The regular museums got cleaned out before the Getting Out, meaning they could not have been in a regular museum.

"Well," asks Hector. "What're we waiting for?"

"What do you mean?" I ask, all glum.

"Jeez, Chickpea Brain—what do you think? You heard the Fiche—there's a written record."

"Yeah, in books. You got any idea how many books there are here about Ohlone Indians and stuff?"

"No," he says, "but that thing does." I turn to look at him. He is smiling through his face fur and pointing at the Fiche. Light from the reading lamps gleam off a pair of shades he's pulled on and I wonder why the hell he's wearing the damn things indoors at night. Hector is muy bizarre.

He's right, of course. The Fiche has an Index of all the books on every subject. In short order, we got all the seventy some odd books on local historical societies and the thirty some odd books on the local native groups and are checking them out for pertinent refs.

We are down to our last ten books when Creepy Lou puts in an appearance. He doesn't read, but he watches us do it for a while before he asks, "Watcha doin?"

"Trying to find something," I say.

"Find what?"

"Some Ohlone stuff."

"Like as in Doloreth?"

"Yeah. Like that. We gotta find it before Chen does."

"Bu hao," says Creepy Lou. "Is thith like a quest?"

"Yeah, that's right—a quest," says Hector.

"Whath the stuff?"

"Shaman stuff," I say, peering at a fuzzy black and white picture of a group of Ohlone in front of a house made of tree branches and mud. "Magical stuff."

"Ceremonial implements," adds Hector, like this is gonna mean squiddle to Lou. "That's—"

Lou is nodding eagerly. "Like Chickpea'th rune can, right?"

"Yeah, okay. Only in this case, it's a rattle and a pipe and some other stuff." Hector waves a hand at Fiche's display, never looking up from the National Geographic he's squinting into. Doug, who is sitting next to him, waves a bough at Lou.

"Oh, yeah. That stuff," says Lou, returning Doug's wave. "Why d'you want it?"

"'Cause I think it can save the Dolores and us from Chen," I say, "and John Makepeace. Well, that is, we can save the Dolores from both, and us from Chen. I don't know if anything can save us from John."

"So, why all the bookth?"

"I told you," I say, kind of wishing my dear bud would go back to wherever it is he goes when he's not dogging my tracks. "We're trying to find references to the shaman stuff."

Hector shakes his head and Doug waves at Lou again—trying to get him to zhou off, most likely.

"T'find out what it does?"

"We know what it does," says Hector. "We need to figure out where it is."

"Oh, I know that," Lou says.

My heart flutters. Hector and I both look at him at once. Then we look at each other. I see myself reflected in Hector's shades.

"Where?" I ask.

"In that creepy place on the wharf with all the frozen people."

Hector's mouth disappears into his beard. Oh boy.

"The frozen people," I repeat.

Lou nods. "Creepy," he says.

I nod back and open another book.

Lou is staring at me and twitching a little. "Well?" he says.

"Huh?" says Hector.

"Don't you wanna go there?"

How to put this kindly? "I don't think that stuff is this stuff."

"Yeah, it is." Lou's left arm does a wild salute and his head jerks back. "It *is*," he repeats and stomps his foot for emphasis.

Doug's boughs flutter and bounce.

"Lou," I say, "this is real serious. I don't think these Ohlone artifacts are gonna turn up where there are . . . frozen people." Whatever the hell that means.

"But they're frozen Doloreth, Del," explains Lou plaintively.

Weird as this is, he has my attention. I mean, Lou's crazy and all, but he's not usually delusional.

"How—frozen?"

"You know, like statueth—like Tin Hau or-or Thousand League Eyes."

"Gods?"

"No, people. But they're not made outta statue thtuff. They're made outta somethin' softer. They're real-like. They got real hair and eyeballth and . . ." He pauses to scratch around in his scraggy hair. "Their eyes kinda follow you all over . . . creepy. The

Doloreth one looks a lot like that guy." He jigs his head toward Fiche's display.

I put down the book I'm holding and stand up. "And this Dolores one has the shaman stuff?"

"No," Lou says and my heart dips a little. "The padre has some of it."

Now, Hector is on his feet too. "Is this dude for real?" he asks me.

I barely hear him. "Show us," I tell Lou.

The place is on the Wharf, or nearly so. The building looks almost like a funky old movie theatre with one of those ticket booths in front. The glass is pretty much shot—literally. "Wax Museum" is written across the front in fading letters about as tall as my forearm.

Inside, the place is a lot like the back hallways of the Mission —or the crypt, my brain tells me. Which is to say, it is dark, damp, dusty and generally unpleasant in a very claustrophobic sort of way. On top of all that, it smells funny—like a cave, but oily. Ooga-booga, in my book. And on top of all that, are the frozen people. Wax dummies or statues or whatever of just about anything you could imagine. They are posed in little groups behind moldy velvet rope, doing things of historical import.

Turning on the sputtering lights doesn't help much in my humble estimation. They flicker and fade almost to off in cycles and make Lou's frozen people look like they're not so frozen. This is especially creepy as some of them are missing important body parts—like heads and arms and such.

There is a headless Abe Lincoln giving a silent address, his top hat sitting right down on his shoulders. There is a wax Babe Ruth getting ready to swing at a pitch from an armless pitcher. His bat has a spare hand on the end of it in which is the baseball. The Babe looks mighty perplexed. Further along, in a painted Western saloon around the corner, a one-armed John Wayne with a patch over one glass eyeball is dressed like a cowboy, but is also wearing an army helmet and war medals. Not too far away, leaning crazy-angle against a jeep carcass, is another Duke, who's got on the rest of the army uni along with a sheriff's badge. He is wearing the cowboy hat, which has a stuffed prairie dog perched in the crown.

Somebody—and I gotta suspect it's Lou—has been having a rare old time with these guys.

Everywhere I look there are cobwebs, thick and gauzy. They float in the little puffs of breeze that ooze in from every which where. Creepy Lou is right about all those glass eyeballs—it feels like they're glued to my back. Even Doug seems to be weirded out by it. His branches flutter and flap so much I can hear the whispering of the needles above the beating of my own heart. The deeper we get into the twisty hallways, the more my skin tries to crawl off my bones. It doesn't help that Doug's wagon decides to take this time to beg for oiling.

I want to zhou the hell out of here, let me tell you, but I realize we are getting to the part Creepy Lou wants us to see, 'cause I am suddenly surrounded by the evidences of Mission life. Most especially, I seem to be surrounded by padres. I see a handless one offering benediction to a group of Ohlone children, another inspecting the catch of shapeless fish being held out by a couple of braves, while two more watch over industrious Ohlone women at crude looms.

Then I see what is supposed to be the Mission Dolores Church. There is a wedding taking place in one corner—the bride's head is tucked under her arm, the groom has exchanged heads with the priest. A muy peculiar image.

Then I see what Creepy Lou has brought us here to see: In an alcove lit by a single old lamp that dangles by its cord, swaying, spooky, in the breezes, is the main altar of the Mission Dolores. Shadows creepy-crawl over the figures gathered beneath a painted mural of the wall-o-saints. There are a pack of padres and natives, too, but in the middle of it all are a priest and single Ohlone man.

The priest is holding his hands out to the Ohlone; a cross is in one, the other is empty, though it looks as if something might've been there once. The arms of the Ohlone are crossed over his chest. When I get close, I can see that they are not empty. When I am standing face to face with the Ohlone, who I know must be the Tuibun shaman, Paguin, I can see clearly what the padre is demanding of him. A beaded piece of cloth is folded against his chest and a clay pipe is clutched in his fist.

I look into his glass eyes. They are defiant—or at least, I imagine they are. Paguin doesn't want to give up the shaman's shirt or the clay pipe. And maybe, in his heart of hearts, he never does give them up. Maybe he just makes room next to them in his heart of hearts for the cross the monk holds.

This Paguin has been holding onto his magics for more years than I been in business. I gotta figure out how to get him to give them up to us. As it turns out, there is no gentle or dignified way to do this. We must bend and break the shaman's arms and hands, which is terrible, though I keep reminding myself he is not Paguin, but only a wax figure of Paguin. The spirit of the Tuibun shaman is not in him, but somewhere else, presently waiting for some ditzy Embarcaderan merlin to set him free. Still, I murmur prayers under my breath the whole time we are breaking the wax man apart.

The shirt isn't so much a shirt as it is a vest, like in the photo-display Fiche showed us. The fabric is damp and gritty and smells of mildew, but it's all there. The pipe has an accidental hole in it, but it looks pretty good otherwise. My hands shake with relief when I finally hold these things. Now, I wonder how I can protect them from Master Chen.

"I thought you said the padre had some of the stuff," says Hector to Creepy Lou, while I am considering this.

"Uh-huh," says Lou. "The watchamacallit."

"Rattle," says Hector. "So, where is it now?"

When I catch the significance of this question, my breath gets stuck halfway out of my lungs and I choke on it. I been so buzzed just to see this stuff, I have forgotten the spirit rattle. I jerk my head up to the padre's empty left hand.

"Oh that," says Lou. "It's in my cozy. Kinda decorative, ni dong."

Decorative. I unclog my lungs and let loose a sigh of relief. "Let's get the rattle," I say and Lou pops up like Jack B. Nimble, pulls his wrinkled old hat out of a pocket, crams it on his head and leads us out of the creep-fest.

Lou's cozy, it turns out, is up a flight of very windy stairs from the creep-fest. There is no way in God's Golden Mountain I'm gonna lug the Fabled Tree up that staircase. Once again, Hector comes through, volunteering to stay downstairs with the Tree while I go upstairs with Creepy Lou.

At the bottom of the windy steps, his foot on the bottommost tread, Lou pauses and scratches around under his hat. "Huh," he says apropos to nothing and then goes on up.

The cozy is a clutter of stuff, kind of like I imagine the inside of Creepy Lou's head. I see Abe Lincoln's noggin. It is home to a collection of dried flowers and bird feathers. It looks right at home next to the head of a Spanish padre, who has a pirate's bandana tied over his tonsure like an old lady's babushka. Both are propped up on an old dresser with a shattered mirror. It doesn't quite cover one of two windows in the cozy. A cold breeze whistles through the gaps around the edges of the mirror.

I see all sorts of other stuff Lou has brought up from the Wax Museum, too. What I don't see is the spirit rattle.

At almost the precise moment I open my mouth to comment on this fact, I hear a clatter and a scrape and a bump from somewhere, and Creepy Lou says, "Uh-oh," and leaps to the uncovered window in this jumbly place. It's not much of a window—all frame and no glass to speak of—and he sticks his head out and then just as quick, pulls it back in.

"What?" I ask, suspecting I will not like the answer much.

Lou gives me this hang-dog look and points at the window, out of which I stick my own head. This is what I see: An old dude with long, scraggy hair is crab-crawling down over the rooftop below Lou's cozy. His crab-crawl is especially sloppy 'cause of the hairy gourd-on-a-stick he's got clutched in one grubby claw.

Squint.

As he reaches the edge of the roof, he cocks his squinty little eyeballs back over his shoulder and grins and shakes the rattle at me. That grin got one message for me (and possibly for th' Alcaldes new merlin, Hector) which is that revenge is sweet.

I pull my head back in the window. "He'll head for Lord E," I tell Lou. "We gotta zhou."

We start by zhouing downstairs to rendezvous with Hector. I fill him in while I make up my mind about how to protect the magical stuff while I'm busy chasing Squint. I pull off my shirt, put on the shaman's vest and put my shirt back on top. I tuck the pipe into my belt.

Then I point at Lou, who jumps and just about salutes me. "You get my wife and have her scramble her best knighties to Potrero with eyes out for Squint. You tell her what happened here, you got that?"

Lou is nodding like crazy as I bend down and prayerfully remove from Doug a branch like a three-fingered hand. I stroke his nodding top boughs, 'cause I don't know when I'll see him again.

"Take the Tree with you," I tell Lou.

"Got it! Got it!" he says, grabs the tongue of Doug's wagon and zhous most prodigiously. The wagon squeals in protest.

Last I see of Doug, he is waving all his branches at me.

I tuck the three-fingered branchlet into my amulet bag and am out on the street. Hector is right behind me, and together, we are, I hope, right behind Squint.

twentieth: will the real demons please stand up?

 EVEN AT FULL-TILT GALLOP, we cannot seem to gain on Squint. Block after block, I see his coat-tails flapping at me from just around a corner. I am about to wonder if he's in really great shape for an old wheeze, or if he's got some truly serious magic, after all, when he scoots across an intersection three blocks ahead of us under full, if flickering, lamp light.

"Aw jeez," says Hector, eloquently, and I stop dead in my insignificant tracks.

Squint is riding one of those big ten-speed tricycles the Wharfside knighties sometimes use on patrol, and he is pedaling like crazy.

"That sucks," Hector sums up, panting. "You got any wheels around here?"

"There's the Royal Mercedes, but that's at the Presidio with the Majesties. Besides, I don't know how to drive it."

"What do you know how to drive?"

"A Vespa," I say. "The knighties use them as emergency vehicles."

"I'd say this qualifies as an emergency, wouldn't you?"

I would. We head over to the Wharfside Squad House. It does not take much splanifying to shake loose a couple of the little electric scooters. Within minutes, Hector and I are mounted up and purring down the road to the Border. I am fuming, because I got not idea one how far ahead our squinty avenger has fled.

As we cross the new bridge over the Trench on Guerrero, I pray to see Squint, though I do not expect to see him. But when we are half a block from the Mission Dolores, heading into a trailing bufandong, I do see him, and he is no longer pedaling away from us. Instead, he is pedaling toward us and he is hollering bloody mayhem.

"What the hell?" asks Hector.

We stop our scooters, blocking the street as much as possible. Squint, seeing us, does not flee in the opposite direction, as I expect, or even try to blow by us. He hollers all the louder and skids to a stop, with the result that his trike heels over and dumps his ass on the broken pavement. He rolls halfway to his feet and scrambles toward us, still hollering.

Finally I catch some words: "Banshees and woggles!" he's wailing. "Ghoulies and ghosties! Save me! Save me!"

"What's with that?" asks Hector.

In the next second or so, we find out, 'cause all of a sudden Guerrero is full of ninjas.

"Aagh! Demons!" shrieks Squint.

An understandable mistake. These guys are black on black; their faces are covered up to the eyes, and their eyes—I jink you not—are glowing a sick shade of green. The effect of this in this grimy, foggy darkness is truly awesome.

"Jeez!" says Hector.

My thoughts, exact.

The ninjas don't introduce themselves. They just head for poor old Squint, leading me to the obvious conclusion that they know he has the rattle. Accordingly, I leap from my Vespa and catch Squint by the lapels of his ratty old reefer coat. There is a brawl the like of which I have seen only in old baseball videos. I have never been in one of these brawls, naturally, so I do not know the protocol. I quickly decide to let Hector fend for himself. I wrap my arms firmly around Squint, making like an octopus on an oyster. I am kicked, chopped and pried at, but I do not give in. I incant octopus spells, thinking only of my oyster's hairy pearl, which I can feel digging into my chest.

My eyes are closed, so I do not see what causes the sudden stoppage of the aforementioned violence to my person, but I hear it. There is the rattle and hum of Vespas, first of all, and their little engines make this weird 3-D whine, bouncing off every brick, cobble and concrete slab within 50 yards. Then I hear the engines cut out and the shouts of knighties and the patter of hi-tops on asphalt.

I crack open my eyes. The ninjas are suddenly otherwise engaged. That is, except for two that seem to have been left behind with instructions to try to drag me and my oyster into an alley. I resist and incant, throwing out as deft a Chouyan as I have ever incanted. The ninjas loosen their grip and utter Chinese swear words and then I hear Hector's voice shout, "Hey, you guys! Over here!" And they are gone.

I am alone with Squint in a grove of Vespas. I tug at his coat. It rattles.

"Uh-uh," he says, clutching it closed over his chest. "Mine."

"Not yours," I say. "This belongs to the Dolores."

"Who the hell's that?" He yanks on the coat, but I am still in squid mode; this oyster's goin' nowhere if I can help it.

I give him the hairiest eyeball of which I am capable. "The Haunts of the Mission Dolores," I tell him. "You heard of 'em, I'm sure. The disembodied spirits of five thousand dead Ohlone Indians. This—" I shake the coat, making it rattle. "—belongs to them, and they want it back . . . Wilbur." I produce his name (given to me by a certain faux merlin) with a flourish.

His eyes are big as horse chestnuts and I feel his grip on the coat start to slip.

"You know my real and secret name!"

"And I'm not afraid to use it. By the way, what I know, the Dolores know." (Could be true and therefore, not technically a lie, but merely wishful thinking.)

"Now, now, children. No need to fight over this old relic. The Ohlone no longer need it. It belongs, by divine right, to me."

I know, before it oozes all the way out, who the Voice belongs to. This is himself, the Red Dragon, in the flesh, as they say. I turn and find him standing so near, I almost back up a step. I don't though, 'cause that would be a severe breach of merlinly protocol and would give him the psychological advantage.

He is wearing plum colored robes, long and priestly, and a strange tall hat with tassels and bells that I realize are now singing —incanting, no doubt, on their master's behalf. This guy is loaded for magical bear, that much is clear as bluesky.

I force my eyes away from his face and find myself looking at the ninja who has appeared next to him. Before my gaze can beat another hasty retreat, I realize that the ninja's eyes aren't glowing at all; they're smudged underneath with some kind of phosphorescent green stuff. It's not magic, it's makeup. This mundane discovery has a weird effect on me. First, hope springs eternal that I am not deadjim; after all, it is a poor wizard of any stripe who must resort to flim-flam to promote abject awe. Second, I am disappointed.

Of course, it is about this time that I notice something else about the ninja's eyes. They got that same, black hole stare I've seen on other folks who hang with Master Chen. I begin to suspect he's got himself an entire army of these ninja-golems. Just as I have this horrendous thought, the ninja smiles. Ooga-booga.

I pull myself as upright as I can without letting loose of Squint, and say, "I'm Cicerone Del, merlin to—"

"Yes, yes. Merlin to Hismajesty, King of Embarcadero. I know who you are, little wizard. And I know *what* you are . . . and what you *could* be."

Against my will, my eyes are pulled to his face. He smiles. By Vespa light I see that it is not a pleasant smile and that his face is not the face of an old man; it is the face of a dragon, ageless and ancient. His eyes are dragon's eyes—so black they're purple, so live, they seem to turn like ferris wheels in his head. They got all the colors in the universe and they got no color at all. They are black holes, sucking up all the light on Guerrero street just the way they've sucked all the light and life out of his ninjas and monks.

At this moment, I am convinced that they will suck up all the light in my world if I don't do something quick.

"I seem to have the advantage, merlin," he says. "I know you, but you do not know me."

He leans toward me, dragon-eyes glittering, sucking at my face.

"You're Master Chen," I say.

"Ah, but that is not my name, merely one of my titles. That knowledge will do you no good. It seems you have some small magic to command. Were you my ally, I would offer you a kingdom of your own to command. But you have placed yourself in opposition to me. So, you will receive only this riddle: I am unity and I am duality. I am one and I am legion. Before the Flood, I sired a nation; after the Flood, the soul of a nation. Because of me, all spirits cried in agony, as the innermost secrets of nature were revealed by my command. Immortals fear me, for I have quested and sought out the elixir of their wealth—and, behold, I shall seize it."

He pauses for me to admire his little poem, then says, "In the tradition of riddles, I give you three guesses. I expect it will take you an eternity to discover my name and, while I have that kind of time, you do not. For now, Hearer of Whispers, bow to the inevitable: Give me the rattle."

While my chickpea brain tries to deal with the fact that he

knows about the Whisperers, he makes this strange beckoning gesture. His grotesquely overgrown fingernails catch the light like as if they got diamond dust on, and a banner of mist wraps around his arm and wags its tail in my face. It hits me that he is trying to spell me and my insides almost freeze up. My eyes are glued to those damn fingernails.

Then, I wonder how he changes his underwear.

This makes me laugh, which sort of jinks up Chen's spell. Just to make sure it stays jinked, I wonder how he does a couple of other homey things. Then, I prepare to let loose some spells of my own.

Squint the Squeamish, however, has other ideas. He isn't so much mesmerized by Chen as he is scared spitless of him. He makes this funny squeaking sound and dives butt first toward the asphalt. Next thing I know, Squint is in full retreat and I am holding an empty coat. Well, not quite empty. The rattle is in there. I can feel it. Huh. Suddenly, I know something Master Chen doesn't.

I fold the coat against my chest, praying it won't rattle. It doesn't. I gesture at Squint's fleeing backside. My arm stirs a banner of mist and it licks Chen's face.

"Rattle's yours," I say, "if you can catch it."

Chen's mouth wriggles like he bit into some bad kim chee, but his eyes are loaded guns. Neither I nor Scrawl nor even Hismajesty got an eyeball half as hairy as this one. This is beyond hairy. It reaches down into my immortal soul and just about sucks it right out.

"Impudent," he calls me and disappears in a swirl of robes. And I do mean disappears. It's like he's there, then he's not, and moreover, his ninja is gone with him.

I move over into the yellow light from my scooter and carefully peek into the coat. Through gold-washed bufandong, the horse hair from the rattle is peeking back at me from the top of the long inside pocket.

Neon.

I start yelling for Firescape. I hear an answering yell from up the street toward the Mission. Then I hear footfalls. Lots of footfalls. I guess not all of Firescape's knighties are ninja-chasing. After a moment of thought and much grimacing, I slip into Squint's nasty old reefer coat and turn to wait for the knighties. With the adrenaline wearing off, I realize how tired I am—almost asleep on my feet. I straddle my Vespa, sucking up cold bufandong, trying to stay wakeful. When this doesn't do a whole lot, I pull open my amulet bag and snuff up some Doug. Muy better— my eyes almost focus.

I look up, then, and see folks moving toward me through the stringy mist. I am about to wave when it occurs to me that they don't look right: they are carrying lights and they are too big to be knighties.

My dull senses scramble to sharpen themselves. I fire up the Vespa, wondering if I should just peel out of here, and in the next instant, in the web-weave of scooter headlamps, I see that these big guys are carrying more than lights, they are carrying alien weapons.

I'm outta there. I rev the Vespa and start to move, when one of the aliens fires into the air. A beam of orange light screams through the twisted banners of fog with a sound like the sky is ripping. This gets my immediate attention. I jerk the scooter to a stop and look up to see big old John Makepeace coming toward me, looking like some dingy angel-o-doom. At the end of his beefy arm (the one that's not holding a laser rifle) is my own beloved wife.

"Jade!" I cry, terrified into uttering her real and secret name. I am answered by a stream of Chinese invective and thank God she is alright.

In short order, we are hustled off the street and into the Mission Dolores compound. All the way there, I am hoping we will be rescued at the last minute by knighties or Hector or even Creepy Lou. When we are safely tucked away in John Makepeace's winnebago, I am forced to face reality.

"What the hell was all that?" John Makepeace asks me when we are alone in the winnebago with him and Ty and some big guy with a truly nasty set of pectoral muscles.

"All what?" I ask back.

"That guerrilla war you staged on our front porch."

"Pardon me, John," I say politely, "but the Mission is still in Lord E's domain and so, technically speaking, is *his* front porch, not yours."

"Don't be flip with me, kid. Is that who you were fighting— Lord E?"

Kid. I forget sometimes that I still look like a kid, though I'm pushing twenty pretty hard. It's tough to get people to take you seriously when you look like a kid. I wax as sober as I can.

"No," I say, "we were fighting the Minions of Darkness."

"The what?"

"We were engaged in battle with the forces of Master Chen. The selfsame demons who have been haunting this very Mission."

John Makepeace makes a face at me. "You were fighting demons?"

"Well, they're not really—" I steal a glance at Ty, whose eyes are as big as walnuts.

I'd started to say that they're ninjas, not demons, and I wonder if it would lying, strictly speaking, if I just sort of leave that out. I have trouble with lies, ni dong, but I'm good at fantasies. Fantasies just roll off my tongue like they don't even check in with my brain first. I decide demons come up on the fantasy side and that not saying something true is not really the same as saying something untrue. So, I simply don't visit the issue of whether the ninjas are demons or just brain-dead guys in black outfits.

"Your men have seen them. I heard Gino say so—Ty, too."

He gives Ty a look. "Yeah, right. What were you really doing?"

I shrug. This turns out to be an error on my part; Squint's coat (my coat now) rattles.

John Makepeace's eyes narrow. "What was that? And don't ask what—you know what."

"Just my ceremonial rattle," I reply. "Merlin stuff, ni dong."

"No, I don't dong. Show me."

"Trade secret."

"Bull shit. Ty, get the rattle."

Ty starts, blinks and looks at me sheepishly. "Uh, look, John, I . . . I hate to—"

John Makepeace makes a sound like a crab pot boiling and lunges at me across the table. My dear Jade lunges too—for his throat—but is jerked back from behind by the guy with the pecs.

Me, I get dragged across the table by John Makepeace, while he violates the privacy of my newly acquired coat. He pulls the rattle out and holds it up in the light. It is a sad-looking old thing, really. At least it probably looks pretty sad to these alien dudes. The hair is dull and limp and the paint on the gourd and stick is fading and chipped.

It looks pretty sad to me, too, actually—until I get a whiff of Doug from the amulet bag that John M has mashed in one big paw. It's like putting on a pair of enchanted glasses. Suddenly, I can see that magic still drips from that old rattle like fiery dew. And I am aware of the pipe, which is digging into my hip, and the vest, which is clinging damply to my skin. There is magic there too, magic I can see and feel; the three things are connected to each other by gleaming phantom threads. I can even see the magical aura of the absent headdress trailing off into the distance. I gotta hope that when it comes to native magics, three out of four ain't bad. Right now, my immediate problem is getting the elusive and much sought-after rattle out of alien hands.

Any hope I have of John Makepeace not knowing how important this stuff is flies out the winnebago window when I see how his eyes have lit up. For a wild moment, I think maybe he sees the magical threads too, but then he says, "Is this authentic?"

It is clear that an actual lie is in order. However, I expect the truth will seem weirder to John Makepeace.

"Yes," I admit. "This is a genuine artifact of great spiritual import. We were attempting to return it to its rightful owner."

My beloved Jade rises to the occasion. "Yeah, right," she says. "Only my man here believes its rightful owner is a 500 year old Ohlone wizard." She makes loco loops around her shell-like ear. "A dead Ohlone wizard. I guess you could say we run sort of a delivery service for restless spirits."

John Makepeace frowns. "Is it real?"

Firescape rolls her chocolate-almond eyes and snickers. "About as real as he is," she says, making eyes at me.

I hold my breath. John Makepeace is clearly not sure what to think. He is looking from the rattle to me and back again. Finally, he looks at Mr. Pecs.

"Go get Professor Hollowell."

"He'll be asleep, sir."

"Then wake him up. I need his professional opinion. If this artifact is real, he'll thank you for waking him."

Pecs nods and leaves.

I eye the door. Okay, one down and two to go. I wonder how to get rid of John Makepeace and Ty. When the lights flicker and go out, I suspect maybe Someone Else has that covered.

"What the hell?" asks John Makepeace.

I recognize this as a Rhetorical Question. It is answered pretty quickly by shouting from outside. I glance out the window. A ghost moon is spilling milky light through the Mission Dolores' eternal shabu dong. Other than that, I see nothing.

John Makepeace swears colorfully and feels his way toward the front of the winnebago. The next thing I know, he has done something that brings lights back on. They are dimmer than before, but I can still see that John Makepeace is pretty damn mad. Outside, the shouting gets louder and fuller, and then there are shots—laser guns and AKs both. The door opens and someone sticks his head inside.

"You better come, John. Someone's messing with the satellite dish."

John Makepeace moves a lot faster than I imagine he can. He pulls out a hand gun, drops the rattle into the little metal sink across the narrow room, and is gone.

Ty watches him go, then turns his head back to look at me and Firescape. We stare at each other in silence for a moment, then he says, "So, this is your wife?"

I glance at Firescape and nod. "Her name is Jade."

Said wife jumps and her mouth pops open, but she doesn't drill me for my indiscretion. She knows I am only trying to show Ty that we trust him, and therefore, he can trust us.

"You . . . you're having a baby, aren't you?"

"Yeah. In a while." Firescape pats her little belly, pretty obvious in spandies.

He nods, looks at the floor, looks out the window, looks at us, then exits the winnebago without another word, leaving the door hanging wide open.

Needless to say, I suppose, we are outta there in no appreciable time. I snag the rattle as we flee, then I Chouyan like I have never Chouyaned before. We hit the ground under the winnebago and take refuge behind a wheel. We are not alone long. In about two shakes of a Doug bough, Cinderblock is hunkered down next to us.

"Thought he'd never get out of there," she whispers. "Let's zhou."

We follow her into the graveyard, creeping low to the ground, bellying under winnebagos to avoid flying feet, lightning bolts, and bullets. I do not breathe until we are safely in the graveyard. And when we are in the graveyard, close to the Ohlone, close to Pedro, I feel the tug and tingle of the Ohlone spirits. I can't begin to tell you what I'd give for just a little bit of time to talk to them —to him. But there is no time. We gotta go. Already Cinderblock is heading for the rabbit hole.

Just before we drop into the hole, I hear a vast sigh from the very ground beneath my feet. *Good*, it says, and I feel a rush of something big and warm fill up my insides. I smile into the thick darkness. So far, so good.

Cinderblock lets out a series of cutting whistles, which I know means, "objective achieved," or words to that effect, then we are down the hole. We recon in the intersection of 16th and Mission, where a handful of knighties await us with the scooters.

"What next?" pants Firescape when we have stopped scurrying, and are sitting astride our little metal steeds. I have never seen her so short of breath.

"Next," I say, "I go to the Mountain."

"You mean we," says my wife. "*We* go to the Mountain."

I lower my voice. "Jade," I say, "you're going to be a mother."

"And you're going to be a father."

"It's dangerous."

"Oh, yeah. And this means you should go alone? Duh. I'm going with you, Cicerone. No arguments."

"Yeah, me too," says Creepy Lou. He has appeared out of nowhere, bouncing like a channel buoy. "No argumenth."

"Anybody else?"

This is a rhetorical question, ni dong. Facetious, even, but Cinderblock takes it seriously. "Me," she says, pulling her Vespa around in front of us.

This time, it is Firescape who objects. "Sorry, Lieutenant. Somebody gotta take care of the Majesties and keep track of the aliens."

Cinderblock leans close in and whispers, "Jade, I'm not jinkin'—you need me."

"Yeah, here." Firescape puts her hand over Cinderblock's and says, muy seriouso, "Lieutenant Guinevere Fred Cinderblock, I, Jade Berengaria Flannigan Firescape, hereby award to you a field commission to the rank of Colonel, effective as of right this moment, as God and Merlin Cicerone and Creepy Lou are my witnesses. Now, you get your fanny back down to the Mission and find out what John Makepeace is doing."

"I'll tell you what he's doin'," says a new voice from out of the fog.

Around us, knighties shift into defensive position. I hear safeties clicking off.

"It's okay!" I yell, but softly, ni dong. "He's a friend."

Hector emerges on cue from the bufando, which is no longer dong. He saunters up to us and repeats, with great and merlinly aplomb, "I'll tell you what John Makepeace is doin'. He's cadging for spare parts."

He pulls his hands out of his monkish sleeves and holds them out to us.

Firescape flicks on the headlamp of her scooter. The yellow light falls on a wad of metal and plastic and wire with silicon chips dangling here and there.

"What the hell's that stuff?"

"This," Hector tells us, "is the guts of a genuine alien satellite relay. I got curious about what makes that sort of machinery tick and, well . . . this is what makes it tick. If ET wants to phone home now, he's gonna have to send smoke signals."

"How did you know how to—" I start to ask, but stop, because I am a mental sneeze away from realizing something truly portentous. My mouth is hanging open and my face is doing something muy silly, I'm sure, 'cause Lord E's ex-merlin laughs and says, "It's just another kind of radio, Chickpea."

"Yeah," I say, feeling like the knee-weak, foolish (but really grateful) recipient of a legit miracle. "And you were always good with radios."

Hoot/Hector laughs at me. "What took you?"

I thought you were dead sounds awfully rude, so I don't say this.

"You've changed," I mutter.

"You haven't."

"Shit," I say. "You damn well better be back for good. You disappear again, and I'll—" I can't finish.

He laughs again and throws his arms around me. I recipro-
cate. The satellite junk digs into my back. Like I care.

"What's with you two?" my wife wants to know. "Del, who is
this guy, really?"

"I told you about Hoot," I grunt from inside Hoot's bear
hug. "This is the very dude."

In the stark light, Firescape's eyes are huge. "You said he was
dead."

"I thought he was."

Hoot chuckles. "Me too. On any number of occasions."

"Yeah, well, I'm really happy for you boys, but we gotta get
this magical stuff to the Mountain before Chen or Makepeace or
some other collector of antiques makes a move on us." Firescape
kills her headlamp. "We gotta zhou, Del."

I know she's right, but having just found Hoot again, I surely
hate to take a chance on losing him. We quickly determine that
four of us will go to the Mountain together—Hoot, Creepy Lou,
Firescape and me. A half-dozen nighties will come along to watch
our back trail while Cinderblock personally guards Doug and the
Majesties.

As we push our Vespas to the Border in preparation for
mounting up and zhouing, there is something I just gotta know
from Hoot.

"Your name really Hector?" I ask.

"Yep," he says. "After some jake on my mother's side of the
family. She always called me Heck."

I ponder this. The possibilities for puns, jokes and generally
cruel word-play are endless. "Damn," I say.

"You're not kiddin'," he says. "Don't spread it around,
though."

"Wouldn't think of it," I promise, and we roll our Vespas in
silence for a while.

"To the Wiz?" asks Firescape.

"No time." I already know we will be followed, and it's not
John Makepeace or other aliens I worry about.

"Don't you need a map?"

"I have a map," I say, "in my head."

This is true. I have stared at photos and maps and elevations of the Mountain over the last weeks until I think I could walk there in my sleep. Which, as I think of it, is just about what I'm going to do. There is one big, fat, glaring problem with my map. That is that the neat little lines run through a whole lot of Big Unknown, the first major chunk of which lies smack in the middle of the Bay Bridge.

Treasure Island.

twenty-first: treasure island

YOU EVER HEARD of the Loch Ness Monster? The Flying Dutchman? The Bermuda Triangle? Well, the Bay Bridge is sort of all those things rolled into one. I can't even begin to tell you what it feels like when we drive our little Vespas out onto it. Fog and some sort of mossy-looking stuff hang on it like party festoons and its big towers just seem to go up into nothing. Then there's the matter of all that salt water a mere 200 feet below. I'm pretty sure we all keep that in mind as we dodge pits and holes and loose pieces of roadway.

The weirdest thing is that in the stiff breeze that's blowing, the whole damn thing vibrates. The slower we go, the more we feel this and the more we hear the moaning the wind makes as it tangles itself in the big metal cables that connect the towers. Needless to say, we go faster, so as not to hear or feel or see much of anything.

I am reminded of scarecrows and tin men and cowardly lions —most especially of cowardly lions. What amazes me most is the way the folks behind me just follow me right on out there like as if there's no friggin' big deal about any of this. I wonder if they got any idea how scared I am. I sure hope not.

The sméagols at the bridgehead have assured us that there has been no activity whatsoever on the Bridge itself. Last check by binoculars showed some lights among the trees on the Island, but that was all. Now, the whole span is locked in a wu that is muy dong and it's beginning to rain. If there are Treasure Islanders on Treasure Island, I figure, we won't see them until we're just about on top of them or under them, as the case may be.

The Island is like a giant sleeping tortoise in the dark and fog. Even though this night has been just about endless, and I know it's got to be getting on toward sunrise, the only hint of this is that the Island can be distinguished just the tiniest bit from the fog it's curled up in. It looms big and black and scary right in front of us and there's nothing in the world we can do but go right through it. We see the lights of fires in the trees as we draw up close and then we see what I've been dreading all the way across—the Tunnel, which we gotta drive through in order to get across the Bay.

We stop just short of the Tunnel to recon and calm our jinking jitters. Suddenly the Island don't look like anything so benign as a tortoise. It looks like a dragon—a great, sleeping dragon with diamonds on his hide and his big old mouth open right in our faces.

I think of Chen. I've met the Red Dragon—well, here's his bro, the Black Dragon. Only comfort is, in Chinese lore the Black Dragon—Oo Loong—he's the good guy. I pray this Black Dragon holds true to type.

"We gotta go in there," I say, as much to me as to anybody else. "There's nothing for it. It's the only way to get where we gotta go."

Around me, I hear weapons being checked and safeties coming off.

"Let's go," says Firescape.

"Yeah, let's go," echoes Hoot.

We go.

In Vespa light, the Tunnel isn't as bad as I expect. The head-lights chase over the walls and along the pitted road. There's debris ever so often where the ceiling has caved in. It's not so much like driving down a dragon's throat as I was afraid it would be (not that I've ever driven down a dragon's throat, ni dong, but I can imagine). Still, I'm pretty sure if I stretch my imagination just a little bit, I can make stomach growls out of the sound of scooter engines bouncing back off the curved walls. I decide not to stretch my imagination.

We go slowly, so the trip seems to take for ever. But nothing falls on us and nothing jumps up at us and as we get to where I think the end must be, I start to relax. This, as it turns out, is a bad thing. Because I am relaxed, I am not as vigilant as I ought to be and because I am not vigilant, I don't see that there is some-thing blocking the far end of the Tunnel, and because I don't see this, the next thing I know, we are all floundering in a big, old fishing net.

I am up-ended completely and my scooter flips over on its side, taking me right along with it. The net pins me to the wet tarmac. All around me, I hear the bangs and scrapes and cries and curses of the others experiencing the same thing. One by one, the little engines die. I get a whole new analogy for the Island at this point—trapdoor spider—'cause we are trapped. There is a spatter of AK fire and the sound of ricochet and then Firescape whistles for her girls to hold fire.

The torches come out in the silence, woggling toward us across the slick, shiny road. They light up a rabble of people who do not look really pleased to see us. The feeling is mutual. A huge dude wearing an ancient yellow Macintosh leads a smaller band of folk forward to see what it is they've caught. He checks us over one by one, then turns his head and calls out, "This ain't them."

"Well, who the hell is it, then?" asks a voice from the rabble.

I gotta stop and tell you about his voice, cause it's got some serious ovaries. I mean, it's a woman's voice, first of all, and it's got aplomb and command and all sorts of other stuff all rolled up into it, not unlike, in some ways, the voice of my wife when she is equal portions General Firescape and Jade Berengaria Flannigan, which is to say, three different kinds of hot. My bones feel less than solid. This has got to be someone with Power.

The Huge Dude turns back to us. "You heard. Who the hell is it?"

"I'm Cicerone Del, merlin to Hismajesty, King of Embarcadero." I've never had to introduce myself from inside a fishing net before, so this is a novel experience, and rather humbling. "We are on a mission of great urgency. All we ask is that you allow us to pass."

"We mean you no harm," adds Firescape from somewhere to my left, and Creepy Lou chirps, "We come in peath!"

The Huge Dude laughs. "Squids," he chuckles, and calls back over his shoulder. "It's a friggin' merlin—whatever that is—on some sort of mission. He says he wants to pass through."

"A mission is it?" says the voice with serious ovaries. "And what kind of a mission might that be?"

"What kind of mission might that be?" repeats the HD.

"We're on our way to the sacred Mountain—Diablo," I explain, "to try to save our world from Wiwe. I know that don't probably make a whole lot of sense—"

The HD asks his own question this time. "This got anything to do with that caravan that rolled through here a while back?"

I push scratchy strands of fishnet away from my face. "Well, yeah, sort of. They're taking over our kingdom and threatening to do worse."

The Huge Dude straightens and turns back toward the rabble. "You hear that? He says the caravaners are threatening to take over in the city."

Another person breaks out of the pack and moves across the steamy, wet tarmac. Even from this angle I can see that it's a woman. She's tall—almost as tall as the Huge Dude and she's wearing a thick water-proof coat like the kind our fisher-folk wear at home. A long, heavy braid of pale hair is coiled on top of her head. I bet if she uncoiled it, it'd go all the way to her waist. Maybe further. Her face is the face of a Queen, I think. Or even a Queen of angels.

"That don't sound right," she says to the HD, then looks down at me through eyes like a winter storm. "But it does sound like the beginning of a very long and maybe interesting story." She gestures to the right and to the left. "Get them loose and bring them up to the Bridge."

I am filled with terror at these words, 'cause it sounds like her royal eminence has every intention of throwing us all into the Bay. I squawk. "Your Highness, please! I beg you! Don't toss us off the Bridge. We're not the enemy!"

She turns and looks back at me and I can see her eyes are laughing. "I'm not your Highness, merlin. I'm Captain Ahab. Bring them on up, Mate," she commands the HD, and off she goes, out of sight.

Well, we are not tossed off the Bridge, as it happens. We are taken up a steep hill and around the curve of the Island until we come to a stubby lighthouse along the rocky shore. Here we are brought into a large room that is lamp-lit and warm. It's also an interesting shape—kind of like being inside half a cake. That's lighthouses for you. A hand-lettered plaque by the door proclaims that this is The Bridge.

The first thing I do in the light of The Bridge is take inventory. One of the knighties—Rollerskate—is holding her arm funny and looks pretty pale and pinched. Otherwise, we are okay —at least those of us who are here at all. Hoot is missing. As if, by now, this should surprise me. I see that Firescape has noticed the same thing; we exchange glances and I shake my head. I'm of the firm opinion we should not mention the absence of Hoot.

While we are silently agreeing upon this, Captain Ahab enters the room. And I do mean Enters. She has a Way about her, as Bags would say, and she's not afraid to use it. She comes in through this little side door and heads toward a platform along one wall that

holds what I s'pose is a Captain's chair. Every eye in the place just
sort of goes to her and sticks there, even Creepy Lou's. And he
does not stomp, snort or jerk one time as she makes her slow and
sinuous swagger to her throne. She is no longer wearing the thick
coat, but what she is wearing's not the least bit captainly. How
many whalers've you seen all tricked out in green velvet catsuits?

"Meow," says Firescape, and I can tell by the tone of her voice,
she don't mean it kindly.

At the end of her swagger, the Captain gets up on her platform and turns to face us all. The Mate moves to stand right next
to her platform, but I notice he doesn't get up on it with her. I
also notice that his eyes do more than just follow her; they sort of
rub all over her as she moves. I am familiar with this behavior,
having given Jade some serious eye massages in my time.

From the platform, Captain Ahab gives us all the once over.
"Who's responsible for the women?" she asks.

Firescape steps forward. "That'd be me, General Firescape of
the Embarcadero Guard."

"I see one of your girls is injured, General," she tells Firescape.
"I'd let your wizard see to it, but I'd prefer to keep him where I
can see him. I'm going to have our Bones take a look at it, just to
show you we're not savages here."

Firescape gives me a questioning glance. Bones is sailor-talk
for doctor, so I nod and Firescape passes the nod to Ahab, who
follows the whole deal with narrowed eyes.

One of the other knighties, an older girl named Mushu, steps
forward before Ahab's guards can reach Rollerskate.

"Let me go with her, sir," she says to Firescape, then gives
Captain Ahab a cool eye. "She's my little sis."

Firescape looks to the Captain and the Captain makes it so
with a wave of her hand. Me, my guts quiver. For all that Captain
Ahab lays claim to being non-savage, I still worry we may never
see Rollerskate or Mushu again.

Ahab gestures at our dwindling group. "So, what's this—the
wizard's harem?"

Firescape's dark eyes are glittering like chocolate diamonds. "It's not a harem," she says. "It's an armed guard. These women are trained knighties of the realm. And they're here to protect him." She jerks her head toward me with a swish of red.

"Ah." Captain Ahab rocks back in her chair. The velvet ripples and stretches and I swear the Mate's eyes water.

Ahab looks at me. "To protect him. That's interesting. And why does he need so much protecting?" This is to Firescape.

"He told you. We're on a mission. He's the key to its success. If you'd just let us go—"

Ahab raises her lily white hand. "A mission . . . to save your world from—what was it?"

"Wiwe," I say, "but that's a really long story and I—"

She makes a chopping gesture in my general direction, her eyes still on Firescape. "He also said the guys from the caravan were trying to take over the city. What'd he mean by that? What have they done?"

"Well, first off, they blasted their way through a neighborhood and slaughtered some neighbors," says my wife. "Children, women, men—mostly unarmed with anything but bricks and baseball bats."

"They set up camp in an important religious shrine," I add, "seriously disrupting my spiritual channels. Then they captured a full third of our prime agricultural land."

The ice storm flies in my face. "I didn't ask you," the Captain says. "I asked the General. What he says is so?" She jerks a thumb at me. "These guys took land, food?"

Firescape is apparently a little nettled by this offensive behavior toward my person and does not bother to keep the nettles out of her voice. "If he says it, it's so. My man isn't in the habit of lying," she adds. She does not mention that I am in the habit of invention, which is similar, though not, strictly speaking, the same thing.

The Captain's eyes flit from Firescape to me and back again. "You're pregnant."

Firescape nods, putting a protective hand over the little Flannigan.

"His?"

Firescape nods. "You care?"

"Does he? Dragging you off on some man-mission—that doesn't seem very lover-like. Don't you think you'd be better off someplace safe?"

Firescape revs it into full gear. "Look, Captain, or whatever you are. I'm along on this mission 'cause I'm the one most qualified to protect the muy important ass of Hismajesty's prize merlin, who as noted, is also the father of my child. Under such circumstances, I'm not likely to let him out of my sight. Meaning, your Captaincy, that I volunteered for this tour of duty and neither my merlin husband nor any other force on this planet is likely to have kept me someplace safe if there was someplace safe to be kept. Which there isn't, and which is why we're on this mission in the first place."

"Th' alienth are eatin' the Gam Thaan," adds Creepy Lou mournfully, then salutes smartly and stamps his right foot three times.

Ahab and her entire entourage stare at him.

"He queer in the head?" asks the Mate.

"He's got special abilities," I improvise. "Sort of like a seeing eye dog."

Ahab's cold gaze sweeps us again. "So the aliens, as you call them, are taking over your property. To what end?"

"To our end," I say. "They mean to drive us out of the Gam Saan altogether so they can bring their own people in. Hundreds of them, thousands."

Ahab and her First Mate eye each other, and I hear a ripple of something uneasy murmur its way through the Islanders.

"Why would they do that?" asks the Captain.

"To get rich," I explain, and my blood starts to boil. "They want to turn the Gam Saan into a place for their tourists to go and spend money seeing historical places and cultural shrines. We're in the way. So, they're trying to push us out."

"Look, we know they came through here," says Firescape. "Didn't they do pretty much the same thing to you?"

This sets up some more murmuring among the rabble and gets Ahab and her First Mate into a whispered conference that results in the whole confab coming to an abrupt end. We are taken to a set of smaller rooms on the first floor of the long two story annex that attaches to the lighthouse. It's pretty spartan, but has a bunch of cots, a bathroom and a barracks-style shower like out at the Presidio. There are windows, but they're barred from the outside; no hope there.

The knighties immediately begin casing the place for other escape routes while Lou flops out on a cot and commences to snore. I never seen Lou sleep before. Somehow, I think I imagined he didn't. Me, I feel like I've gone beyond the need for sleep.

We discover that we are a long way from the ground and that even if we could squeeze through one of the tiny bathroom windows, which are not barred, we would most likely be dashed to pieces somewhere below. This side of the annex has a lovely view of bone-crunching breakers.

Firescape and I closet ourselves in the shower for what we intend to be a tactical conference. Then we discover that this shower has hot running water and soap, and even some crude excuses for towels, so we put it to good, thorough, and possibly improper use, which goes a long way toward making us feel like ourselves again. All this questing and life or death stuff can put one hell of a strain on a relationship. There's nothing like a little hot water and steam to sort of focus things.

When we are done focusing, we discuss where Hoot might've gone, where our scooters might be, what sort of folks it is we've fallen in with and how we might fall out again. I confer with the Doug bough, but I am the recipient of no nose visions. Finally, Firescape and I flop out on a cot together. I sleep even as I am thinking that I can't.

I don't know how long we sleep, but we are awakened when someone kindly brings us food and a report on Rollerskate. It's daylight, more or less, and a soft rain is falling.

"Arm's broken," the woman tells us. "Bones says it's just a hairline fracture so she put it in a sling. The girl's resting easy."

"When can we talk to the Captain again?" asks Firescape.

"Captain's in a conference with her officers," the woman says. "You spewed some pretty outrageous spindrift last night. Captain's just trying to figure out how much of it is so."

"It's all so," I insist through a mouthful of stew (somebody here's a bueno cook). "Every last bit of it."

"Yeah," agrees Creepy Lou. Biscuit crumbs tumble from his mouth. "Who'd make up thtuff like that?"

"I guess that's what the Captain is trying to figure," she says, and leaves us to our breakfast or whatever.

When I've stuffed myself pretty effectively, I go to a window and peer out. There's nothing to give me clue one as to what time of day it is. We might've slept for three hours or thirty. My body informs me that, however long it was, it wasn't enough and my brain, that it was too much. There is mush between my ears. I wonder where Hoot is and what he's doing. I wonder how many Ohlone Dolores John Makepeace has dug up while we been here.

But no one comes to tell us what time of day it is or anything else. The woman comes back to take away our dishes, but all she'll say is that the Captain will talk to us soon. "Soon" is a relative term here, I come to find out. The weepy sky is going from silver to pewter and still no one has come for us.

"Do thomething magic, Del," Lou tells me, but I seem to be all magicked out.

I try to initiate a nose vision, and manage to catch a glimpse of Hoot skulking somewhere on the premises, but that's all. Still, it's enough to get everybody a little buzzed. We begin to hatch wild plans about what we'll do when they take us out of here again. We agree whoever gets a chance to escape will. We send thoughts of mercy and compassion to Captain Ahab. And then one by one, we fall asleep again.

I am just dozing off when the Mate arrives at the door. He beckons to Firescape, who is curled half on top of me on our cot.

"Come," is all he says.

She doesn't want to come, however, and says so.

The Mate flexes his pecs but his words are mild. "I need to talk to you, General. If you ever want to get out of here, you'd best cooperate."

She goes with a backward glance at me and my gut twists itself into a neat little granny knot. I don't have long to stew, though, before a couple of strangers arrive and take me away to see Captain Ahab. This surprises me, 'cause I get the distinct impression that Ahab considers me to be a lesser lifeform. I am further surprised when I am taken, not to The Bridge, but one level higher to what must be the Captain's private quarters.

As my escort leads me out onto a circular landing, I look up— sort of a natural when you've been trucking up a spiral staircase. I realize that there is yet another landing above this one. Through the stairwell I can see that, muy higher, the spiral goes up without a break, all the way to the light chamber on top.

Off the landing, there are several doors. My escort takes me to one of them and knocks. Captain Ahab answers the knock herself, signals me in, and closes the door behind us.

The room, which is sort of fan-shaped, is softly lit by candle and lamp, making everything a little fuzzy and me sort of fuzzy right along with. The Captain is no longer wearing the velvet catsuit. She is wearing a soft, blue, clingy gown that doesn't close well in the front. I win my bet about the braid. Falling over one shoulder, it ends somewhere below her hips. I realize these things vary from culture to culture, but I have the distinct impression that the Captain is, shall we say, ready to rock. With a total stranger. I gotta wonder why.

I look at her with as much aplomb as I can muster. "You wish?"

"To talk," she says, and motions me to a giant pillow in front of a wood stove. The door is open and cheerful flames leap about inside like circus acrobats.

I sit. She sits. Then she just looks at me for a long time, playing with the end of her braid. I'm patient. I wait.

Finally, she speaks. "You said the aliens killed people in the city. Is that so, or were you just trying to scare us or get our sympathy?"

"It's so. They killed about fourteen people—that we found."

I remember the moment pretty intensely all of a sudden, which makes me squeeze my amulet bag. I smell Doug. So does she. She leans closer.

"What's that smell? Pine?"

"Doug fir. It's sort of a talisman. Keeps me focused."

She smiles, tilts her head. When a woman does this, I know from experience, the situation is serious. "And do you need to keep focused right now?"

"Yeah. We haven't seen death like that in Embarcadero since Lord E took the Buena Vista. I was a kid when that happened, so I guess I never really have seen death. Every time I think of that—those people—I get sucked back there."

She backs off a little, peering into my face. "Are those tears?" She wipes one away, which gesture reminds me of Jade, which makes me real tense suddenly, 'cause Jade is with the Mate.

I lick my lips. "Listen, Captain Ahab . . ."

She leans in again. "Yes?" Smells like she just had a shower, only her soap smells less like soap and more like cedar.

"About Firescape. Your Mate came and took her away just before you sent for me . . ."

She nods. "And you're worried about her. Sweet. Don't be worried. She's fine. He's only going to ask her some questions. Like I'm asking you. That's all. Now, tell me some more about these aliens. Did they really cut off your food supply?"

"Yeah. They took a piece of land we call The Farm. My folks run it for produce. Train apprentice farmers, grow fruit and nuts and greens mostly. The aliens drove them off at gunpoint. Kaymart and Bags—they're my folks—they're real worried about the crops. All the aliens have done so far is trample on them. They're sure not taking care of them. Kaymart—she's sort of our all-purpose scientist—she experiments with new strains of vegetables. So we can grow more food in less space which will be seriously helpful as the population grows." I stop myself. "Of course, if John Makepeace has his way, the Gam Saan is going to grow in a whole 'nother way that don't include us."

"Makepeace," she repeats and nods. "You catch any other names?"

"Yeah. Gino, Ty. There was this guy with outrageous pecs, too, but I didn't get his name. Oh, and they had an archaeologist with them named Dr. Hollowell. Never met him, though. They captured me and Firescape. Ty helped us get away, so I guess they're not all greedy SOBs."

"Greedy SOBs," Captain Ahab repeats and looks real thoughtful. "And you're pretty sure they mean to open the area up to the outside?"

"Oh, yeah. That's a surely. John Makepeace was real clear about that. They got Backers—people where they come from with lots of money. If they can show them some salvaged treasures, they figure they'll get more money and salvage more treasures and bring in more people and—"

"And then the whole cycle starts all over again," she murmurs. Then, she changes the subject drastically. "You have to try real hard to get your woman pregnant?"

Try real hard? My pants tighten. "We just, uh, did the usual things and she got pregnant."

"I been trying to get pregnant," she confides. "But no luck. Don't know whether it's the First Mate or me. The Islanders, they expect me to have an heir. Problem is, if I pick another Islander to be Number One, I'll have to give up this Mate, 'cause that's how it is when you're Captain, and that would be a pretty tough thing for me to do."

She smiles. Even her smile's got ovaries. She fingers the collar of my coat. "Mate's a hell of a guy. You wear an awful lot of clothes, Cicerone Del. Why don't you take some of them off?"

She tugs the coat off my shoulder and it rattles. "What was that?"

Here we go again. "My spirit rattle." I pull it out and show it to her right up front. "I gotta get this rattle and a ceremonial pipe and a vest to the sacred Mountain real soon, or all hell is gonna break loose in the Gam Saan."

"What's this got to do with the aliens?"

"The aliens want to throw the moldering bones of 5,000 Ohlone Indians into the Bay. Only if they do this, the Ohlone spirits will just disappear—*poof*! And then there's this Red Dragon Wizard named Chen who wants to grab the Ohlone magics—that's this stuff—and use them to lord it over everybody —living or dead. I got one chance of stopping any of this and that's to get these magics to the sacred Mountain they came from. It's the only way to stop Chen from getting his hands on them and save the Ohlone spirits from Ultimate Annihilation. The longer I stay here, the closer Chen gets to becoming an Immortal and the closer John Makepeace gets to rolling the bones."

Ahab sits back and gives me this long look. While she is doing this, I try to assess the situation. I'd have to be totally jingbing not to see where all that stuff about getting pregnant and Islander expectations and too much clothes is going. I am facing a decision of scriptural proportions, which is—what am I willing to sacrifice for this muy righteous quest?

I return Ahab's long look. I gotta admit, there are ways in which "sacrifice" isn't quite the right word. Then I think of Jade. Maybe "betrayal" is the right word.

"You're serious about this, aren't you?" she asks.

I nod.

She leans toward me again and looks right into my eyes. My hair stands on end. A bit more than that stands on end when she kisses me full on the mouth.

This is it, Chickpea, I think. *You got one big decision to make, here.*

No. There's no decision here. I open my mouth to say 'no,' when Ahab pulls away and smiles again, sultry and slow.

"You know," she says, "you're real cute, and I'm willing to bet making a baby with you would be a hoot, but I gotta have a mind for the gene pool, honey, and you're just plain crazy."

She gets up then and goes and opens her door. There are two guards right outside, waiting to escort me back to the holding pen.

"I hope my Number One has better luck with your lady friend," she says, as I'm led away.

Her Number One, as I recall through my haze of stunned relief, was going to ask Firescape a few questions just like Ahab was going to ask me a few questions. The very thought makes me more crazy than Captain Ahab thinks I already am. Crazy enough to try something. So, as my escort escorts me down the spiral stair with me in front and them behind, I do something muy loco. I turn, give the foremost escort a good shove, then grab the inside railing and swing on over.

It's a ten foot drop before I land on a lower portion of the spiral with a loud clang. Adrenaline pushes me down the stairs as fast as my miraculously unbroken legs will carry me. Faster, even —I'm leaping stairs by the time I hit bottom.

First thing I see is a door to the outside, which I kick open. Second, I see the dark corridor that leads into the lighthouse annex, where the holding room is. I disappear into it. Lastly, I tuck myself into an even darker recess and begin to Chouyan.

The escort hits bottom about five seconds later. They see the open door and barge out into the darkening fog without so much as a glance at the corridor. With them gone, I dart out and take a quick peek into The Bridge. No luck. I go back into the annex and try the holding room, next, praying, among other things, that the Mate has already taken Firescape back there.

One prayer is answered; there's no guard. The door has an

iron throw-bolt on the outside, I notice, though there's not so much as a knob on the inside. Definitely a room of Limited Purpose.

I throw the bolt and slip in. The knighties are immediately on their feet. No Firescape—my heart does a Titanic.

Lou gets up grinning. "Good timing, Chickpea," he says. "We were juth trying to come up with a plan. You got one?"

The only plan I got for yours truly is to find Firescape. I say as much. "The rest of you try to lay hands on some kind of weapons and find Hoot, although, most likely, he'll find you. We need to get the Vespas and zhou the hell out of this place."

"What about Rollerskate and Mushu?" asks one of Firescape's girls—her name's Fresca.

"Try to find where the doctor hangs and get them out, if you can, but if we get the rest of us together and can't find them . . ."

"Understood," says Fresca, and looks grim.

We split up. They go outside, where the sky has gone from pewter to leaden gray. I stay in. I decide pretty quickly I can't do this alone, so I take a moment to get down on my knees on the floor of the holding room. I pray like I have never prayed before in my whole life. I pray for smarts, for wisdom, for intuition, for divine intervention. And while I pray, I break a whole bunch of Doug needles under my nose. What I get is a nose vision of Ahab's rooms. It tells me something I don't expect. I been thinking that since the Mate is, well, a mate, he'd most likely share quarters with his Captain. But when I envision Ahab's rooms, I realize that there is nothing remotely male in there, at least not permanently. The Captain's quarters, says my nose vision, are the Captain's quarters.

The vision takes me out of there, onto the landing and back to the spiral stair. My brain wants to look down, but my nose says to look up, 'cause there's that whole other floor just above the Captain's. That's where I go, following my vision back into the lighthouse and up the spiral stair, past The Bridge, past the floor where Captain Ahab is. Before I can quiver myself into a puddle, I manage to make it up to the third floor landing and step off. Like the Captain's level, this one has a circular gallery with a series of doors. These rooms will be smaller than the ones down on the Captain's level, but probably the same odd shape.

I pick a door and go to it and listen. Nada. I go to the next. Zero. I go to the third. I hear the murmur of voices from within. Shaking like the Regency Palace in a 4.8 temblor, I try the door. It's not locked. I open it as quick as I can and step inside.

I find myself looking right at Jade. She is sitting on a trunk facing me, her face golden in the lamp light, her eyes raised to the First Mate, who is standing over her, flexing his pecs. He's talking, but I don't wait around to hear what he's saying. I grab the first heavy object in reach and go for him with it.

The heavy object happens to be a foot stool (at least, I think it's a foot stool—it's got three legs which are too short to qualify it to be anything else). It's a very heavy object, as it happens, and throws me way off balance so that it, and not me, is leading the attack on the Mate.

He turns just as I reach him and the foot stool catches him in the chest, which is a good deal lower than where I'd meant it to catch him. He makes a good, satisfying *oof*! anyway, loses his balance and goes down against the trunk, which Jade has hastily vacated.

"Del!" she cries and starts toward me, but the Mate grabs her ankle and drops her. She flips over and starts kicking at him, but he's every bit as strong as he looks. Her feet don't get anywhere near their target.

It's up to me this time. I glance around the room, panicking and trying not to. I know that in a moment like this, I really gotta see what I'm looking at. What I see is that this place has a wood stove, too, and that next to the wood stove is a box of, well, wood. I lay both hands on a piece of this and go for the Mate. He is bent half over, Jade kicking and squirming in his arms as he tries to straighten up. He's fumbling with something in his belt and I realize with a cold shot of terror that it's a knife.

I got no time left and no options, 'cause in the next second, he's got it out of his belt. I charge, split log in my hands. The knife whispers past Jade's neck and she cries out, which wreaks havoc on my nerve endings. The knife comes up, but the hilt is caught in Jade's hair. She screams and I take a swing. I connect. The Mate roars, the knife flies and I swing again, this time at his head. He ducks, but Jade kicks his shin. When his head comes up, I swing a third time.

Third time, as they say, is a charm. The wood catches him in the side of the head and he sags. In two shakes, Jade is out from underneath him and in my arms.

"Mi Corazon," I whisper in her shell-like ear and she sighs and trembles a little. "Are you alright?" I ask.

"Dui. You?"

I wonder if she knows anything about my brief encounter with Captain Ahab. I look down into her face, but don't see anything but relief and love. Naturally, I kiss her.

We have little time for this sort of thing, however. Unlike in the videos, where you can count on your adversary being out long enough for a tender and passionate reunion, reality's got no such perks. Already, Number One is groaning and merely groggy.

We flee.

"He bribed his way over," Firescape pants, as we scamper down the stairs. "Makepeace. He gave them clothes and food and all kinds of stuff to let him squat on the backside of the Island long enough to repair the Bridge. He made all kinds of promises, too, about what he'd bring next time. He passed himself off as some sort of trader. That's why all the questions— they didn't want to hear that their windfall was going to back-fire on 'em."

An interesting mix of metaphors. Through which one thing is clear: The Islanders don't think of Makepeace as an enemy . . . yet.

We hit the bottom of the staircase at a dead run. The bottom landing is a pool of light, which we dash across straight through the Doorway to Freedom. We do this without thinking, ni dong.

Especially without thinking that there might be someone waiting for us when we come out into the dark of another night.

There is someone, though, and we are both yanked to a sudden stop to find gun muzzles in our backs.

"Move," rasps a voice in my ear and we do.

I glance at Firescape. She glances back, looking more defeated than I've ever seen her.

There are two of them, both dressed in the thick, hooded fisher coats of the Captain's rabble-guard. They nudge us back into the lighthouse where we take a left turn and enter the annex. Back to the holding room with us, I guess.

Only I'm wrong. We go right past the holding room and out a door at the very end of the annex. We're on a cliff-side walk now, with a line of trees to our left and a railing to our right. Below is roaring surf. I wonder if that's where our escort intends us to end up. But we keep on walking, moving away from the shoreline eventually. We pass a number of Islanders who give us no more than an interested glance, or in Firescape's case, an interested leer. Even in the semi-dark, she is a sunrise. Wherever we're going, I'm glad we go there together.

We come to a long, low building that was white once upon a time. Our escort nudges us up a short, rickety flight of stairs and into what feels like a warehouse or a barracks. There's no light at first; we wait while our guards fire up an oil lamp.

While one of them fumbles with the lamp, I try to make conversation. "Look," I say, "could you at least tell us where you're taking us? What you're going to do with us?"

The one with the lamp makes a sudden chopping gesture and his partner grunts out, "Face front 'n move," and spins me about with the muzzle of his gun. The lamp flares and we are prodded forward again to an inner door.

"Open it," says the talkative one.

I do. On the other side of the door is an open warehouse room. In the middle of the room, beneath a dim light, are nine Vespas and six Embarcadero knighties. The door closes behind us.

I am speechless.

"Your carriage awaits, Chickpea," Hoot says in my ear, then, "Let's roll!" to everyone else. He's on his way to the scooters already, stripping off the Islander garb.

I look at our other guard. Creepy Lou grins back at me from inside the hood.

Will the real merlin please stand up?

We quickly determine that Mushu and Rollerskate will head back to Embar while the rest of us go on to the Mountain. Then we mount up, Hoot riding double with me until such moment as we can retrieve his scooter, which is hidden just uphill from the mouth of the Tunnel. We open the warehouse door only enough to let out one of us at a time, then roll, single file, out into the rainy night.

It's Hoot who leads us now; I'm just driving the bike.

The road slopes and winds most of the way down to where it meets the Bridge, so we won't have to fire our engines until we're almost there—unless we're spotted. The Vespas' electric engines are quiet, but when you get this many in one place, the whine sounds like a giant wasp. I think we're all holding our breath during that endless roll. Every scrape and squeak our battered Vespas make sounds like thunder.

Hoot's bike is parked up under some ancient cedars and so well hidden, I don't have clue one of how he even recognizes the spot. He's just flung his leg over the thing when sudden light pours down on us from somewhere above.

"Dios mio!" yells Mushu, "they got a search light!"

We scramble. At least, everybody scrambles but me. My bike doesn't want to start. I keep hitting the starter, but it just whines briefly, then falls silent. Over those pathetic whines, I can hear the footsteps of Islanders on the hillside above me. I glance down the hill and see red tail lights. I glance up the hill and see torches and, against the glare of the search light, the silhouettes of a whole lot of people.

My heart's about to give out when the Vespa finally comes to life under me. I almost cheer. That is until I realize that someone else's hands are also clamped on my handlebars—very, very big hands. I look up into the face of the First Mate, who makes a truly prodigious roadblock.

We are frozen like that for an instant, then he draws back a fist. I close my eyes and pray.

"Yo!"

The voice comes from the hillside.

A quick glance shows that it's her, Captain Ahab. From this angle, back-lit by the searchlight with her yards and yards of silvery hair flying loose in the rising wind, she looks like the Angel of Death—what's her name?—Izrá'il?

"Let them go," she says.

Huh. Well, maybe it's a different angel, then.

"He tried to kill me!" objects Number One.

"No. He tried to save *her*." Her head tilts down hill where the red tail lights have all but disappeared. "Let him go, Mate. There's no sense in keeping any of them here. They can't do us any harm whether they're lying or telling the truth. But if they are telling the truth, they aren't the enemy. The enemy is on the other side of that Bridge."

After a moment of thought, the Mate takes his hands off my handlebars, straightens and steps out of my way. With a last glance at Ahab, I rev my bike and light out down the hill, putting Treasure Island behind me.

twenty-second: diablo

**THEY ARE** on their way back up the hill when I meet them. What's left of them, anyway. Mushu and Rollerskate have already disappeared into the Tunnel. I explain as coherently as I can what happened with the Islanders; after that we don't talk much at all, but just make our way to the end of the Bridge.

Here, I stop, 'cause I can barely believe the sight that meets my eyes. Coiling away from us into the darkness are wet, gleaming rivers of concrete. It's like being in a giant's bowl of chow mein. After a long moment of awful staring, I consult the map in my head, choose a noodle that points Southeast and we go.

I got ooga-boogas running up and down my spine the whole time, 'cause beyond our headlamps there is a murkiness unbroken by any manmade light. A lazy huichen dong makes a filmy bubble around us, scooting fore and aft—now close, now far. After a while, we enter into a canyon of sorts. The walls are manmade and pretty tall. Over the tops of them, I see occasional pinpricks of light up in the hills, but that is all. If there are people here, they stay out of these canyons at night. I gotta hope we don't find out why.

The only sound we hear is the purr of Vespas, which makes me suddenly aware that if the sun don't shine through the fog on this quest, it may be a lot shorter than we hope. Each bike's got an auxiliary battery, but both aux-bats and bikes are solar.

Ever so often, one of Firescape's knighties glides up from behind to signal that there is no one on our back trail . . . yet. What they mean is, they can't see anybody, but I know Somebody is there. Nothing I can do about it. All I can do is follow the map in my head and pray that we have enough of a head start.

We are out of the strange canyon when the huichen becomes a polvo and then dries up and just stops. So do we, 'cause such a sight as we are seeing demands some boggled ogling. A moon is up and it has laid a silver blanket over hill and dale. There is, in addition, one hell of a lot of hill and dale. A lot more than is suggested by any of the maps I been studying. Above us, there are stars—more stars than I've ever seen, and muy, muy brighter. With the lights and fog of the Gam Saan, and the smoke of Potrero, you sometimes forget they're there at all. Now, over our heads is this humongous black bowl full of glittering lights.

I have a moment of prodigious vertigo and shut off the engine of my scooter. One by one, my traveling companions do the same. Then, we hear something I realize we have never heard before— complete and total silence. The Farm is pretty quiet, ni dong, but that's a close, cozy quiet in which you can hear the wind singing lullabies and animals going about their animal-type business. You can wrap yourself up in the quiet of the Farm. This is a big, wide-open, cold, awesome quiet in which there is no sound whatsoever.

"Whoa," somebody says.

"Amen," says somebody else.

"Can you see the Mountain?" asks Firescape, then, "Which one is it?"

The answer to this is I don't know, 'cause nothing looks at all like the map in my head. I scan the awful darkness, but see nada that makes any sense to me. There is the black of the sky, which is looking more and more like a watercolor, bleeding purple at the horizon. And there is this other black that is immense and looming. Those are the mountains, but I can't tell one monster lump from another.

I remember seeing a vid at the Wiz about high-tech field glasses that let you see long distances in the dark. I sure wish I had a set of those now. But I don't. What I do have is that I am wearing a ton-o-magic and Dougness. I also have Pedro's story. Pedro talked to the Mountain. More to the point, the Mountain talked to him. As I am a shaman of sorts (or at least, Pedro says I am), there is an outside chance I can talk to the Mountain, too.

Well, duh—of course I can talk to the Mountain, it's the reciprocal that's problematic.

While I am chewing my lip and stewing on my lack of shamanly aplomb, Fresca glides out of the huichen at our collective backsides and whispers to Firescape (loud enough for me to hear), "There's somethin' back there, General. Behind. We best zhou."

Firescape nods, but holds up her hand. She is watching me like she expects I'm gonna do something miraculous like maybe smack a 97 mph fastball into the Bay in a one run game at the bottom of the proverbial ninth. Instead, I pull the rattle out of my inside coat pocket and the little Doug bough out of my amulet bag. I crush two tiny needles on one finger of the branch and inhale, holding the rattle up before me like I've seen old-time knights-o-the-realm hold their swords. Believe it or not, the Doug branch twitches.

This brings a thought into my head, which is that if Chen thinks a combination of magics will work for him, it might just work for me. I lay the Doug branch alongside the handle of the rattle and hold both out in front of me like I'm dowsing. The end result of this is that I start twitching.

Yowza, as Mr. Lopez-Alvero was wont to say, what a rush! I am hot and cold and tingly all at once, and I feel like I'm getting ready to levitate. *Neon*, I think. But then I gotta wonder what good all this twitching and tingling does if I don't get clear instructions from on high.

I send my mind back to the smoky dream lodge, where I sit across from Pedro. *The Mountain came to you, Pedro*, I think. *How can I get it to come to me?*

Shaman! whispers a Voice like many voices.

I sit up straighter on my scooter. "Yes," I answer.

Behind me I hear someone ask, "What's he doin'? Who's he talkin' to?"

Would you become a shaman?

"He's envisioning."

"You betcha." No disrespect to Pedro, but I can surely learn from someone else's mistakes.

Come to the Mountain.

"He alright?" someone else asks.

"Lead me," I say.

"He's fine," says Hoot.

Then I feel the tug, sure as I've ever felt any tug—Doug's or Jade's or Chen's. This, though, this is like double-Doug, triple-Doug even. This is a whole mountainful of Doug.

Holding out the rattle, which is chattering like a squirrel 'cause I'm shakin' so bad, I start to turn around in a circle just like the incomparable Inigo Montoya does to find the Man in Black in one of the classic tomes of Questing. I let the Mountain tug that old rattle and that little Tree branch wherever it wants to. When it's done tugging, I open my eyes.

In front of me, across the fields and hills, I see The Mountain. It is bigger, blacker and loomier than anything around it, and it is wearing an aura of light. The road we're on is a long, glowing silk ribbon and all the turns we will have to make are written on the back of my eyes. A trail of magic leads from here to there. All I gotta do is follow it.

I put the Doug bough next to my heart, wedge the rattle into the handlebars of the Vespa and fire it up. In a heartbeat, the other scooters are humming too. I lead off again, hair and coat tails flapping in the breeze, the others strung out behind me on the gleaming tarmac.

Definitely a Moment.

Music pops into my head: *We don't need another hero; we just need to find the way home.* Yeah. Mad Max on Vespas.

This strikes me funny and I laugh, feeling for a little bit like I'm flying above a river of molten glass. Okay, so the glass got potholes, weeds and tar bubbles, but I feel very cool and very electric in spite of this. With Hoot to my one side and Firescape to my other and Creepy Lou straggling along right behind like always, I also feel very put back together.

Funny what moonlight, a righteous quest, and lack of sleep will do for a guy.

twenty-third: the size of his magic

BY THE TIME we reach the foot of the Mountain, the sky is the color of the Bay. And here, as we pause at the edge of a dead little town to switch our aux-bats, a muy strange thing happens. A green-tea mist comes sneaking up behind and around, and pretty soon we are up to our eyeballs in moist silky stuff.

It is very like a shabu dong, which makes me feel . . . comfy somehow. But I gotta say that out here on this Mountain, it takes on a whole different personality. The natural shapes of bushes and trees and rocks are a lot spookier than the angles and planes of the stuff people make. For one thing, natural stuff moves when the wind blows. This makes me feel as if there are a thousand ninjas watching from just where I can't see them. I can't help but twitch a little as I recall Fresca's warning about Something being on our trail. Neither, I guess, can Hoot, for when he takes a reckoning of all the Vespa batteries, he makes a defensive suggestion.

"I think we need to consolidate our shit, Chickpea," he tells me, and then proceeds to expand upon the nature of this consolidation.

In the end, we leave Firescape's four knighties where the road begins to climb seriously, taking their aux-bats with us. They can recharge their primaries in the sunlight. The knighties have instructions to fire off flares if they see pursuers and are unable to stop same.

This reasoning is sound enough, it's just that I have a small attachment to affording the magical stuff (and our collective asses) as much protection as possible. Now Hoot is in immensely good shape for a man in his mid-to-late-twenties, but beyond that, our protection amounts to a pregnant woman, a slightly crazy dude with a twitch and a pint-sized merlin with delusions of shaman-hood. I mention this, but Hoot is derisive.

"A merlin," he tells me, "is not to be judged by the size of his person, but by the size of his magic."

I recognize this speech. It's one of Bags favorites.

"You," he continues as we prepare to ascend, "are letting your natural tendency to self-deprecation influence your confidence level. You got a self-esteem problem, boy. And you gotta lick it right here and now, or you're not gonna be any use to Pedro or the Mountain, or anybody. So, remember—it's not your size, it's the size of the magic. How big's the magic, Del?"

I look up at the Mountain. It looms like a lumpy pyramid. Even in the fog it's got one awesome Presence. The road snakes away into the curling fog, the yellow stripe down its middle gleaming in the Vespa light. This bothers me, for some reason I cannot put my finger on, but I'm pretty sure it has nothing to do with the size of the magic, which is huge—bigger than me, bigger than Pedro, bigger than Chen even (I hope).

It suddenly hits me and knocks me about off my scooter that I have let the smallness of me limit what I think the magic can do. I have a muy strange and paradoxical revelation, which is that there is such a thing as too small an ego, and that having too small an ego can cause as much trouble as having too big a one.

"The magic," I say, "is as big as this Mountain."

For which Hoot slaps me on the back and says, "That's the spirit!"

"Yeah!" echoes Creepy Lou. "Thaththethpirit!"

We go up. And we go up. And we go up some more. We are on the northwest slope of the Mountain, so sunrise, which I think is in progress, is having damn little effect on our foggy little world. The purr and whine of Vespa engines sounds, in the fog, like a hundred very happy cats in the company of a swarm of wasps. The wheels turn, but that is the only sign we are really moving.

We have gone some miles when the shifty gloom ahead is lit up as if by an army of flashlights. Suddenly we are facing a spread of headlamps that would do any alien craft proud. The very fog rumbles.

Then It is upon us—a Vehicle such as I have never seen before. A veritable Behemoth. It is yellow and looks like any sensible person's worst nightmare. It's roaring like a storm and trembling the ground like a 4.5 roller and worst of all, it is astride the yellow line—there is no place for us to go that will not be in Its way.

This is all happens so suddenly, all we can do is hug the uphill side of the road, with me in the lead and praying like there is no tomorrow, appropriately. I swear I can feel the hot breath of the thing all over us. In an act of desperation, with the Beast almost upon us, I grab the spirit rattle out of my handlebars and hold it aloft. The Behemoth answers with a blast of light and sound.

I think I can speak for all of us when I say that I have never in my life heard such a sound. It shreds the air and rattles my teeth and makes my eyes water. Every spell and incantation I know flashes before my eyes. None seem appropriate to the occasion.

You ever notice how, in a crisis, time sort of turns itself into pulled taffy? This is happening now, as my spells flash through my head along with various prayers (Remover of Difficulties upper-most) and my whole Universe collapses down into the space between the headlamps of the Beast.

That's when a little road opens up just ahead and to my right. I almost don't see it 'cause there are tree limbs hanging down, but the trees are Doug firs and as I draw near, they beckon me to the road between them. I hit my brakes once, put down a foot and spin that scooter for all I'm worth. Meanwhile, I pray that everybody else makes the turn too.

I go up the little road some yards and spin back, trying to swallow my heart. I'm barely turned around when they pop out of the fog—*poot! poot! poot!*—Hoot and Lou and my Jade, like the Horsemen of the Apocalypse, only on Vespas.

I go to jelly. "Damn!" I say, and that's all I can say for the next five minutes or so. In fact, that's all any of us can say. So, we sit and "damn" each other for a while as the world lightens up around us.

"What," pants Jade when we are all damned out, "was that?"

"Some kind of alien vehicle . . . I think," I pant back.

"Thought it was something else for a moment there," admits Hoot.

"I thought it was a dragon," says Lou. "Dragonth live on mountains, don't they? That's what the Books of Kingdom thay."

Creepy Lou with a case of nerves is a lot like a leaky faucet. You can't stop it, so you might as well just get used to it. While the rest of us catch our breath, Lou gives forth a rolling commentary on the mysterious ways of dragons. This is really okay, 'cause listening to him has a strangely soothing effect. In the back of my mind, though, I gotta wonder where that thing came from and if there are any more like it at home. It occurs to me, now, why that yellow line was so bothersome. There used to be yellow lines on the streets around the Gam Saan, too. They wore off a long time ago cause no one kept them up. These lines clearly do not suffer from that kind of neglect.

Creepy Lou finally runs down.

A while after, Jade asks, "Anybody catch why the Treasure Islanders were trolling for trespassers when we came through their Tunnel? I mean, it occurs to me to wonder why, if they were so happy to do business with John Makepeace, they were setting traps along his back trail."

"Precaution," answers Hoot. "While he was visiting and

handing over trinkets for toll, some of his guys got a little high-handed with the village maidens. According to Mushu and Rollerskate, who had it from the doc, Captain Ahab just wanted to make sure the appropriate payment was exacted upon Make-peace's return."

My wife snorts. "Like as if that fishnet was gonna stop a winnebago."

"Not stop it, maybe," agrees Hoot, "but it'd surely slow one down."

"We gotta go through there on the way home?" asks Creepy Lou.

"Yeah," I answer, "we do. But let's cross that bridge when we come to it."

Then Jade asks, "How far?"

"Huh?" I ask.

"How far to the Place? How do we know we're there?"

Well. It occurs to me at this auspicious moment that I have not clue one of where "there" is. I been following my nose, I realize, for the smell of Doug is sharp and tangy in the moist air.

"I don't know how far," I admit, "but I'll know when we're there. They'll tell me."

"The Doloreth?" asks Lou awfully.

"And this." I hoist the rattle and give it a shake.

I can feel everyone's eyes on me and on it and on magic I don't even know if they can see. I can see it, bouncing every-which-way, charging the fog with silver light that is not light at all, if you know what I mean.

We are caught in a Moment . . . or at least I am. When at last I look at them again, Firescape has her eyes closed and Hoot is checking out the scenery. The Moment collapses, just like that.

I look at Creepy Lou. He smiles, scratches his head and says, "Wow."

Before I can ask why, Hoot says, "You know, this road goes straight up through the trees for quite a bit. Wanna ask your invis-ible compadres if it's worth a look?"

I peer in the direction Hoot specifies. The road does just what he says, it goes straight up into the trees and disappears. It don't look like much, just chewed up tarmac trail covered in leaves and needles. In the middle of it, a sea gull pecks at a fir cone, looking seriously out-of-place up here in the piney woods.

Is this it? I ask Pedro and Doug and all their respective kith and kin in the worlds of tree and spirit. *Is this the road to the Sacred Place?*

Perhaps there is no such place, says a Voice from a dark corner of my head. There is a momentary scuffle in my noggin between it and me. I determine to win.

Of course there's such a place, I tell it (or tell myself, depending). I take a deep sip of the fir-tangy fog and try to picture the Place, and suddenly I see it, clear as if I'd been clobbered on the head by a fairy godmom: An overturned bowl made of branches and patched with mud spills smoke into a clearing in the middle of a grove of trees. I know that, inside, the Place smells of smoke and evergreen and sweat. I been there. I also know that there is not here.

"Let's go," I say and lead on up the road. The sea gull squawks at us, all indignant, and flaps away, fir cone and all.

We drive the Vespas as far as we can, then, when the road gets too rough, we walk them and walk them and walk them and walk them.

"When will be there?" asks Firescape.

I want to tell her "soon." But, the vision has faded and I am tired and cold and sweaty and my throat is on fire. So, this simple question hits me sideways and I realize in this big, chilling, awful Moment that I just don't know if we'll ever be there, or if there's even anywhere to be. Yeah, sure, I had this epiphany and all. But I have epiphanies every day, and the fact is, I'm not sure how real they are. I mean, it strikes me suddenly that a lot of the stuff that happens to me is a little weird and that I'm the only one who hears the whispers of Douglas firs and dead Ohlone.

Well, okay, supposedly Lou hears dead Ohlone, too, but

somehow I don't find this terribly comforting. I'm willing to bet I'm the only one who sees dead Ohlone, and magical threads and even Chinese Dragon wizards. And that's the most awful thought of all: I realize with the suddenness of lightning that I am the only one who has ever seen Master Chen or heard his Voice.

Okay, except for Squint, you might object. But Squint is not here for me to consult, ni dong, so that does me squiddle in my present frame of mind.

But the shrine! whimpers my brain. Creepy Lou saw the shrine, and the monk who told me about Chen, and the ninja who told me Chen was sleeping. And someone has to *be* before he can be asleep.

This is not helping. I seize on the fact that Jade saw the monk, too. My brain wracks itself trying to remember if she heard the monk tell me about Chen and wondering what would happen if I just asked her. Meanwhile, a more collected part of me informs the various uncollected parts that we don't have time for this.

This is when I have another sort of epiphany: It strikes me that even though I am the only one who has seen Chen or talked to Pedro or heard and understood a Whisperer, these people have followed me up this Mountain as if I knew what the hell I was doing.

Great. Now I got guilt on top of a stunning lack of self-confidence. On top of both, I am suddenly scared spitless. What if there are no Whisperers and no Chen? What if Doug is just a garden variety fir tree?

I've had doubts before, ni dong. But they were doubts about me, not about stuff that counted. Not drag-the-earth-out-from under-my-feet doubts. Now it's like I'm standing in a North Beach undertow with Whisperers inside my head, only these Whisperers are from the Dark Side of Cicerone Del.

I am having a crisis. Problem is, my Collected Part is right: I don't have time for a crisis. There are people looking at me, believing in me, waiting for me to do something, to lead them somewhere.

You may lead them straight to hell, says that nasty Voice from the Dark Corner of Chickpea's brain.

I tell it to shut up, to go away, to friggin' frag itself. Then take a deep, shaky breath. Fir perfume rides in on it and my life flashes before my eyes. I scramble to take inventory. Since it'd take too long to go over it all, I just hit the high points: Mi madre y padre, Hoot, Bags, Kaymart, Doug, Jade, the Dolores, Pedro. I see, immediate, that all the high points of my life are people (if you interpret "people" pretty loosely). Then, I see all the connections between them and me and realize that those connections are a lot like the threads that bind the magics together. You can't see them —not really—but you know they're there.

A question forms in my head. I look at my friends and my wife—who are still waiting for me to say something—and say, "Do you believe we're gonna find the Place?"

There's this truly awful silence, during which Jade's lovely brow furrows most prodigiously.

"Duh, Del," she says. "I only asked when we'd get there."

Well.

"It's a shortcut," I say, and head on up.

twenty-fourth: a righteous quest

 SOMETHING ABOUT WALKING in silence makes the brain work. This is because this really cool mechanism called autonomic reflexes knows how to put one foot in front of the other over almost any kind of terrain, so the brain, which might otherwise be busy directing footwork, has nothing to do but take in scenery. In a shabu dong, there ain't much in the way of scenery to take in, so the brain is at loose ends and finds itself something else to do.

In this case, my particular brain starts to work on Chen's riddle. I fall back beside my inestimable mate and pant, "I am thinking about who Chen is, or at least, who he thinks he is."

"Sounds like a good think," she says, not panting much at all anymore.

"He gave me a riddle to solve," I say. "Wanna hear it?"

She spocks an eyebrow at me. "When'd he have time to give you a riddle?"

"Tonight—I mean last night—in the alley, while all hell was breaking loose and ninjas abounded."

"He was in the alley?"

"Yeah. You were otherwise engaged, or you might've seen him. Squint sure got an eyeful of him," I add, and try not to make it sound as if I am defending my grasp on reality. "Which is why I ended up with this coat and the spirit rattle. Chen went off after Squint."

She nods. "Let's hear the riddle."

I recite: "I am unity and I am duality. I am one and I am legion. Before the Flood, I sired a nation; after the Flood, the soul of a nation. Because of me, all spirits cried in agony, as the inner-most secrets of nature were revealed by my command. Immortals fear me, for I have quested and sought out the elixir of their wealth—and, behold, I shall seize it."

"Sounds like a bad case of multiple personalities," says Jade.

"Or past life regression," offers Hoot from just behind us. "He's talkin' like he's been a bunch of people."

"I'm not sure it's past lives, exactly," I say. "He made some crack about being around before the Gam Saan. And then there's that bit about the wealth of the Immortals."

"Which'd be immortality," says Hoot.

"You'd think. So, he's been legions of people, but right now he's one. I mean, he can only be one at a time."

"We hope," says Jade Berengaria Firescape with some feeling. "'Cause he also says he's two."

"Well, then maybe he is talking re-incarnation," I say. "The body takes a dive, the spirit repeats."

"But why two?" asks Firescape.

I don't have an answer for that, so I forge on. "He says, 'Before the Flood, I sired a nation; after the Flood, the soul of a nation.'"

"As in Noah's Ark?" asks Lou.

"No!" says Firescape, her voice sounding amped up. "The Great Flood of China. The Yellow River overflowed its banks bigtime for years, says the history. So, it sounds like he's saying he was a pretty big deal on both sides of the Flood."

"Yeah, I'll say," snorts Hoot. "You'd have to be a pretty big deal to sire a whole nation."

"No, no, no!" Firescape bounces a little. "He's the father of China! Huang-ti, the Yellow Emperor! He was the one who unified China, who made laws and set up trade. Before the Flood."

"Okay, father of a nation," says Hoot. "Kinda like Jerry Steinmetz is the father of Embarcadero. But what about the soul of the nation? Did he, like, found a religion or something?"

Firescape shakes her head and tugs at her lower lip. "Not Huang-ti. But he's somebody else after the Flood, right? Lemme think on this,. I know this."

"What about the crying spirits?" I ask. "What's that about?"

Firescape waves her hand as if I'm a pesky mosquito. "That's about Huang-ti, too. Or it's about his minister, anyway. The legends say this minister made the spirits of all things cry out by revealing their innermost secrets."

"How'd he do that?" asks Lou.

"Same way we do, I guess," says my no-nonsense wife. "In books."

"Did they have books in ancient China?" I ask, then, thunderclap, blinding flash of insight. "He invented *writing*!"

"Yeah. Huang-ti thought it'd help unify the people, so he commanded that the language be written down. Now if you guys don't mind, I'd really like to think, okay?" She sweeps us all with an especially pointy look.

We decide unanimously that it's best to observe silence while Firescape thinks. During our silence, Lou and Hoot get ahead of me and Firescape—so far ahead we can't see them any more. But we hear them when my good buddy Creepy Lou yells, "Looky-dooky!" at the top of his lungs.

With a glance at each other, Firescape and I hustle our bikes up the trail as fast as we can. At the top of the grade, we burst out of the trees and onto the edge of a road. It is a shiny black road with a bright yellow stripe down the middle and it gives up a tarry aroma. I suspect this might even be the same road we were on earlier, just doubled back.

Across the shiny black road from where we have come up are twin pillars made of white stone. Between them is a black wrought-iron gate. A big gate. It's closed over the smooth, black tarmac and it is what has beckoned to Hoot and Lou.

"Blackhawk," says Firescape. She is reading from the larger-than-life gold letters on a huge polished boulder. "Is this the place?"

I don't think this is the place, as it happens, but Hoot and Lou obviously think it's something, because Lou is bouncing up and down on his Vespa like he's spring-loaded, and Hoot is standing in front of the closed gate, tinkering with something on the front of it where it meets the left-hand pillar. Before I can yell out a wherefore, the gate glides open and Lou just up and scooters right on through. Hoot throws a leg over his bike and takes off after him, leaving me and Firescape sitting there, across the road, staring at each other.

Naturally, we mount up and follow.

Inside the gates and around a curve is this little house. Two guys in dark blue unis are leaping all over its itty-bitty patch-o-grass and gesturing up the road in the direction we are going. As we whiz by, they commence to yelling. I suspect they are border guards and are excited because we have just invaded their barrio. I feel bad about foregoing protocol, but I figure this is an emergency. I gotta wonder, though, about their lack of weaponry and knightly aplomb. The thought of Embarcaderan knighties jumping around like toads while their border is penetrated by guys on Vespas sends me into a fit of giggles.

Damn, but I'm tired.

The giggles stop most quickly when I see the kind of place this is. It is a barrio of castles and palaces, each one with its own Farm. I can't get a clear look at any of these palaces, ni dong—only a ridge-pole here, a chimney there, a row of windows or pillars. But I can still tell that these are unlike anything we got even up on the

Knob. These are like little Camelots, and I gotta wonder if the aliens come from a land of kings and queens with very tiny realms. Maybe these are the homes of John Makepeace's mysterious and mythical Backers who, according him, are pretty loaded. If this is so, I also gotta wonder how these folks maintain their realms with guards as feckless as those guys in the little guard house.

Maybe, I reason, this is what happens when dudes become knighties. I mean, women are much better suited to this function as they got finely tuned protective instincts, are truly crafty, and are not overly impressed with hardware. It's a rare jake who can handle the power invested in a knightie without getting a little jinked up by it. This is why most Embarcaderan knighties are women and why we have such a well-disciplined police force.

My giggles are long gone when Firescape cries out and comes to a stop. I see right off what has caught her eye—in front of a righteously Tudorian castle worthy of the Arthur, hisself, our missing compadres are confronted by two golf carts topped with flashing lights. They are painted like black-and-whites—an Old World police vehicle which I have seen in videos—but in form they are, well, golf-carts, just like the ones Felicidad uses out on the Presidio to tool around and about his fields. Hoot is talking to one of these Peace Officers—a female, to my relief—and gesturing about, while Creepy Lou bounces up and down and twitches extravagantly.

These knighties have weaponry, I note, which is presently sheathed. Not for long. The alien knightie sees us and draws her weapon, after which Firescape whips out her magic AK and Hoot waves his arms and shouts.

"Outta here!" I yell, spin my Vespa and give it full throttle. I hear no shots. Firescape and I buzz back out the way we came in, past the border guards. They are no longer leaping, toad-like, but shake their fists at us as we putter by.

"Damn kids!" one of them cries.

Behind us, I hear something that sounds a lot like John M's singing demons only tinny. I am galvanized. Unfortunately, this galvanization is not communicated to my Vespa. At what seems a crawl, we escape through the gates and swing uphill—which I immediately think is a tactical error. Fear does a wild tap dance through my veins. But the song of the demons stops at the Blackhawk gates. The little black-and-whites do not come out, and their officers seem to think chasing us is less effective than simply closing the gates behind us. Neon.

Still, as they might change their minds, and as I have a quest to get on with, when I see a little dirt track running almost straight uphill, I go there. Hoot, I know from experience, can take care of himself. I'm gonna trust he can take care of Creepy Lou right along with.

The track I've chosen is narrow and made of hard-packed earth, and I know before we've gone 50 feet or so that the Vespas won't make it. I also know, without knowing how I know, that this is The Way. I stop my scooter. Firescape pulls up on my tail. There's not enough room for us to ride side-by-side.

"These scooters aren't going to make it," I tell her.

"Okay," she says and glances back down the hill. "I guess we can back them down to the road."

"No. This is The Way, Jade."

She gives me her LOOK. "Okay, so we leave them and hike it."

"I hike it," I say. "You . . . stay and—"

"And what—guard the friggin' Vespas?"

"Well, yeah . . ."

"Like someone's gonna steal 'em?"

"Jade . . ."

"No sale, Cicerone. You really do got a chickpea brain if you think, for one molecule of time, I'm gonna sit here like a lump while you go off questing without me."

"Jade, you're pregnant," I remind her.

She rolls her eyes, granting me a moment of respite from being glared to a cinder. "So you keep reminding me. Look here, husband: Nobody on this planet knows I'm pregnant more than me. And the fact of the matter is that I'll be in better physical shape when I'm nine months ripe than you'll ever be, 'cause you don't eat right and you don't sleep enough and you're always doin' dangerous stuff like pokin' your loco nose into the affairs of wizards. I hate it when you do stuff like that and then try to leave me eating dust in your tracks. There is no way in this wide woolly forest that you are gonna go any further up this Mountain without me. You got that?"

Yeah, I got that. It simultaneously warms the cockles of my heart (whatever the hell those are in a ventricular context) and scares real tears out of me. I nod and salt water trickles down my cheek.

"Oh, jeez-Louise," says General Firescape, and grabs my face between her capable hands and kisses me very convincingly.

Thus inspired, I lead the way up the narrow trail . . . which somehow manages to get narrower as we climb. It twists around a lot, too, running almost level in one direction, then doubling back the other way for a while. The trees thicken until they form an awning overhead. I wish Doug could be here to see this. Not, ni dong, that I regret not having to drag his pot all over this Mountain, but you know what I mean.

It occurs to me, even as I have this wistful thought, that he is here, only I have got him tucked away in a sack. I open the amulet bag and take the Doug branchlet out, carefully straightening the little firry fingers. Then, in a fit of inspiration, I guess, I decide to tie the branch to the spirit rattle. I go through my pockets in search of something to do this with. Nothing. Next I try to yank out a handful of my hair. This does not work and it hurts like hell.

"What're you doing?" my wife wants to know.

"I need a knife," I say. "You got a knife?"

"Does Hismajesty have an ego?"

I use the knife to cut off a hank of hair, then hand back the knife and start braiding. As I walk and braid, I start thinking about Chen's riddle again, as we never did finish deciphering it.

"So, he thinks he's Huang-ti."

"Once upon a time," says Firescape, following my thought as if we've been chewin' on this without hiatus.

"So is it re-incarnation or something else?"

"Re-incarnation," she says. "Gotta be. Look, it's like this—he wants to be immortal, right? Which means he isn't yet. And he's sure not going to get there like a normal person with faith and work and all that. He's looking for a shortcut—the elixir of the Immortals' wealth."

"What's that got to do with the soul of a nation? Maybe he thinks he was Confucius . . . or Buddha even."

"No, that's not it," says Firescape, and I can tell by the sound of her voice that her mind's caught on something. "It's Lao-tzu."

Okay, I know Lao-tzu founded Taoism—the religion, not the philosophy. But I wonder why Lao-tzu and not Confucius? Then it hits me. "Lao-tzu is supposed to have never died, but only disappeared!"

She pokes my shoulder. "Not only that, but he was supposed to have known the secret of eternal life. And get this—for some reason the histories aren't real clear on, Huang-ti and Lao-tzu got combined into someone called Huang-Lao. So the formula for the elixir of eternal life is called the Learning of Huang-Lao. Which the second Emperor Huang-ti sent his minister, Fu-Hsen, to search for across the sea."

This part of the story I remember. "I studied that. They say he took hundreds of children with him. I guess he was hoping to start a whole country of Immortals."

"Yeah," says Firescape in her best ghost story voice, "and neither he nor any of the children were ever seen again."

"That's his name, then—Huang-Lao."

"Huh?"

"That's what the riddle's about. Chen's challenging me to figure out his real and secret name."

"That must be it," says Firescape. "I mean, that's his quest, isn't it? Beating death?"

Damn. I feel pretty good all of a sudden. Not such a chickpea brain after all, I guess. Although, I have to admit, my well-studied wife did most of the actual thinking.

So, Chen thinks combining magics is gonna be a shortcut to the realm of the Immortals. Oh, and he by-the-wayly wants to get rid of Hismajesty and become Emperor of all he surveys. From the way Pedro's gone on about him, I gotta believe his plans include turning all of us into mindless, black hole drones like his monks and ninjas.

I stow my new knowledge and the Name, finish tying the rattle and Doug branch together, and concentrate on the trail. This is becoming necessary, for though the Sun is rising higher in the sky, we are beset by fog again. Not just any fog, mind you, but a shabu dong the like of which I have only seen in one place.

I duck under a tree limb and find I am gazing up a long, wide clearing bordered by a stream on one side and a jagged line of boulders on the other. The ground is lumpy with random humps of moss-covered rock. The fog creeps in and around the clearing like cats checking out the alley behind a Gee Gah butcher shop. I have been here before. I know this as surely as I know that I have not been here before. I raise the hand that holds the rattle and the place begins to morph.

First, a shadow seems to sweep over the clearing and the shabu dong waxes restless. It also begins to gleam like powdered silver, and before my eyes the whole clearing starts making with this eerie light. The grass glows green, the trees brass, the rocks gold.

I move forward, rattle held high, and that's when I see it. It grows out of the fog where one of the mossy rock piles was. It is a muddle of tree branch and pine thatch and rock and mud, and a ghostly banner of smoke flies from its crown. And I know that the insides of this upside-down bowl are gonna be hauntingly familiar.

twenty-fifth: undertow

 I **EXHALE** the breath I have been holding forever. "This is it," I say, but then get a cold shot of the doubtfuls. This is nuts, that's what it is. For a strange, dizzy instant, I feel that undertow again and I wonder if I haven't gone completely and seriously napoleon. My upper lip is sweating and itching like crazy and my eyes are wonkier than they've ever been in my whole life.

"Jade," I say to my conspicuously silent wife, "what do you see?"

"I . . . I'm not sure," she says, and her hushed, uncertain voice puts tears in my eyes.

"Do you see . . . do you see the clearing and the shabu dong?"

I feel her nod, 'cause she's pressing into my back. "Yeah."

"Do you see the Dream Lodge? And is the whole place glowing?"

There's a pause, or at least I think there is. Then she says, "Yeah. Yeah . . . glowing."

I lick my very dry lips. "This is it, isn't it?"

"Del, if you say this is it, this is it. What do we do next?"

The undertow lets up and some confidence flows back. I

don't know if she can see the Lodge or the Technicolor grass—she believes I can see it, and that's enough.

"The Lodge," I say and step into the glade.

I expect Something to happen at this auspicious moment. I mean, after all, the magics are here, right? Something really ought to happen. But nothing does; the glade is still waiting for something.

Okay, maybe if I get closer to the Lodge; maybe if I go inside. Maybe then, the Dolores will come out. And Pedro. I want Pedro to be here. I want that so bad I can taste it. I want it so bad, I see someone standing in front of the Lodge. I move faster, Pedro's name on my lips.

But it's not Pedro at all.

"Chen!" cries Firescape, and before I can do more than croak, she brings her AK up and fires. Or at least, she tries to fire, but instead of a spray of bullets, there's just this funny mechanical cackling.

Chen echoes it pretty effectively. "Pathetic," he says. "Did you honestly think you could kill me? Obviously, you still don't know me, or you'd understand how futile your puny, mortal weapons are."

"Damn!" says Firescape with much gusto. She checks the magazine, hits it with the flat of her hand, then gives me this apologetic look.

Me, I'm just glad she can see this jake. More confidence flows.

"You're Huang-ti," I tell Chen. "Yellow Emperor and father of China. And Lao-tzu, father of the soul of China."

He nods his head. "Clever. I was once known by those names. No longer. You have two pieces of the puzzle, and you have used up one of your three guesses. But my name is not Huang-ti or Lao-tzu."

"Then," I say, "it's Huang-Lao."

I guess I expect him to go up in a puff of smoke or melt into the ground crying, "What a world! What a world!" But he doesn't do this. He just smiles at me in that irritating Red Dragon way of his and says, "Was that guess number two?"

"Sonofabitch," says my wife and launches herself in the general direction of Chen's throat.

He points one of his fingernails at her and says, "Jade," in a Voice like a little storm.

She stops like she's just run into an invisible wall. You ever play Red Light-Green Light? Like that. A growl rumbles in her throat. Chen just laughs and beckons with another fingernail and out of the shabu dong come these two ninjas. They grab Firescape, disarm her, and pull her to where she cannot come between me and their Dragon Master.

I try to leap into action. I fumble with the rattle and nearly drop it.

"Del!" Firescape cries. "Get the hell out of here!"

But I can't get the hell out of here without her, so I face Chen mano y Dragon. "Let her go," I command, as if this will actually make something happen.

What it does is make Chen crow like a damn rooster. "Your soft spot, merlin?" he cackles, then waxes philosophical. "One who wishes to hold real power must not have such . . . faults. Yes, weaknesses are like that, are they not? As faults underlie this land, so they lie deep in a man's spirit and make him weak and able to be shaken."

He makes a chopping motion toward Jade and spits her name like a curse. She cries out and crumples like she's been gut-punched.

I think of our baby and it's all I can do not to throw myself at Chen and try to disassemble him, which, of course, is just what he wants. Tears leap to my eyes. For the first time in my life I wish I had spells that could kill. What spells I do have are suddenly locked up tight somewhere in my Scarecrow brain.

Chen smiles. He's got a hook in me and he knows it. "You only postpone the inevitable. Come here, Cicerone Del, and bring me the magics, or your pretty young Jade and your unborn child will die."

Jade cries out again on cue, and the hook in my soul gives a demon yank. I fight, but Chen is reeling me in, step by step.

"Del." He says it with much power, curling his fingers, and the hook digs in deeper.

The air around us shimmers and darkens. The colors of the glade drain away and I see dark, huddled shapes that don't belong here. They come with the smell of incense and the sound of chanting, which is not a sound made by your average forest. Suddenly, I tumble to what Chen is trying to do; he is trying to magic us off the Mountain and back to his shrine over the Tin Hau where he will be in complete control and where, no doubt, the headband waits for the other artifacts. The chanting I hear is the voices of monks, dark and smoky, heavy and sweet.

Showered in cold fear, I sweat. I feel my immortal soul being sucked away, pulled off the Mountain. That's when I remember again how big the magic is. It's as big as the Mountain, and the Mountain is under my feet. I inhale evergreen and think Tree. I root my thoughts in the rocky soil of the Mountain and I dig down.

"Come, Del," says Chen again, pulling up on me, trying to shake me loose. He sounds a little ticked, like this is taking longer than he'd like. "Del!" he commands again and the glade loses some more of its color.

No! I think. *I gotta be better than this! I gotta have more than this!*

I dig deeper; my thoughts are roots; my roots are firm. They go down forever into the soil and rock. The wind sways me, but I barely bend and I don't break. I am the Mother of All Trees and my roots go down to the heart of the Mountain. For a moment—just a moment, ni dong—I think I hear it. The Voice of the Mountain. Calling me down.

My thoughts are roots.

Then I hear this other voice, this sweet, angel voice that says, "Del" in a way that has always turned my insides warm and runny, and I remember that I also got Jade. She speaks to me again.

"Del!" she says sweetly. "Del! Snap out of it!"

Something smacks me upside the head. Hard. It's Chen, and now he's got both hands wrapped around the rattle. I try to hold on, but my head is a mish-mosh of incense and evergreen and pain. There are shouts and the sound of footfalls coming hard behind me.

Someone grabs me from behind, yanks me half backward, then reaches into my coat and drags the pipe out of my belt.

I fall, and when I fall, I let go of the rattle and Chen lets go of my soul. My roots come up out of the Mountain and what's left of the Tin Hau rips away from around me like wet silk and disappears into the shabu dong of the mountainside. Chen stands over me, holding the rattle high, but he is not gloating, as I expect. He is glaring at it, as if it has just called him a very bad name, and he is swearing loudly in Chinese.

Someone grabs my shoulders and drags me up.

"Up!" Hoot shouts into my face. "Zhou!"

Where can I zhou without the rattle? I give the glade a frantic glance and see Creepy Lou, of all people, standing in front of the Dream Lodge grinning at me. He waves the pipe over his head. Then he turns and disappears into the Lodge. Just like that. I boggle, 'cause in the back of my mind all this time was the idea that the Lodge wasn't, you know, real.

Chen is boggled, too. "How has he disappeared?" he demands. "Where has he gone?" He has the rattle tight in his claws and is shaking it like nobody's business.

I gotta guess he wants to get that magic going right this minute. I also gotta guess he can't get it going—not without the vest, which I am still wearing, and the pipe, which has just disappeared into a place he can't see. I do the thing that makes the most sense under these circumstances. I dash for the Lodge and dive in.

This Dream Lodge is different in some way I don't get right away. I am wrapped in mist and dark. So far so good. I smell the Ohlone incense of smoke, pine, and sweat. A fire crackles and paints the mist with its colors. But this is no itty-bitty upside-down bowl I'm in here. This place is bigger on the inside than it is on the outside—really big, like I got the whole Mountain wrapped around me.

I move toward the fire, a warm, bright, hazy spot in the big dark. There is someone waiting for me there. No surprises this time; it's Lou.

"Yowza!" he says, his face all crawly with firelight. "This is pretty cool, huh? Is this where the Whithpers come from?"

"Yeah," I say, and I wonder where the Whisperers are now. "You got the pipe?"

He hands it to me and it tingles my hand to touch it. The vest answers with a tingle of its own. A ghost-thread reaches out to join the two magics together. The mist around us eddies and the Mountain sighs, or the Lodge does, or Something in the Lodge does.

Okay, I think, *something's doing here, after all.*

I pray I have blundered fortuitously. I've got two pieces of the magic in here and Chen has the third piece out there. In order for him to get what he wants, he's gotta come in here, and in order for me to get what I want—which is for the magics to be united in the right spot—he's gotta come in here and I gotta get the rattle away from him. For once, I seem to have a pretty clear agenda.

I say all this to Lou. "Problem is," I add, "I don't think he can even see this place. You should've seen the look on his face when you popped in here."

"But you thaw it and I thaw it," Lou observes.

"Maybe 'cause the Dolores wanted us to."

Lou shrugs. "Then maybe they can make him thee it too."

Sounds good to me. I address the Whisperers accordingly. "Pedro and company, I'm not sure, but I think it might be a good thing if the appropriate persons can see the Lodge so that the rattle might somehow make its way inside. My preference would be for Hoot and Firescape to get the rattle away from Chen and bring it in here, but if having Chen bring it in is most do-able, that'd be fine, too."

The mist is eddying again, looking most Spielbergian. I pray, bite my lip, and tuck the pipe back into my belt. I have barely finished this little task when Chen appears like one of those little, winky fake candles. *Flash-pop!*

He doesn't waste any time, but comes right at us, his lips doing mumbo-jumbo at light speed and his fingernails making julienne out of the mist. I tuck in shoulder-to-shoulder with Lou, which puts the spirit-fire between us and Chen, and spread Chouyan incantations all over the place. The mist thickens toward shabu status.

I am Chouyaning, hoping to confuse Chen, when the Dragon speaks my name. I feel the hook sink into my soul and send shivers down my spine. He says it again, and again. My bones go cold to the marrow and my feet shuffle underneath me. I hear a groan building in my throat.

Before I can think Tree, Lou's arms are all of a sudden wrapped around my shoulders. "Del!" he says. "Del!"

I am boggled anew, 'cause my good buddy Lou does not just say my Name of names, he says it with power. This is not the same as just speaking a name, you know. You gotta know how to speak it, and Lou apparently knows how, 'cause Chen's hook slips a little.

The next thing I know, I'm in the middle of a tug-o-war. They pull my name back and forth, while I bob around like a channel buoy, trying to think tree-like thoughts. The shabu gets thicker and I see, clearer and clearer every moment, the little ghost threads of magic that bind the three relics together.

I see something else, too. I see that Chen, for all he is big and terrifying in his Dragon robes and priestly hat and with magic dripping off his fingertips, is having a problem with the rattle. It keeps shaking in his hand, which is going every-which-way—up, down, around. At first, I think Chen is doing the shaking, but when he keeps throwing it these weird looks, I realize something else is going on and Chen is being distracted by it.

Finally, with this wheezy roar of rage, he stops waving his fingernails at me and grabs hold of an amulet he's wearing around his neck. It's one of those Egyptian things—an ankh—and it glows jade green through his fingers. He spouts a long stream of Chinese mixed with some language I don't get and next, I'm looking out at the world from inside a dense, dark, velvety fog. I can't see Lou anymore; I can't hear him chanting my name. Instead, I hear the voices of the Tin Hau monks and smell their sweet incense. The air shimmers and the ground under me feels suddenly not so grounded. In the freezy marrow of my bones, I know that if I lose the Mountain, I lose everything.

I try to send down roots again. It takes all the will power I got, but I manage to tear my eyes from Chen's glowing amulet put them on the threads of magic between the artifacts—on how they seem to get brighter and fatter the closer Chen gets to me. But Chen is strong. He makes me want to look at him; at the glowing amulet.

I gotta not do that. My eyes on the threads, I reach for my own amulet bag. But there's no Doug sprig in it any more and my hand closes on a flat, hard lump of stone.

The Mountain moves under my feet. I raise my head and look the Dragon straight in the eye.

"Shen!" I cry. "Your Name of names is Shen!"

His face is red with fire and surprise. He gasps, staggers, roars my name aloud.

I roar back; so does Lou, and so do two other voices from somewhere in the dark around us. A moment later there are two solid figures—Hoot and Firescape—moving toward us through the mist. They are chanting Shen's name.

I don't know if they're a power or just an annoyance, but the strange dark fog scrams. The shabu dong that lives in the Lodge swirls and dances. The swirls pull into spirals and thicken into columns and a sighing breeze licks at my face and at the fire, which leaps up to tango with the mist. I hear Whispers now—many Voices that are one Voice.

Shen, they say, *Shen*. I think even the Mountain says it.

The Red Dragon falters, stumbles, and drops the rattle. It hits the ground with a shower of sound and rolls to my feet. I snatch it up, expecting all hell to break loose, but nothing happens except that the connecting threads glow brighter. Strange thing is, one of them still connects to Shen.

I get this at the same time I get that he's not finished with me yet. Leering like he knows a whole lot I don't, he tears the amulet from his neck, casts it into the fire at my feet and shrieks a Chinese incantation at the top of his lungs. Then he hurls himself at me.

In two heartbeats, we are in a bubble inside a bubble inside the Mountain. The fire is between us, but everyone else is outside the bubble looking in. I can see the Dolores (sort of) and Firescape and Hoot and Lou. Their lips move, but no sound comes in here.

We are alone, Shen and I, and we know each other's names.

But I got the magics, I tell myself. I got the relics. Why isn't he outta here?

As if I've said this aloud, Shen smiles at me and raises his arm, shaking back the long sleeve of his robe. The shaman's headband is wrapped around his hand. A bright ribbon of magic connects us. The air inside the bubble tingles.

"You make a habit of underestimating me, young merlin," he tells me. "You may have stolen the power of my name for the time being, but you will not defeat me. Your magic is so . . . transparent. You thought you could hide in this place from me because it was, itself, hidden in the coils of Time. Yet I pried it from its secret place into plain view."

I wonder if this is an auspicious moment to tell Shen I actually asked the Dolores to let him see the Lodge, but before I can impart this info, he goes on. He doesn't just want to win, ni dong. He wants to rub it in.

"This place I have brought you to," he informs me, "is outside of time. It is a place into which neither your mortal friends nor your spirits can reach. I have constructed it carefully, so that we might have our final . . . conversation."

He lets out this weird little sound that's half wheeze and half laugh. "This body of mine is failing. It is time for me to move on. True, I will have immortality when I have done here, but who would want to face eternity in this?" He taps a golden fingernail to his breast. "Better to have a young, virile, healthy body. One pleasing to the fairer sex. One like yours."

Whoa. What's he chewin' on here—body snatching?

He cackles at me again. "You think I can't do it? Hmm? You think I can't acquire your body, if I wish? However do you think I've lived this long? In my second incarnation, as Lao-Tzu, I discovered the secret of transferring my Self to other forms so that I would not be bound by Laws that compel other mortals to shed the material form for the immaterial at the end of life. Only my body disappeared into the mountains—my real existence continued, after a fashion. I have lived a myriad lives—I have been Khan and king, emperor and storyteller, philosopher and astronomer. I took whatever form lent me the most power. It was immortality of a sort, and very handy, I suppose you might say. It saved much time in the way of having to relearn the basic capacities of thought, speech, action. It saved the toil of having to learn who I had been and ferret out what I had known. I'm sure you appreciate how much time could be wasted in such activity, not to mention childhood. Much better to let someone else waste the time."

"Then," I ask, suddenly curious, "how did you get here?"

His mouth goes all twisty. "A miscalculation. This body belonged to a scholar whose force in the community I overestimated."

"Yeah, okay, but why bother with this other stuff? Aren't you basically immortal now?"

"I have not beaten Death, merlin. I have merely cheated it, tricked it, outrun it. I would spend eternity in one body, holding all of the knowledge I have acquired, keeping all of the skill, without ever having to relearn any of it. You see, even with the ability to transfer my Self, I still must invest much time in making each new body uniquely mine, and in getting the mind of its owner to acquiesce. Then too, sometimes I am not in a position to choose propitiously. I have to take what the gods place in my path. I do not take kindly to being at the mercy of the gods. This time, the choice is mine.

"You should be honored, Cicerone Del, merlin, that you will become the vehicle for my complete victory over Death. Your knowledge of the arcane will be added to my own and yours shall be the form that is known as the Sovereign Lord of a united Gam Saan. You will be pleased to know that my first actions after toppling Hismajesty and his inane counterparts will be to drive the alien invaders from my Empire and to construct a Great Wall that will forever deny them access."

My Alice bone tickles. "I can see how jakes like Lord E might wrinkle your universe, but what've you got against Hismajesty?"

"I have against him that he and his forebears have weakened my people. We are buried in the Gee Gah, our virility sapped, our power depleted, our ancient Tongs demoted to mere community service groups. We should be rulers of the Gam Saan, not its scurrying servants."

He is silent for a moment, already decorating the Imperial Palace, I bet, and I wonder how much of this stuff is for real.

"Bullshit," I say—I mean, what've I got to lose, right? "You don't fool me. You're the one who's been demoted, Shen, and you don't like it much. You don't like it so much, you've gone shining, napoleon, and seriously fruit-cake."

"Del!" he snarls.

"Shen!" I cough.

He waves a foot-long hand in my face. "Enough of this nonsense. Playing for time will do you no good. You will never possess as much of that commodity as I do. And let me squash any hope you have that your friends will fight me. They won't, because they'll see you emerge from this noplace victorious. While the being they knew as Master Chen will be seemingly annihilated. But, in truth, I shall be the victor. I, Shen Ah Nen, shall be the only true Immortal. I shall have conquered Death utterly. So you see, you may as well give up. Give me the relics, Cicerone Del. Surrender, and perhaps I shall leave a part of you alive, give you a corner from which you can watch your world through my new, young eyes." He gives up this big, sigh and adds, "It has been a long time since I have held in my arms a woman as beautiful and courageous as your Jade."

Well that just does it, you know? I mean, my eyes have glazed over by now and anything else he might've said would've just gone in one ear and out the other, but that—I mean, the thought of this creepy old Dragon getting his claws on Jade—even if they're my claws materially speaking—is just too much.

In a heartbeat, I am beyond mad. Through this wave of high and righteous dudgeon, I see that the threads of magic between the artifacts have become fat, bright, virtual ropes of magic. This gives my Alice bone a sharp poke, and I hold up the rattle and say, "Say, Shen, what do you see?"

He looks annoyed, but says, "I see an ancient spirit rattle, which I want." He opens his hand and smiles as if he really expects me to just give it up.

"That's all? Look again. Don't you see it glowing, Shen?"

He chuckles. "No, I don't. And don't imagine that you can make me see something that isn't there. You are no match for me, merlin. Cease these futile games. Surrender."

He moves closer to the fire, and spirit flames leap toward his face. He doesn't seem to notice.

"Um, watch out for the fire."

"There is no fire, merlin. Come. Your time is up."

Okay, that clears that up. I gaze at the fire for a moment, then I step into the flames. These are spirit flames, ni dong, so they don't burn me, but they do amazing things to my eyesight. I see Shen as the Red Dragon he is, jaws wide and hungry, eyes bright and hot, with a black, rotten peach pit for a heart.

Whoa. Don't go there, Chickpea, I tell myself. I focus instead on the blazing cords that bind the magics—on the ghost flames that now leap over my head.

With a cackle of satisfaction, the Red Dragon steps into the fire he cannot see and grabs the rattle with the same hand/claw that is wrapped in Paguin's headband. The two relics connect and things happen. Shen's dragon mouth opens wide on a shriek like a gale force wind, but it's lost in the sound of heaven and earth splitting wide open. We are hit with a shock of light and heat and wind and the Mountain twists and opens up under our feet.

And then Shen is just gone, like he got sucked right out of his dragon scales down into hell. His out-of-time bubble collapses.

Prodigious.

I am still standing in the fire, but I am fully back in the Dream Lodge among family and friends, with a whole lot of fully-formed Dolores looking on. Pedro is there, and there are two other guys next to him. One looks a lot like Pedro, only younger, and the other I know without asking, is Paguin.

The spirit shaman steps into the fire with me.

"Honored," I say, and mean it.

The shaman raises his hands, palms up, and I know it's time for me to give back his stuff. I tuck the rattle into my belt, take off my coat, my shirt and the vest that is underneath them. I fold the vest ceremonially and lay it across Paguin's hands. Then I lay the pipe and rattle on top of that and, last, I fetch the headband, which is lying across the toe of my boot.

Then I wait.

Paguin looks at the things, smiles and bows his head to me. Then, it's like he just dissolves down into the fire. Well, the artifacts got burned after all, which means I did obey Pedro's wishes, after a fashion.

I turn to Pedro. "Is that it? Did we do it? Did we save the world from Wiwe?"

He nods gravely. "The world is safe from Wiwe. Your magic is as big as the Mountain and your wisdom is the wisdom of the Mountain, for you listened to the Mountain, where once, I did not." The corner of his mouth seems to twitch. "But, you did not listen when I told you to burn the magics."

"I listened," I say. "I just . . . improvised a little." There's something I just gotta ask. "Shen said that he was gonna take my body and . . . and pretend to be me. How do I know that hasn't happened?"

Pedro laughs. Really laughs. "Only you, Cicerone Del, shaman, would ask such a question, and so, answer it. Shen is now in our world; he is no longer in yours. Go now. You have done well."

"You found your son?" I ask quickly, in case he means to suck himself back from whence he came.

He nods and tilts his head toward the younger version of himself. "I have found my son. He is in my world, as your son will soon be in yours."

There is a vast, silent Moment and then Pedro and the Dolores and the Dream Lodge and the fire are all sucked away by the cosmic Vacuum of Time and the rest of us, me and Firescape and Hoot and Lou, are left standing in a foggy clearing on the side of the sacred Mountain. There's no sign of Master Chen's ninjas. There's no sign anything but trees and rocks and grass. Birds chant instead of monks or spirits.

The Sun chooses this cosmic Moment to slip through the clouds and turn everything to emeralds and diamonds and gold.

"Wow," says Creepy Lou.

"Amen," says Hoot.

Firescape just runs into my arms and cuts off my air for a

minute or two. After that, Hoot comes and slaps me on the back, and then we are all hugging and laughing and back-slapping.

When we turn to go back down the Mountain, my foot nudges something on the ground. It clinks. I pick it up. It is an ankh on a silken thong, one the late Master was wearing around his neck not that long ago.

"What is it?" asks Firescape, peering over my shoulder.

"A souvenir," I tell her. I pocket it, and we go back the way we came.

twenty-sixth: one down and 324 to go

 **GOING BACK,** it's down hill all the way. It's about time something was down hill all the way. Even Vespas are pretty sprightly on a thirty degree grade. I am not surprised when the knighties at the bottom of the Mountain report no Chen sightings. I somehow get the feeling our man Chen didn't get up the Mountain on a motor scooter. I do gotta wonder what happened to his ninjas, though. I mean, did they just poof right alongside their lord and master, or did they turn back into regular guys? And what about all those bespelled monks back at the Tin Hau?

In my mind's eye, I got this weird image of a humongous bubble bursting and sunlight and little songbirds pouring into Chen's dark shrine while all the monks and ninjas, stretch and blink their eyes and say, "My, what a curious dream!" Then there's music and dancing and firecrackers and much celebrating.

Okay, stupid image. But it makes me guffaw, so I share it with the others, and it makes them guffaw, too. So it is a combination of laughter, relief, and adrenaline that carries us as far as Treasure Island.

We approach with caution. I know Captain Ahab said we weren't the enemy and that it didn't make any sense to hold us, but I'm still a little woggly as we draw on up to the Tunnel. There are no Islanders to be seen. Nor is there any longer a fishnet over the Tunnel exit. After a hasty conference, we zip inside. The day is gray, but there's enough light that we can make out the Embarcadero end of the Tunnel as a silvery beacon in the dark. Before we reach the Black Dragon's mouth, though, we see some brightly colored flags fluttering from saw horses along the sides of the road. Muy peculiar.

This causes us to slow down and proceed with even more caution. Which is a good thing, since it keeps us from driving headlong into the flag-covered rope that's stretched loosely across the Tunnel's maw. It's obviously not meant to stop anyone coming from this side, just slow them down, and after a quick recon, the reason becomes clear. Where yesterday there was a full roadbed, today there is something much less than that. The Treasure Islanders have gone and blown out the span again.

However, on the bright side, they have done it in a most inventive way. We, on our little Vespas, can putter safely, if slowly and trepidatiously, across the quarter-mile of half-lane wide sidewalk the Islanders have left along the seaward rail. John Makepeace, with his winnebagos and sundry big machinery, is going to either have to find a new way home, or perform another patch-it job on an exposed piece of Bridge with less than friendly Islanders for neighbors.

As we clear the newly busted up section, I feel Captain Ahab's sea-storm eyes on us. I wave, knowing she's watching from that stubby lighthouse. I wish her the best of luck with her domestic problems and reflect that it's not such a bad thing to be loco after all.

It's afternoon when we pull up to the Regency Palace. Cinderblock meets us and drags the whole story out of us before she'll tell us any more than just "Status is quo." After we've generated the appropriate oohs and ahs and sent sméagols and knighties scurrying with the news that we have saved our spiritual bacon, Cinderblock reports that God seems to have put a bookmark in the saga of Our Alien Encounter.

I'm surprised, 'cause it feels like we been gone an ice age and I half expect to find everything changed. But the Royal family is still out at the Presidio, Elvis is still shivering in his Potrero planetarium, and the aliens have not spread beyond their current encampments, which now number three.

In fact, according to the sméagols reports, they've been strangely quiet. Deadend suspects they are still recuperating from the damage Hoot has done to their communications system. I hope his suspicions are well-founded, 'cause I can think of other things they could be doing that we would like a lot less.

In our room at the Regency Palace, the first thing I do is embrace my Tree. If it weren't for that little branch, which has now moved on to the spirit world with Paguin's rattle, I don't know what we would've done. One thing I know—among all the things I don't—is that what we just did was a Group Effort, and Doug—for all his totality was sitting up here in the Palace—was in the heart of same.

I push my face into the soft branches, close my eyes, and smell his smell. It's the perfume of home and family and safety and happiness—none of which may last much longer if John Makepeace has his way. Tears come out of my eyes. When I open them, I marvel—a droplet of fir sap has squeezed out of Doug's topmost bough. He has missed me as much as I have missed him.

Doug and I sit for a while in what they call companionable silence, watching the sky redden toward evening. Then Jade comes, fresh from a warm bath, and tells me it is time to sleep. I barely make it from Tree to bath to bed, but as I slip away into Dreamland, I realize suddenly how lonely it is inside my head. There are no Whispers there anymore. Nada peep. At least this time, I know this is a good thing. Pedro and company have made it safely to the Abhá Kingdom and I got to have a part in that. Feels good. I can also feel good, I tell myself, about still having

Jade and Doug and a Flannigan-to-be. That oughta be plenty to keep my chickpea brain occupado.

I don't dream. At least not portentous stuff. I just go back over the Great Trek up Diablo, during which I am mostly trudging uphill through fog. Huh. Not so different from daily life in the Gam Saan.

General Jade has given Colonel Cinderblock explicit instructions to wake us after six hours, so naturally, she lets us sleep for sixteen. It's hard to be real twigged at her over it, but Firescape does some prodigious scowling at her anyway.

"What if the aliens had gone on the offensive again? We'd've been caught flat on our backs."

"What—I got lo mai for brains?" argues the Colonel. "Th'aliens haven't budged, and if by some happenstance, they did budge, I'd've waked you up, pronto."

"It's been quiet, huh?"

Cinderblock gives her commandant a weird look. "There's more goin' on in the Mission Dolores crypt than there is in those alien camps. It's like they're all locked down or somethin'. Yesterday morning, they looked like they were gearing up to spread out some more, but then they just hunkered down instead. Little bit ago, I got some recon from Berk's team over at the Dolores. He says they've stopped working on anything but that satellite whatsit your pal Hoot hacked."

This is heartening news. I realize that sooner or later, John Makepeace and his buddies are gonna come roaring out of their encampments and overrun us like kudzu, but just maybe we can take advantage of this pause to set up some worthy defenses. Maybe there's something we can do to the aliens before they get their satellite dish working and call in reinforcements.

Jade and I have sat down to snarf a muchly appreciated breakfast of baos and rice when Cinderblock informs us of a late-breaking development out at the Presidio.

"Hismajesty wants a debriefing yesterday," she says. "He's one confused monarch right about now. I had Goldfinch and Luz try to explain what happened the other night up on the Mountain, but I don't think he got half of it. It seems he needs a little hand-holding at this especially trying time."

She is looking at me, but it's Jade who shakes her head and gives answer. "Del don't have the time to go hold His M's cold, clammy little hand. He's got another miraculous rescue to plan. I'll take care of the Majesties." She turns to me as a sort of after-thought and gives me the old melting-chocolate gaze.

Damn, but I'm a sucker for that look. Fact is, though, I'd been sitting there trying to think of some way to get my bride up to the Presidio anyway. Just in case all hell were to break loose here. Let someone who's not hauling Chickpea-lets handle the warrioring.

I smile and nod. "You're better at soothing Mercedes twitchy breast than I am, anyway," I say.

"But you'll let me know the minute anything breaks," she commands.

I glance at Cinderblock, who glances back. We smile and nod.

Once General Firescape has headed off for the Presidio, I call a council of war with my confederates, trying to ignore the feeling that this is one battle we can't win. Cinderblock is there, along with the commanding officers of all the Embarcaderan guard units. I bring Hoot, Lou, Deadend, Berk and, of course, Doug.

We gather in the Pit of the Regency throne room to hear Berk give the latest breaking report from the front. As Cinderblock has duly noted, the aliens have circled the winnebagos. Not so much as an alien whisker is glimpsed beyond their perimeters.

Huh. And all because of a handful of silicon chips and wires.

I gotta admit this situation makes me muy nervous. Mostly 'cause I don't like waiting for stuff to happen—especially bad stuff. Now, you'd think a guy who's just faced down a major spiri-tual nemesis would be a little less twitchy about the idea of facing a merely human enemy armed with nothing more deadly than laser rifles, but I feel a severe need to take action. Question is: what action can we take that won't make a lot of innocent folks deadjim?

I am pondering this when I realize that, once again, all eyes are on yours truly.

"We gotta find a way," I say slowly, carefully, "to drive the alien menace from our fair land. And the only way we can do this is to raise an army from every barrio of every kingdom on the Peninsula."

"A tall order," says Hoot. "I can tell you, right now, old Elvis ain't gonna go for any joint effort. Not unless you can convince him it's a win-win situation. Elvis, he likes to go with a winner and he's got this jingbing idea that our weapons are no match for alien laser rifles."

"Yeah, but we got magic," argues Creepy Lou. "The alienth don't got magic. They don't even believe in magic."

"Any sufficiently advanced tech is indistinguishable from the aforementioned," paraphrases Hoot. "Arthur C. Clarke. Elvis can't tell the difference. Even if he did believe we got magic— which he don't—he thinks the aliens got more of same. Elvis is somewhat of a pragmatist."

Such discouraging words from my most bosom buddy make me want to whine. I don't. I just say, "We gotta try," real calm. Calm is not how I feel, ni dong, but it's how I gotta act.

Hoot raises his eyebrows. "Well, hell yeah! I mean, if you can convince Elvis and his fellow monarchs and elected reps to do something together, that'd be a miracle—part of your stock in trade, Chickpea."

Hoot has a good point, and immediately my head fills up with visions of winnebagos driving off into the sunrise as we, citizens of every nation—Embarcadero, Potrero-Taraval, Bernal, Merced, and Excelsior—watch, united and victorious.

Yeah, right.

"Then, we're gonna try, right?" asks Creepy Lou.

Berk and Deadend just exchange looks.

"What good's it gonna do to drive 'em off?" asks Deadend. "I say we gotta wipe 'em out."

This pronouncement makes my heart drop to my boot tops. I

don't want anybody's blood on my hands, not even alien blood. I wonder for a moment if that's how the Ohlone felt when they realized the invaders' plans for them did not include their continued existence as a people. I wonder if there's any other way to deal with someone else wanting something you got and want to keep. In the middle of this quivery quandary, I remember something I heard John Makepeace say to his guys.

I say: "The aliens are here 'cause they told the folks at home this was going to be easy. They've got these people called Backers who pay for their stuff. They've got to convince the Backers this renovation is a good idea that's going to bring in lots of tourists and lots of money. If they have to run home with their tails draggin', their Backers aren't gonna waste any more money to try again."

"Are you sure about that?" asks Splendid, Commandant of the Union Square Brigade.

I'm not sure—not precisely sure—but since that was the gist of what I overheard, I nod solemnly.

"What if they never get home?" asks Berk. "Same difference, right? I mean, their Backers aren't likely to send any more of 'em, right?"

I start to open my mouth, but Cinderblock beats me to the punch. "Difference is, fish-head, that we don't have to kill 'em. Which means we don't gotta deal with the possibility of revenge. It'd be better to scare the cojones off 'em."

Berk subsides a bit and nods. "Okay. So let's s'pose if we can get a multi-national fighting force together, we can drive the aliens off. I'd say we're gonna have to scare the cojones off the alcaldes, too. If we want 'em to haul ass together, we may have to give 'em an idea of what it's gonna be like if they don't."

"A pogrom?" asks Deadend, dryly.

"The worst," says Berk, missing the sarcasm.

Sometimes Berk's thoughts get so thick I think it's hard for him to see through them. This means he misses a lot of what goes on outside his own head. Surprise is, he's actually a pretty good sméagol in spite of it.

"We'll do a little of everything," I decide. "We'll threaten a little calamity and promise a little utopia and pray they'll believe the magic will come through again."

Hoot grins. "If they could've been up on that Mountain with you, they'd believe."

"Yeah, well, I wasn't on the Mountain," says Deadend, "So, I'm not sure what to believe. And you can't send the Mountain to the monarchs."

O, out of the mouths of sméagols.

I summon knighties to the Palace and assign four teams of six. Each team has a letter from Yours Truly bearing the Royal Seal of Embarcadero that briefly lays out our collective problem, our intended solution, what benefits will accrue if we succeed and what horrors will result if we don't. From Doug, I humbly and reverently remove four branchlets, which I bind to the rolled-up letters with braided locks of my hair.

Hey, look—you find something that works, you go with it.

Cinderblock, meanwhile, mobilizes our troops and stations them at ready positions near the alien camps. Then we wait. While we wait, my curiosity gets the better of me and I end up tugging Doug down to the Tin Hau. Once I'm in the hustle-bustle part of the Sang Yee Gah, I get stopped about every ten feet or so by someone who wants to know what's happening with the aliens.

All I can say is, "We're working on it."

I realize something really funny (as in head-twisting funny, not amusing funny or oo-ee-e-oo funny). This is that not very many people have clue one about what really happened on that Mountain the other night between me and Chen. Oh, sure, the grapevine's been activated and sméagols and knighties have spread all sorts of tales, but mostly folks've heard the tale, said, "Wow, that's neon," then, settled on the aliens as the problem de jour. Naturally, they are waiting for someone to do something about it.

It's kind of like Moses, you know? I mean, here He is, telling the Israelites that God's talking to them again and has all sorts of spiritual glory saved up for them, and all they can say is, "Yeah, but can you do something about these Egyptians?" Not that I am in any way comparing myself with Moses, ni dong. I'm a mere merlin, not a Buddha, but you get the idea.

Most of the folks I talk to don't get that the Spiritual Battle has been fought and won; they just want the Powers that Be (meaning me and the Majesties and the knighties) to get rid of John Makepeace. If we can't get rid of John Makepeace, Hismajesty Mercedes will go down in history as a monarchal flop, I will flop right beside him, and what should have been a Golden Age for the Golden Mountain will be spoken of by future generations as the Dark Ages.

I kick myself right about here, 'cause I know I'm being unduly hard on the good citizens of Embarcadero. They don't deserve me ragging on them; they deserve me doing my damnedest to defeat the alien menace.

The Tin Hau is pretty much the same as ever. The monks pray, the offerings char, the incense smokes up the place real good. Doug and I hang inside the doorway of the sanctuary for a moment, wondering what do next, when one of the monks comes over, smiling.

I gotta clamp my jaw shut to keep it from dropping—it's Brother Howin, whom I last saw getting psychically battered by the late, great Master Shen Ah Nen. He is noticeably un-bespelled. I can tell because when I look into his eyes, there's a light on, if you know what I mean.

He bows very low to me and Doug and says, "Nin hao, most illustrious shaman. Nin hao, most excellent Tree. To what do we owe this kind visit?"

"I just wondered how you guys were doing," I say, and notice that other monks are beginning to gather around us. Once upon a time, this would have made me muy nervous. "I mean, I wanted

to make sure you were all right after, um, after Master Chen . . .
uh . . . left."

Eloquence incarnate.

The young monk's smile deepens. "We are well, great shaman,
for which bounty our Master, Ho, would like to thank you."

The cluster of monks nod and smile, reminding me of a flock
of pigeons cadging bread crumbs.

"Master Ho?" I repeat.

"Come," says Brother Howin, and beckons me to follow him
through the dragon-screened door.

I gotta admit, this gives me serious pause. I tremble a little as I
go down the hall toward the stairs that lead up to the shrine of
Shen Ah Nen. But the stair is no longer hidden, the door is wide
open, and sunlight tumbles down the stairs in fits and starts. The
monks cheerfully carry Doug up the long flight, while he waves
like some kind of conquering hero—which, in a manner of speaking, he is.

The doors to the shrine are open too, and I can see from here
how much the place has changed. It's still ornate and rich in
colors and smells, but the imperial din is gone and so are all the
little stands and tables with their pilfered relics. There is only a
simple altar, and shelves full of books and herbs. A monk is at the
altar setting out candles when we walk in.

"Master," says Howin. "They are here."

Wow. Like we were expected or something.

The Master turns and greets me with eyes that sparkle like
apache tears. It is the old monk who gave me the shen, without
which . . . who knows? There is much bowing and mutual
thanking and then the monks melt away, leaving Doug and me
alone with Master Ho.

"Many thanks, shaman," says the Master and it strikes me that
no one's called me 'merlin' since I got here. Seems as if I been
promoted. He waves a hand at the room. "I wanted you to see
that where Shen had sown darkness, you have reaped light."

I remember just about then what's cluttering up the pocket of my jeans. I pull the slightly singed shen out by its thong and hold it up.

"You knew," is all I can say.

"His name of names?" He tilts his head. "He revealed it while trying to ensorcel me when he took over this Order. He was an arrogant creature, one who liked riddles and icons perhaps too much for his own benefit. He was never without one of these hanging about his neck." He touches the shen with a fingertip and sets it swaying. "The gods love irony."

"Why did you send for me?" I want to know. "Why did you give me the shen?"

He smiles, gap-tooth, reminding me of Lou. "I am a monk, not a shaman. I have no magic, only faith. My faith informed me that you have both. It appears my faith was well-informed."

I blush all the way to my toes. "It wasn't me," I say. "It was Doug and the Ohlone Dolores and Firescape and Hoot and Creepy Lou . . . and you. You were on that Mountain with me too, in spirit, I think."

He holds out his hands palms up. "You are the fulcrum upon which other elements balance."

Oh, boy. Monk-speak. I feel my brain start to quiver. "Look," I say. "We gotta go. We, um, kind of got another war going on. Material plane kind of stuff, nothing real important in the cosmic scheme, I s'pose, but well, if some aliens show up in a while and try to evict you, you'll know we lost."

"Ah. These aliens you speak of are the men who seek relics of the past, yes? Not unlike Shen in that way, though their goals are material ones."

"Yeah. And to them this city is one big fossil."

"But they are wrong, are they not?" says Master Ho. "The city is a live thing. And a live thing has both a soul and a will."

My brain is close to poached by the time Doug and I are back down in the Sanctuary, saying good-bye to all the monks, who crowd around, wanting to touch Doug's boughs.

"Doug," I murmur as we squeeze toward the entrance, "if I

ever understand what a monk says, I'm going to be very concerned."

twenty-seventh: uneasy alliances

"THAY CHICKPEA!" cries a muy familiar voice, and I look up to see Creepy Lou and Cinderblock in the door of the sanctuary.

Wrong knightie, but deja view, anyway.

I suddenly miss Jade most painfully, and wonder if we'll ever be able to just—oh, I dunno—sit in front of Bags' and Kaymart's fireplace together on a cold summer evening, with a cat, maybe.

Creepy Lou is as full of bounce as ever, but he lets Cinderblock do the narrating.

"The emissaries are in, Chickpea," she tells me. "Excelsior says 'yes.' The Tsarina Khabaroff is sending out her crack troops. Prime Minister Tewksbury of Merced, however, wishes to delay his decision, pending further developments. There's no word from Lord E and the Bernalis aren't biting. The Sultan thinks it's a trick to get him to leave the borders of his tiny republic open to attack."

"One huzzah and three damns," I say. "What are our chances?"

"Last count puts the alien incursion at three-hundred twenty-four. We can top that, troop-wise, but we don't got the weaponry. For every AK we got, they got a laser rifle or a canon, whereas we got nothing bigger than the semiautomatics. The Tsarina's knighties aren't any better off. According to sméagols, they got about thirty AKs between all of them and ordnance is a major problem." She gives this big sigh. "Nothing like a real enemy to make you realize how little defense you really got."

"Oh, by the way," she tells me as we make our way out of the Sang Yee Gah, "your old buddy Hec—I mean, Hoot—has taken off on some sort of mission. He wouldn't say it right out, but I think he's gone over into Potrero-Taraval to try to scare up some support among them as don't care much for Lord E."

"Hell," I say, "that'd be half the populace."

I get a glance at her face, then, and realize that something about this scenario is really jinking with her head. I take a wild guess that somebody's been getting better acquainted with somebody else while I been busy elsewhere.

"Hoot," I comment, "is a rare dude. He can talk hisself in and out of just about anything."

"Thilver-tongued devil," agrees Lou.

Cinderblock just grimaces.

When we get back to the Palace, there is still no official word from Lord E. No surprise there—it'd be most un-Elvis-like to pick a side before the body count. I review our forces. Cinderblock is right. Even with the troops from Excelsior, we're still holding the short end of the stick.

I take a moment to pull Doug aside and cast runes. I don't know what else to do what with no Dolores to whisper at me any more. The center of my rune spread is a bottle cap with a little gold crown on it. Well, that's pretty clear. I get Cinderblock to send knighties to bring Hismajesty out of the Presidio. A king, the runes say, should be at the head of his troops at a time like this. I try to disregard the fact that it will bring Firescape out of the Presidio as well.

As evening settles, so does a dense, truly nasty fog that is unlike anything I've ever seen. It's like all thirty-four known varieties rolled into one humongous ground-hugging wu dong frio of epic proportions. It's the kind of fog that makes everybody talk in whispers and look over their shoulders.

It's the kind of fog that makes Berk the Sméagol wax poetic. "Damn," he says, peering out of the Palace windows during our next council of war. "You could lose yer socks in that stuff without 'em ever leavin' yer feet."

We discuss the timing of any raids we might pull off. The Tsarina's General—an ex-sméagol named Nab—is all for clobbering the daylights out of our enemy in one big night time free-for-all. Cinderblock, Splendid, and Sweetie—veteran Captain of the Richmond Guard—recommend lightning fast hit-n-runs followed by a prolonged siege.

"They gotta run out of food," says Sweetie. "And when they run out of food, they gotta come out. And when they come out— *whammo!*" She slams one leather-bound fist into the opposite palm. "We got 'em."

"And when we got them," asks Dragonboat—she's from Wharfside, "what do we do with them?"

"Nuke 'em," opines General Nab.

"Run 'em out of town in their underwear," says Sweetie. This has always been her favorite way of punishing miscreants.

"I don't want to nuke them," I interject, "I want to drive them out so they don't want to come back and their Backers won't pay to send them. Listen, they're not all like John Makepeace. Some of them feel kind of guilty about what they're doing. One of them—a dude named Ty—helped me and Firescape get out of captivity the other night. They don't want to kill us either."

"Hell, no!" sneers Deadend. "They don't want to kill us, just snatch our kingdom right out from under us. Whether we starve or get lightning shot, we're still dead."

"No, Cicerone's right," says Cinderblock, giving her magic weapon a sharp rap on the floor. "If we kill them, more might come to even the score. We need them to leave here and never want to come back. And we want them to tell everybody back home that the Gam Saan is bad news, your worst nightmare and otherwise unfit for tourism."

Sweetie snorts. "Don't matter to me whether it's the Grim Reaper, guilt, lack of funding, or sheer humiliation—I just want 'em gone."

"You just wanna pants 'em," sniggers Dragonboat.

I find myself staring at her. She is a traditionally beautiful Chinese girl, sans red hair, but still reminds me powerfully of my Jade. I think, again, for just a moment, about sitting in front of that fireplace in the Farm House with a cat in my lap and Jade in my arms and our baby snoozing peacefully alongside. I sigh.

"I still say we nuke every last mother's son of 'em," says Nab, clenching his fist around a handful of air.

"Me too," agrees Sweetie, and the ruby in her eye patch glitters like a drop of blood. "I say if none of 'em makes it home, the legends about the Lost Cities will grow, and that will keep their kith and kin from pokin' their alien noses into our turf."

"And I say," says a voice from the dark beyond the Pit, "it'll crank their kith and kin up for some serious revenge." My wife steps out of the shadows with Hismajesty at her side. "Merlin Cicerone and the Colonel are right. We get them out of here with as much finesse and as little loss of blood as we can."

My heart leaps to see her, then falls flat on its keester, 'cause I know she's gonna want to lead her knighties into battle. Cinderblock's face is as screwed up as mine by this realization. We exchange worries in a glance.

Firescape and her cohorts waste no time. It seems only minutes before they begin to settle on strategies that they will begin to implement as soon as weather allows. Me, I mouse out and pray that the fog holds until I can produce a miracle.

In the midst of the war council, a wiry little knightie in Richmond yellow comes streaking into the throne room to hold a harried whisperfest with Firescape and Cinderblock. Next thing I know, they're all three in my face.

"Somethin's afoot, Del," says Firescape. "Hear this report." She nods at the wiry little knightie, Bustop by name, who unloads the tale.

"There's fighting going on inside the alien camps."

"Inside?"

I imagine a coup perpetrated by Ty against his leader. It takes a lot of imagining.

"I been attached to the unit at the Mission Dolores," Bustop goes on. "It's quiet as a graveyard in there, then, all of sudden, there's shouting and shooting and general panic and all these big lights come on. It's like as if they're lookin' for something. Of course, we can't get a good gander inside, ni dong, 'cause those damn sirens'll go off."

I can only boggle. I try to think, but nothing comes. I look at Doug. He rustles and trembles. Uh-oh. I know that look. Somethin' really *is* afoot.

"Is Hoot back yet?" I ask.

Cinderblock roughs up her wild crop of hair and grimaces. "No, and I think your buddy Lou's gone off after him."

"You think it's them raising this ruckus?" Firescape asks.

"Hell, I hope not!" says Cinderblock. "Damn gonzo, jingbing half-wit!"

I appreciate for a moment that true love can happen anywhere at anytime to anyone, then I make a command decision. "I'm gonna do some personal recon. Maybe I can magic up some answers." I turn to my wife, trying to think of a way I can talk her out of going with me.

Cinderblock is one step ahead of me. "General Firescape, we gotta get back to the war council, finish our tactical plans."

Jade glances from me to Cinderblock, then at the Pit where Hismajesty is pacing in circles. Then she kisses me with enough heat to make my jeans tighten up and says, "Take Bustop with you." Then she turns to go.

"Wait," I say. "I gotta know—are you planning on leading the raids?"

"Hell no," she snorts. "I can't brace my AK against this." She pats the growing Flannigan and winks at me. Then she and her Colonel go back to Our Twitchy Majesty.

At the Mission, Bustop and I are far from enlightened. From outside, we can't see squiddle, just a huge patch of bright fog from which come occasional spatters of laser fire. Bustop wasn't jinkin'—the aliens got every light in the place turned on. We go inside, but the view from our rabbit hole isn't any better. In the hour we lie among the crumbling statues of the garden, all we see is the occasional random shadow, stretched, spider-like, in the fog.

It is as we wriggle back toward the hole that something happens. A sound we've been hearing without hearing just stops and all the lights go out. There is a moment of gaping, dark silence, then all hell cuts loose. There is yelling, gunfire and general panic, much as described by Bustop in her report. The weird wu is sliced to ribbons by alien power torches, but I doubt the aliens can see whatever it is they're shooting at. The shouting gets louder and louder, but eventually, one voice wins out.

"Hold-your-fire!" roars John Makepeace. Sounds like he got a bull-horn or something.

There is another sudden, dark quiet, and then some lights come on. From the way they spear the fog, I know they gotta be winnebago headlamps. Huh. Those aren't gonna last long.

"The generator cut out," I whisper to Bustop. "It's gotta be Hoot."

She shakes her head, something I can barely see even though she's hunkered down right next to me. "Why would this jingbing jake decide to take out the aliens single-handed? That's loco."

"It's also muy Hoot-like. Besides, I suspect he's double-handed. I think Creepy Lou's with him."

Bustop whispers a raspberry. "Like that'd be a help."

"Yeah, it would be," I defend Lou. "Lou may be a little gooey between the ears, but he's got this . . . special sense. I don't know what it is, but it's number one jade. If I got to go into a bad place alone, Lou's one dude I'd surely take with me."

"Who's there?" someone yells and a bolt of laser fire screams over our heads.

We are, understandably, outta there—behind the cedar bough, under the statue, into the ground. I hear the gallop of alien feet as I slither into the earth. We don't stop to catch our breath until we're safely out in the street. Behind us, a flurry of power lights whip through the fog over the garden.

"If they find that hole," says Bustop, "they're gonna fill it in and your buddies are gonna be trapped."

"Then pray they don't find it," I say.

The words are barely out of my mouth when the flurry of power lights gets really wild and gunfire rips loose again.

"What the hell is going on in there?" asks Bustop. "What could your buds be doing that'd get the aliens so riled up?"

"Don't' know," I answer. "But we're not going to find out here."

The fog does not lift by morning. The military types move their troops around, working them closer to the alien camps. When they get close enough to hear the outbreaks of weirdness, they settle down to wait some more. If they wait forever, there won't be enough of them. Nab and Sweetie agitate to lay siege, pick off anybody who comes out. I hope cooler heads will prevail until I can figure out what it is Hoot is doing and what I can do to help him out. I can't shake the awful feeling that he might've gotten himself and Lou trapped inside the Mission.

In fact, I've about settled on this theory when there come confirmed reports that the same weirdness is going on inside the other alien camps, too. Including the conspicuous malfunctioning of some of their equipment. This makes me suspect that maybe Hoot was able to raise some Potreran recruits after all. It also makes me worry about casualties. Just like Hoot not to coordinate efforts. Damn jingbing buckaroo.

Eventually, the waiting gets to me and I head up to the rabbit hole once again. The street end looks the same as always, so I don't think twice about slipping on down. I think three times, but in the end, I do it anyway. I'm just at the part where the tunnel starts to slope up into the garden when my foglite, which I got clenched in my teeth, picks up the first piles of dirt and rock. Four feet later, I realize I'm gonna have to back all the way out. John Makepeace has found the hole and filled it in.

Backing up on the flattest part isn't so bad, but when the slope gets steeper, it's really tough. I try not to think about where I am; I tell myself I can smell fresh air, that I'm really close to the surface, that any second now, my feet are gonna be swinging free. Then they are. I almost cry out in relief. That's when something grabs my ankles and hauls me out of the ground like a ripe carrot.

When I'm right-side up again, I find myself staring into the muzzle of an alien laser rifle.

twenty-eighth: history

WE DON'T GO in through the main gate. We go in through a little gate in the side wall. The moment we step inside the place, I get how weird things are. Above the Mission is a patch of wu luz that filters the sunlight just enough to give everything in the place this kind of angel glow. It's like being in the eye of a storm. I didn't know fog had eyes.

Faces peer out at us from winnebago windows. The guys I'm with seem real edgy, too, eyes going every-which-way. It's clear there's no work going on in here.

We're almost to John Makepeace's personal winnebago when a silky banner of mist drifts across our path and the guy next to me slices through it with his laser pistol and a wild shriek.

Weird.

John Makepeace himself slams open the door of his winnebago, reaches down with both hands and hauls me up the stairs by my collar. He flings me so hard across the little room, I flip over the table and into the bench seat on the other side. It's not a smooth landing, 'cause my hands are tied behind my back.

Next thing I know, I'm right-side up again and looking hard

into John M's face, which at this moment is almost as red as his beard.

"All right, you conniving little bastard. Call off your dogs or, I swear, we'll drop every one of them."

"My dogs?" I repeat, wondering if John and I are on the same planet.

"You heard me. Tell them to cut the crap or—"

"I don't get it, John. I don't have any dogs."

"You know what I'm talking about, you little hair ball." John's face is getting redder by the second. "The spooks, the haunts. You remember them: First you pretended not to know about them, then you decided they were the Minions of Darkness. Well, I think it's pretty clear whose minions they are. And I've never heard of ghosts that tinkered with machinery. Now, I'm going to take you out there"—he nods toward the door— "and I want you to tell your buddies two things: One, they stop this harassment of my crews right now, or they're going to end up with their sheets full of holes, and two, they give back the components they took out of the satellite dish."

I blink and try to look muy innocent. "You mean, it's broken?"

"You're damn right it's broken."

"Then, you can't phone home and call in reinforcements." I give him a certain look, hoping he will see that his situation is deteriorating.

He does. And he reacts to this observation by rapping my skull against the window behind me and snarling, "Look, weirdo, my crews are cut off from home, sitting on a fault line, and surrounded by fog, legends, and a pack of schizophrenic indigents who have exploited their every nightmare. I've offered them extra pay and bonuses and paid time off—you name it—but right now, every other one is ready to quit. Ty's threatening to take his crew and bug out right now and . . ."

He fumes for a moment, then finishes, "—and I just lost contact with the group in Golden Gate Park. Either they've been put out of business, or they've broken camp. Now, I'm telling you, Ciceroni, you are going to show these boneheads that these spooks are bogus before somebody really gets hurt."

He hauls me to my feet and aims me at the door.

"So, no one's been hurt, yet?" I ask.

He shoves me out the door before answering. After he has picked my sorry ass up off the flagstones, he says, "Actually, a few of my guys have managed to break some bones and singe each other. Naturally, they blame it on the spooks and not on their own careless stupidity."

He commences to dragging me toward the sanctuary. Shabu dong pulls apart before us like gauzy curtains and glides back behind.

"So you . . . you haven't shot any of the haunts?"

"Not yet. But if they don't stop their haunting, we will."

"I don't get it, John," I say, 'cause I don't. "Coming in, you didn't have any queasies about wiping out a couple city blocks of Potrero-Taraval, Potreros and all. I know. I buried some of them. Burying the kids was the hardest."

I check out his face. He looks pretty grim.

"You're lying," he informs me. "We didn't target any kids. Only people who were attacking us."

"No, John. I'm not lying, and I think you know I'm not lying. It doesn't matter that you didn't target them. They still ended up dead. Collateral damage, I think they used to call it in wars. So, I gotta wonder what you're waiting for here. I kind of think if you could shoot these haunts, you would. So, why don't you?"

He doesn't answer, just drags me up to the top of the sanctuary steps, turns me around and addresses the shabu dong thusly, "Listen up, all you ghosties and ghoulies. I've got your feckless leader here. Make no mistake, this is a threat. You pack up your bed sheets and get the hell out of here or people are going to get hurt—starting with El Loco, here."

The shabu dong has been minding its own business up to now, eddying here and there, sniffing at our heels a bit. At the end of John M's pronouncement, there is a sudden stoppage of dong. The courtyard is so quiet, I can hear water dripping from the church roof and pigeons mumbling under the eaves. Then, weird stuff happens—stuff I seen before real recently, only not in a real place as I recall. The shabu gets muy, muy dong and begins to coil into columns and spirals that I suspect are going to look very human before too long.

Huh, I marvel, not Hoot and Lou after all.

A couple of laser bolts zing across the courtyard. One hits a tree, another zaps the corner eave of the church and sends plaster flying away in scorched chunks.

"Hell," mutters John Makepeace, then bellows, "Hold your fire!"

He gives me a hard shove, then yanks me back by the rope around my hands, obviously forgetting that arms don't bend that way.

"Tell them," he snarls. "Tell them to get lost."

"Sorry, John," I say, "I'm afraid I can't do that."

I feel the muzzle of his laser pistol glide, cold, alongside my neck.

Yow. "I mean, yeah," I say quickly, "I can tell them to get lost. I can tell them anything you want, but I don't s'pect it'd do any good. They're not my guys. I can't control them."

I can't control my face, either. It just starts grinning bigtime. Master Ho was right, the city does have a soul and the Ohlone are part of it and probably always will be.

Whoa. I have understood monk-speak. Anything is possible. I laugh—an untimely and ill-advised move.

"What are you laughing at, you nit-wit?" roars John Makepeace and clobbers me upside the head, then grabs a fistful of my hair to keep me on my feet. "What do you mean, they're not your guys? You mean they belong to that moron, Lord E?"

"No, I mean they don't belong to anybody. They're spirits."

"Aw, jeez," John M says, then adds a few more colorful comments, taking the names of several Prophets in vain. "Are we back to that crap about the Minions of Darkness? Are you going to pull that old Chinese wizard out of your hat again?"

"I don't own a hat and the old Chinese wizard is out of the picture," I explain, my eyes on what's shaping up in the courtyard.

I wonder which funnel-o-fog is Pedro? I wonder if his son, Delmar, and Paguin the Shaman are here, too.

"This isn't the Minions of Darkness, either," I add. "This is the Dolores."

"The who?"

"The spirits of this place. The soul of the Gam Saan."

"That's bullshit! There are no spirits. You've got some sort of technology you've been hiding from us. You—" He breaks off and glances sideways at me. "Damn. What the hell am I saying? You're such a backward bunch of— If they're not your people, why would they defend you?"

"Maybe 'cause we're like them and you're not. Or maybe they just don't wanna see history repeat on itself."

He gives me this long look, then pokes his pistol into my neck again. "Talk to them."

I shrug and turn my attention to the courtyard, which is beginning to be a very scary place for people who don't believe in ghosts. The fog is moving, changing, clumping up around the winnebagos and other places I suspect aliens are hiding.

"Ohlone!" I say loudly. "John Makepeace wants you to cease and desist as you are interfering with his plans to turn the Gam Saan into a tourist trap and make oodles-o-bucks. Now, I figure since you are the landlords of this chunk-o-real estate and it's up to you who you'd rather rent to—"

John Makepeace stops me with another jab of his ray gun. "Cut it out," he says. "Just tell them to leave."

"John Makepeace wants you to leave," I say. "Now. What d'you say?"

The Mission holds its breath for just a moment, then things go from weird to weirder. The foggy shapes are suddenly legitimate wraiths—totally Lost-Arkian. They are as fully-formed as they were in the Lodge; I can make out faces and arms and legs. They move, too, not on the ground but above it. Not swiftly, ni dong, but in that slow, inexorable way that ghouls do in those old movies (which makes you wonder how they ever catch anybody). These wraiths go right for the hiders. Winnebago doors crash open, laser bolts fly and human forms dart among the ex-human ones.

As for John and me, we are forced to go to ground, and all the shouting he does about holding fire does squiddle. It doesn't take long before the aliens lose track of each other in the swirl of fog and spirit. There are screams of pain as their lightning starts striking random targets.

"Shit!" says John Makepeace. "They're going to massacre each other! Shit!"

Now he moves, dragging me backward through the doors of the sanctuary. The pistol goes to my head and I hear it click and whine.

"Give me one reason I shouldn't blast a neat little hole through your head."

"Because I don't think you really want history to repeat on itself, either," I say. "'Cause that'd make for really bad karma. And maybe 'cause you know we didn't do anything to you. You chose to come here. We just tried to hang on to our lives and our home. Now our home is trying to hang on to us. That's the core of it, John—even if you kill me, the Gam Saan will still fight back."

Outside, a winnebago engine roars to life. Then another and another. John Makepeace freezes. This seems like an auspicious moment to give him some travel information.

"By the way," I tell him, "you can't get back across the Bay Bridge. The Islanders blew it up again. You might want to go south."

"Shit," he says again. Funny how fear reduces the vocabulary.

He gives me a hard look in the face, then pulls off his belt, cinches it around my ankles, and shoves me to the floor. When I manage to struggle into a half-sitting position, John Makepeace has disappeared out into the Dolores fog, leaving me on the hard, cold floor and the doors swinging open on their freshly oiled hinges.

The shooting is dwindling now, and out in the courtyard is a regular winnebago chorus. There is a vast rumbling as they pull out. There are some crashes, too, but eventually, the rampage of metal elephants stops, their bellows fade and the place goes quiet.

I peer from the doors and see the shabu dong has stilled and begun to clear—except for this one, lone swirl of fog and sun-motes that's doing a dance right in front of me. It thickens, slows and becomes Pedro, sitting cross-legged across from a fire pit that is and isn't there.

I have the weird sensation of being in the Ohlone Lodge and the Californio sanctuary at the same time. I can almost feel the warmth of the spirit fire on my face.

Pedro smiles at me. At least, I think he's smiling. "The first aliens met the shaman when they climbed the mountain," he says. "They have met him again. They will tell their people you are their Devil."

"So, history repeated on itself after all," I say.

"The first aliens didn't go home," he says.

He stands up, or maybe rises is a better word, and turns to the open church doorway. I can see right through him; the graveyard's ragged, leaning headstones, the rocky grotto, the devil/saint. There are no more ghosts.

"When I told the Indian agent I was the last one," Pedro says, "I was more wrong than I knew. Now I see that the spirit of my people has never left this place—will never leave it."

"So that's why?" I ask. "That's why you came back to help us?"

He begins to fade; I can see sunlight washing the graveyard. "And because you are right in what you said to John Makepeace."

"That we're like you? Or that you didn't want history to repeat?"

But he's gone and I'm still tied up like a fat duck in the Gee

Gah. In the videos, they untie you. Sometimes life isn't a whole lot like the videos. I settle back and watch sunlight play across the grey and white and weathered brown of the graveyard. Eventually, Firescape will come for me. She always does. And I'm sure she'll know right where to find me.

Now I'm thinking about our son who will soon be in this world, and I'm thinking that his name will be Pedro. Pedro Delmar Flannigan. Well, Pedro Delmar Flannigan whatever his mother eats or sees or hears or thinks of at the moment-of-his-birth. That's tradition. And, I think, it's something the spirits of this place will understand.

Appendix 1: A Gaam San Vocabulary

- Alcalde: a king or ruler
- bao : a steamed bun filled with meat and/or vegetables
- bueno : good, nice, cool
- Bu hao! : No good! That's bad! That stinks!
- chen : vast, great
- Chun jie : Spring Festival
- coolies : from kuli—bitter toil
- deadjim : Really, truly dead
- Duanwu jie : Dragon Boat Festival, late May, early June
- Du Pon Gai : DuPont Street, the site of an open air market
- fanguan : a noodle shop
- Gam Saan : Golden Mountain, San Francisco
- ha gow : wrapped shrimp
- hao : good, okay, fine
- ho : the good
- howin : a loyal swallow
- jin : gold; also, spirit
- jingbing : crazy, silly, nuts
- jink : to mess with something or someone, to play games with someone's head
- jinked : messed up, screwy
- liko : Buddhist nun
- loco : mad as a hatter
- luz : light
- mushu : a crepe filled with vegetables and meat
- muy : very, much
- napoleon : severely egomaniacal
- nen : primordial waters
- neon : really, truly cool

- ni dong : you understand, you know
- number one jade: the best imaginable
- Wo dong!: I understand! I get it!
- shen: (Egyptian Book of the Dead) amulet placed at the feet of the dead
- siu mai: pork with shrimp
- shining: mad, over-the-edge, crazy
- sméagol: a spy
- Suti: (EBD) god who carries away the soul, Guardian of Darkness
- wu: fog
- Yuanxiao jie: culmination of Chinese New Year in February
- Zhangqui jie: Moon Festival, full moon in late September, early October. Celebrants watch the moon and eat moon-shaped cookies
- Zhou!: Hurry! Scram!
- Zhende?: Really? You don't say?

Appendix 2: An Index to Varieties of Fog

Drop down, O fleecy Fog and hide her skeptic sneer, and all her pride!
— Francis Bret Harte (1836–1902), *San Francisco from the Sea*

	Static	Moving	Warm	Chill
HEAVY				
Consistent	wu pesado	wu pesadong	planchar	planchar frio
Billowy	zhentou (pillow)	zhendong	chunmao lana (wool)	helado (ice cream)
Wispy	bufando (scarf)	bufandong	tonzi (blanket)	sabana
MEDIUM				
Consistent	wu gauze	wu dong	wu caliente	wu frio
Billowy	lazy nube	nube dong	nube caliente	nube frio
Wispy	seda (silk)	silk dong seda dong	seda caliente	seda frio
LIGHT				
Consistent	powder polvo	polvo dong	gun powder	
Billowy	dust huichen	dust dong huichen dong		
Wispy	shabu	shabu dong	hot silk	shabu frio
OTHER	Static	Moving	Warm	Chill
Lit by Sun	wu luz			
Almost rain	jin rain			
Ground mist	ditan	bowu	lucha (green tea)	niunai (milk)
high fog	wu gao			

read a sample from a princess of passyunk

One: If Market Street Flooded

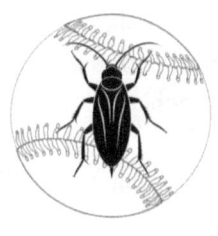

"If Market Street ever flooded," said Stanislaus Ouspensky, "South Philly would be an island."

He contemplated this possibility over a bowl of chicken soup in a postage-stamp-sized deli on South Tenth Street between Cross and Tasker.

Across the counter, the deli's owner, Izzy Davidov, looked up from the newspaper spread across the worn linoleum of his countertop and raised a graying eyebrow. "How so?"

Ouspensky straightened from his soup and flung his arms wide, dripping chicken broth across the counter. "Just look. Water on three sides; history on the fourth. All it would take is a little push"—he demonstrated on the lone matzo ball still bobbing in the bowl—"and we're cut off from the present. Because Time gets confused in South Philly."

At the end of the counter closest to the door, Ganady Puzdrovsky and his best friend, Yevgeny Toschev, locked eyes over their root beer. The boys had heard Mr. Ouspensky hold forth on this subject before and knew that Mr. Ouspensky believed Time flowed into Philly and eddied there, unable to find a way out again. At least, that's what he claimed to believe.

Stanislaus Ouspensky, who had lived in a walk-up on 20ᵗʰ Street across from Connie Mack Stadium since the Creation, had watched many baseball games from his rooftop before the notorious 'spite fence' went up in '35. To Ganady and Yevgeny he had privately intimated that because of these so-called time-eddies, he could *still* watch them. At the ambiguous age of sixteen—stranded midway between childhood and adulthood—neither boy could completely discount the claim. Neither was sure he wanted to.

"Confused?" repeated Izzy, eyeing the golden beads of liquid on his previously spotless countertop. "How does Time get confused?"

"Abigail Adams's Bed and Breakfast is how," said Mr. Ouspensky. "The Betsy Ross Museum is how. Time slides down the Broad Street Line and finds these places, and it eddies around them and gets stuck. Do you know what you get when Time gets stuck?"

"No," said Izzy, rattling his paper. "But I suspect you will tell me."

"Windows into the past. Windows into *history*. That's what you get." He glanced at the two boys out of the corner of his eye and winked, making them parties to his theory.

As indeed, they were. Thanks in large part to Mr. Ouspensky and his philosophical ramblings, their Philadelphia was not circumscribed by the neat grid of streets or a modern façade. Their Philly wasn't merely trapped in Time, it was sinking back into it.

This meant there were times when Izzy's deli was a tavern at which thieves and pirates gathered in the wee hours. And Saint Stanislaus' Church was a grand and massive cathedral gone to weed, in which sad monks carried out their daily rites, and at night worked for an unspecified Underground.

"Windows?" repeated Izzy, his eyebrows just visible above the edge of the newspaper. "I'll tell you what I know about windows, Ouspensky. I know that mine haven't been washed for above a week thanks to that *hulyen*, Nikolai Puzdrovsky."

Ganady snorkeled into his straw, root beer exploding up the sides of the bottle. Hearing his elder brother referred to as a "hell-raiser," even in Yiddish, was not without humor. Lazy, Nikolai might be called, careless, maybe—but a hulyen?

The hulyen himself appeared just then as if magically summoned, stepping through Izzy's door with the sharp April wind nipping after him. He closed the door in its face and said, "Hey, Mr. O. Hey, Izzy. Can I get a grape soda?"

Izzy's eyebrows rose again at the sound of his pet name coming from Nikolai's lips. Neither of the other boys would have dared address him in such fashion, but Nikolai was seventeen and as of this past winter, considered himself to be sufficiently grown up to experiment with such adult privilege.

"How do you do, *Mister* Puzdrovsky?" asked Izzy mildly. "I'll be happy to see to your soda as soon as I've finished my business with Ganady."

Ganady's ears perked up at this, for he had no idea that business was being done with him.

Izzy said, "So, Ganady, since my windows have gone unwashed this week past, I am wondering if you and your young friend might be interested in a bit of work. One could do the windows, one the floors..."

Nikolai reverted swiftly to his youth. "Gee, Mr. Davidov, I was going to do them Friday, but...well, I had to make up some homework, and then it was getting dark, and you know how Mama is about us being out after dark."

"My windows don't know from homework," said Izzy. "They're just dirty. Perhaps Ganady doesn't have homework that must be made up?"

Ganady glanced at Nikolai, whose entire thought process was writ publicly on his lean face. Certainly he wanted the money, but having to do windows on Friday afternoons instead of all the other things that could be done...

Nikolai took a deep breath. "I'll do them Wednesday. I promise. Right after school. Will that be okay, Mr. D.?"

Izzy grunted what Ganady assumed was an affirmative and poked his long nose back into his paper. "You know where the soda is. Help yourself."

Nikolai did just that, swinging around the end of the counter to the beaten-up little icebox where Izzy kept his cold stuff. He was back out again in a moment, swigging a grape Nehi. "Seen any good ballgames lately, Mr. Ouspensky?" he asked.

"A few," said the old man coyly, dunking the hapless matzo ball with his spoon. He did not elaborate.

In days past, he would have waxed poetic about the games, but Nikolai was no longer of the inner circle. To Ganady's chagrin, his elder brother had begun to change with the onset of this, his junior year, until by now, in early April, he seemed as blasé and unimaginative as his peers.

For his part, Nikolai merely grinned, sucked his soda and said, "Mama sent me to bring you home, Ganny. And Eugene's wanted up at the restaurant."

Yevgeny's eyes shot sparks of perfect delft blue onto his freckled cheeks. "Don't call me that," he said.

Nikolai shrugged his shoulders. "Suit yourself. All I know is, your Mama wants you to help out in the kitchen."

Unlike Yevgeny, who resisted Americanization with every fiber of his being, Nikolai had become relentlessly American, his interests running more and more to cars and leather bomber jackets and chinos and high-school dances. Mama and Baba were the only ones at home who could call him "Nikolai" or "Nikki" these days; everyone else must call him "Nick." He had unilaterally decided that Yevgeny would be "Eugene" instead of "Zhenya" or some other standard diminutive. He had also coined the shortened version of Ganady's name on the grounds that the Polish version—"Genna"—"sounded girly." Everyone had taken to using it—even their Mama on occasion. Ganady couldn't find it in himself to care with anything like the passion Yevgeny did.

Nick said South Philadelphia was an antique or a museum, or worse, a human rummage sale. Further, Ganady and Yevgeny with their heads full of time eddies and magical windows were *yentas* who might just as well be doing needlework and sharing neighborhood gossip with Baba Irina's *glayzele tey* society.

He rarely joined the other boys on their rambles these days, and when he did, Ganady knew he was only along for the ride. He never brought his imagination with him. To hear Nick tell it, the only reason he spent any time with the younger boys at all was to keep them from dropping permanently through one of Ouspensky's magic windows, leaving him to explain their disappearance to the elder Puzdrovskys.

Root beer bottles drained, the two younger boys followed Nikolai from the deli.

"Saturday?" asked Mr. Ouspensky from behind them.

"Saturday," said Ganady and Yevgeny in unison.

And Izzy Davidov muttered, "Mr. D!" and rattled his newspaper.

"Saturday, what?" asked Nikolai as the boys made their way up the street.

Ganady shrugged, thrusting his hands deep into his pockets, trying to lose the root-beer-bottle chill. "Oh, nothing. We're um..."

Yevgeny said, "We're going to help Mr. Ouspensky put up a new clothesline."

Nikolai smirked. "You mean you're going over to watch ghost baseball with him. You been going over there for a month of Sundays. You ever seen any old ghost-ball game?"

"The season hasn't started yet," said Yevgeny. Mr. Ouspensky says it's a matter of timing. He says what we want is a Saturday afternoon just after Opening Day."

Nick shook his head. "You two are such *shlubs*. And Mr. O knows it. He's just fooling with you."

"No he isn't," said Yevgeny defensively. "He says there's a spot
—*The Spot*. He knows how to find it. And if we get there at just
the right time—"

"You might see a twenty-year-old ballgame?" Nick finished for
him. "That's dumb."

"Baba says there are magic spots like that all over Poland," said
Ganady. "Why wouldn't there be magic spots here, too?"

Now Nikolai's eyes rolled. Baba Irina, he'd be thinking, still
thinks she's in Keterzyn, and that Poland is still an imperial force
—or ought to be. All he said was: "This is America. The New
World. There's no magic. There's movies."

"But Baba remembers—" Yevgeny began, and Nick's eyes
made another circuit.

"Eugene, you've known Baba all your life and you still don't
get that when she says, 'I remember...' she's about to tell a *boobeh
myseh*? I bet you still believe in fairytales, too, huh?"

Yevgeny winced at this abuse of his name, but Ganady had
barely heard his brother at all, for something had called to him
from the corner of 21st and LeHigh.

"You know what Mr. Ouspensky says is magic?" he asked,
looking away over rooftops and telephone poles. "A five-four-
three triple play."

The other boys considered this. Then Yevgeny nodded
agreement.

"You," Nick disparaged, "are obsessed with baseball. You and
Mr. O, all three."

"You sleep with your mitt under your pillow, *Nikki*," said
Yevgeny. "Same as us."

Nikolai blushed crimson to the roots of his dark hair. "Don't
call me that," he said, but he didn't deny where his fine, red
leather catcher's mitt spent the hours between dusk and dawn.

A Princess of Passyunk—updated version released May 20, 2025
from Book View Café.

about the author

Maya is the New York Times Best-selling author of *The Antiquities Hunter (a Gina Miyoko Mystery)* and *Star Wars Legends: The Last Jedi* (with Michael Reaves). She became addicted to science fiction when her dad let her stay up late to watch *The Day the Earth Stood Still.* Since then her short fiction has been published in *Analog, Amazing Stories, Century, Realms of Fantasy, Interzone, Paradox* and *Jim Baen's Universe.* Her debut novel, *The Meri* (Baen), was a *Locus Magazine* 1992 Best First Novel nominee. Since, she has published over a dozen speculative fiction novels.

Maya lives in San Jose where she writes, performs, and records original and parody (filk) music with her husband and awesome musician and producer, Chef Jeff Vader, All-Powerful God of Biscuits. The couple has produced seven music albums: *Retro-Rocket Science, Aliens Ate My Homework, Grated Hits* and *Shrödinger's Hairball* (parody), and the original music CDs *Manhattan Sleeps, Möbius Street, I Remember the Rain* and *Labyrinth.*

Visit Maya's writing website Making Reality Behave: htpp://www.mayabohnhoff.com

You can find Jeff and Maya's music at Band Camp: http://www.jeffandmaya.com

You can find their parody videos at: https://www.youtube.com/@mysticfig

more books by maya kaathryn bohnhoff

THE ANTIQUITIES HUNTER
(A Gina Miyoko Mystery)
Pegasus Crime, 2018

STAR WARS LEGENDS: THE LAST JEDI (Coruscant Nights Book Four)
Del Rey / Lucas Books, 2013
with Michael Reaves

STAR WARS LEGENDS: SHADOW GAMES
Del Rey/Lucas Books, 2011
with Michael Reaves

The Mer Cycle:
THE MERI
TAMINY
THE CRYSTAL ROSE

SHAMAN
(A Collection of Short Science Fiction)
Book View Café, 2013

ALL THE COLORS OF TIME
(A Collection of Short Science Fiction)
Book View Café, 2014

Gina Miyoko Stories:
"Tinkerbell On Walkabout"
a Book View Café novelette, 2015
"Tinkerbell and the Storybook Murder"
a Book View Café novelette, 2021

copyrights & credits

Chickpea Del & the Fabled Tree of Destiny by Maya Kaathryn Bohnhoff

Book View Café 2025

ISBN: 978-0-98284-406-9

Copyright © 2009, 2025 Maya Kaathryn Bohnhoff

Project Coördinator: Maya Kaathryn Bohnhoff

Cover Design: Maya Kaathryn Bohnhoff

Art credits: Anna Griessel, Hanna Hrytchyna, Roman Sotola, Anatoli Korniakov, Travelscape, Dreamstime

Formatters: Vonda N. McIntyre and Jennifer Stevenson

Digital edition:

20140818vnm

20221111jks

20240830jks

Book View Café

304 S. Jones Blvd.

Suite #2906

Las Vegas NV 89107

www.bookviewcafe.com